Garry Douglas Kilworth was raised in South Yemen, the son of an RAF sergeant, and later served in the RAF himself. He has won many awards for both adult and children's fiction, and divides his time between Suffolk and Spain.

ATTACK ON THE REDAN

1855: The port of Sebastopol is still under siege by the allies, with the Russians putting up a vigorous defence. Jack Crossman and his hardy band of malcontents find their own ways to harass the enemy in the hills and valleys around the city. But these foxhunts serve merely as a warm-up to the British attack on the Redan, a fortification guarding Sebastopol. The British attack, when it does come, is ill-planned and ill-advised, ending in total disaster and forcing Crossman to bear witness to the wholesale massacre of his fellow soldiers. Two months later, the French and Sardinian forces foil a massive Russian counterattack and Sebastopol is left to the allies.

Books by Garry Douglas Kilworth
Published by The House of Ulverscroft:

THE WINTER SOLDIERS

GARRY DOUGLAS KILWORTH

---◆---

ATTACK ON THE REDAN

Complete and Unabridged

ULVERSCROFT
Leicester

First published in Great Britain in 2003 by
Constable, an imprint of
Constable & Robinson Limited
London

First Large Print Edition
published 2004
by arrangement with
Constable, an imprint of
Constable & Robinson Limited
London

British Library CIP Data

Kilworth, Garry
　　Attack on the Redan.—Large print ed.—
　　Ulverscroft large print series: adventure & suspense
　　1. Crossman, Jack (Fictitious character)—Fiction
　　2. Crimean War, *1853 – 1856*—Fiction
　　3. Historical fiction 4. Large type books
　　I. Title
　　823.9′14 [F]

　　ISBN 1–84395–353–6

Published by
F. A. Thorpe (Publishing)
Anstey, Leicestershire
Set by Words & Graphics Ltd.
Anstey, Leicestershire
Printed and bound in Great Britain by
T. J. International Ltd., Padstow, Cornwall

This book is printed on acid-free paper

This one is for Bill Fedden —
who served with me at Masirah and
Strike Command — a warrior
on the golf course

1

'There must have been an army.'

This enigmatic statement had erupted very suddenly from the lips of Sergeant Jack Crossman of the 88th Connaught Rangers, an Irish regiment with a drinking problem. The statement and the problem had little to do with each other, except that in a nearby sutler tent there were some rangers carousing the night away. Their sometimes bawdy, sometimes sentimental songs had been interfering with the conversation between Fancy Jack and his close friend Rupert Jarrard, an American war correspondent. Consequently both men had settled back in their chairs, one with his beloved chibouque pipe, the other with his cigar, and had slipped into separate reveries.

'What?' answered the startled Jarrard. Jarrard stared at the shining face of his companion. The American had been somewhere else. On the island of Run, to be precise. He had been reading recently about the nutmeg and its subsequent influence on world history, and his imagination had taken him to the source of the nutmeg tree, a small

1

island in far eastern waters. He had actually been standing on a cliff buffeted by balmy breezes, picking precious nutmegs, which in a distant century would have made him a very wealthy man, when the eruption had occurred from the mouth of the sergeant. 'What are you yelling about man? You almost had me swallowing my cigar.'

'Sorry,' said Crossman, leaning forward, 'it just occurred to me. Look, when the three wise men, or the three kings, or whatever you want to call them — when they travelled to the birth of Christ, they wouldn't have made the journey alone. No. They would have had an army with them. We don't think about that. We don't depict it in our illustrations.'

It was a warm clear night, without any dew, the moon shining mistily through a thin layer of cloud. Fireflies turned a nearby drystone wall into a miniature universe of swimming stars. Crossman never failed to be fascinated by fireflies, which seemed to him to have the secret of a natural source of energy. The horsedrawn carriages of the siege railway which now passed through Kadikoi on its way up from Balaclava harbour had come to a standstill during the dark hours, but the two men could hear the clink and clatter of tools in the distance where the Russians, under their inventive engineer Colonel Todleben, were busy repairing the damage caused by allied guns. The Sebastopol defences were attacked daily with vigorous intent. Every night the Russians doggedly patched up the holes.

Jarrard tapped the ash off his cigar. It fell like fine snow through the beams of the lamplight to the stone floor of his small room. 'I should be used to these outbursts from you, but I'm not. You and Archimedes would have made a fine pair, with your eurekas. All right, tell me. Why was there an army with the three wise men?'

'Look at it logically. They were, if not great kings, very important chieftains. They were carrying priceless gifts. Their journey would have taken them through all kinds of landscapes — bandit country, deserts, foreign places where they were not known. There would be hostile tribes and lone robbers. They would pass through areas where they were likely to be attacked by wild beasts — lions, bears, that sort of thing, drawn by the scent of the domestic livestock, if not the men. They would need an escort to guard them and their precious caravans . . . '

'Why do you assume a caravan?'

'Oh, Rupert, it's obvious! If it isn't three men, riding hell-for-leather through the night, which for reasons I've already gone into it

3

wasn't, then there has to be a retinue. Animal-transport needs fodder, people need food. There would have been a herd of goats, which naturally brings in goatherds. Fowl for eggs and meat. There would have been camels to carry the fodder and firewood, for they would need fires during the freezing desert nights, and of course to cook their food, boil any suspect water. Camels need handlers. Things break, things snap. A blacksmith, perhaps, certainly a saddlemaker and a harness maker, to repair the tack . . . '

'Wouldn't one man suffice?'

'No, Rupert, a saddlemaker and a harness maker have different skills.'

'Not on the Frontier,' snorted the American. 'We could turn our hand to anything out there.'

'Yes, but we're talking about a proper ancient civilized society, Rupert, not your rough-and-ready wild west of the Americas. No, there would have been both, perhaps more than one of both. There would have been cooks to prepare the food, tent carriers and erectors — all right, I grant you, these *could* have been the same men. Then these wise men, these kings, would need to be served. Possibly by young maidens. Such normally pampered creatures would have been waited on, hand and foot, back in those times. They would not be used to fending for themselves.

'There would have been some sort of pagan priest with them — Christianity, after all, was but a newlyborn nestling in stable straw at the time — they would need a holy man to see that the travellers observed the correct rituals and properly followed the rules of society. There would have been a scribe to keep a journal of their travels, to mark the names of slaves now close to their home country who escaped in the dead of night, to note punishments handed out to idle servants, hostlers, grooms. Do you see where I'm going, Rupert? The list builds and builds. When you get caravans of this size, carrying gold, frankincense and myrrh, you need to protect it in the dangerous lands through which you have to travel. There would have been an army, Rupert. An army of some considerable size.'

Rupert Jarrard sighed, impressed in spite of himself. His musings on the nutmeg, on the battles it had caused between powerful nations, on its unique, humble origins, had been interesting enough, but Jack had the edge with this army thing. It was always the army with Jack. It was as if he were trying to justify his choice of career. He was forever trying to make others see the importance, the

5

necessity of armies. Only the other day, Jack had spoken at length about the warrior cult, the warrior worship, of most civilized nations, pointing out that the plaques and plates on the interiors of church walls glorified two main professions: the clergy and soldiering. Bishops and generals, rectors and majors, vicars and captains. The clergymen were there because they owned the place. Why were the military there? Jack thought it was because the warrior was universally admired.

'All right, Jack. There was an army. I grant you that. Why, d'you think, Matthew and his crew didn't mention it?'

'Because it didn't *need* mentioning, Rupert. Where you have kings, you have armies. You don't waste words on the obvious.'

'And you, in your pipe dreams, were riding beneath those desert stars, that one bright star, a trooper in a king's army.'

Crossman smiled. 'I was, Rupert. I was there, consulting my astrolabe, navigating, finding the shortest route over the mountains . . .'

At that moment, Jack Crossman's words were completely drowned in a crashing which had the farmhouse juddering and shaking on its meagre foundations. The noise, and the earth movement it caused, made both men turn white with shock. Rupert pulled out his pocketwatch and stared at it for a moment. Four a.m. A barrage had begun. Out there on the lines some 800 allied guns had roared forth their message to the Russians: we are going to pound you. There had never before in history been such a cannonade. The Russians would know, if not by their spies by the very strength of the barrage itself, that an assault on their defences was coming. Their angry reply was not long in coming, from the mouths of the enemy's cannons.

When he could, during one of the infrequent lulls, Jarrard asked, 'Is your regiment going in, Jack?'

'Reserve,' replied Crossman with a little asperity. 'We're being held in reserve.'

'Still, that might mean action.'

'Yes, it might. But we won't have been the first to go in. It's the Redan, after all. One of the two keys to the city. I know, the 88th helped to take the Quarries, but that won't loom large in future discussions on the Crimean campaign, believe me. The attack on a fortification like the Redan will. The Russians think it's impregnable. No fortress ever is . . . ' The guns crashed and thundered again, covering the tail end of his bitter words.

Crossman was, as were most of the soldiers

and civilians in the Crimea, convinced they were in the last stages of the war. Sebastopol was about to fall. Spies like Crossman had witnessed carts of straw being taken into the doomed city, presumably in readiness to set fire to the houses and boats that the Russians did not want taken. There were the French trenches in front of the Malakoff, full of French soldiers ready to take that other key to Sebastopol's defences. Just as the British parallels held their own troops, around a third the size of the French army, ready to storm the Redan. The portents were good, the French Caesar and the British Caesar had steeled themselves, and the final act of the war was about to be written, so they thought.

'Will you be with the 88th reserves?' asked Jarrard, in another relatively quiet period. 'Or shall you watch from afar?'

'I'm told to be in a high place and watch. Major Lovelace and I will be glued to spyglasses, attempting to note any weak points in the enemy's defences. My men will be there though. You should hear Wynter whining about it. Peterson, Yorwarth, they're ready enough. Yusuf Ali will be with his irregulars. Gwilliams will be where he wants to be, of course, being only attached to the British army.'

At the mention of the other American who

graced the life of Jack Crossman, a barber-and-bone-man, clever with a razor in all its various uses including the nefarious ones, Rupert Jarrard scowled. Crossman believed they were jealous of each other, the two Americans, neither necessarily more educated than the other, but definitely from different social backgrounds. Americans were of course few and far between in the Crimea, though there were all kinds of nationalities there amongst the civilians. Jarrard would have enjoyed being unique, as would Gwilliams. It is a failing of men in general that they wish to be regarded as special.

Crossman noted the frown and said quickly, 'And you, Rupert? Where shall you be when the final attack takes place tomorrow.'

'Today, Jack. It is already tomorrow.'

'You're right, of course. But where shall you be?'

'Oh, with the crowds, watching. I shall go for the human story, as well as the battle. I don't think my readers will really care much who wins. Of course there will be new immigrants — Russian, French and British — who will take sides, but for the most part they're dispassionate observers of a foreign war . . . '

'Oh, I think you're wrong there, Rupert,'

interrupted Crossman, taking a final puff of his long-stemmed chibouque. 'I think your countrymen will be very interested in the action.'

★   ★   ★

A few hours later and Sergeant Crossman was on his high place with his commander, Major Lovelace. The pair were not bosom friends, but they understood one another. The fact that Crossman came from a family of aristocrats helped to surmount certain obvious barriers, the difference in rank being the greatest of these. Both had been to Harrow school, at different periods. Both were army men to the core. They believed that the warrior was necessary for the stability of civilization. One was coldly ruthless in his professional attitude, the other constantly questioning and forming arguments for the distasteful methods he needed to employ in his work. One had chosen his role as spy and saboteur, the other had been thrust into it.

This work they did, sometimes involving assassination, was both as old as time, yet as fresh as last spring. It was constantly changing. The attitudes towards it in high places varied between utter contempt and complete belief in its necessity and place in a modern army. One cared about this, the other did not. Lovelace was a modern soldier, one who would go to the ends of the earth for information and destroy anyone who got in the way of his mission. Crossman, though he believed himself up to the mark, was simply a frustrated inventor and engineer, who held old-fashioned ideas about a soldier's honour. Although he was not one of those who still believed a soldier should stand up and be shot in order to waste the enemy's ammunition, he did not believe the end justified any means. War was changing its face, he could see that, but he wasn't sure that the new face was better than the old, or that it was an honest one.

'Look at that mob of civilians down there,' muttered Lovelace, peering through his spyglass in the dull greyness of the early dawn. 'Ghouls. Vultures. Some of them aren't happy unless they go home to bed having seen soldiers blasted to pieces, arms and legs flying in different directions, heads taken off shoulders by round shot.' He swatted at a cloud of flies in front of his face, momentarily distracted. The flies were a menace. Those in the trenches waged constant war on them and considered them as much the enemy as the Russians. 'I see Mrs Durham amongst the ghouls,'

'My God, sir. Some of the French are going in already.'

It was Crossman who had spoken. He had been viewing the ground in front of the Malakoff, which the French were due to attack in thirty minutes, to coincide by agreement with the British attack on the Redan. Lovelace swung his own glass round to the scene indicated by the sergeant.

'Hell and damnation!' he exclaimed. 'What the devil are the French playing at? Someone's blundered — again. What is it with these commanders? Can't they ever get anything right for once?'

Indeed, it seemed that one of the French commanders, jittery with nervous tension, had mistaken a mortar shell for a signal rocket and had taken his men in ahead of the attack time. These mistakes were becoming more common as the war progressed, leaders being so terrified of criticism and rebuke, fearful of being accused of tardiness or cowardice, they listened to their hearts, not their heads. Thus the worry of things going wrong caused them to go wrong. Here was a prime example of a commander giving rein to his fear-driven instincts rather than obeying his orders.

'Oh — Lord — save us,' murmured Lovelace, as his spyglass caught the waves of

12

French washing forwards, to be cut to shreds by the wall of grapeshot which came out to meet them from the Russian guns. Two batteries blazed into the hapless soldiers. Men were left staggering amongst the bodies of their comrades. From where Crossman and Lovelace were standing they looked like puppets with broken strings.

A second wave went in towards the Malakoff. Some of them miraculously managed to escape being seriously hurt in the storm of metal from the guns. These actually reached the ditch surrounding the Malakoff, but were exposed to fire from the riflemen ranged two deep on the parapet of the fortifications. They began to go down now in ones, twos and threes, instead of dozens and scores. There was no shredding of bodies, no flying limbs, but a simple crumpling or felling of a brave Frenchman.

And they were brave. So very brave.

Crossman watched a party of blue-jackets carrying a long, heavy siege ladder. Several of them started out. One by one they dropped away, as they were shot or stepped on a fougasse, until only one man remained. The ladder was of course too heavy for him. Nevertheless he tried desperately to drag it nearer to the walls of the Malakoff through the mud. It hardly went more than a few inches before this last bold fellow was shot and the ladder was left forgotten, as French soldiers ran past it, first one way, and then later — by then a great deal fewer in number — the other. Crossman felt the frustration. He itched to be down there, picking up that ladder, calling for others to help him, so that he could take it forward and scale the walls of the enemy.

He then took in the view of the ditch before the Malakoff. It was choked with dead and dying men. The scene was appalling from this vantage point. So much worse than actually being in the battle. Down there one saw comrades fall in ones and twos, but the heat of the battle, the yellowy haze that hung over the field, the smoke from the guns, the very real fear, the daze of not quite knowing what was happening around him — all these served to limit a combatant's vision and awareness. Here, on a cool hilltop, with the clarity of a boy playing soldiers on the floor of his bedroom, Crossman could see what an ugly mess guns and rifles could make of a mass of soft human flesh. It was carnage on a grand scale. It was obscene.

'They're not going to make it,' said Lovelace, finality in his voice. 'No — they're turning back. What an impossible task . . . '

Crossman's spyglass was on the British

lines. He said, 'Our chaps are going in, regardless.'

Lovelace swung round muttering venomously, 'Where are our guns? Why aren't our guns pounding the Ruskies while we advance? God damn the Staff. I could have run a better war when I was six years of age. It's nothing short of damn butchery.'

The pair could see the Russians standing four deep behind and around their guns on the Redan. The guns blazed away from the earthworks on the advancing British with something like contempt. Clearly the pounding from the allied barrage the day before had done little to damage the Russian batteries.

The Rifle Brigade skirmishers went down like hares at a hare shoot at first, before meeting that curtain of swishing grapeshot and canister which chopped them more finely. Those behind them, men of the regiments of foot, rolled in and out of shell holes in the scrubby grassland, more going in than coming out.

Small things caught Crossman's eye.

There was an abattis in front of the Redan. A young ensign was trying to climb through it, getting tangled in the branches of the felled trees, becoming infuriated when his uniform snagged. The young man dropped his weapon in order to use both hands to snap away dead twigs that impeded his progress, now being hopelessly caught and more concerned with freeing himself than killing the enemy. Crossman then saw something with wiry legs flash from the face of the youth, as the boy was finally hit in the head. Whatever it was went flying like a silver spider with bright eyes through the sunlight. It was a moment before Crossman realized they were spectacles which had flown from the lad's face and now dangled on a bough some twenty feet away from the nose on which they had once rested.

'Poor boy,' Crossman murmured. 'Some mother will grieve.'

There were other soldiers draped in the branches of the abattis, hanging like dead birds on a gamekeeper's gibbet.

A senior officer with drawn sword ran out in front to attempt to urge his men forward and was shot stone dead.

A woolbag man who looked remarkably like Crossman's old form master at Harrow tried to protect himself by holding his bag in front of him, only to have it punctured by accurate musket fire. The dead man's fall was broken by his soft load.

The Naval Brigade was fighting well and gave some hope to Crossman's fluttering heart, but even they collapsed in the end. Canister and shot did for them as it had done for others. They could no more survive a blizzard of metal than could their comrades.

'It's a lost cause,' said Lovelace, removing the glass from his eye and refusing to watch further slaughter. 'Lost, damn it.'

Crossman, feeling emotional himself, was nevertheless amazed to see the major wipe away tears from his cheeks. What a harrowing experience this voyeurism was. Yet down below gentlemen travellers, women from various classes, camp followers, civilian traders — all had gathered to watch the battle for entertainment. Crossman's erstwhile lover, Mrs Lavinia Durham, wife of a quartermaster captain, was down there somewhere in the crowd. How could they do it? It was terrible having to take part in a battle. Worse not being able to. Worse still having to stand and watch the bloody mincing of a thousand courageous young men.

★   ★   ★

After the battle the heavy losses were such that a quiet period followed for Crossman and his band. No one, including the usually zealous and irrepressible Colonel Hawke, felt like raising any initiatives. Even his steel soul was not immune to the air of torpor that hung over the allied camps. This heavy mood of depression in the Army of the East permeated from Raglan himself right down through the ranks to the lowest new recruit. Any activity was performed in a listless, apathetic way. Some could not believe the attack had failed, others had merely had their own fears confirmed. Many mistakes had been made. Criticism from London was fierce. There was talk that Lord Raglan would be replaced as commander in chief. He was ill, some said with the cholera, and needed rest and care in a more pleasant environment. The short-lived air of optimism before the battle, when everyone thought they might be going home, had now evaporated completely. They felt they would be in the Crimea forever.

Several days later Crossman and Lovelace were in the farmhouse office of Colonel Hawke, their senior in this cell of spies and saboteurs. The lean and sharp-eyed Hawke stared down gloomily at the top of a desk made from old barn wall planks and rafter beams. Crossman had never seen his superior looking so defeated, so sorely oppressed by events. Usually the colonel was an optimist, preferring to see the advantages rather than the setbacks.

'Lacy Yea is dead,' said Hawke. 'He was a fine officer — one of our finest. Sir John

Campbell fell. Colonel Shadforth, gone too. A particular friend of mine, Captain Forman.' He looked up. 'Sir George Brown has a lot to answer for.'

'Can we blame one man?' asked Lovelace. 'I mean, he commanded, it's true, but there were others who could have prevented it.'

Hawke seemed not to have heard him. 'Half a thousand men, gone at a stroke. We can't afford such losses. Thirty-one officers! Thirty-one. What a mess. There'll be no bloody poems about this blunder, that's for sure. Total humiliation, for both us and the French. To expect 2000 soldiers to cross a quarter of mile of shell-battered glacis without artillery support? Surely they must rid us of that meddlesome field marshal now? We need strong leadership, not damn obsequious clerks running the war.'

Crossman felt awkward. He did not like being in a room where senior officers were criticizing generals and Staff. He was, after all, only a sergeant. It didn't sit right with him. This sort of talk should have been for the ears of Lovelace only. Yet Hawke seemed quite oblivious of the presence of a sergeant from a line regiment. The colonel continued to rant, in between praising the courage and actions of the officers, and rank and file, who had taken part in the attempted storming of the Redan.

'Brown and Pennefather are said to be going home. They should take that senile old man with them.'

'Sir . . . ' began Crossman, his discomfort having increased.

Hawke looked up through misty eyes and seemed to see Crossman for the first time.

'Yes, sergeant?'

'I — nothing. Is there something you wish me to do, sir? Do you have a fox hunt for me?'

'Do I? Oh, yes. Yes, I do. The menace of the Russian sharpshooter is ever with us, sergeant. Sadly it looks as if this war will continue, though we had thought it might end today. I don't know what the plans of the high command are, but I imagine we'll be licking our wounds for the next few weeks before trying again. In the meantime, there will be sharpshooters thinning the numbers of our picquets and soldiers in the trenches. I want you to devise of way a thinning *their* numbers.'

'The sharpshooters.'

'That's what I said, didn't I?'

Crossman did not like to point out that the statement had been ambiguous, that the colonel could have meant the Russian troops and not just those few who took vantage points and picked off unwary allied soldiers.

'Yes, sir, I believe you did. Will that be all, sir?'

'Yes, for now.' The iron-grey colonel stared keenly at Crossman from behind his desk. 'I need not emphasise the need for you to remain silent on the manner and content of the conversations that have taken place in this room.'

Lovelace said, 'I think I can vouch for the sergeant's discretion, sir. He is one of us.'

Hawke looked thoughtful. 'Yes, he is, isn't he? Heart and soul, I hope. Well, let me know what you come up with, sergeant. Here's a chance to reveal what ingenuity lies between those ears. A sergeant, given a chance to use his own resourcefulness! There's a thing in this modern army.'

'Yes, sir.'

Crossman left the farmhouse and made his way to the hovel which he shared with his small band of men in Kadikoi village, just outside Balaclava Harbour. He found Peterson there. Peterson's gender was not a secret amongst the *peloton*, though hidden from the army in general. She was one of a rare breed of women wearing the uniform of a soldier. At that precise moment she was staring disgustedly at a shiny new rifle-musket which lay on her cot. Her face was as sombre as a

21

November day at Stonehenge.

'Peterson?'

The lance-corporal looked up and said glumly, 'Oh, hello sergeant.'

'You didn't need to leave the trenches today?'

'There was a need, but no we didn't go, sergeant. Good job. We'd have been shot to bits, wouldn't we?'

'Where are the others?'

'In one of the drinking huts.'

Crossman nodded, looking through the glassless window at the sutlers' bazaar, which had various names and had grown from a few tents into a large hutted settlement in the last year. Since Crossman's band came from an Irish regiment they called it Donnybrook. Apart from brothels and drinking huts there was every kind of trade practised there: shoemakers, tinmen, bakers, saddlers, cheese-sellers and there was even a shilling library. For the most part though, it was the more seedy elements which attracted Crossman's men of an evening: the rough women and the even rougher gin.

'That seems fair, after this morning, even if you were only held in reserve.' He knew the tension and the pressure of waiting to go into battle. Actually going in relieved all that, to a certain extent, while not going in meant it was still there, pent up inside. 'You didn't want to go with them?'

'No, sergeant.' She could not seem to take her eyes off the weapon on her bed. 'Not much point in me going with that lot, is there?'

'Something wrong, Peterson?'

'It's this,' she sighed, flicking her fingers. 'One of the new rifles. The lieutenant took away my Minnie.'

Peterson was the best shot in the *peloton*, a sharpshooter who even Captain Goodlake acknowledged was something special. Peterson had begun a love affair with her rifle-musket from the moment it was in her hands. Since the first weapon given her had been the Minié rifle, an accurate, reliable firearm which far outshone the old smooth-bore Brown Bess musket, she thought her search for the perfect partner had ended. Of course it may have done, had she not been in the army, where change is inevitable. New weapons were coming along all the time. Most soldiers were rejoicing at the introduction of a new rifle, which had the words ENFIELD or TOWER stamped on the locking plate. They considered it a superior weapon. Peterson was wedded to her Minié though and this replacement was not welcome in her house.

'Can you do something, sergeant?' she pleaded. 'Can you ask Lieutenant Pirce-Smith if I can have my Minnie back?'

'Not yours, Peterson. The army's.' He paused for a moment, then said, 'I'm sure the lieutenant thinks he's doing you a great favour, by getting you that weapon. So far as I understand, the only division which has been issued with it is the 3rd. I'm sure Lieutenant Pirce-Smith went to a lot of trouble to obtain that rifle. You should be grateful, Peterson.'

'Well I'm not,' she retorted hotly. 'Look at this,' she held up one of the balls for the new rifle-musket, 'it's smaller than my Minié bullet.'

'That's right.' Crossman, who liked to be up to the mark on the newest inventions of the age, had talked with Jarrard about this particular shoulder arm. Jarrard had a friend in London who kept him informed of developments in the weapon field. 'Point 577 calibre, as opposed to point 702. Being smaller has its advantages, Peterson. Many leading gunmakers have been consulted in its manufacture — Lancaster and Purdey to name but two. Do you know that Major Lovelace thinks that Purdey will sit on the right hand of God when he goes to meet his creator? A smaller bullet doesn't necessarily mean that the weapon is less accurate. Think how much lighter your ammunition pouch is going to be.'

'I don't care about my ammunition pouch. How can a bullet go as far if it's lighter? Stands to reason. Look at a cannonball, how far that goes, because it's heavier. This new bullet will just pop out of the end of the barrel.'

'Yes, but — look, the Minnie bullet is heavier, so the trajectory has to be higher.' He swept a half-circle through the air with his hand to illustrate the said trajectory. 'But the bullet of that weapon is lighter, so the arc is less pronounced. The curve of the bullet's flight is flatter. That's a distinct advantage, Peterson, in trying to hit the target.'

'I don't have any trouble hitting the target.'

Crossman shook his head and sighed. 'You may be a wonderful shot, Peterson, but your science is wild. I can't sit here and discuss trajectories, barrel lengths, rifling, charges and weight ratios with you, but I can assure you that you'll find this new rifle-musket as good, if not better, than the old. If you don't, then I'll personally intervene for you and get the damned Minnie rifle back.'

Peterson's eyes brightened and her bulky form quivered.

'Will you, sergeant? Will you really?'

Sometimes Crossman felt he was dealing with children, rather than adults.

'I've said so, haven't I?'

At that moment there came the sound of singing from a group of men walking along the mud road which ran beside the railway track. Crossman could hear Lance-Corporal Wynter's voice above the others, horribly out of tune, hoarsely grinding out, 'Drink Old England Dry'. After this song was mangled it was followed without a pause, by 'John Barleycorn's a Hero Bold'. In both renderings the lyrics were not only murdered, they were chopped to pieces and the parts scattered over boggy ground.

Wynter was drunk. No rare thing in an Irish regiment, except that Wynter was not Irish. There was no telling what his ancestors had been since he was born in the workhouse without a father to give him a proper name, but Wynter had been raised in England. The English could drink too, of course, but they usually did it with less noise than the Irish rangers. Not Wynter. He loved to draw attention to himself, always for the wrong reasons, and could get into a drunken brawl over nothing at all.

Peterson, on hearing the noise, got off her bed and picked up Major Lovelace's cricket bat, which stood just inside the door. She hid on the opposite side of the door, the bat raised. Crossman could see exactly what she was going to do.

'Peterson, you cannot strike Wynter.'

'Why not? He's kept me awake for the last two nights with his drunkenness. I plan to cold-cock the sod.'

She certainly had the strength to do it, having put on a good deal of brawn since she had been in the Crimea. Others had taken it off, but somehow Peterson thrived on the diet.

'I can't allow it. It's a shame I came back too early, but there it is. I'm here now and there will be no cold-cocking of Wynters or summers in here.'

'A joke,' muttered a disgusted Peterson, throwing the cricket bat into the corner. 'I can do without your jokes, sergeant.'

Wynter then came through the door, his face flushed, his eyes full of gin-lustre.

'Whoa-ho! It's the sergeant. We've bin in the trenches, sergeant. Entitled to a bit of fun after the trenches.'

'You're lucky to be alive Wynter. If you hadn't been down in a dirt hole you'd be lying in front of the Great Redan now, half your head missing.'

Yorwarth, the Australian, nodded his head sagely. 'He's right, y'know. Did you see them poor bastards? Got shot to pieces. I'm glad I wasn't out there. They didn't stand a chance.'

'You'll get your chance,' growled Wynter, sourly. 'It won't be the last charge at Sebastopol, you can bet your purse on that.'

Wynter fell on his cot and was mercifully asleep within a few seconds, his throat rattling with phlegmy snores. Peterson heaved a sigh of relief. There were others now who came in behind the first two. Yusuf Ali was bringing up the rear, along with Gwilliams, the civilian barber from the United States. These two were arguing about various breeds of horses and their merits.

'I say you can't beat the South American paso fino horse,' Gwilliams was saying. 'He's got a strong body and hard legs, and *three* separate gaits.'

'Every horse has four,' replied Ali. 'Walk, trot, canter, gallop.'

'No, you disunderstand me,' Gwilliams argued. 'Gaits is not walk or trot. It's moving at cross-country speed. *Paso fino* is one gait. Then *paso corto* — you can cover a deal of country with a steady *paso corto*. Then last is the real fast *paso largo*. Got fire in its hooves, the paso fino, I tell you, Turk. You won't find a better little horse than the paso fino anywheres.'

'I had a tarpan once that could not be

28

beaten. I would race your paso fino into the ground, America. You find one. I get a tarpan from the steppes people. We race together, some day.'

'Some day,' replied Gwilliams. 'You bet.'

Crossman gathered his brood together. He was glad Wynter was asleep, because that man always disrupted any discussion, especially when he was drunk on gin. First he would be belligerent, then maudlin, and finally complaining. It was good to have a rest from him. The others had been drinking, but were not too far gone to listen and contribute.

'We've been given a task,' said Crossman. The air around the lamp on the table was swimming with bugs and moths. He turned the wick down, then lit another lamp, placing it at the far end. He wanted a mellow atmosphere, to encourage deep thinking, but he didn't want anyone falling asleep in a dark corner. 'We've been asked to thin down the sharpshooters on the other side.'

Peterson blinked. She was a sharpshooter on *this* side. Sharpshooters were a despised breed amongst soldiery. They killed from a safe distance, coldly and mercilessly. Any soldier in the trenches would cheerfully lynch a sharpshooter, if he could get his hands on one. A vendetta against sharpshooters made Peterson feel uncomfortable, even though they were talking about the enemy. She felt her calling was being criticized.

'Now,' continued Crossman, 'we're not going to get near them during the day. So we have to think about night operations. I want you all to put your minds to this one. It's open house. I know you've all had a few gins, or rums, or whatever, but let's have a smoke on this . . . '

Crossman took some pipe tobacco from his pocket and handed it round. They took out their various clay pipes and filled them. Crossman and Ali had their chibouques. Bowls were filled and tamped down. A taper was lit from the oil lamp and the pipes were soon glowing. Men settled back comfortably. Woman less so. Crossman sucked in the smoke and filled his lungs. He could not envisage being able to devise plans without the assistance of tobacco.

The atmosphere was perfect, except for Wynter's snores.

Ali got up, put a huge calloused hand over Wynter's mouth. Wynter stopped breathing, went a strange colour, then coughed in air when Ali let him breathe again. Ali flipped the drunken soldier on to his stomach. The snoring had now given way to a heavy breathing sound. Mercifully, Wynter had not woken during this swift smooth exercise.

For his part Crossman was glad the snoring had ceased, though for a few seconds there he had thought the Bashi-Bazouk was going to suffocate the sleeping soldier. The Turk was even less fond of Wynter than the sergeant himself. It would not have taken much encouragement for Ali to put an end to Wynter's complaining for good.

'Now,' said Crossman, after a lengthy period in which they had all sucked ideas out of their pipes, 'any thoughts?'

Yorwarth spoke first. 'What we could do, sergeant, is sneak up there at night and somehow get a light on the Ruskie sharp-shooter. We know Peterson here has tried firing at the flash, when the sharpshooter takes a shot at one of our blokes, but he always jumps away from the spot after firing, and Peterson ends up shootin' at thin air. If we could give Peterson a light to aim at, why she'd get him right between the eyes, dark or not.'

Gwilliams snorted. 'What, walk up with a lamp and say, 'Scuse me while I illuminate you for purposes of shooting your damn head off'?'

'No. Not that, but some way — say, toss a lit cigar, or fuse — something like that. It doesn't need to be a lamp. Just a light of some kind. Get it near him, so's Peterson can put a hole in his head.'

Peterson blinked again. She was a brilliant shot. She rejoiced in having this rare skill. But she did not like to dwell on the outcome of her actions. Once the bullet had left the muzzle of the rifle it ceased to be her responsibility. The damage it caused was not her concern. She did not like to consider holes in hearts, heads, or any other part of the human anatomy. Such thoughts were ugly. The less she thought about them the better.

They pondered on Yorwarth's words for a while. Getting some Russian uniforms so that they could move amongst the enemy was no problem. There were hundreds to be had, taken from bodies after battles. But Yorwarth's plan was full of terrible holes. It was too flimsy, too likely to end in a chase across no-man's-land, the *peloton* with the Russians on their tails.

Peterson said, 'It doesn't have to be me. Why can't we go as a group behind their lines. Then we can jump on the sharpshooters and — and — '

'And cut their throats?' Gwilliams finished for her. 'I like that.'

He took out a shaving razor, opened it, studied the gleaming edge for a moment, then replaced it in his pocket. There were no fussy feelings about Gwilliams. He would do before he was done to every time.

'That's no good,' Crossman said. 'I'm sorry lads, but we'd only get to one or two of them before we had the whole Russian army on our tails. It's got to be like a lit fuse. We've got to be out of there before they start missing their sharpshooters . . . '

At that moment Major Lovelace came through the doorway. He brushed some persistent moths off the shoulders of his uniform. Then he looked up into the faces of Crossman's men.

'Insects, moths, the air's full of 'em. Forgive me, but I couldn't help overhearing your discussion. You're planning your mission, of course. I've been thinking about that since Hawke spoke to you, sergeant, and something has occurred to me. *Lampyridae*. You should do something with those flying *coleoptera*. There are millions of them out there. Got to be useful for something other than flitting about, don't you think?'

Crossman nodded slowly. The major smiled and went up the stairs to the room he shared with his sergeant on the first floor of the hovel. Crossman considered his major's words carefully. Lovelace had a keen brain, that much Crossman knew. He also knew that the major had used the Latin name for the nocturnal luminous insects so that Crossman alone could think about what he had said without involving the rest of the men at this stage. If Crossman thought the idea too wild or unworthy of further consideration, he could abandon it without anyone losing face amongst the men. On the other hand, if he decided it was worth taking further, and he would not be met with a wall of incredulity, he could throw it open to the rest of them and see what came out of it.

He decided to test the *peloton*'s ingenuity.

'Fireflies,' he said, flatly. 'Any ideas?'

Gwilliams still looked blank, until Yorwarth told him, 'Lightning bugs, to you.'

'Oh.' Gwilliams nodded. 'Them.'

'Well, what about 'em?' asked a bewildered Peterson. 'We call them *blinkies* in Rutland, but I don't see . . . '

★ ★ ★

Crossman and Yusuf Ali were dressed in merchant seamen's clothes. Crossman was a German sailor. He didn't particularly like this disguise, since there were parts of him — his hands — which had obviously never hauled on a rope or turned a capstan, but travelling under the guise of army or imperial navy was so much more hazardous than posing as a

34

civilian seaman. Ali was, to the Turk's great distaste, supposed to be Greek. Both men spoke passable Russian, which was why they were on their own. They wandered through the barracks and work areas of the Russian soldiery attracting very little attention. Mariners of all kinds had been gathered up by Colonel Todleben and put to work on building and repairing the defences of Sebastopol. There were others of a similar kind strolling or hurrying about the place, exciting no military suspicions.

A sentry was lounging against the wall of a church, guarding the entrance to the crypt. Crossman wondered whether a general or some lesser rank was using the crypt as a headquarters, it being a natural shelter below the ground and relatively safe from the allied bombardment. Not for the first time Crossman envied the Russians their solid lodgings. The sergeant filed this information in his mind for further consideration. For the moment they had to concentrate on the task in hand.

The sentry's eyes narrowed as they approached him, but when Crossman gave him a cheery grin, he seemed to relax a little. There was no answering smile, but the wariness had gone from his eyes.

'Corporal,' said Crossman, 'forgive us for

approaching you like this, while you're on duty, but we have a question.'

'Yes?'

'We're looking for a tavern or drinking hall where the sharpshooters meet to talk over their exploits. Do you know of such an establishment?'

The soldier shrugged and yawned, before asking, 'Why do you wish to know this?'

Ali said, 'We are great admirers of these sharpshooters. Being seamen we have little to do with firearms. The sharpshooters are the great heroes of this war, wouldn't you say?'

The sentry stiffened a little and a scowl appeared on his face.

'No, I wouldn't. I'd say those of us who fought at Alma and Inkerman were bigger heroes. Just because a man's born with the eyes of a hawk doesn't make him a hero in my book. He's just lucky.'

'I suppose so,' Crossman agreed. 'I mean, they get a soft bed, don't do picquet or guard duty and get treated like royalty. I know what you mean. Yes indeed.'

'They don't even eat with the rest of us,' complained the sentry, who scratched his unshaven chin as he stared at them. 'They get a mess hall all to themselves. You'd think they shit gold coins the way they're pampered. I think your admiration is poorly placed.'

Ali nodded. 'Perhaps you're right. Maybe we won't seek them out, after all. So, you were at Alma, sir. You look as if you've seen a battle or two. Was it so bad?'

'Worse than bad. I wasn't at the Alma, but at Inkerman.' He lifted his trouser leg to show them a healed gash. 'Got a bayonet through my calf. I had to crawl half a mile before I got any attention.'

'I hope you blew the brains out of the man who gave you that ugly wound, sir. I see now what you mean about heroes . . . '

'Oh,' the guard looked a little embarrassed now, 'I didn't mean me — I'm no hero, sailor. I simply say that sharpshooters aren't either — they have it easy. It's a soft life for them.'

'Sharpshooters don't have to face bayonets, do they?' scoffed Ali. 'I'll give you that much.'

'They don't face *anything*, friend. They have their cosy little killing nest and they simply walk from there to the mess hall . . . '

Crossman looked around as if the guard were pointing out the establishment in question. He wasn't of course. But now he did, indicating a large square building which looked like a museum or art gallery.

Crossman became a little incautious. Having got the information he wanted so smoothly and easily, he reached out to shake the soldier's hand. Too late he remembered that his hands were soft giveaways. Yet the guard was now feeling good about himself and shook the proffered hand with great enthusiasm. 'It's well to know we common soldiers are appreciated,' he said, 'and you — you do a fine job, helping to rebuild our poor tortured city.'

'We do what we can,' said Ali, shrugging. 'It's not our city — not even our country — but when you get shelled day in, day out by those devils over there,' he pointed towards the allied lines with his chin, 'in the end you take sides, eh? I look forward to the hour when they're overrun and we can go about our normal lives. A ship is all I want. Even a Black Sea coaster would suit me at the moment . . . '

A bombardment began with the allies firing into the city and the Russian guns answering them. Crossman put a finger to his forehead by way of salute to the corporal, who now had anxious eyes on the sky. Ali and he walked away, heading for the hall where the sharpshooters messed. One or two more questions found them inside a dusty bare hall, the walls lined with dark oil paintings, mostly figures exuding pomp. There were over a dozen soldiers eating at a long table. One or two of the soldiers — sharpshooters of all ranks who had come from their night holes — glanced up when the two men entered. A cook came hurrying from behind a servery, wiping his hands on a filthy cotton apron, an annoyed expression on his face.

'What do you want here? This is out-of-bounds to ordinary personnel. Didn't you read the notice outside?'

'No, no, you don't understand,' said Ali, smiling. 'We came to see the sharpshooters — brave men.'

One of the sharpshooters in question looked up from his soup and said, 'Are you mocking?'

Crossman decided to leave all this to Ali and simply stood at his side like one who has agreed to accompany a friend.

Ali looked shocked. 'Of course not. I have an older brother who is a sharpshooter in the Greek army. I have always admired his skill with a firelock.'

'What do you want here?' asked the cook, intervening. 'You must leave before I — you — get into trouble.'

'Just to give you these.' Ali took two jars of honey out of his trouser pockets, one from either side. He handed these to the cook with an abashed air. 'My friend here and I, we have been keeping these. They were part of our cargo, but why should the officers have everything? They eat like kings while the rest of us go hungry. I have more, but I thought, for my brother's sake, it would be a good gesture to bring these here, for the sharpshooters.' He let out a little laugh. 'I'm sure some of them have a sweet tooth.'

The cook's eyes bulged a little. He took the jars of honey and nodded. 'I'm sure they'll appreciate the gesture, friend. I thank you.'

One of the men at the table called out, 'Don't you go hiding them away, Rolschoff. I want to see them on the table tonight.'

'Enjoy it,' said Ali. 'Good to see you, gentlemen.' He waved towards the sharpshooters, still hunched over the table. 'Keep up the good work.'

The pair then left, hurrying out into the city streets.

The honey had actually come from Lovelace, who had purchased it from a fellow officer. The idea was a wild one, but approved by Lovelace, who had something of the same in mind when he had suggested that fireflies might be the answer. Lovelace, not greatly interested in beetles himself but in contact with a keen collector, had learned that fireflies ate nectar. Honey was not nectar, but it was the closest thing they could get to it. There was the hope that the scent of honey would be enough. Insects were often attracted to sweet sticky substances and honey in particular.

Ali and Crossman, now used to slipping back and forth between the allied camps and Sebastopol, made their way back to their lines.

★ ★ ★

That night Crossman and Ali were in a forward position with Peterson and her new Enfield rifle-musket. Ali and Crossman had spyglasses, not terribly effective in the dark, but certainly they could pick out bunches of fireflies with them. They scoured the skyline for their targets. Crossman was the first to give Peterson's coat an excited tug as he indicated a small cloud of fireflies, concentrated around a particular spot. The fireflies occasionally exploded into a larger space. The cause for this movement was undoubtedly due to some irritated person flicking at the cloud with his hand, trying to wave them away.

Peterson took careful aim and squeezed the trigger. The shot rang out, shockingly loud. She was rewarded with a cry, then the clatter of a dropped weapon.

'Got him!' she whispered, excitedly. 'This new rifle isn't half bad.'

They moved from their own hideout quickly, for fear of reprisals from enemy sharpshooters who might have seen the flash from the Enfield's muzzle. Throughout the night they hunted small clouds of fireflies, firing into their midst. Some of those shots would have been unsuccessful, others, they were certain, had hit their target. Whatever the case, the Russian sharpshooters would be severely shaken. It was not often their numbers were culled with such efficiency. Crossman sometimes wondered, afterwards, whether the the survivors of that night ever guessed that it was the honey they'd eaten for supper which was responsible for the deaths of their comrades.

The following day, Colonel Hawke sent for Crossman.

'Fancy Jack, my lad,' said the man with short iron-grey hair, 'you did very well. Major Lovelace has received reports from his spies in Sebastopol that five — *five* — Russian sharpshooters were wounded or killed last night. Top men. Crackshots, as some would say. What do you think to that?'

The colonel leaned back in his creaky, rickety chair, in grave danger of tipping over and falling on his back.

Crossman cleared his throat. 'I'm very pleased, sir.'

'Brilliant idea,' cried the colonel, coming back upright again with a crash as his chest hit the edge of his desk and he slapped both palms on its surface. 'Absolutely. The honey I mean.' He gave a little chuckle. 'Ambrosia! That'll send the bastards to sleep for a long time. Who thought of it — you?'

'Well, it was a sort of combined effort. Actually it was Major Lovelace who put us on the track. Gwilliams had heard something about honey, insects and the American Indians. Yorwarth was sure the native Aboriginals in Australia used it to attract ants to eat, or something of the sort, so between us all we came up with our little plan.' Crossman was feeling rather good about himself. He had never seen Hawke in such a good mood before. The colonel was positively merry. His normally storm-clouded face, though not hostile, rarely allowed any sunshine to break through.

'Team effort, eh? Better and better. I don't like individuals to get *too* clever, y'know. Makes 'em uppity. Much better when the plan comes out of several heads. Well, so? Out again tonight, eh?'

Crossman's pleasant thoughts shattered immediately.

'Er, tonight, sir?'

'Yes, bag a few more of the buggers. Maybe

not five again, but a brace here, a brace there. Soon mounts up.' He could have been talking about grouse. 'I'm told they have about thirty really top sharpshooters all told. Prime riflemen. Probably Siberian bear killers or something. If we can get that down to about ten, we'll make them spread themselves rather thin, eh?'

Crossman drew a deep breath. 'Sir, I don't think it's advisable to go out again tonight.'

Hawke scratched his grey scalp. 'Why not?'

'Because, sir, I believe they'll be waiting for us. Even if they haven't caught on to the honey trick, they'll know something's afoot, won't they? You don't lose five sharpshooters in one evening by sheer bad luck. They'll be sitting there thinking it through, trying to come up with the answer, and they'll certainly be laying a few traps in case we try it again.'

'Can't you shoot 'em from here? From the trenches?'

'We can't see the fireflies at that distance. In the daylight, Peterson could certainly hit a target the size of a man from the trenches, but we need to be closer to see the fireflies.'

Hawke sucked in his breath and stared at his desk top. Finally his head came up. 'I understand what you're saying, sergeant, but I think we have to go at least one more time.

44

You could be wrong, you know. They might be putting it down to a one-time effort by us. I'm sorry, but I have to send you out again tonight. If you meet stiff resistance, then we'll stop the forays, but until there's positive proof of such, I want you to continue.'

Crossman saw it was useless to argue. The colonel had thought it out, there in front of him, and had made his decision. There was nothing for it but to go again when darkness came round. Perhaps the fireflies would not be out. Then there wouldn't be any point in repeating the exercise.

'Yes, sir. As you say, sir. I shall take Peterson out as soon as the fireflies make an appearance.'

'Good. But you don't have to go yourself, do you, sergeant? You have a corporal? Wynter? Why not send him?'

'He's not that reliable, sir, as a leader. Oh, he's fine when he's told what to do and where, but I wouldn't trust him to lead an expedition. No, I think it best I go myself, along with Yusuf Ali. Ali is a most resourceful man, sir, who uses his initiative and cunning with great skill.'

'Your Turkish irregular. Bashi-Bazouk, isn't he? So I understand. I also understand he considers himself your personal bodyguard and would kill a general if one ordered you to your death. I'm only a lowly colonel, so I'm sure he would dispose of me for a much lesser crime.'

Crossman was horrified, the hair on the back of his neck standing on end. Ali was fond of promising to kill people if they betrayed his sergeant.

'Ali hasn't threatened you, has he, colonel?'

'No, no.'

'That's a relief. He means no harm, sir . . .'

Hawke roared with laughter. 'Oh yes he bloody well does. Don't come it, sergeant. But don't worry, I approve. These units we're forming, these little *pelotons* of spies and saboteurs, they have to be made up of men like him. And men like you. You need these bonds, to survive in such work. Your soldiers are a bit like the old Anglo-Saxon warriors — the hearth companions or housecarls of half-kings such as Bryhthnoth. Those thanes, or nobles, were the leader's bodyguards and would fight and die for their lord, without question, even over his dead body if he was struck a mortal blow during the battle. They were totally loyal.'

Crossman had no idea what Hawke was talking about and must have been looking blank, for the colonel explained.

'Have you never read *The Battle of*

Maldon, sergeant? Old poem. Oldest poem in the English language, I believe. An Anglo-Saxon ealdorman and his warriors defended a causeway near the town of Maldon in Essex, against Viking raiders. That was in AD 991. It was a famous defeat. We're fond of our famous defeats, aren't we? Bryhthnoth, the ealdorman made a mistake, let the Vikings cross the causeway, and was subsequently killed in the action that followed. His housecarls fought over his body and saved it from the clutches of the enemy, though they lost the battle itself. Some booby of a thane took the half-king's horse and fled the field and that accounted for the subsequent defeat, the warriors thinking their leader had fled the field followed suit. You should read it, you know, sergeant.'

Crossman stood there, thinking, what is the damn colonel talking about? His thoughts must have crossed his face like clouds on a fine day. Hawke nodded.

'You're wondering about the relevance?'

'Yes, sir, I'm afraid I am.'

'You, sergeant, are a half-king. I am the king. I have several half-kings who fight in the field on my behalf. These half-kings have their housecarls to assist them in their endeavours. In the sort of situations you find yourself in, you half-kings, you need unswerving loyalty.

Your Bashi-Bazouk would die for you, yes? That's the kind of loyalty I'm talking about, sergeant. The loyalty of a housecarl!'

Crossman left the colonel's farmyard with his mind buzzing. Hawke was certainly an interesting man, but not one Crossman would have chosen as a friend outside the war. Their ways of thinking were too diverse. Something struck Fancy Jack Crossman and he let out a whoop of laughter, causing soldiers on the road to turn and stare. It had just occurred to him that Wynter had been compared to a housecarl, a nobleman bodyguard whose loyalty to his leader was unquestionable. The idea was so ludicrously funny Crossman laughed all the way back to the hovel. There the first person he was confronted with was Wynter, looking sour and testy.

'What've you got to be so jolly about, sergeant? They sendin' you home, or what.'

'No, Wynter, just out to kill more sharpshooters tonight.'

'What?' cried Peterson, looking horrified. 'What's so funny about that? You're going mad, sergeant.'

'Yes, I think I am, Peterson.'

He left them, looking worried, and went up to his room. There he found Rupert Jarrard, lying on his cot smoking a cheroot. The

American looked up at him as he entered the room.

'Rupert?'

'Sorry, Jack, this was the only piece of furniture I could find and I didn't know how long I had to wait.'

'That's all right, but what are you doing here?'

'Came to warn you,' replied Jarrard, darkly. 'That captain we sent to India. He's back, and spitting blood and fire, naturally.'

It took Crossman more than a short while to turn this over in his mind before he came up with the answer. Captain Sterling Campbell had been a cardsharp, a gambler who fleeced Crossman's half-brother, James, and would have reduced him to penury if Crossman hadn't done something about it. Crossman had disguised himself as a lieutenant and had tried to win the money back from Campbell, only to lose yet more of the family fortune. Finally, it had been Jarrard who had tricked the gambler on board a ship about to leave for India by promising him an interesting game of cards with some naval officers. The naval officers had been under the impression that Campbell was travelling to India with them and *Antigone* had set sail, carrying the half-drunk captain to foreign places, where he would no longer be a menace to Crossman's older brother.

'Oh my God, Rupert. He'll blow your bloody head off.'

'He will if he catches me. Fortunately I saw him first and ducked away. He's been asking for me all over the place since then. You should see his face. Grim death ain't the phrase for it. He'll be after you too, so I'd be a bit scarce if I were you, sergeant.'

Crossman shook his head. 'All he knows of me is that he beat me at cards. If you remember, I was simply a lieutenant who got into a card game with him. He won't connect me with his abduction.'

Jarrard stared at Crossman for a moment, then nodded. 'You're right. I'm the only one he's after. Now is that fair, Jack? I don't want to have to kill the man.'

Jarrard was a crackshot with the Navy Colt he carried. Crossman had seen him in action and knew he was quite deadly. However, Campbell too was reputedly good with a duelling pistol. Crossman was not sure who was the better, though Jarrard was always brimming with confidence when it came to such matters.

'I wouldn't want to put this to the test, Rupert. This is my fault. Maybe I should just go and own up. He won't want to fight me. I'm a lowly sergeant.'

'No, but he'll have you court martialled for impersonating an officer. I seem to remember you called yourself Lieutenant Tremaine, of the Rifles. You wore Rifle Greens, anyway.'

Crossman nodded. 'Yes, and it will probably end in a flogging. I've never been flogged, Rupert, and I never want to be. It's not the pain of the punishment I fear . . . '

'The humiliation, I know. Ghastly bloody practice, tying a man to the wheel and whipping him in front of the troops. Sickens a proud man to the pit of his stomach — the watchers as well as the victim. No, we can't have that, Jack. I took it on myself to kidnap Campbell, without discussing it with you, so I must take the consequences. If I kill him, I'll have to leave the Crimea and may even lose my job on the *Banner*. If I don't, I'll be singing Negro slave songs with the angels. Best to stay out of his way, if I can. It hurts my pride, but it would seem the most sensible course of action.'

Crossman was relieved. Jarrard could be a fiery individual where he thought his honour was being questioned.

'Campbell's in the 93rd, Rupert. All you have to do is stay away from Kadikoi and Balaclava.'

'But what about you, Jack? What if he recognizes you?'

51

'I'll keep a good watch for him. If I see him coming I'll duck out of sight. Shouldn't be a problem.'

'Well, I hope it's not.' Jarrard rose from the cot. 'I'll be off now, Jack. Come over to the French lines occasionally. I'm finding it a bit cosier over there at the moment. It's not so bad. There are ladies over there. And the food is better, of course. And the wine superior — in fact I don't know why I've stuck with you people so long. I should have moved into the French camp the moment I arrived.'

'We speak English, Rupert. You do not speak French.'

'There is that, of course.' He grinned. 'I'm a lazy son-of-a-bitch when it comes to languages.'

'Just don't upset any French officers.'

'Me, Jack?' cried Jarrard, in mock innocence. 'As if I would.'

He left the room, leaving Crossman deep in thought. The sergeant knew he really would have to keep a keen eye out for Campbell. It would not be a happy meeting if they should chance upon one another.

2

The fireflies were in evidence. Crossman damned their bright bottoms, as they flitted with their fairy lamps around the landscape. Ali and Peterson were with him as the three of them made their way over the rough ground in front of the Quarries. They had passed through the forward picquets with the watchwords 'Admiral's Lady', which was some army commander's idea of annoying any naval personnel since the response, 'Nelson's Jade', was a clear reference to a Lord Hamilton's wife.

The three men had to scramble through the rocky terrain, disturbing wildlife and, occasionally, loose rocks. The closer they came to the Russian lines, the more desperate they became to prevent noise. At one point they were in a deep gully, unable to see over the top. They passed down this steep-walled groove in the countryside until there was a place where they could climb up and take a peek at the Russian defences. They found they were so close to the enemy they could hear them talking to one another, even though the voices were low. Crossman

53

scanned a parapet just a few yards in front of him and noticed a cloud of fireflies. He tapped Peterson on the shoulder and she went to her task.

The shot crashed out.

There was no answering yell, or clatter of falling weapon. Crossman slid back down into the gully. The other two followed with alacrity. They needed to be somewhere else very quickly. There were only two choices: to retrace their earlier journey, or to continue along the gully in the opposite direction. Crossman decided on the latter. He led the way. They really had to find another way up to the top quickly, before the Russians sent a patrol down into the gully.

In fact, they were already there. Groups of Russian soldiers had been posted in various locations in front of their own lines. Half a dozen men in the gully must have heard Crossman and his companions moving towards them, and sent enfilading fire along the natural tunnel.

Miraculously, none of the three were hit.

'Quick! The other way,' growled Crossman.

They turned, Peterson in front, then Ali, followed by Crossman. They had gone about twenty feet when Crossman heard labouring breath behind. Someone was almost on him. He turned just as a hand with a bright lamp came around the last corner. The sergeant reached inside his coat for his revolver, a five-shot Tranter he always carried. In that instant a Russian soldier rammed a bayonet into his stomach. Crossman had on a thick leather belt with a brass buckle. As fortune would have it the bayonet point struck the leather at an angle, slid along it and went under the buckle. The bayonet bent, as Russian bayonets were wont to do, and twisted almost to a right angle, not harming Crossman but trapping the soldier's rifle.

The Russian yelled something and jerked his rifle back, pulling the hooked Crossman with it. Crossman fell on top of his attacker and they scrabbled about. Crossman knew he could not reach his pistol while pressed against the soldier, so he reached down into his boot and withdrew a hunting knife. He managed to stab the struggling soldier several times in the chest. The man began screaming. The victim's wounds did not stop his efforts, but seemed to redouble them, as he let go of his musket and gripped Crossman by the throat. Someone else was now thumping a musket butt into Crossman's back. Crossman leapt up and smashed his elbow into a face. Then he was off, running down the dark passageway of stone. Something was impeding him for a while: the musket still hooked on to his belt. Then it hit a boulder and clattered away from him. Crossman kept running.

When he was some way along the gully, he then reached into his coat and withdrew his revolver. He sent four shots crashing down the ravine behind him, hoping to hit any pursuers. It was too dark to see if he'd been successful. Crossman hoped he'd unnerved them, made them more cautious. Then he climbed the sheer wall of the gully like a cat: claws into soil and cracks in the rock face. It was a feat he wouldn't have been able to do had he not been afraid for his life.

Once out of the gully, he gulped for breath. He looked around him. At first, as he cowered amongst bushes, there were shouts coming from every direction, and lamps in evidence. But then the British picquets began firing at the lights and those carrying them put them out. Darkness returned. He found he still had the bent bayonet caught in his belt buckle. He tried to remove it, but failed. Leaving it there, he began crawling back towards his lines, wondering what had happened to his companions. He had not heard or seen anything of either Ali or Peterson, not since that Russian had rammed into him with the bayonet.

Halfway back to his own lines the guns

began roaring from the British lines. There was answering artillery fire from the Russians. Suddenly, Crossman felt tremendous pain in his right shoulder. He fell forward thinking he had been hit by shell or canister, but when he investigated he found no blood and decided it was a delayed reaction to the blows he had received from the soldier thumping him with a musket butt. Crossman lay there in the dirt for a while, allowing coruscating mortars to fly over him like meteors from both directions. Gradually the pain in his shoulder eased. It would have been pleasant to stay where he was until Sebastopol fell, but he realized he would have to make a move sometime. He dragged himself to his feet and continued, yelling the passwords as he passed through the area where there would be British picquets. It would have been foolish to be killed by soldiers wearing the same uniform as himself.

Eventually he realized he had passed the 5th Parallel, close to and following the edge of Middle Ravine. The guns ceased pounding a few minutes later. Their noise was replaced by the clinking of stirrups and bridle rings. The occasional stamp of a horse's hoof on hard earth. Someone was sitting on his mount nearby, waiting for something. The rider moved off, back towards the Col, a field officer perhaps, or cavalry man.

When Crossman's ears had cleared properly he could hear French voices to his left and British voices to his right. He knew he was safe from harm and his body went limp. It was only then he was aware that his clothes were soaked with sweat and that his right boot was full of grit. He emptied the boot and allowed a cool breeze to dry the tension sweat from his upper body. Finally, he managed to unhook the bent bayonet. He threw it away, angrily, hearing it clatter amongst the stones.

In the next few minutes he tried to relax and recollect what had happened. It was human nature to wonder about his responsibilities. Was he in any way to blame for the failure of this mission? Turning over the events in his mind he could not find any great fault with his actions, except for the fact that he had lost contact with his two men.

Should he have searched after the scramble with the Russians? Where would he have looked? One moment Ali and Peterson were with him, the next they had gone. Hopefully they had scampered away and saved themselves. That did not sound like Ali, but anything could happen in the heat of the moment, especially in the darkness. Gathering his faculties together he walked the half mile back to a British battery, where he had agreed with Ali and Peterson that they should meet in the event they were separated. When he got there he questioned one of the gunners.

'Have you seen a Turk? A Bashi-Bazouk?'

'No, I ain't,' came the reply, with a curious look at Crossman. 'Sergeant, is it?'

'What about a lance-corporal? 88th Foot?'

'Ain't seen 'im, neither. We just finished tossin' a few balls over there,' the man nodded towards the Redan. 'Nobody's come.'

At that moment Ali arrived looking dishevelled and a little wild-eyed.

'Sergeant!' There was relief in the Turk's voice. 'You get back.'

'Yes. Are you all right?'

Ali made a gesture with his palms, looking down at himself.

'No wounds, I think. You have Peterson with you?'

Alarm bells jangled in Crossman's head.

'No — not with me. Isn't she — he with you?'

'I lose her in the ravine, sergeant.'

'Well, then, let's wait here. Peterson will turn up. Let's just wait.'

They waited. They stayed by the battery for three hours, until even Crossman realized there was no hope for it. Peterson was in the hands of the enemy. He could not think she

59

was dead. Apart from those first few shots, when the three of them were together, there had been no more firing except from Crossman's revolver. Of course, there had been the guns, later, and they could have disguised the sound of shooting. Or perhaps she had been bayoneted or clubbed? In fact, Crossman thought, she might be better off dead than alive. When ordinary soldiers got hold of an enemy sharpshooter — what they saw as a despised cold-blooded distance-killer — they worked horrors on them before someone in authority saw fit to intervene.

It did not make a great deal of sense to form a hatred for a man who was doing much the same job as an artillery gunner, killing from a place of relative safety, but there is no logic to such things. The unknown face of the hidden sharpshooter was loathed by the soldier in the trench or on the parapet. Perhaps it was because they killed during dead calms, when all was tranquil and peaceful, dropping a smiling man in mid-sentence, blowing half his head away in front of an unsuspecting friend. It was the shock of such incidents, coming as they did, without warning. Harry might be saying to his chum, 'Hey, John, have you got some pipe tobac — ' And suddenly Harry's head would explode. Only afterwards, the sound of the shot: the full stop at the end of '*Take that*'. It was a terrible shock, that unexpected missile, and the sender was considered abhorrent, less than human.

'Poor Peterson,' murmured Crossman. 'Come on, Ali. We can't stay here all night. If she gets away, she'll go back to Kadikoi.'

The two men began the walk back themselves, with Ali asking, 'You have no wounds, sergeant?'

'No, no, I'm fine. Stiff shoulder. Got clubbed, that's all.'

When he entered the hovel, Crossman was half-hoping to see Peterson sitting on her cot looking shaken. She was not there. Wynter, Gwilliams and Yorwarth were there. Yorwarth was lying re-reading a letter he had received — the first since he had been in the Crimea — and was completely absorbed by the words on the page. Wynter was in conversation with Gwilliams. They were talking about women.

'I think it's about time I found meself a wife,' Wynter was saying, lying back on his blankets. 'I need some creature comforts, see. A wife can give you those. Oh, yes, she takes some of your money, but it's worth it for a good one. Someone to bed — every night if you fancy . . . '

'If *she* fancies.'

'Well, that too, but some of us are roguish

men. They like a rogue, women do. They'll do anything to hang on to a man like that. And I always choose saucy wenches, me. It's something I do. I don't mean a strumpet — I steer clear of strumpets. Just one that knows how to flick her hips and come out with a bit of breezy talk, to get you goin' like.' He paused before adding thoughtfully, 'Some men don't like their wives to be saucy, but that's 'cos they're scared they're goin' to run off with the gunner's uncle. Not me. I can hold on to my women, saucy or not.'

'I thought you was already hitched,' Gwilliams said. 'You said you had a wife back in England.'

'Not so much a wife,' came the vague reply. 'I an't heard from her in more than a year or so. We wasn't married regular, not under the law nor the church.'

'You mean you just lived together?' This wasn't an accusation of immorality, but simply a statement of fact.

'Not even that. The house weren't big enough, bein' just two rooms, one up, one down, and there being seven of 'em in her lot. No, I just used to visit, after a night at the Duke of Wellin'ton. Sometimes twice a week, when I was feeling like it. Oh, there you are, sergeant.' He had just noticed Crossman standing in the doorway. 'Come on in, don't

62

stand on ceremony. Treat it like your own home. We don't mind, do we, Gwilliams?'

'Shut up, Wynter!' snapped Crossman, furiously. 'Just keep your mouth closed.'

For once Wynter did not argue. He could see from Crossman's face something was badly wrong. Yorwarth and Gwilliams said nothing. They too were aware that something awful had happened. They sat and waited for Crossman to tell them. Had the Russians broken through? Was there to be an attack on Sebastopol?

'Has anyone seen Peterson?' Crossman asked.

It was a forlorn question and he knew the answer.

'She went with you, sergeant,' Wynter replied, quietly.

'Yes, but she hasn't returned?'

'Well, I an't seen her.'

The others shook their heads.

Crossman went from the doorway to the stairs and began to ascend. Halfway up, he stopped, and said, 'If she comes in, during the night — wake me.'

★　★　★

When he opened his eyes the next morning the sun was slanting through the window. A dazzling object hovered above the chest-of-drawers which Lovelace used for his sewing and shaving kits. Phantom echoes of the brilliant circle jumped from wall to wall around the room. It was a moment or two before Crossman realized that the brilliance was due to the fact that the item was a mirror and it was in the hand of the major. Lovelace was looking into the glass, inspecting his chin, presumably for any hairs which might have escaped the sharp edge of his razor. The mirror flashed its last message and was then replaced on the chest.

Crossman went up on his elbows. 'We lost Peterson,' he said.

Lovelace turned. 'Oh, you're awake.' Then gravely, 'Yes, I know. I have people in there, asking questions.'

'People?' He queried the word, but he knew exactly who Lovelace meant. Paid informers in Sebastopol. 'When do you think . . . ?'

'Oh, today, I'm sure. They'll get word out today.' Lovelace paused. 'Do you believe her to be alive?'

'I don't know. I think I would know if she'd been killed there and then. I've spoken with Ali about it. One minute we were all together, the next it was chaos. You know what it can be like, a surprise attack in the darkness. If she's alive . . . '

'I know what you mean, sergeant. She. The fact that Peterson is a woman might work against her, not for her.'

'Of course, they won't know she's the sharpshooter,' Crossman added, the thought only now coming to his mind. 'It could have been any one of us.'

'They'll get it from her.'

Crossman thought about this. 'Yes, they will, won't they? And once they do, she'll be in for a terrible time. Damn, I told Colonel Hawke . . . Sorry, sir.'

Lovelace brushed his shoulders with a silver clothes brush.

'Calcutta Hawke is his own man, sergeant. He probably regrets this as much as you do, now. He doesn't know Peterson personally, of course, but he knows he's lost a valuable soldier, his best sharpshooter. I found him in a very reflective mood this morning.'

'If she's alive, we must get her back.'

'I agree. Once I hear from my sources, I'll let you know.'

'Thank you, sir.'

Lovelace put on his cap and left. Crossman knew he could do nothing for the moment. He got up, washed and dressed, and then thought about going to see Hawke. It was what he should do, after a fox hunt, especially one that had ended in disaster. But instead he felt the need for empathetic company. Calcutta Hawke might be 'reflective' but he wasn't going to sympathize with Crossman and his fears for Peterson, whereas Lavinia Durham and Cousin Jane most certainly would.

Lavinia Durham was an old flame of Crossman's and Jane Mulinder (a *pretend* cousin, the daughter of a family friend) was rapidly becoming a new one. Lavinia was married to Bertie, a quartermaster, and was accompanying her captain husband. Jane had recently been jilted and had come to the Crimea to assuage her wounded pride. The two women were old friends and, here in the Crimea, inseparable companions.

Lavinia wanted Jack to love Jane, for reasons of her own. Jack was smitten but held back because of past sins. He did not want to make the same mistake twice. Jane had been hurt once, very badly, and was keeping her own confidence. Since Crossman had done much the same to Mrs Durham as Jane Mulinder's beau had done to her, he was not in a great position to be outraged and swear to avenge Jane's wrongs. This was his great problem. The women held no secrets from one another. He had wronged one of them himself and he didn't want to put himself in the position where he might wrong the other one.

Things were further complicated by the fact that Jack Crossman had joined the army under an assumed name, to avoid being discovered by his father, a Scottish baronet and an ex-major of the 93rd Foot, the Sutherland Highlanders. Crossman had been christened Alexander Kirk, had found out that he was the bastard son of his father and an English maid, and had deliberately joined the ranks rather than let his father purchase him a commission. Father and son did not get on.

He found that Jane was out riding with Rupert Jarrard. Crossman bristled for a moment, then let it go. Lavinia was studying his expression, keenly.

'Alex,' she said, using his real name since they were alone, 'you mustn't consider Rupert a rival, you know. Jane likes him as a friend, but it's you she has a fondness for.'

'I didn't come here to talk about Jane,' said Crossman. 'I've just lost a woman to the enemy.'

Lavinia's eyes widened. They were in a lodge down by the quayside, to the east of the waterfront. Through the window they had a view of the Black Sea stretching beyond a rocky harbour towards a grey-green horizon.

There were ships and boats in the scene. Sailors were at their various tasks on decks or in the rigging, polishing lamps, coiling ropes, doing things that mariners did when time was not of the essence. Fishermen were drying nets on wooden racks. The activity was domestic and unhurried, almost charming: it did not feel to them as if they were in a war zone.

'I'm sorry, I don't understand. What woman, Alex?'

Crossman now realized how it had sounded. 'Oh, one of my men. That is to say, a woman who joined the army disguised as a man. You've seen her. Lance-Corporal Peterson. She is one of my best. Was. We went out on a mission last night and she was either captured or killed.'

'The burly one? Of course. But Alex, how did she contrive to keep it secret?'

'She didn't, of course. It was successfully kept from the army proper, but we knew. I've known for a long time.'

'And she was taken last night?'

'Yes.'

Lavinia put a hand on the sleeve of his coatee. 'And you feel responsible.'

'Yes, of course. I *am* responsible.'

'But they're not children, Alex.'

'In a way, they are. No, no, that's very

patronizing. But I'm just trying to decide whether I could have prevented it. I just feel — well, Lavinia, what do you think will happen when they discover what she is? One hopes they will behave, but no matter how much I tell myself they will, I have terrible fears. Poor Peterson. She's quite vulnerable, you know. A simple soul. Nothing of your grit, Lavinia. You, I know, would meet fire with fire, but she's a delicate creature, despite being a soldier.'

Lavinia's eyes suddenly went very deep.

'I'm not sure in the circumstances that I would be any braver or more worldly than the picture you paint of Peterson. I shudder to think what they might do to her.'

If Crossman thought he had come to Lavinia Durham for comfort, he was sadly mistaken, for they were a little out of tune this morning. He suddenly realized he was indulging in self pity. Peterson was a soldier. She had joined the army in the full knowledge that she might be captured or killed by any enemy the politicians chose to send her against. Hers was the responsibility, not his. The responsibility for the fact that she was a woman in uniform might be shared between several people, including Peterson, since it would have taken but a word in the right ear to have her thrown out of the army

69

at any time. Crossman *should* have reported her. So should half a dozen commissioned officers. That part was cause for regret.

'Thank you, Lavinia. You have clarified my thoughts on the matter.'

'But I've said very little.'

'What little you said, your reactions, were enough. Now, tell me, are you happy? What are you and my cousin doing with each other?'

'Happy is not a word I have used since the day we parted, Alexander,' said Lavinia with a little quiver to her lips. 'However, we contrive to be comfortable.'

Sometimes these little melodramatic statements from Lavinia were really felt and at others she was merely toying with him. The trouble was, Crossman could never tell which it was. Today he decided she was just being petulant and he wasn't going to feed that petulance.

'Fine, I simply asked. In future I shall keep my curiosities to myself.' He looked about him. 'What a glorious day. Halfway through the winter I believed the Crimean peninsula was actually hell, but now the June weather has arrived, it is very pleasant.'

'You may change the subject, Alex, but I am quite serious.'

In spite of himself he found he was playing her game after all.

'You are also quite married, Lavinia, and whilst I regret the past I can do nothing to change it. I have told you how sorry I am a million times. We were young, very young. It is true I was very much in love with you and I can see now, now that you have grown even more beautiful, what a fool I was to let you go — but I did. You can surely forgive the caprices of a youth? It is I who am the greatest loser, for while you have only lost this ragamuffin creature you see before you, I have lost a jewel.'

She smiled now and those magenta eyes sparkled.

'There, I knew I could get you to say it. You loved me! I am all vanity, Alex. It was all I wanted from you today. And such a pretty speech to go with it! I never believed it possible. I thought your head was full of horrid noisy engines and inventions. There were times, Alex, when I wished I were a device invented by one of your heroes like Isambard Kingdom Brunel. I'm sure if I had a name like that you would have married me. But there, you have told me I am a jewel, and it was spoken so sincerely I'm inclined to believe you.'

'But you have to like engines too — James Watt declared it.'

Lavinia looked utterly mystified and

Crossman enlightened her.

'James Watt, of steam engine fame? He once said, 'The velocity of violence and horrible noise of the engine give universal satisfaction to all beholders, believers or not.' Now I know you are not a believer, but surely Watt was right?'

'He most certainly was not right,' replied Lavinia, indignantly. 'I hate the sordid things.'

At that moment there was the clatter of hooves outside the cottage, then the door was flung open. Jane came tumbling into the room, her eyes revealing distress. Her riding hat was askew, her lacy cravat in disarray, and she was clearly in a state of upset. Crossman immediately jumped to conclusions. He was ready to rush outside and challenge Jarrard to fisticuffs at the very least, a duel if the assault on Jane had been serious. However, it was a good thing he did not follow through these rash assumptions, for Jane suddenly blurted out the reason for her obvious passion.

'Lord Raglan is dead!'

Lavinia's hand went to her mouth and she uttered a little, 'Oh.'

'What was it?' asked Crossman, knowing that though Raglan rarely left his farmhouse headquarters these days, he did occasionally emerge. It was possible he was hit by a cannon, or even a sharpshooter. 'Was it — on the field?'

'His illness took him,' said Jane. 'We have just heard it from a staff officer. Jarrard has rushed away to copy something . . . '

'You mean, write his copy,' said Crossman.

'Yes, that was it.'

Tears sprang to Lavinia's eyes. 'Oh, that poor man.'

'Many poor men have died here, Lavinia,' Crossman pointed out. 'There were plough-boys just as worthy.'

'No, no, I didn't mean that. Of course every death is regretted, Alex. I meant he died broken. It was the last straw, the failure to take the Redan. If the attack had been successful, he might have had the strength and the will to win over the disease. After the 18th he had nothing to live for. I am certain the protracted nature of this ugly war sapped him beyond his capabilities. He was such a nice man.'

'Too nice, for a commander in chief,' Crossman said. 'I know, I know, he was a gentleman through and through, but we actually needed a savage lion here, not a noble antelope. It's a shame he ever took on the task. I'm sure he regretted it a thousand times over. He was no Wellington, that's certain. But I can see by your looks, ladies, that I must not speak ill of the dead, so I'll add that he was an inoffensive man, an aristocrat who was caught up in a tangled net of duty and honour. It is a great shame, for I think he did his best, as he saw it. Let's hope the cabinet back home now send us someone with a bit of fire in him, someone competent, a warrior with a keen sense of purpose . . . '

'There is talk of a General Simpson — Sir James Simpson.'

'Don't know him, but he's got to be a better general than Lord Raglan,' said Crossman. 'Sorry, sorry, I shall say no more.'

Crossman took his leave of the ladies and went back to the hovel, where he found the only subject of talk was the death of their marshal.

'What's goin' to happen now?' Despite Wynter's constant battle with authority, his rebellions over the least little thing, he found himself worried at any hint that order and the status quo were in danger. God had toppled dead from his perch. Did that mean chaos followed? He wasn't sure. He felt insecure and vulnerable. 'Will we all go home?'

'No, o' course you won't,' growled Gwilliams, who was polishing a knife blade. 'Generals is two a penny. They'll ship another one over, quick as you please. They got more generals than rats in a barn. What they ain't got, is good ones. Good ones is hard to find.'

Crossman said, 'Gwilliams is right. Good generals are worth their weight in ammunition. Ali, can I see you outside for a minute?'

Ali rose and followed Crossman away from the hovel, where they would not be heard by the others.

'Do you believe Peterson is still alive?'

Ali nodded his head. 'I think so.'

'Then we've got to get her back. If it were me, I'm sure you'd come after me. I certainly would come after you. Peterson will be suffering.'

'I think so. We keep an ear.'

'Major Lovelace has promised to seek information.'

'Good. We wait for the proper information, then we go and get her.'

'That's my feeling too. I'm glad we're together on this.'

Ali grinned. 'We go together on everything, sergeant.'

★ ★ ★

Lovelace and Hawke were sharing a quiet drink in an officers only drinking tent. Hawke had it on the best authority that Sir James Simpson was going to be appointed commander in chief. His information had come to him via the telegraph and was quite up to the minute.

'Simpson,' he said, bitterly, 'I ask you. Another Peninsula veteran. We've simply exchanged a dove for a pigeon.'

'Yet who else is there?' asked Lovelace. 'There are no eagles to be had at the moment. We must rub along with these old men. I hear Simpson has been with Napier in India.'

'Well, that's something I suppose, but I wager he'll prove no better than his predecessor.'

Lovelace agreed, not because he wished to, but because he wanted to end the conversation. The major felt uncomfortable speaking about a superior officer, a general, in the presence of other officers. To change the subject, he asked Hawke, 'What's happening at Kars?'

The question concerned the main fort in Turkish Armenia, which had been besieged by Russian forces. Inside Kars were thousands of trapped Turks, in very bad conditions. It was the situation in the Crimea reversed, with the allied forces suffering malnutrition, disease and constant battering from enemy fire from within their defences.

'Oh, the gunner is holding out.'

From the way Hawke said it, it sounded as

if there were one man inside the fortress town. He was in fact referring to a Colonel Fenwick Williams who had been sent to Kars as Lord Raglan's liaison officer with Zarif Pasha, the commander of the Turkish forces. Another gunner, Major Teasdale had gone with him. Between them Williams and Teasdale had tried over the past few months to raise morale and improve the town's defences. An Irish general who was serving in the Ottoman army, General Gunyon, had appraised them of the situation several months previously and the pair had gone in and immediately requisitioned grain and other necessities. They were becoming something of a legend amongst the Crimean officers, some of whom would have changed places with Williams or Teasdale in a second, simply for the fact of their celebrity status.

Not only was this mirror image of the Crimean war going on at Kars, close to the Turkish border with Russia, but the British navy had been busy on various waterways too. In the Pacific there were two British squadrons at work, one under Admiral Stirling, the other under Admiral Bruce. They had harried Russian shipping in their region, just as Admiral Dundas's fleet was blockading ports in the Baltic. The effort to end the war was being made on more fronts than one, but soldiers in the field are concerned with their task only. There was not really any great interest in men like Lovelace and Hawke for the good work the navy was doing. Soldiers like them were concerned only with the fall of Sebastopol, and they wanted their contribution to that fall to be seen and appreciated.

'Good, good,' replied Lovelace, listlessly. 'If you'll excuse me, sir, I'll be getting back. I want to go into Sebastopol tonight. I'm sure the Russians are cooking something up. It's in the wind. I need to go in and have a look for myself.'

Hawke raised an eyebrow. 'A retaliation attack on our trenches?'

'I don't know. Something. I must go in and see what I can discover.'

'Take the lieutenant with you. He still needs field work.'

Hawke was referring to Lieutenant Pirce-Smith, an ex-Guards officer who had transferred to a less elite regiment to escape underhand treatment by officers from aristocratic families. Despite his grand double-barrelled name, Pirce-Smith was from a humble background, which did not fit well with the Guards.

'All right. I know he prefers to come with me, rather than with Sergeant Crossman, who I'm told bullies him.'

Hawke laughed. 'Fancy Jack. Yes, I'll wager he does.'

Lovelace downed his drink and then, after a little thought, said to the colonel, 'Sir, I wonder — I would like to do something for the sergeant. Some sort of recognition. What do you think?'

The colonel's eyebrows went up. 'What were you thinking of?'

'Oh, you know — *something*. Something fairly grand.'

'Ah. Yes. Well, I'll see what I can do. I'm not without influence, these days. Now that Lord Raglan has gone, perhaps it'll increase. So far as I am aware, Simpson does not regard our work as the skulking of scoundrels, as our former commander did. You never know, he might approve.'

'Good. Thank you, sir.'

Lovelace knew where he would find Pirce-Smith.

The lieutenant was fond of shooting, it being the sport of gentlemen. Pirce-Smith went out of his way to do anything and everything like a member of the gentility, his father having been the resident vicar of a chapel attached to a large wealthy country estate of a nobleman. Pirce-Smith had been raised with the son of the house, Stanhope Winslow, who had also joined the Guards.

Stanhope had not been one of Pirce-Smith's tormentors, but had done nothing to discourage his brother officers. The pair had parted on cool terms. A few days later Lieutenant Winslow had been killed at Inkerman, his legs shot away from him. He had bled to death over the course of several hours, unable to reach help. Pirce-Smith now wished they had parted on better terms with one another. There is nothing a man can say to his friend once that friend is dead.

Although he would not admit it to himself, one of the reasons Pirce-Smith disliked Sergeant Crossman so much was because the sergeant was from the kind of family Pirce-Smith envied — would have given his eye teeth to be part of — yet Crossman had rejected it all. Here were two men desperate to cast off their fathers: one because his father — though loyal and true to wife, friends and employers — was not genteel; the other because his father was an aristocratic tyrant who made every effort to own people as well as property. They would have swopped places in an instant, these two young men, and walked away with sunny thoughts in their heads. Neither knew his place in Victorian society, both preferring another station.

Lovelace went into some foothills, at the entrance to which was a graveyard. He passed, on the way, a very young and desultory looking private by a line of corpses still left for burial a week after the attack on the Redan. The cadavers were bloated, lying as they were in the sun, and the apathetic private was walking along the row piercing their stomachs with a bayonet to let out the gases. Lovelace, not ordinarily one for niceties, felt a great distaste for this treatment of the dead.

'Is that absolutely necessary, soldier?' he asked.

The private stopped, blinked, and then said, 'S'orders, sir. Them mioght burst on un, an' then where's we be?'

'I'm sure the corpses won't explode.'

'Oi'm just doin' the orders, sir. One hofficer tellt me.'

'All right.'

The bayonet went in again with a *phut* sound and the ballooned belly of a soldier deflated visibly. Lovelace winced. If he had a son lying there he would have been utterly appalled. But things went on behind the backs of civilians which would have horrified them. He remembered the corpses in Varna harbour. The dozens, hundreds, of soldiers who had died of disease on the way to the Crimea. They had been weighted and cast into the sea to dispose of them quickly, but the gory bodies rose to float around, bumping against the boats. Ghastly business. He remembered the ships full of wounded men, crossing the Black Sea from the Crimea to Scutari Hospital in Constantinople. They had left without doctors or surgeons on board, and with dying men crying for water. The hospital itself was awash with rats and fleas. In the beginning there had been no bedding for the patients, no proper sanitation, no one to change bandages which remained in place for months. He recalled the nights after the battles, when the sorely wounded still lay out there on the field, screaming for attention, yet no one able to go to them, bring them in, give them any kind of nursing or comfort.

This is how we treat our dead, he thought. Men of courage, who had died for their country, their regiment. Men who had left their families in an Irish village, a Welsh town, a Scottish city, an English hamlet, and who had fetched up on this foreign shore. Many had died slowly. Many had died swiftly. Few had gone out intact. Those who died of the cholera, or dysentery, or some lung disease, had left with all their body parts. Others had been scattered over wide areas. Some had simply ceased to be.

Lovelace wondered if those who sat in parliament had any idea what real war was like these days. It was no longer a game. It was a serious business, too serious to be in the hands of amateurs. Most of the senior officers had no idea what they were doing. Many of them were there because they came from the nobility or were wealthy. The best general in the army was not leading it, because the best general in the army was probably a cobbler's son, or a farrier's boy, and therefore a private or NCO.

Not that families of breeding did not throw up the odd brilliant soldier: of course they did. Lovelace himself was proof of that. Natural soldiers came from every walk of life. Just as a duke could be a wonderful carpenter and a goose girl could run a country estate. There was natural talent in any human being, from whatever station in life. But the system did not allow for it, could not use these skills to their best advantage. In the beginning, when British warriors were rough tribesmen, the biggest and the toughest and the cleverest man rose to become chief. But then, as always, dynasties were formed, oligarchies carved themselves a niche, and hereditary rights became more important than natural skills.

Some men in the government, Lovelace supposed, must have seen war. Those who were ex-soldiers and sailors. Yet still wars continued to be bungled in a most appalling way. Lovelace hated inefficiency, loved expediency. He was an open admirer of Machiavelli. A woman he had once known had compared him to a well-made sword. 'Clean, bright and deadly,' she had said. Lovelace did not mind that. He was an Englishman and the English made superlative blades. He had studied English sword-making and knew it to be a superior craft, even an art, in his own country. Anglo-Saxon sword-makers had been forging peerless blades long before the Spaniards of Toledo or even the now renowned Japanese.

If he were a sword he would use his cutting edge to the best advantage. His skills were not best used at the front of the battle, but working behind the lines. Intrigue, sabotage, information gathering, assassination, forming secret armies within the enemy army. If he could turn enemy soldiers against their officers, that was for the better. If he could remove a great general with a pistol shot from the shadows, so be it. His skills were not universally admired, he knew, by gentlemen of his own class. Dash, verve, blind courage, élan. These were beloved of his kind. Talents that lay open to observation in the bright light of day. His were closed, carried out in darkness, secretive, cryptic. His brilliance had to be shaded in polite company. But he knew they were necessary tools in modern warfare and he was determined to use them to their full.

'Lieutenant!' he called now, on climbing a slope and seeing Pirce-Smith, wearing tweeds and shooting boots, a long old-fashioned sporting gun under his right arm, walking along like some earl out looking for his Sunday lunch. 'Have you bagged anything?'

Pirce-Smith looked up and saw his superior officer. His eyes gleamed with great pleasure. The lieutenant was one of the faithful, one of the followers of the creed of Lovelace, and he admired the major above all creatures on the earth. Of course, as with Crossman, Lovelace did not let Pirce-Smith see all his facets, for the young man would have melted away in horror, and anyway, that was the major's stock in trade, keeping secrets, especially about himself. No man knew him well. No man knew the whole Lovelace. No man ever would.

Pirce-Smith held up a brace of hares. 'Dinner,' he said.

'Well done. Let me see that piece, will you?' Lovelace reached out for the sporting weapon, but Pirce-Smith smiled and kept it tucked beneath his arm.

'No, no, sir. I'm mindful of the rule you

have taught me. Never let yourself be disarmed, even by someone posing as a friend. You're testing me, I'm sure.'

Lovelace's face darkened. 'Don't be a damn fool, lieutenant. I'm a sportsman too. I merely want to see who made it . . . '

Pirce-Smith was upset. He passed the weapon to the major.

'Sorry, sir, I had thought . . . '

Lovelace smiled now and shook his head sadly, and tutted, while turning the firelock over in his hands. 'Lieutenant, you must learn not to take notice of sudden mood changes in bullying majors. This is your property, you should have insisted and held on to it. How am I ever going to teach you? One day someone is going to wander up here, take this out of your hands, and blow your head off. Sergeant Crossman would never have allowed me to take the only weapon in his possession. You are in the business now and are fair game for any assassin.'

Pirce-Smith was now thoroughly miserable. 'Failed again, eh, sir?'

'I'm afraid so. But never mind, you will learn, eventually — if you're not dead by then.'

Pirce-Smith reached into his pocket and pulled out a pistol.

'Ah.' The major laughed. 'You *are* learning,

just a little, but I would have beaten you to the cock, you know.'

'The gun is not loaded, sir. The pistol is.'

Lovelace nodded again, this time thoughtfully. 'Good. But this monster — how do you hit anything with it?' He looked down the barrel. 'It's archaic.' There was no rust on the hunting weapon, but it was black with age, the stock was worn almost to a stub, the barrel was slightly loose and the hammer was pitted, corroded.

'It was my grandfather's. We're not a wealthy family, sir. I'm very fond of it.'

'I'm sure you are, but wouldn't you like my matching Lefauchaux shotguns? Pinfire. The very latest. Well, not *the* very latest, because my Purdeys have arrived and they're actually just a little superior to the Lefauchaux.'

Pirce-Smith's eyes widened in disbelief.

'You're offering to sell me your shotguns? But sir — I am most grateful, most grateful indeed that you should offer them to me first — if I am the first you have asked — but I'm afraid I just haven't the wherewithal. As I said, my father is not a wealthy man and I have no money of my own.'

'They're a gift, lieutenant. Say no more about it.'

The eyes widened even further.

'Oh, I couldn't . . . '

'Of course you damn well could. Now stop looking at me like a newly-born calf at its mother. The guns are yours. You'll make good use of them, I'm sure. Shooting is a passion with you, isn't it? I enjoy it too, but that's mostly because I like playing with precision-made instruments of death, not because I delight in potting hares. It's the machine that excites me, the action, the noise and the destruction it creates. Blue gunmetal. The smell of expensive gunpowder. Now you sir, are the true hunter amongst us. I am the popinjay who likes the show of the thing.'

'Well, I shall accept your gift, sir,' said Pirce-Smith, stiffly, clearly overwhelmed by this show of generosity, 'but you must allow me to give you something in return. I'm not sure what.'

'Oh, a pleasing bottle of Chardonnay will suffice, man. I'm always up for that. Now, we have work to do. Peterson has gone missing in a raid. There's a chance she's alive. We need to slip into Sebastopol and ask a few questions.'

'Right, yes. Lance-Corporal Peterson, you say?' Pirce-Smith looked doubtful.

'I know what you're thinking, but don't say it, or you'll spoil a flowering relationship, lieutenant. Peterson is one of our own. We look after our own.'

'Yes, yes, of course.'

⋆ ⋆ ⋆

The two officers returned from their mission later and went to see Crossman together, in his room above the hovel.

'Bad news, sergeant,' said Lovelace.

'She's dead,' said Crossman flatly.

'No, she's not dead. She's being held. In a farmhouse, north of here.'

Crossman blinked. 'Not in Sebastopol? But why . . . ?'

'Tell him, lieutenant.'

Pirce-Smith explained, 'We came by the information too easily, sergeant. It's clear they *wanted* us to know. Our informants said that their informants . . . '

'You know we keep several buffers between us and the actual source,' interrupted Lovelace, 'or we wouldn't last a day.'

'Yes, of course, sir. What you're saying is that Peterson is being used as bait, to draw someone?'

'You, we believe,' replied Pirce-Smith. 'She's been given to the Cossacks. As I say, they have her at this vineyard to the north. It's our belief that they want you to go and try to rescue her. All the indications point in that direction.'

'The bloody Cossacks,' muttered Crossman.

The sergeant had had several run-ins with Cossacks and so far had come off best. They had their spies amongst the many civilians in the British and French camps, just as Lovelace's spies walked the streets of Sebastopol. They knew he was responsible for several deaths, off the battlefield, amongst their numbers. There was an incident at a French-owned farmhouse, where Crossman's *peloton* had killed a few Cossacks. And they had crossed swords several times in the Fediuokine Hills. He had subsequently foiled an attempt on his life, killing his would-be Cossack assassins. They hated him for it. There was a price on his head and the blue warriors, those famous horsemen of the steppes, were determined to even the score somehow.

'Now,' said Lovelace, as Crossman was absorbing this piece of news, 'clearly we can't leave her there. I shall get together some people — Captain Goodlake will help — and we'll go and get her.'

'They'll kill her as soon as they know I'm not coming,' Crossman said. 'She won't be worth anything to them then. You'll find the farmhouse empty.'

'That may happen, of course.'

Wynter and the other soldiers had been listening intently from their own room and

Wynter shouted up, 'Poor old Peterson. Well, that's war for you, an't it?'

The officers and sergeant knew that Wynter was expressing *his* opinion on the subject. He did not want to walk into a trap, even if he knew it was a trap. Crossman wondered whether the others felt like that too. Ali would go anywhere with him, but Yorwarth and Gwilliams? Perhaps they were of the same opinion as Wynter. Let waiting dogs wait?

'I have to go, major, you know that.'

Crossman's voice was quiet but insistent. Pirce-Smith nodded. Lovelace followed suit. 'All right, sergeant.'

'All right *what?*' cried Wynter, who had crept up the stairs and was now listening outside the doorway. 'I an't going.'

'You'll do as you're told,' snapped Lovelace, angrily. 'Unless you want a flogging, corporal.'

'That's right, that's just it, an't it?' whined Wynter. 'Give us a choice, eh? Flogging or death.' His keen eyes pierced through the gloom and he could now see Major Lovelace's expression. He suddenly remembered he wasn't speaking to his sergeant, who was sometimes lenient, occasionally allowing a certain amount of insubordination in order to give Wynter an escape valve for his frustrations. The major did not require anything from Wynter. His life would never be dependent on the soldier's loyalty. The lance-corporal realized instantly he had overstepped the mark and immediately changed his tone. 'Sorry, sir. Din't mean nothin' by it. I'll go, o' course. I an't sure whether the other two . . . '

Gwilliams snorted in contempt. There was no doubt about his loyalty to the sergeant and his concern for Peterson's plight.

And Yorwarth yelled up the stairs, 'Don't you speak for me, you snivelling worm. The sergeant knows I'm with him.'

Lovelace looked at Crossman. 'Sergeant, I shall go to Hawke directly, and tell him I've sent you to get Peterson. The colonel will understand. Try to be careful. They will know you're coming. On the other hand, you know they will know you're coming. This is as deep as it gets. Use every guile. No heroics. No holding back on this one. This is not a gentleman's war, this fight between you and the blues — it's a deadly business.'

'I understand. No quarter.'

'No quarter indeed. And I'm sure,' the major hesitated for a moment, before continuing, 'well, what I'm trying to say is, you're not going to find Peterson in good health. Be prepared for that.'

'I will, sir. And thank you, for understanding.'

'Just get back in one piece. All of you.'

Over the next couple of hours the *peloton* prepared to leave.

They wore Tartars' clothes and, after nearly a year in the Crimea they looked the part. They were all, to a man, bearded and weathered. Their skins were the colour of seasoned oak, some darker than others. They were muscled: Crossman and Yorwarth tall and lean, Ali and Gwilliams shorter, hard, stocky characters. Wynter was apart, being as short as the latter but thinner even than the former. He was what Gwilliams called a 'whipcord' man, light on his feet, remarkably fast, almost frantic in action, his movements often driven by that self-preserving, essential viciousness that some men possess. They were all strong men with strong eyes. They could stare down a general when disguised and on the road.

Dark men, then, with dark souls. If they had chosen careers as pirates or highwaymen they would have been called Black Jake or Robber Jones. All except Gwilliams, who had a touch of gold about him. Gwilliams' rippled beard and hair were magnificent. His full set gleamed like hammered bronze. Had he been a member of some biblical tribe he would have been chosen instantly as their king, simply because of his imposing bearing, his glorious hirsute pate and chin. Even the contours of his head were regal: a large, marvellous head, the head of a lion. He held it as if it were heavy with a king's crown.

'We all ready then?' said Crossman, as they armed themselves. 'Yorwarth, damn you, what's the matter now?'

'Don't know, sergeant. Woke up with it this morning.' He looked down at himself and then started scratching furiously. 'It's all over. It started in the crotch.'

The others all stared at the Australian youth. His face had a horrible prickled rash covering two-thirds of it. Two eyes stared out from beneath puffy red cheeks. He looked extremely ugly.

'God man, if anyone was to catch anything around here, it would be you. I can't understand why you haven't died of the cholera before now.'

Yorwarth had not long recovered from a broken jaw, which had to be rebroken and reset after Gwilliams had put a strange cage-splint on his face. He still had a bit of a lopsided look about him.

It was Gwilliams who spoke up now. 'I can fix him, sergeant. I got this balm the Huron

Indians give me. I could paste him now — but I ain't doin' his crotch. He'll have to do that hisself.'

'Well, hurry up then. Yorwarth, strip. Gwilliams, find the balm and get to work.'

Ali and Wynter helped Yorwarth rip off his clothes. Gwilliams went to a footlocker and found a large can with a rag for a lid. He used the rag to smear the contents of the can on Yorwarth's skin. The private said it felt cool and nice, and had no doubt he would be cured in no time. Once they had him covered he looked like he had been greased for some diabolical purpose known only to savages about to perform pagan rites. At the last minute Gwilliams told him to stay away from naked flames.

'If'n you don't, you'll go up like a torch.'

'Well, tell me *now*,' grumbled Yorwarth. 'I mean, every damn weapon we use spits bloody fire.'

The suggestion was too much for an impressionable mind like Wynter's and he absently took his clay pipe from his pocket.

'Put that away,' growled Yorwarth. 'You want me to burn?'

'Is it that inflammable?' asked a concerned Crossman of Gwilliams.

' 'Fraid so, sergeant. Worse than lamp oil. Anyone lights a match near him and he'll join his ancestors. The other use is for corpses on pyres, to make 'em go up quick. He'll crackle all right, give him a light. Though it should be all fine, give it an hour or two, once it soaks in.'

'This crazy bunch,' muttered Crossman. 'Why can't I have men about me that are sane?'

''Cos only loonies would follow you, sergeant,' said Wynter, grinning like a dog.

Provided with horses by Lovelace, they set out at a walk along the road, towards the hills. Until they were out of the town they presented a rough-looking picture, dressed as they were, with rifles wrapped in rags to hide the glint of gunmetal. Officers and men of line and artillery regiments, sailors, ladies, sutlers, all stepped out of their way, wondering who these tough-looking irregular forces were. One or two knew them. Jane saw them pass by and her eyes flicked a quick hello-and-farewell at Crossman. She did not openly acknowledge him, realizing he was going out on a mission.

A rather smart officer of Hussars riding down the middle of the street seemed about to refuse to give passage, then looking into Ali's face, changed his mind and he too pulled his mount aside.

Crossman, rather childishly (he admitted to

himself) enjoyed this show of the barbarian warriors going out to do mischief in the hills.

The sergeant had been given an inaccurate map, which showed the farmhouse. It was the only chart available, having been purchased by Lovelace's father at a map shop in Sicilian Avenue, London and sent with others to his son at the front. This, and a compass, were his only tools. But he had Ali, who was invaluable. During off-duty hours the Turk had familiarized himself with the countryside all around the war area, riding out on a small tough horse, making mental notes. Sometimes he had taken his 'companion' with him: a very handsome bare-breasted local woman with broad shoulders, thick limbs and a strong nose.

Wynter was hopelessly in love with Ali's companion, whose virtues were all that he himself would never own: steadfastness, uncomplaining loyalty, inner strength, immense stamina. The Bashi-Bazouk knew of Wynter's adoration — it was hardly hidden in his eyes, fixed as they were on the woman's bare bosom — and it amused him. Wynter would, of course, have died a horrible death if he had done anything about his feelings, and well he knew it, but it didn't stop those longings in him. He suffered in silent joy, feasting from a distance on what he could not have.

Once beyond the town they came into an area of quiet beauty. Wild flowers grew in great variety and abundance. Dragonflies skimmed the wayside herbs and small birds showered the summer grasses. Trees with full foliage studded the rises and brooks, mostly dry at this time of the year, cut through between stony hummocks. Cimmerian Tauri, Ostrogoths, Huns, Khazars, Cumans and Mongols had all ridden this landscape, as the foreign soldiers were doing now, and had admired its contours and wildlife. To the north was the semi-arid steppe, where wheat and cotton fields flourished, sweeping down towards the Black Sea and its subtropical shoreline.

'Say,' Gwilliams spoke to Crossman, as their horses' hooves rattled amongst the loose stones of a slope, 'did I ever tell you? I read once that a Byzantine emperor had his nose cut off by army officers and was exiled to the Crimea. It was a Justinian. Can't remember which number. Second or third, I think. I'm not so hot on the numbers.'

Gwilliams had been raised in a home with books and was always throwing out these titbits to his sergeant.

'Who took the throne after that?'

'One of the officers.'

'That makes sense.'

Wynter, whose rivalry with Gwilliams was becoming a pain in the neck to Crossman, was starved of attention. He rectified this, coming out with his own choice piece.

'See the way they looked at us, riding out of town? We're 88th, I know that, sergeant, but we could make our very own regiment. Just us.'

'You mean, like Crossman's Cut-throats, or Fancy Jack's Fusiliers?' said Gwilliams. 'Yeah, I like that.'

'No, I mean a real regiment, with colours and all. That's what I mean. Of course, there won't be hundreds of us, like in a regular regiment — just us few good men — but we an't a regular bunch anyways.'

Crossman said, 'Much as I like the idea, Wynter, I fear having colours is an expensive business. You count the cost in men. Have you stopped to think how many ensigns and sergeants we lose defending the colours? What a target they make for the enemy. Even lieutenants snatch up the colours when the bearer falls. One after the other. It's a sad way to lose men.'

'Well I agree about the officers, but sergeants is two a penny — sergeant,' countered Wynter. Then he grinned at his own joke. 'No, serious, sergeant, the colours is necessary, an't they? For a rallying point. You need to rally in battle, sometimes.'

'True, but why not let the colours be carried by someone lowly, someone fairly worthless, like a lance-corporal.'

Wynter grinned again. 'Now you're havin' a go at me. Touch, sergeant.'

'As you say, touch.'

Wynter had meant *touché* of course, but Crossman did not correct him. The sergeant already had a reputation of being a bit of an education snob and it did him no good amongst men like Wynter to reinforce this.

When they stopped for the night in a gully clustered with trees, the first thing Yorwarth did was strip off his clothes and start scratching like mad. Far from curing his dermatitis the 'balm' had inflamed and spread it further. Yorwarth's skin was burning with millions of tiny red pinheads. They had to hold him down to stop him from clawing his skin off. He was like a raging madman for a while, until Ali found a waterhole. They took the cool mud from the hole and covered him, giving him some small relief, before throwing him bodily into the water to wash him off. Then Ali set about trying to cure the effects of Gwilliams' 'cure'.

'It's not the balm,' complained Gwilliams. 'It worked on Indian skin and it worked on mine. It's Yorwarth. He's a blamed natural child of goblins and pixies. Nothin' seems to work with him. I make him a good workable face splint and he gets a crooked jaw. When he was in fever I gave him perfectly sound medicine, used on Mexicans and Apache Indians to good effect, and his body heat goes up like he's got a furnace in his chest. I can't be doing with him. He ain't right, that boy. He's from a different place.'

Ali spent an hour collecting herbs and mixing them in a bowl before applying another kind of paste to Yorwarth. They had by this time tied Yorwarth's hands to his sides. His eyes were bulging. He swore at anyone and everyone. Hot tears of frustration ran down his cheeks. He begged, as Odysseus begged to have his cords removed on hearing the sirens' call, to be released to scratch himself. It did not help him any that Wynter kept making jokes at his expense.

'You an't comin' up to scratch, Yorwarth, old chum!'

'I'll kill him,' raged Yorwarth. 'I'll rip his tongue out.'

'No skin off my nose,' said Wynter. 'Plenty of skin off your back though, me old matey from convict-land.'

Crossman put a stop to the jokes but he could do nothing to relieve the stricken soldier's suffering. He refused to release him from his bonds, but said that once Ali's medicinal paste began to work he would consider it. However they found to make matters even worse, Ali's paste attracted the midges and mosquitoes. Before long they were settling on Yorwarth like dark snow, threatening to make his wounds fester. Wynter said he now looked like a skinned boiled rabbit, covered in black pepper.

Yorwarth wept.

In the morning the youth's eyes were black with lack of sleep, but his skin had improved enough for them to untie the ropes. He darted accusing looks at everyone who tried to sympathize with him. He muttered something about being 'bewitched' by one of the 'painted ladies' at Donnybrook. Gwilliams stared at him and said, 'I surely hope you haven't caught some Black Sea pox, for Wynter's sake.'

'Why?' queried Wynter, his head coming up.

''Cause you always share his women,' replied Gwilliams, matter-of-factly. 'You get 'em cheap after Yorwarth, we all know, 'cause the boy's so well endowed and the women is so satisfied they're mellow and warm-hearted. If he's caught somethin', you've got it too, fellah.'

Wynter found himself subconsciously scratching. He stopped and glared at Gwilliams. 'You think you know everythin', Yankee.'

Gwilliams said, 'See here, I will quote you somethin' farmer's boy. Somethin' I learned off by heart from one of the preacher's books. 'In Xamdu did Cublai Can build a stately Palace, encompassing sixteen miles of plaine ground with a wall, wherein are fertile Meddowes, pleasant springs, delightfull streames and all sort of beasts of chase and game, and in the middest thereof a sumtuous house of pleasure.' Now that was writ in 1613, by a Mr Samuel Purchas, whereas that there well-known poem about Xanadu was writ by some Englishman poet just in the year 1816.'

'So what, Yankee?' snarled Wynter, who hated to be spoken down to. 'What are you tryin' to say.'

'Nothin's new in this here world.'

3

Crossman intended to lead his men a long circuitous route, northwards at first, then west, then returning southwards, in the shape of a hook. He had deliberately staged that flamboyant departure from Kadikoi in order that it should not be missed by Russian spies. If they had been torturing Peterson the necessity would cease once they knew Crossman had taken the bait. Word would now have got back to the vineyard that he was on his way and it was to be hoped the Cossacks were not sadists and that now their scheme was in motion Peterson would not be subjected to further hurt.

Crossman did not intend hurrying and he avoided straight lines. The Cossacks would be waiting for him at various points. He had discussed these tactics with Yusuf Ali, who thoroughly approved. Now that they were on the trail they needed to avoid all contact with human society. No one was to be trusted. They stayed away from other farmhouses, orchards and tracks as best they could. Crossman made what he believed to be unpredictable moves, changing direction by whim. In this way he hoped to keep clear of ambuscades. The Cossacks were not good at ambushes anyway. If they had been at one time, now their prowess lay in charging across flat areas slashing with their swords and pricking with their lances.

At noon they came to an old iron mine: a black shaft that went into the side of a rocky hill. The entrance was low and wide. Any miners entering that tunnel would need to crouch double. Ali found goat and wolf droppings close to the opening. When he investigated further, he realized there were still some goats inside the mine. Not hesitating any further he crawled in, took one, and slaughtered it for their next meal. There was a short debate about whether or not to light a fire and Crossman decided there were enough dwellings and herders in the area, with their own fires. If the Cossacks were looking for smoke they would be chasing phantoms all day long.

After providing them with water and feed, they hitched the horses to some stunted pines which stood on the shoulder of the shelf. Yorwarth's chestnut gelding was the largest and most bad-tempered of the mounts, so he was kept apart from the others. Sydney was fond of biting and kicking. However, the tall chestnut was fleet of hoof, and therefore valuable in emergencies. If a messenger was needed, Yorwarth was the man. He maintained that when it came to run and chase, Sydney was always out front, 'too bloody-minded to be caught by any Russian nag.'

'This meat is really good,' said Wynter, the hot fat running down his chin. 'Who'd have thought goat would be so tasty.'

'Not much difference between goat and sheep,' said Yorwarth, scratching his face with a thigh bone.

While they were eating, Gwilliams, who was on sentry duty, gave the alarm. They scattered amongst the rocks, Yorwarth crawling in the entrance to the mine, hiding himself behind a thick shoring timber.

A Tartar came up the hill, a young man with a slight limp and using a staff. He paused on cresting the initial climb, to stare at the wide ledge. He sniffed the air. Yes, there was the fire he had smelled from below. Looking puzzled he proceeded to investigate, staring with a bemused expression at the bones around the fire. Gradually Crossman saw the truth dawn upon his face: someone had been eating his goats. He looked around him quickly, angrily, seeing nothing. Next, he went to the entrance to the mine and chirruped, calling what remained of his goats to him. Out of the darkness of the interior came the muzzle of Yorwarth's rifle to within an inch of the startled goatherd's nose.

'Don't say a word,' ordered Yorwarth. 'Not a sound.'

Crossman now came out and repeated the order in the Tartar's own tongue. The youth was so frightened by the sudden appearance of a gang of brigands he sat down, his face white. They crowded round him, looking down on him.

'What we do with him, sergeant?' said Ali. 'You think we have to kill him?'

Crossman hated these decisions. He had never yet come to terms with this side of the nasty business he was in. He was not ruthless enough for these cold-blooded killings of civilians, even though they threatened his own life. If they let the boy go, he could warn the Cossacks. The Russian cavalrymen might already have primed the local inhabitants, warning them they must pass on any news of strangers. On the other hand, the Cossacks already knew the *peloton* was coming, so if they were out of this area by mid-afternoon, the youth's information would be obsolete.

'We'll let him go, later,' he said. 'Finish the meal.'

'I think we should kill him,' said Ali, sensibly.

'Me too,' said Gwilliams, 'but I don't want

107

to do it. Look at his blue eyes.'

'I can do it,' Ali murmured.

'I wouldn't wager against that,' added Wynter. 'You'd kill your own brother if you had to.'

The goatboy said something in tremulous tones. Ali snapped back at him. Crossman sighed.

'What did he say?' asked Wynter. 'Is he askin' us to let him live?'

Crossman replied, 'He said his grandmother will be angry with him if he's late bringing the herd down to water.'

'So?' muttered Ali. 'Every man has a grandmother. If we worry about grandmothers we kill no one in this war.'

But Ali needed a reason not to murder the boy, this was it, and he said no more. He was annoyed with the youth. But the decision lay with the sergeant and the choice had been made. The risk, as Crossman had said, was not great, especially if they took the boy with them for part of the way.

As the men now continued to munch away on the meat the young man became irritated. He said something.

'What now?' growled Wynter.

'He's berating us for killing his goat,' said Crossman. 'He tells us it is a crime to take another man's property.'

'Well, gee, we didn't know that,' snarled Gwilliams. 'Tell the kid he's lucky to be alive himself, sergeant.'

But the young man somehow knew he was not in the hands of bandits and he continued to mumble away about thieves and how they would have hung if his father had been alive. Crossman asked how the boy's father had died and was told he had been killed by the French and British army at the Alma, when he was delivering produce to the Russian troops. A shell had exploded overhead and showered his father with red hot metal. His father had been a peaceful man, but the foreigners had not cared about that. They had killed him anyway. His mother had gone to fetch the body and bring it home, but had been caught up in the general retreat back to Sebastopol. She had not emerged since then and the boy and his grandmother had not had any word from her. Either she too was dead, or she was being held against her will.

'Your father was not killed on purpose,' Crossman argued, 'it was just the fortunes of war. He was in the wrong place at the wrong time. The British do not kill civilians if they can help it.'

'Then why do they bombard the city?'

'Well, that's different. They're aiming at the city's defences, but some damage is done to the buildings and streets beyond. That can't be helped.'

'I don't understand any of it,' said the youth, sullenly. 'We just look after our goats and the cabbages we grow.'

He understood the boy's argument of course. The Tartars were simply caught up in a conflict not of their making or wanting. But then who *had* wanted this war? Politicians and kings, perhaps, in the pursuit of power. Certainly not the common Russian conscripts. They would rather be at home too. Crossman had to admit the British and French soldiers had not been against the war at first. They had been puffed up by cheering, waving crowds as they left the shores of their countries, destined, they were sure, to be great heroes. But since then disillusionment and a loathing for war had crept in, once they found it was not simply a single glorious moment, but many ugly months that turned into ugly years, dying in wet trenches of gangrene, cholera, hypothermia, and sometimes of a bullet to the heart or brain. Wars seemed to happen whether most people wanted them or not. Human beings and war seemed to rush at one another and collide, no matter that there were more peacemakers than warmongers on the earth.

Once the meal was over they got to their

feet. Wynter buried the ashes of the fire. Gwilliams did the same with the bones. They had dug a shallow latrine which they now filled in. Ali brushed the area with branches. In a short while the camp needed very close inspection to reveal any evidence of their presence.

The boy got to his feet, ashen again, convinced they were going to shoot him before they left. Ali went to him and took his face in his big callused hands, staring into his eyes. He held the youth's head as if it were a pumpkin he was going to crush with his palms. Crossman called to him, from the edge of the track. Ali answered.

'He will slow us up, sergeant.'

'Leave him here then.'

Crossman told the youth to collect his goats and take them down to his grandmother.

'We should kill you,' Ali told the boy, 'but I am a kind man. Do not speak of this to anyone for at least a month. Then you may tell your grandmother you met a descendant of Suleiman the Magnificent, who destroyed the castles of the Knights of St John and spread the power of the Ottomans. You have heard of this man? I am his great-great-great grandson, a worthy successor to my grandfathers, for I too am a warrior of splendid renown. You have been touched by the hands of greatness. Good fortune will follow you now to the ends of your days, if you keep your tongue.'

Ali went to his mount. The harnesses the Turks used were always decorated with horse brasses. There were three main symbols: the crescent moon, a star and a heart. Ali kept his own brasses polished to perfection, even though their shine was sometimes dangerous. Crossman had seen such brasses on British draught horses, such as Clydesdales and Shires — and one he had first seen just a few days back, the Suffolk horse. He knew that in England they were intended to ward off the evil eye. The English might have been Christians since the seventh century, but they still held to certain pagan ways. They prayed to Jesus and the Lord God, but they also kept their horse brasses, as insurance against those who did *not* believe in Christ and still practised witchcraft.

Ali removed one of the horse brasses from his mount's harness and took it to the boy.

'Keep this,' he said, pressing it into the youth's hand. 'This will keep you safe from bad people. Never tell anyone who gave it to you, or it will not work. Secrets are sacred. Keep them, and you will flourish.'

The youth's eyes bulged at these words and

he nodded dumbly, before going to collect his charges from the mine.

Crossman shook his head at the Turk. 'I don't know where you get it all from, Ali.'

'How do you know it is not true, sergeant?'

'I don't — but then I don't think you know, either.'

Ali's broad face broke into a smile.

'These stories my aunt tell me, to get me to sleep at when I was six years old. They come in useful.'

'Come on, you old rogue, we need to be somewhere else.'

The trek began again, as they wended their way through shallow valleys, after hitting the flatlands to the north of the mountains. Here they had to rely on dips and dives in the landscape, to mask their progress over the wide area through which they were travelling. It was a hot coming they had of it, the horses sore of hoof and bad-tempered.

'Could you afford that horse brass, back there?' asked Crossman of Ali. 'You leave yourself unprotected against the evil eye.'

'I have more,' replied Ali. Crossman felt he detected a little nervousness in the Turk's tone. 'I will replace it. One cannot have enough, it is true. The evil eye is everywhere.'

'Too true,' muttered Wynter. 'I've always had bad luck and I put it down to an old woman back home. She put the evil eye on *me*, that's certain, or I would've had more luck.'

There were many Englishmen, and those from neighbouring countries, who would have nodded their heads sagely at this remark.

Wynter had fallen back and was now riding beside Crossman, who suddenly felt the need to talk to the one man whom he could not get to like, no matter what good deeds Wynter performed. Surely there was more under that sallow skin of Wynter's than just base greed, idleness, ignorance and surliness. There had to be more. After all, Wynter had a mother, was once a babe in arms and an adorable infant, wasn't he? Crossman set himself a task to draw out the Wynter behind the Wynter. He was hoping to find, if not a rough diamond, at least a semi-precious stone. Perhaps the soldier had been the victim of tragedies and misfortune all his life?

Crossman said, 'I was thinking, back there, of the Suffolk heavy horse, Wynter. Someone pointed out a pair of them the other day on the siege railway, drawing a carriage. Chestnuts, these were. It's the first I've seen of them. Do you know of the Suffolks?'

'Oh, yes, sergeant. You don't get no other colour but a chestnut — or as we say, sorrel — with a Suffolk. Good tempers, they've got.

My uncle was a horseman. He used to say a Suffolk had the face of an angel and the arse of a farmer. No featherin' round the ankles, like him there, that mount of Ali's, but sort of stocky and tough. Beautiful beasts.'

Wynter's voice was full of animation, just as Gwilliams had been, when he had been talking to Ali about horses. It was a manly subject and men did love to talk of the muscle and grace, the speed and might, of horses. Now that railways were transporting people and goods, the horse was appreciated even more. You couldn't take a personal pride in a railway engine, unless you owned one, and very few men did that. Horses were worked between the shafts of cart and wagon, used for recreation, for battle, for racing, for fox hunting — for just about everything manly and heroic. You could be the most insignificant idiot in the country, but if you owned a good horse, you were somebody. Tattersall's sold prime horse flesh, but you could pick up a fine quadruped in a gypsy market in Lincoln if you knew your stuff. And there wasn't a man worth his salt who didn't think he knew his equine stuff.

'Yes, sir,' continued Wynter, dreamily, 'lovely cart horse, the Suffolk.'

'I was thinking so, when Lovelace brought them to my attention. I'm sure they'd go well on my father's Scottish estates . . . ' He stopped, for he had been absently musing, and regretted those words. Wynter didn't need more ammunition than he already possessed as regards Crossman's genteel background. He took a quick glance at the soldier, but Wynter was looking straight ahead and with nothing but a sweet expression on his face.

'Well, then,' said Crossman. 'Thank you for your advice, Wynter. I — I shall pass it on.'

'Well, then, sergeant. You can use it yourself, can't you? When you inherit them estates off your daddy?'

He might have guessed he was not going to get away with it.

'Wynter, it might disappoint you to learn than I am a younger son and am therefore entitled to nothing under my father's will.'

'A bastard son, too, so's I've heard, sergeant.'

Crossman flushed. 'I'll thank you to keep . . . '

Wynter crowed over him. 'Oh, don't you worry none about that, sergeant. I just heard it, is all. Can't help hearin' things, can I? Never mind. My mum and dad weren't married neither, not under law. So we're sort of bastards together, an't we? Brothers, so to speak, of natural ways.'

Crossman seethed. Why couldn't he learn not to offer sprigs of friendship to Wynter? The lance-corporal was simply not worth it. One day soon there would be reckoning between the two of them. It had to come.

'Sergeant?'

Ali had drawn up alongside him.

'What is it?'

'I think we must swing round. Head towards sea. Then back again. Just to be sure.'

Ali was talking practical matters here. Throwing off any scent. Approaching the farmhouse from an unexpected direction.

'Right. You lead the way.'

The stars came out. It was a clear night, the moon a very pale object just above the horizon. They had travelled, first east, then directly north, so that they had been northeast of their destination. Now they were heading directly west and would then turn back heading southeast. There was a ridge at that point, about a half-mile from the farm. It was Crossman's intention to use this ridge to hide behind while they studied the farm.

When morning came they could see the Black Sea shining in the distance. It looked remote and uninviting, yet at the same time every man in the *peloton* was drawn to it. Soldiers in foreign lands view such waters as the road to home: a place of comfort, love,

117

and blessed peace. Yet the liquid pathways were forbidden, until the last knells of war had peeled. The sight was frustrating, causing pain and anguish in every breast. It was with some relief that they turned away from the shoreline and began heading inland again, away from the temptations of that distant refuge from hell.

After two years away Britain was a land of strangers to veteran soldiers like Crossman. He could not even remember the face of his mother, let alone his friends, no matter how much effort he put into it. He felt detached from that land, with its distinct seasons, its once familiar sounds, sights and smells. He felt as if he had been in the Crimea for most of his life and that other faint part of it was just a peculiar dream. This was real and that other strange life he had experienced was a kind of fantasy.

'The ridge, sergeant.'

Ali again, reining him in from his thoughts. 'Thank you.'

They kept the horses at the bottom of the slope, hidden in a crop of boulders. Yorwarth took charge of them. Wynter and Gwilliams remained at the bottom, while Crossman and Ali climbed to the watershed. Using bushes they carefully remained concealed while they studied the buildings below. Crossman put a glass to his eye and was immediately staring into the face of Peterson. Shocked, he whipped down the spyglass quickly, his heart beating fast.

'What is it, sergeant?' whispered Ali, concerned.

'She's there on the porch, dammit!'

Ali used his own glass. 'I see her. She sits in a chair. Wait, I see the leather strap. She is *tied* to the chair. They offer her to us, to come and get.'

Crossman looked again. Peterson's face was expressionless. He could not see if there were bruises on her cheeks, but he guessed there probably would be. She simply sat there, unmoving. For a moment he wondered if she were actually alive, then he saw her flinch, when a fly settled on her lip. Yes, she was alive, but her spirit had been broken. She looked like a sack of meal, tied there. She sagged forwards, bulkily.

The two men then studied the farm itself. There were around twenty blue-frocked Cossacks in and around the yard. Some were attentive, staring at the hills, watching the single winding dust track that led to the farm gate. Others were busying themselves with various tasks, mostly to do with their precious horses. If the horse was king to an Englishman, it was God to a Cossack. They would spend endless hours grooming their mounts, polishing their tack, training the animal in various tricks.

Next, the landscape around the farm. Again there were Cossacks posted in several key positions. Most dangerously there was another ridge forming a T shape with the British escarpment and two Cossacks had been left their to watch the main ridge. They were looking directly at the bushy strip behind which Crossman and Ali were hiding. The Bashi-Bazouk indicated this watch and Crossman nodded to show he had seen it.

The sergeant intended to do nothing for a while. Peterson was still alive, if very miserable. They left her on the porch the whole while, only releasing her so that she could eat her food and go to the latrine. It was evident they wanted Crossman and his men, when and if they came, to see that she was alive. In that way the British would not go riding home without a showdown of some kind. That was what it was all about: a meeting between the Cossacks and the British crew who had been giving them so much trouble over the last few months. They wanted revenge. They wanted the sergeant, they wanted his men, and they wanted them dead.

So Crossman waited. He could afford to.

'We should've brought a regiment with us,' grumbled Wynter, later. 'We could've marched right in there and took her.'

'If we had, she would not be there to take. They've got eyes and ears, Wynter. And be sensible. Would they let us have a whole regiment to save a single soldier?'

'Well, a company then.'

'Same applies,' said Yorwarth. 'They won't give the sergeant no company. It's up to us, ain't it?'

'So we're just goin' to ride down there and snatch her up, eh? Just like that. An' they're goin' to let us.'

'That's not a bad idea, Wynter,' said Crossman, who had been playing with certain thoughts for a few hours now. 'We'll just ride down there and challenge them!'

'Eh?' cried Wynter. 'I an't going to, that's sure.'

'You'll do what you're told,' growled Gwilliams. 'Me, I'm all for it. Famous charge. Five against fifty. Sounds good to me.'

'Famous *last* charge,' spluttered Wynter.

Yet this was the plan. However, Crossman did not intend to go all the way to the farmhouse. The scheme was to make the charge, down the slope, and straight at the enemy. When his riders were three hundred yards from the house, Crossman and his band would turn and run, drawing the Cossacks away from the farm. Not all of them would come, of course, but certainly most of them would want to be in at the kill. Once the fox breaks cover the whole hunt takes up the chase. It's the excitement of the thing.

Only one or two reluctant and disgruntled warriors would remain to guard the prisoner. Crossman and the others would take off over flatlands, pulling the Cossacks well away from their base. Afterwards, Ali, who would remain behind, would go down and despatch them, take their captive, and run for home. Once the Turk had Peterson the Cossacks would be pursuing a lost cause: Ali knew all the secret places, all the hidey-holes in the landscape. He would dart from one to another, by day and by night, and the Cossacks would be left sniffing his dust.

The raid would be at dawn. Crossman told his men to get some sleep.

'For tomorrow we die,' whispered Gwilliams in the ear of Wynter, just to see him look pained.

Ali and Gwilliams went out just before first light and cut the throats of the Cossacks on the neighbouring ridge. It turned out there were two of them, one a corporal. The corporal did not die easily. With blood pouring from his wound he fought with Ali ferociously, while trying to call for assistance. Ali's first cut had been deep and all that came out was a gargling sound not loud enough to travel to the farmhouse below. Finally Ali broke his assailant's neck. Ali and Gwilliams took a Cossack horse: a gelding which had stood quietly watching the horrific skirmish between his master and the knife-man. They would need this extra mount.

In the dagger-grey dawn four riders came out of the valley mists riding hard at the front of the farm. A Cossack look-out raised the alarm with a shrieking shout. Peterson, still roped to the chair, raised her head with a hopeful expression replacing the bleak look. Bullets began thudding into the farmhouse woodwork. The Cossack next to her spun as a lucky shot — it could be nothing else from the saddle of a galloping horse — struck him in the arm and knocked him aside. He lifted himself up and staggered through the doorway, into the farmhouse.

'Sergeant!' yelled Peterson, as if she were not in plain view. 'I'm here!'

The four riders thundered on, only two of them firing now, the others having spent their single shot weapons. The Cossacks began firing back. The attackers seemingly realized the odds they were up against. Straight away they wheeled, heading back out of the valley again.

Peterson cried out, plaintively, 'Don't leave me . . .'

Cossacks ran for their mounts, standing in rows of six, unruffled by the sound of firing and the commotion. A sergeant shouted something and two men stopped, walked slowly back to the porch. They looked disgruntled.

The two remaining Cossacks stood on the porch, watching the dust cloud rise as their comrades rode hell for leather after the attackers. From sentries on a neighbouring hills came an enquiry.

What had happened?

Why, replied one of the two on the porch, the English assassin and his men had come and were being chased to their death.

Good, good. We will eat breakfast, then come down to the farm.

As you wish.

One of the two Cossacks went into the farmhouse, the smell of freshly brewed coffee having drawn him. The other, a large man with thick, callused hands, fingered Peterson's hair and smiled at her. She looked up at him with a tear-stained face and whimpered, 'No — please — not again . . .'

At that moment a single shot rang out and

the Cossack's ugly smile turned to red pulp. His legs folded under him and he fell heavily, crashing down the steps of the porch. The second Cossack was at that moment halfway through the doorway, carrying two tin cups full of steaming coffee. He stared at his felled comrade. There was a puzzled expression on his face. But his bewilderment did not last long. The next moment it turned to a sensation of agony as a bullet struck him full in the chest.

He dropped the cups, splashing Peterson's ankles with the hot coffee. She yelled in pain, kicking the cup away from her. The Cossack staggered forwards, reaching for a carbine that stood against the farmhouse wall. A third shot struck him in the back of the neck, snapping his spine like a twig. He flopped sideways, fell, and lay twitching, gargling in the back of his throat. By the time Ali came thudding up on his own horse with Yorwarth's Sydney in tow, the body was still. Someone shouted from the hills. Ali answered. A silence followed, during which time Ali had cut Peterson's bonds.

'Get on Sydney,' grunted Ali. 'Quick. We take that right path into the hills. Quick, Peterson.'

'Thank you,' sobbed the young woman.

'Thank you for coming.'

She allowed herself a swift savage kick at one of the dead men. It was a foolish gesture. She almost overbalanced, being still groggy. Then she climbed awkwardly into Sydney's saddle. Ali himself leapt into the saddle of his own horse. The Turk held the reins for her, while she gathered herself together. She was exhausted and emotionally drained, and needed a few seconds to gather the reserves of her torn spirit. Finally she gestured to Ali that she was fit to ride.

A third Cossack now came out of the farmhouse, the man who had been wounded in the raid. Unsteady on his feet, his complexion was as grey as stale bread. He had no firelock, but tried to draw his sword with the wrong hand. It stuck halfway out of its scabbard. He struggled with it, weakly. Ali ignored the man, seeing no threat in him.

Stiff from being tied to the chair, and in no little pain, Peterson was not in good health. She gripped the reins and kicked Sydney into motion. Although not always an obedient fellow, Sydney took off with alacrity, loving nothing better than a gallop.

Ali's own thick-set mount flew forward at the same time. He was a war-horse and knew his work.

It was only as they were riding away that

one or two shots came from high points around the farm. Breakfasts in the outposts had been interrupted and at last the other sentries had drawn the correct conclusions. The rounds were from carbines and fell uselessly in the dust behind the escaping pair. They went as if on horses with wings, flying out of the end of the valley, first north, then east, climbing up into the folded hills behind the farm.

The Bashi-Bazouk had planned their escape with meticulous detail. He knew exactly the trails, paths and goat tracks he wanted to use. Peterson did not question him. She trusted Ali as much as she trusted her sergeant. While they climbed a narrow path the Turk gave her a waterbottle to drink from. Peterson refreshed herself.

Then she asked, 'Can I have that carbine holstered on your mount?' Ali glanced down, then reached for the weapon, handing it to her.

'We must keep the silence,' he said. 'No shooting. Only in emergency. You understand?'

'I understand.'

That night they found a cave, high up in the hills. The place was large enough for the horses and the two soldiers. Ali lit no fires. He took some cold fare from his saddlebag and handed half to Peterson. She took it and wolfed it down, not having eaten for two days. The Turk then noticed something. The index finger on Peterson's right hand was crooked. He reached out and examined the finger.

'They broke it,' she said.

Peterson winced when the Turk felt around the joints of the damaged finger. Then he suddenly grasped it and twisted. She let out a gasp which could have turned to a yell, except that Ali put his hand over her mouth.

'Silence, please!' he murmured.

She was crying now. 'What did you do that for?' she whispered, fiercely, holding her right hand in her left.

'Only broken from joint.'

She looked at her finger again. It was swelling, noticeably, but it was straight now. 'Dislocated?'

'Yes, this is the word.'

'Only that? Will it be all right?'

'In one or two days. They do this to stop you shooting?'

'I think so,' she replied.

'They not do proper job. They only take out of joints. Finger good as new in one week. Now we get some rest. Tomorrow they come look for us, follow our tracks. Sometimes I try going on the bare rock, but not always possible. We must be rested, get good start in the morning. You like the horse?'

'He seems to be as gentle as a lamb.'

'He is and, as you are not well, is better if you ride him tomorrow. Now you get to sleep. I watch.'

'When will you sleep?'

'I wake you four hours' time.'

It did not take long for Peterson to drop into a fitful sleep, despite her pain and her emotional state. Her dreams were jagged affairs which had her tossing and turning all the while. Ali woke her at the appointed time and she took over the watch for the next three hours. He let her sleep after that until the dawn, knowing it was dangerous to continue in the darkness. If one of the horses went lame they would be in serious trouble.

Peterson woke the second time to the sound of birds. She opened her eyes and saw that a shaft of light was cutting across the entrance to the cave. It looked intensely bright to her from within the gloom. She sat up and then put her hand out to heave herself to her feet, only to wince in agony. Her hand was puffed and painful. Using her left hand she managed to scramble to her feet. Outside, Ali already had the horses saddled and ready to go. Silently he handed her some unleavened bread and the waterbottle. She stuffed the bread into her mouth and washed it down with some water. Climbing up into the saddle she still felt as if she had been hit by a coach and four. Her bones ached, her muscles ached, in fact everything ached. The thought of safety and a decent bed was a huge incentive though and she tapped the horse in the ribs with her heels to get him in motion.

The pair began to wind down a long slope to a grassy plain below. Three-quarters of the way down there came the sound of hooves thudding on hard ground. At this time they were passing through a flourishing orchard. The owner was caring for these apple trees even though his house was probably many miles away. Land on the peninsula sometimes consisted of small parcels miles from the owner's farm. In times of intense competition it was not economically viable to work such pieces of land, but at the moment the farmers had a ready market for their goods. If the Russians did not buy the produce, the invading armies would. Tartar farmers did not have to ship the goods out of the Crimea: they could trade on their own doorsteps.

'In the leaves,' whispered Ali. 'Quick — under the branches.'

The outer foliage of some of the apple trees touched the ground at the edges, forming a wide skirt around the trunk. The pair found one of these trees each and hid inside the circle of branches. Peterson's heart was pounding. She did not want to be captured again. She was ready to shoot herself rather than let that happen. Her legs shook against Ali's horse, making him nervous, but she managed to hold him in, soothe him with whispers in his twitching ears. Finally, after what seemed a very long time, Ali came into her quiet little hiding place.

'All right now. They go. Now we go.'

The pair continued their journey.

The next night was spent on a dry river bed. Peterson was scared that a flash flood might come in the night and sweep them to their deaths, but Ali assured her that it would not happen. She didn't believe him. The whole time they were there she kept waking up from a deep sleep and listening hard for the sound of water rushing from beyond the next bend. Peterson was never more relieved when they set off again the following dawn, climbing through scree which had the horses skating this way and that. Once out of the loose rocks they were on grasslands again. The air was pleasantly aromatic. The scent of wild herbs pacified the horses. Peterson filled her lungs, breathing deeply. When trussed to the chair on the porch she had not expected to smell such delights of nature ever again.

That night they slept in a copse of pines.

Eventually they reached their destination and passed through the picquets, to enter Kadikoi. Amazingly, to Peterson, it had not changed in the slightest. There were hundreds, thousands of people, going about their business as if there was nothing happening out there in the hills. It seemed callous of them. Why were they not all fretting and worrying? Some would be, she knew, and indeed she was woken halfway through the morning by a lady wearing a dress of soft grey. The lady's face was pale with concern.

'Is the sergeant not with you?'

'Ma'am? No, no, he's not back yet. I don't think so, anyway.' Peterson looked round to ask Ali, but he wasn't there. She remembered he had climbed on his horse as soon as he had delivered her to the hovel. Ali would now be riding hard, back to the *peloton*, to see if they needed his help.

The lady was agitated. 'You know me?'

'Yes — Miss Mulinder, the sergeant's cousin.'

'Then you can tell me where he is, can't you? Is he safe, still? I'm to be trusted, you know.'

Peterson sat up, feeling miserable. The lady had a fragrance about her, whereas Peterson knew that she herself stank of sweat and many other even more unpleasant odours. The lady kneeling by her bed must have been quite strong not to reveal how offensive she must have found Peterson's smell. Peterson shook her head to try to get rid of the buzzing sound in her ears. She was still muzzy from the horror of her experiences. Then she caught Miss Mulinder looking at her swollen hand.

'They tried to break my finger,' she explained. 'To stop me from shooting.'

Jane winced on being shown the blue-black injury.

'You're a sharpshooter, is that correct?'

'Yes. Look, the sergeant — well, the rest of them are still out there, somewhere. I don't know where, or I'd tell. They drew the Cossacks away from the farm — I was being held at an old farm — and then Ali came and got me. But I don't know where they went.' Peterson touched Jane's hand. 'He'll be all right, miss. He knows how to get away from them.'

Jane stood up. 'I'm sorry, I shouldn't have come.'

'It's all right.' Then, looking up into Jane's sympathetic features it suddenly became all too much for the female soldier. Peterson burst into tears. She touched Jane's ankle with her good hand, weeping freely, and said, 'They were dirty with me, Miss Mulinder. I hate them. I hate them. They did nasty things to me . . . '

Jane was almost as distressed by these shocking words as Peterson herself and she knelt down and put her arms around the soldier. She was unaware of the coarseness of the uniform or the foul smell of the person who was wearing it. Her heart had been pierced by the woman's words, the hurt cry of a wounded fellow human being.

'Oh — oh, you poor thing. How awful. How dreadful. Come on, let it out, let it all come out.'

Peterson sobbed, taking comfort in another woman's arms.

★ ★ ★

Crossman had already picked out a spot to make his stand. The difficult part was in reaching it before the pursuing Cossacks caught up with them.

But the horses held out. The soldiers made the semi-circle of rocks with little time to spare. Shots had been exchanged from the saddles, but no one so far had been hit on the chase, not Cossack nor ranger. The mounts were taken behind a tor and hobbled to keep them from bolting. There was a small beck nearby, dribbling down a rocky channel. It was enough to keep the *peloton* in water, whereas the Cossacks, now ensconced in a tangle of trees lower down the escarpment, had none.

Crossman had chosen his 'fortress' well. They were higher than the enemy, who had to shoot up the slope and were therefore at a disadvantage. There was good cover and they could not be encircled, since there were serious drops on either side of the gradient. A man might get round, but not on his mount, and any Cossack who tried to get behind the group would be stark against the landscape and would make an easy target. Cords of firewood had been stashed in the rocks earlier, so that fires could be lit at night and catch any stealthy movements in their light. Each man was carrying more than 120 rounds of ammunition. They had supplies in their saddlebags and were prepared for a siege.

Allowing themselves to be governed by natural inclination — they were after all cavalry — the Cossacks first attempted to charge the position with their superior numbers. They were beaten back by the fierce firepower of the *peloton*. Unfortunately for the rangers, who were fatigued from their ride, their aim was poor due to unsteady hands. Also, they were excited by the charge and therefore blasted away frantically, firing at everything and nothing. The air was thick with bullets but only one Cossack was hit and he was only wounded in the shoulder. Still, the intensity of the fire, combined with the difficulty of the slope, forced the Cossacks back to the trees.

Crossman heard an argument ensue between the various members of the force down below him.

'What're they sayin', sergeant?' asked Wynter, performing the difficult operation of reloading while lying down. He withdrew his ramrod and sheathed it back on the stock of the Enfield. 'Are they comin' again. I'm a bit more ready for 'em, this time.'

Yorwarth and Gwilliams were already taking beads on the edge of the trees, waiting for the next charge.

'No — no, I think they're going to bed down there,' muttered Crossman, listening hard for the snatches of loud conversation that floated up on the breeze. 'Yes, their sergeant is insisting on it. He doesn't want to lose any more men at this stage. Gwilliams?'

'Sergeant?'

Crossman pointed. 'See that ledge over there? It commands a view down the far side of the hill. If they go for reinforcements they'll have to head out that way. I want you to get up on that ledge and shoot any rider that makes a break for open country. Can you do it?'

There was a chimney of rock leading up to the ledge in question and Gwilliams felt he could make it safely to the flat stone which was angled away from the trees and therefore presented cover.

'I'm on my way,' he said, snaking across the dusty ground towards the chimney.

'Take some water,' said Crossman, tossing him a leather bottle. 'And some salt beef.'

Gwilliams grinned. 'Got some in my pocket, sergeant.'

The barber continued to wriggle to the rock face and, once there, began to wend his way up the granite channel to the ledge. Shots came from the trees, smacking into the stone face of the hill. Wynter and Yorwarth started to return the fire, furiously, while Crossman watched anxiously until he saw Gwilliams make it to the slab of stone above their heads.

'Well done,' he said, then joined the others in firing down the hill into the fence of trees.

For the next few hours the battle raged in earnest. A goodly shower of meteors flew through the air, humming, zinging off stones.

Yorwarth got stone splinters in his cheek from a ricochet, which drew a quantity of blood, but he was not seriously hurt. He was the only casualty during that fierce exchange. So far as they knew, there were none on the other side, either. At that point both commanders realized they were simply wasting ammunition and almost simultaneously the intensity of the firing dropped to the odd few sporadic shots.

'You look as if someone's drawn your cork,' said Wynter, dabbing at Yorwarth's face with a rag. 'That's a prime claret comin' out there. Here, you've gone an' got some chips in you . . . ' Wynter found his bayonet and began picking the gravel out of Yorwarth's face with the point. 'Yell if it hurts.'

Yorwarth took the opportunity of the break to have a furious scratch at his chest and genitals, and anywhere else his nails could reach.

'Don't worry about that,' he growled, 'it's this bloody rash that's turning me to a lunatic.'

'Stop that!' ordered Crossman. 'You'll take your skin off.'

'I wish I bloody could. It ain't much use to me like this, is it?'

At that moment, Gwilliams cried, 'One going off!' The sound of a horse's hooves came to the ears of the rangers. There followed a shot from the ledge, then a satisfied, 'One out of the saddle.'

'You got him?' queried Crossman.

'Knocked him clean off.'

'Dead?'

'Looks like it. Good as, anywise.'

Crossman nodded. 'They won't try that again. Nice shot, Gwilliams.'

'Couldn't miss. He filled the skyline.'

'Good work, anyway.'

Twilight arrived not long after this incident and this heralded a lull in the fighting. Neither side was making any impact on the numbers of the enemy. Yellow firelight appeared in the bank of trees below. Soon the smell of cooking came wafting up to the rangers. Crossman ordered the lighting of two fires, one either side of their position. He knew they would illuminate the rangers' camp, but they needed to view the slope. Fortunately for him and his men a huge moon rose in a clear sky. If the Russians had thought they could send a rider out in the darkness, they were mistaken.

After eating, Yorwarth changed places with Gwilliams, and the American tucked into some heated food with relish. They also made tea on this third, smaller kitchen fire. There was a short interlude in the festivities when lumps were noticed attempting to crawl unseen up the escarpment and had to be fired upon to drive them back to the trees. Then the meal was resumed, pipes were lit behind the shelter of the rocks. Conversation turned to things other than the current dire situation.

'What got you in the army, Wynter?' asked Gwilliams. 'You took the shillin' for a pint of ale and a game of skittles? Or did the recruitin' sergeant offer you a soft bed and waiter service for the rest of your life?'

Gwilliam's tone was jocular, but Wynter replied in all seriousness.

'No,' he said, 'I always fancied the military, see. I didn't want to be no horny-handed son of the soil, like they called the other farm lads. I mean, there was no space for me in the cruck an' I always saw meself as a redcoat.' He inspected one of his weathered, threadbare sleeves, now turned a dark purple hue. 'It were red in them days, of course, with lovely white pipe-clayed straps. An' even the shako seemed pretty to me then. The army gave you a musket, free of charge, an' boots — I'd never had boots on before and they hurt like buggery at first. All that stuff they give you. And all to the tune of beatin' drums and the trilling of the fifes.'

'You pay for much of your kit,' pointed out Gwilliams.

'Yes, but they give me the money to do it,' replied Wynter, with his usual warped logic. 'Anyways, soon as I was fourteen I joined the militia. I went for the Yeomanry, but they wouldn't 'ave me, bein' as I wasn't from a family with a trade. So I upped and joined the Volunteer Rifles. They give us a weapon, which we had to keep in the guildhall, to save us from usin' it to hunt rabbits and such. I wanted to shoot Frenchmen of course, they bein' the last enemy we had, but there weren't no invasion and never was goin' to be one, so next time the army came I upped an' took the shilling.'

'You regret it now, though, don't you?'

'Naw, not really. I moan a bit, I know . . . '

'A *bit*?' snorted Crossman, listening to this exchange with some amusement.

'We-eeell, I weren't never given to followin' discipline,' argued Wynter. 'It's against the grain of my nature, so to speak. I'm like a roe deer, I am. Free-spirited. It don't come easy bein' told what to do, when you're a man like me.'

'Everyone has trouble takin' orders,' replied Gwilliams. 'You just have to learn it. Now take me, I wouldn't join no army again. Not because I don't favour taking orders, but

141

because you have to swear allegiance. I'm alleged to no man but me, an' that's a solid fact.'

'You're a bloody mercen'ry, you are,' scoffed Wynter.

'Too damn right.'

The conversation had to stop there as flashes and bangs came from wood below. The Cossacks were shooting at the fires, trying to scatter the logs. They gave up this pointless activity after a very short while, when they saw that even if they hit something it was soon replaced. Everyone settled down for a quiet night. Morning was soon enough to raise hell.

Normal fighting was resumed the following day. In the early hours a Cossack rider managed to get away. He had led his mount down beyond the tree line and was at a distance before the ledge sentry, Wynter now, could get a shot in. Wynter was never the best of riflemen anyway and he missed. By the time he had reloaded the Cossack was out of range. All the rest of the day Crossman expected to see a horde of Cossacks come riding back, hellbent on the destruction of the *peloton*, but none came for some reason. He could only guess, as the evening came round, that something untoward had happened to the rider. There was also the possibility that the commander to whom the rider had reported had decided not to risk any more of his troops. It was something of a puzzle. Of course, the reinforcements might arrive the next day, but Crossman had a feeling this would not happen.

This must have infuriated the Cossacks in the wood because at about three o'clock their frustration overcame them and they began blazing away like fury at the group in the boulders above.

The rangers, excited by the amount of metal in the air, responded in kind, with Wynter screaming, 'Bloody barbarians!' during every lull in the shooting.

'Keep your breath, Wynter,' ordered Crossman.

This was followed by a desperate charge from below. This time the Russian cavalry almost made it. One trooper, sabre flashing, reached the edge of the rocks before he was blasted from his saddle. The Cossacks retreated again, with Wynter still crying, 'Barbarians!'

Another quiet period followed this heart-racing action.

Wynter asked, 'Where the bleedin' hell do they come from anyway, these Cossacks? Farm boys, are they?'

'A bit more than that,' replied Crossman,

reloading his Tranter. 'Barbarians, possibly, but I wonder if *they* consider themselves a barbarous race. They were indeed outlaws and fugitives at one time. There's some Tartar and Kipchak blood in there. Ukrainians, mostly, but there are others — the Ottoman Cossacks are Polish I believe — and there are the Zaporozhe Cossacks, cousins of the Don Cossacks. In the Middle Ages they ranged over the areas on either side of the River Don . . . '

'So that's why they call 'em Don Cossacks!'

'Well, it would seem so, wouldn't it? I know they are intensely proud warriors, dedicated to force. You and I are merely part-time fighters, Wynter. A Cossack is *born* a warrior. There's no wondering about whether he might be a carpenter or cobbler, as there is with us. Cossacks believe themselves to be the natural guardians of the Russian plains. There's a traditional courage, a fearlessness that goes with being one of those men down there, of which we ought to be very cautious. It took a few weeks to turn you into something vaguely resembling a soldier, Wynter, while it took centuries of fighting to make one of those Cossacks in that wood. Their skill with the horse is legendary. Their sabre-talent, equally so. We may call them barbarians, but they are the sort of barbarians that soldiers admire.'

There were no further charges. That night was as black as gunpowder and yet another courier was sent out from the Cossack camp. Crossman heard the hooves pounding on the hard ground. He put on extra security, the four men taking watches in pairs, in case the Cossacks sent up a party with knives. However, enemy numbers had been thinned somewhat and perhaps the Russians felt they ought to wait for their reinforcements. It was their style to attack and overwhelm, rather than sneak up and slit throats. Cossacks went for flair and there was no glory in night assassinations.

There was a heavy dew on the ground the next morning, even though they were now deep into summer. The heights had something to do with it. Supplies were getting low, but more importantly ammunition was running out. The cavalry charges the previous day, along with the blistering firefights between, had depleted stores of cartridges. Now there were only a few cartridges left between the whole group of rangers. Crossman cursed himself for not keeping a better watch on the ammunition.

He realized now he had drifted off into that

nether world where concentration and focus almost disappears. It was one of those situations — indeed, like the war in the Crimea itself — where conditions on either side hardly changed from day to day. Quite soon one slipped into the false state of mind whereby one believed they would never change, that the status quo would remain until some outside agency arrived to alter it. Well things had altered now, without any external intervention. The rangers had very few bullets left. Crossman wondered whether the leader of those Cossacks below was a step ahead of him. Perhaps the tactics yesterday were, 'Get them to waste as much ammunition as possible and tomorrow, when they've run out of ammo, we'll just ride in and take their heads'? Crossman could have booted himself up the backside. The more he thought about it, the more he was convinced that was what the Cossacks had in mind.

'I've got three cartridges left, sergeant,' said Wynter.

The others had similar amounts.

'Looks like this will be the last day,' Gwilliams said, grunting. 'I won't be shaving no more famous people.'

'You never did shave famous people,'

growled Wynter. 'That's a load of old horseshit, that is.'

Gwilliams shook his head. 'You're a poor specimen of a man, Wynter. God made you from the bits left over, when he'd finished making the camels and yaks.'

'Very funny.'

Yorwarth giggled and said, 'I think it is.'

Crossman stared down the slope.

'Looks like they're getting ready for a final charge,' he said, aware that he had only two bullets left for his Tranter revolver. 'At least their reinforcements haven't arrived. But they've had a good breakfast and now they're going to finish us off.'

Wynter shook his head angrily. 'How do they know we're out of peas?' he snarled. 'They can't know that.'

'They can be pretty sure — I would be.'

'Yes, but sergeant, we could have stashed a whole box full of cartridges up here. I know we didn't, but they don't know that.'

'What do you suggest, Wynter?'

Wynter's brow furrowed, but the idea was as far as he could go.

'You're the one with the big learnin', sergeant. You tell us. You're the one who went to a real school, an't you? You must have read stories about things. You must know some tricks used by other soldiers in the same road

147

as we're in now. Come on, you're the damn leader, use your noddle.'

Crossman flared. 'Don't be insolent, Wynter.'

'I an't bein' insolent,' shouted Wynter, 'I'm tryin' to spur something out of you. Anyways, who cares if I'm bein' insolent or not? What're you goin' to do about it? Put me on latrine duty? Throw me in the stockade? Flog me? We're all about to die, dammit.'

Wynter was right. Crossman's authority was almost gone: dissipated by the fact that they were all about to meet the great leveller. There were no sergeants in heaven or hell. There were only lost souls and they were about to become just such creatures. The jaws of death were open wide and they were all about to be swallowed.

Wynter's spur had done it though. Crossman's anger had helped to hone his thoughts, had sharpened points on them. He recalled now an incident in military history that his father was always recounting at dinner, the old man having very little social graces or skill at intercourse, but relying on a huge fund of anecdotes and stories.

One of the tales the major was fond of telling was the story of the Duchess of Tryol, who lived in the fourteenth century. This Amazon warrior-queen, intent on expanding her territory, had encircled Castle Hochoster-witz in the province of Carthinia, intent on breaching its walls. Just when the duchess thought the castle was out of provisions a roasted ox, its belly stuffed with barley, was tossed over the walls into her camp. An enemy soldier yelled from the battlements that the duchess's men might like a good hot meal, because they had a long wait if they thought they were going to lift the siege in anything like the near future. The duchess lost heart and broke the siege, leaving with her army and returning to her own province.

'Of course,' the major would add, with a wry chuckle, 'that ox and the barley was the last food in the castle. The commandant was a wily old fox like myself. He had nothing to lose and he knew the value of a trick.'

'Well, Father,' muttered Crossman, 'you may be good for something after all, you old boaster.'

'What?' cried Wynter. 'Oh, Lord save us, the man's lost his mind. He thinks I'm his pa now.'

Crossman shuddered. 'Never that, Wynter, even in lunacy. Right,' he became brisk. 'Give me that black bottle you brought with you, Wynter.'

'My ale?' Wynter gasped. 'I was savin' that.'

'A lot of good it'll do you in hell. You can drink it now.'

Gwilliam's eyebrows shot up. 'He can?'

'Yes, and quickly, they're gathering below.'

Wynter took the bottle of beer from his saddlebag and began guzzling it. Gwilliams whipped it off him, took two swigs, and then handed it to Yorwarth. Yorwarth put it to his lips and then said, 'It's warm from the horse's arse,' and handed it to Crossman. Crossman finished off the last few dregs. Then he tossed the empty bottle down the slope. It rattled and bounced amongst the stones, grabbing the attention of the Cossacks on their horses.

'Right,' said Crossman, 'first one to break that bottle gets the drumsticks of the quail hanging from my harness . . . '

He himself began banging away at the bottle with his pistol, missing every time, bullets zinging from rocks. Gwilliams began whooping, American style, and fired at the bottle, just chipping the base. Yorwarth tried, at the same time yelling his head off. Wynter looked around him, amazed at the scene, and then fired one off himself.

They all reloaded, frantically, as if the bottle were running away on legs of its own. The air was full of their cries, their chirrups, their high-spirited yells. Finally, Yorwarth hit the bottle and it shattered, the glass flying everywhere, tinkling amongst the stones of the escarpment. A hoarse ragged cheer went up from the doomed men, now completely out of ammunition. They stood up with smoking rifles, staring down at the Cossacks, who were now milling around, silently, witnessing this crazy spectacle with narrowed eyes.

Crossman pretended to reload his pistol, indicating his men should do the same with their Enfields.

He shouted cheerfully down the slope in Russian, 'Ho, boys, come on up now. We've had our target practice for the day and we're ready to put more holes in you. Don't take your time though, we don't like a slow moving target. Too easy. There's a brace of quail's legs running on this one. First to get an empty saddle. What do you say? Coming up?'

At that moment a shot rang out from another high point nearby. A Cossack dropped like a stone from his saddle. Then another shot came, and another. The Cossack commander, now down to a corporal, fired back with his carbine at this point. Wynter, the only one with a shot left in his barrel, fired at the corporal and took his furry hat off.

The Cossacks had finally had enough. They

dug their heels into the ribs of their mounts and rode away and out, down the track the way they had come, riding like maniacs. They hurled insults over their shoulders at Crossman, telling him they were going to get him one of these days, and they would hang him by the heels from a tree and use him for lancing practice. They would take out his eyes, they yelled, they would take off his nose. He would be meat for the choughs circling the hills.

'Bugger off, you bloody barbarians!' screamed a delighted Wynter, into the wind. 'Go on, fuck off, or I'll kick your Russian arses for you!'

'That's enough profanity for one day,' said Gwilliams, sternly.

'S'not profanity,' argued Wynter. 'I didn't mention the Church once — it was just plain cussing.'

After a short while Ali came down on his stocky horse from above, clattering amongst the loose scree. He was grinning broadly. Arriving in the camp he swung his portly figure from the saddle and he and Crossman embraced. 'Well done, old friend,' said Crossman. 'It was you who got the riders they sent out for reinforcements, wasn't it?'

'I am guilty of that, sergeant,' the Turk growled, still smiling.

'Well, you did a good job of chasing that lot away too.'

'It weren't that,' Wynter told the Bashi-Bazouk, excitedly. 'I'm sure it helped a bit, but it was the sergeant's plan that did it. I — I was the one who inspeared . . . '

'Inspired,' Crossman assisted.

'Yep, inspired him. That was me. I told him to think sharp and he did, and there we had a result. They thought we had a deal of ammunition left, but we an't got none. Not a bullet between us.' He laughed uproariously. 'Not a single cartridge to our names.'

They broke camp now and headed out towards the plains. There was a need to put miles between the siege hill and themselves. Wynter couldn't help chattering, going over their trick countless times. Crossman and Ali rode together, exchanging news. Crossman wanted to know about Peterson, whether she was all right.

'She has bad hand — and they rape her.'

'Oh my God.' Crossman was horrified. Poor Peterson. He knew she must be utterly broken by such an experience. 'Why did they do that? They are bloody barbarians.'

Ali shrugged. For him it was to be expected. Amongst the conquerors there was always a pig, one who took his pleasure from the pain and misery of others. There were

153

British soldiers who would have done it, given a reversed situation. It did not mean that all Cossacks were bad, but he did not say this to the sergeant. He knew it would not help for the moment. The sergeant needed to vent his anger, to feel hate. The situation there, on the hill, had been dire. The sergeant and his men had been close so close to Death they could have shaken hands with him. That kind of experience needs an escape valve. So he said nothing. He simply shrugged.

4

The exhausted band of men arrived back at Kadikoi to find Peterson recovering from her ordeal. Crossman learned that she had been visited by both Lavinia Durham and Jane Mulinder. He had expected to find Peterson in pieces but it seemed that the ladies had helped to bolster her spirit in the way that only women can. That is not to say she was perfectly well, but she had not descended into a pit of despair. Words of comfort and sympathy — help and understanding — had kept her from falling into a dark place from which she might never crawl again.

'Peterson,' Crossman said one night, when they were alone in the hovel. He automatically slipped into that formal mode of speech he used with the opposite sex, especially when talking of subjects draped in petticoats. 'I am sorry for what happened to you. I cannot imagine the pain and anguish it caused and I wish you had not had to experience such a thing.'

Crossman was clearly embarrassed and upset at having to talk of such a subject to a woman whose soul he hardly knew. He and

Peterson had been in a war together. They had fought side by side, had spent nights around camp fires talking, had been constant companions for months. Yet still they knew very little of each other's private feelings. Even if their differences in class, rank, or the reserved nature of the nation had not prevented them from revealing confidences, the fact of the army definitely would. In the army you only let people see what you wanted them to see. Any weaknesses in character, any deeply felt views or passions, any skeletons in the cupboard, you kept strictly hidden. You showed your comrades only your battle-face and you kept a whole mass of secrets tightly sealed inside.

'I know, sergeant.' Peterson was more than embarrassed. She was writhing inside. She could not imagine what images were in her sergeant's head and she did not want to. 'Sergeant,' she was visibly writhing now, 'do people like Wynter know — know . . . '

'Wynter knows nothing. Only myself and Ali are aware. The Turk is an insightful man. He guessed what had happened to you. Be assured that the secret will remain amongst those who think well of you, Peterson.'

Her eyes went a little misty, but then she held up her bandaged right hand. 'My finger's getting better.'

They were both relieved to slip into another subject.

'Excellent! You'll soon be able to shoot again.'

At that moment the door was flung open and a half-drunk Wynter strode inside, his eyes unnaturally bright.

'Congratulate me!' he cried. 'I'm goin' into double harness again.'

It took a moment for the other two people in the room to comprehend what it was that was exciting the lance-corporal.

'You mean you're going to get married?' said Peterson, flatly.

Wynter flung his arms up. 'Yep! Me, hitched. Told you I would. Found this saucy Orkney girl. She belonged to one of them in the Highland Brigade, but he died of the cholera. Now she wants me.'

'I wonder why?' said Crossman. 'Has she lost her reason?'

'No, an' she's not blind nor stupid neither,' growled Wynter. 'She just wants a good man to look after her. Well, I'm a good man, see. I'll take care of her, just see if I don't.' He was quiet for a moment, then added, 'Likes a drink too, just like me. We suit each other. You want to meet her?'

Without waiting for an answer he opened the door and yelled, 'Mary! Come on over, meet the sergeant.'

A dumpy woman in a rough skirt and dirty blouse came sidling into the room a few moments later. It was difficult to guess her age, but Crossman would have put her in her mid-forties: probably twice the number of Wynter's years on the earth. She had a pleasant, if doughy face, with dark-ringed eyes dulled by gin. Her hair was mostly grey, with some of the original darkness in patches: it was tied up in a loose bun from which thick dirty strands had escaped and hung over her shoulders. On her feet were a pair of Russian soldier's boots, cut to fit her larger size. The bare ankles above the boots were thick and covered in sores.

As poor soldiers' wives went, after two years away from home in a place where proper sanitation and ablutions were non-existent, she was a reasonable catch for a man like Wynter. Mary had probably been lured away from similar conditions in a croft in the Orkney Islands — neither better nor worse than many other homes in the United Kingdom — and had spent a hard time in scratching a living in the army. No doubt before that her life had been somewhat harder and her life expectancy shorter. As any army wife she had to wash clothes and look after her man, probably several men, but she did not have to dig flinty soil and plant potatoes year in, year out. She did not have to carry firewood dozens of miles, nor spend her life in a dank scullery the size of an army officer's toilet. Here her diet was a little more varied and the entertainment decidedly more sparkling.

'Hello, sir,' she said, curtsying to Crossman. 'Very pleased to make your acquaintance.'

'You don't 'ave to call him *sir*,' laughed Wynter. 'He's only a sergeant — they're two a penny.'

'I ken that,' she flashed back at her husband-to-be, 'but I speak as I would be spoken to.'

'Well said, Mary,' Crossman intervened, hoping to avoid a domestic scene. 'I hope you know what you're doing, marrying that reprobate.'

She touched her grey hair and gave Crossman a look which implied that her choice was limited.

Wynter crossed the room and threw up his arms again. 'Mary, what d'you think of your new home? Eh? Palace or what?' He turned and indicated his cot. 'This is our bed. I'll hang a blanket up, for the sake of modesty an' all that. Save them lot gawking at us.'

Peterson rolled her eyes and made a retching sound.

'Well, not you maybe,' said Wynter, 'but that there Gwilliams. And Yorwarth — bloody hell, here he is!' Yorwarth entered the hovel, raking his nails over his neck. 'Yorwarth, you've broken out again — you scratch 'em like that and you'll bleed to death. Now Mary here, she's good at curin' things. She could probably make you some decent ointment.'

Yorwarth said, 'I've had enough of damn ointments.'

Crossman asked, 'So, when do you tie the knot?'

'We're jumpin' the broomstick this afternoon, at three. You're invited, sergeant. And you, Peterson. It's goin' to be quite a do. All the girls from the black tent are comin'.'

'You're going to have those harlots at your *wedding*?' cried Peterson. 'Mary, is this true?'

'Oh, I don't care. He can have who he wants.' She sounded weary, as if she had been through this a dozen times already.

'They're my friends,' argued Wynter. 'The trouble with you Peterson, is you're jealous. You don't have friends like me. Plenty of booze, that's the secret. I'm goin' to have the time of my life . . . '

The day did not quite work out the way Wynter planned. He did indeed get married. There was no vicar of course, the pair did not even consider a chapel wedding, but he did

160

jump the broomstick with Mary Robertson and declare his intention to be married in front of witnesses. Nothing more was required. Mary was now his chattel. In turn she would be fed and given shelter. Any more than that was dependent on Wynter's benevolence. Mary did not expect anything more than her basic needs to be met. Wynter was not stingy with the gin, once he'd had a skinful himself, and she appreciated this generous streak in his otherwise mean nature.

By six o'clock Wynter was dead drunk.

He and a friend from the 88th loaded a rifle with a ball-less cartridge, stuffing sea-salt crystals down the barrel for the ammunition. They planned to fire the salt like pellets of shot at another soldier in the regiment. Wynter had a sour history with the victim, a young Irish private, who had once taken money from him at cards. Wynter had craved revenge ever since the fleecing and his wedding day seemed liked the perfect time to get even with his enemy. Since it was summer the men working in the docks and around the camp had taken off their shirts to work. This was important. Wynter had to blast bare skin so that the salt would be driven into the man's body. It was an old trick used by Corsican and Sardinian farmers on poachers.

The result of the salt entering a man's

bloodstream was the raising of the victim's temperature for a few days. It would in effect cause the man to experience the same symptoms as a high fever. Death was seldom the outcome of such an act. In almost all cases the victim recovered, though for quite a long time he would be weak and sickly. Wynter wanted his man to know he couldn't 'cheat' Wynter and get away with it forever.

Wynter, grinning evilly, stepped out of the shadows and confronted the unwary soldier with, 'Sullivan, d'you want some salt in your beef?' He then fired at the bare chest of the startled man in front of him.

Unfortunately for the bridegroom an ensign came round the corner just as he squeezed the trigger. Wynter was so drunk his aim was off. A certain amount of salt struck Sullivan, causing him to scream in pain. At the same time a little of the blast caught the sleeve of the ensign. Sullivan ran off, his chest streaming with rivulets of blood. The young ensign — not more than eighteen years of age — stood with wide, disbelieving eyes and then yelled hoarsely for assistance, genuinely thinking he had been shot at by a disaffected soldier running amuck.

'Help! Ho! Murder here!'

The ensign kept inspecting his coat, trying to find out where the bullet had entered.

Men came running. Wynter was disarmed and secured by two or three strong soldiers. A colour sergeant slapped his face, telling him to come to his senses and that he had committed a heinous crime against a superior officer.

'You'll hang for this!' said the colour sergeant.

Wynter's friend had disappeared like the morning mist. Wynter himself was taken into custody. He tried to explain to a rather unsympathetic captain what he had been trying to do, but after a beating was cast into a makeshift prison. He managed to get word out to Crossman, who had already heard a fragmented story from the wedding guests. Major Lovelace was consulted and with a great deal of negotiation and diplomacy on his part the attempted murder charge was dropped. The ensign however, and his superiors, were determined to exact a strong punishment on Wynter. Lovelace agreed that Wynter's acts, both on the soldier and in tagging the ensign, required that he undergo punishment. 'A lesson needs to be taught.'

'Don't let them flog me, sergeant,' said Wynter, when Crossman went to see him. The miscreant soldier was white with fear. 'They're talking about fifty lashes. I can't take no fifty lashes. I'm a sick man.'

'The sickness is very temporary, Wynter. The result of your overindulgence. If you will drink to excess . . . '

'Oh, shut that gentry-talk, sergeant. I'm in trouble. I had a few too many rums, that's all. You can get Colonel Hawke or Major Lovelace to get me off. It was my weddin' for Christsakes. I didn't mean no harm.'

'You shot at an ensign. Major Lovelace has managed to get the charge of attempted murder dropped, but you can't expect him to involve himself any further. You're an idiot, Wynter. A complete fool. I can't do anything more for you. You'll have to grit your teeth and take your punishment. Other men have taken as much and walked away laughing. By the by, Sullivan is in a bad way. You'd better pray he pulls out of it, otherwise there's nothing I or anyone else can do for you.'

'He'll be all right,' grumbled Wynter. 'He an't gettin' no fifty lashes, is he?'

Sullivan did go through a bad time, his temperature soaring as it was expected to do, but he recovered from the attack. Wynter received his punishment. Crossman went to watch. Wynter passed by him, giving him a sidelong glance. The lance-corporal's face was ashen. Those watching could see his legs were unsteady. No one blamed him for this, nor when he screamed out after the sixth stroke. The whistle of the lash made the man tense for the actual strike, which was all the worse for him. Wynter passed out three-quarters of the way through his punishment. When he was taken down, his back was flayed and he was insensible. Gwilliams and Yorwarth carried him on a stretcher to Mrs Seacole, who rubbed some healing ointment into the wounds and gave the pair instructions on further treatment.

On opening his eyes, the first person Wynter saw was Crossman.

'You bastard,' he groaned. 'You could've stopped that.'

He tried to roll over on his back, forgetting that's where the wounds were, and yelled in pain.

Peterson said, 'Don't be a goat, Wynter. The sergeant couldn't do anything. You took that on yourself, when you shot that private.' Peterson paused a moment, before adding, 'Oh, and you've been stripped to a private again yourself.'

'What?' cried the beleaguered man. 'That's me money cut, an't it? I can't afford to be married now.'

'It's a bit late for that,' said Yorwarth. 'You should've thought of that, before.'

'Well, where's me new wife, anyways?' He

tried to lift his head. 'Where's that cow got to?'

'Saying she's a cow makes you a bull, does it?' Peterson said. 'I don't think so. Wynter, when're you going to get it in your head that no one is going to run around after you, even your new wife. She's gone out drinking, so I heard. She said if you woke up before she was back to tell you she'll bring you some eggs . . . ' But Peterson stopped here, because Wynter had slipped into unconsciousness again.

Colonel Hawke sent for Crossman. The sergeant was halfway to the colonel's 'office' when he noticed a certain captain heading towards him. Crossman recognized him instantly as Captain Sterling Campbell, the officer with whom he had once played cards. Crossman was quite evidently a sergeant, whereas Campbell had last seen him in a lieutenant's uniform. There was little Crossman could do to avoid the captain, however, and as he passed he threw up a salute. Campbell was in a world of his own for he did not even acknowledge the sergeant.

Crossman drew a deep breath and hurried on. Seeing the captain again caused him to wonder whether there had been any sort of showdown between him and Jarrard. Perhaps Jarrard was still 'amongst the French' and had managed to avoid meeting with Campbell. Jarrard was no coward, but the trick of sending Campbell to India had been for Crossman's benefit and there was no reason why Jarrard should fight a duel over the matter. In fact Crossman would have felt duty bound to interfere if it did come to that.

Hawke was pacing the floor when Crossman entered. He looked up, staring down that powerful nose of his.

'Ah, sergeant. Come in.'

'Thank you, sir.'

Hawke's bushy eyebrows knitted for a moment as he continued to walk up and down at the back of the room. He suddenly stopped and looked up. 'And how is Lance-Corporal Peterson?'

'Recovered, I think.'

'That was good work, sergeant. I wondered at first — it was a risk, you'll agree — but now I think I approve of looking after our own. These small groups, they're very new, but they're like families, aren't they? A family looks after it's own. Normally one would say that when a soldier is taken prisoner, in a battle for instance, that there would be an end to it. That soldier would be more or less forgotten. But with these bands, these *pelotons*, each member seems to be important to the whole. Yes, that was well done.' He laughed. 'I hope you would do the same for me.'

'Naturally, sir. In a flash.'

The colonel's face darkened a little now. 'On the other hand, this business with Wynter, that was *badly* done. Is the man an idiot?'

'Not far off, sir. A useful idiot.'

'You think we should still keep him in the *peloton?*'

Crossman saw a wonderful chance of ridding himself of Wynter, but found he could not mouth the right words. 'That's up to you, sir.'

'What do you recommend?'

Crossman sighed. 'Perhaps give him another chance? He's been with the group for the whole war. One of the founder members. It would be churlish of me to suggest you throw him out at this point, just when the war seems to be drawing to a close.'

'I suppose so. Well, then, I take it he mends? Now, to get down to business. Something exciting for you. Zumbooruck! What do you think?'

There was a triumphant note to the colonel's tone that Crossman did not like the sound of. Crossman furrowed his brow wondering what he was *supposed* to think. What was that word the colonel had used? It sounded Turkish, but it meant nothing to the sergeant.

'I'm afraid you'll have to enlighten me further, sir.'

'Ha! Caught you out, eh, sergeant? Well sir, a zumbooruck is a swivel gun, mounted on the saddle of a camel.' He frowned as if musing, then corrected himself. 'Or it might be the whole thing, the camel *and* the saddle-and-gun. That's neither here nor there. The important thing is, they use 'em in India. Saw them in action myself, when I was there. Very effective. Scares the hell out of the enemy. Elephants are better of course, for making them wet their pants, but zumboorucks can do it too. This one was brought back by a captain from the 93rd. In fact . . . '

'That wouldn't be Captain Campbell, sir?'

'You know him?'

Crossman could have bitten off his tongue.

'Well, as to that, you may recall, sir, that the 93rd was my father's regiment, and that of my older brother, who was sent home sick a few months ago.'

'Ah, there's the connection. Yes, it was Campbell. Poor chap was abducted and shipped off to India. Somebody's head is going to roll for that one day. Now where was I? Oh, yes — not only did Campbell tell me about these zumbooruks, he brought the

169

equipment back with him. Won it in a game of *chemin de fer*, apparently. Campbell's rather good at cards, but if you know him, you'll be aware of that. It's not a great secret. Over there, sergeant, in the corner of the room behind you. What do you think of that then, eh?'

Crossman turned and looked. In the dim dusty shadows of the far right-hand corner stood a magnificent object. It was a gleaming brass swivel gun mounted on the front of a polished leather saddle. The saddle itself was a work of art, being etched with symbols and hanging with tassels, and folds of embroidered Indian cloth, both colourful and decorative. Leather straps splayed out from the saddle like the tentacles of a stranded octopus. There were leather knobs on the front and back of the saddle and a carved, curved wooden supporting frame, rather like the skeleton of an upturned boat, gave the whole thing a sense of rigidity and stability.

'Beautiful thing, isn't it?' said Hawke, dreamily. 'Exotic and deadly. Some call 'em *falconets*. No idea why. Not into semantics. So, I've got a man out looking for a decent camel. Not sure what condition it'll be in, you know that beasts of burden are hard to come by here, but I'll purchase him outright and have him sent over to you with a handler. I want you to test this idea out, sergeant. Make it work. Could be useful when we go into Sebastopol.'

'Sir?'

Hawke gave Crossman a look as if to say that his patience was rapidly thinning.

'If we have to fight street to street, we won't be able to use the RHA, will we? Some of those streets and alleys are remarkably narrow. But a dromedary could get down them. Think man, we could be pioneering something new in the way of skirmishing in built-up areas! This is your chance to shine, sergeant. It's something I *could* put you forward for. The other work, sabotage etcetera, we have to keep under out hats. But the general staff would approve of something like this.'

Crossman tried to wriggle out from under. 'Are you sure we're the right people for the job, sir. I mean, the cavalry . . . '

'The cavalry are already too big for their boots. This is *our* project, sergeant. I'll speak with you again later, when you've had a chance to assess things. Dismissed.'

Crossman gave his colonel a steady salute and marched out of the room.

When the camel arrived it was not the *he* that the colonel had continually referred to, but was definitely of the female gender. It stood in the doorway, blocking any entrances or exits by humans. Its handler, a young Tartar boy, was outside squatting on the ground, looking through the creature's legs at the interior of the hovel. He seemed to Peterson to be a little possessive, for his eyes kept flicking towards Gwilliams, also on the outside of the room, who patted the camel's neck affectionately.

Yorwarth, on the inside with Peterson and the still bed-ridden Wynter, said, 'Peterson, you won't be so lonely now — there's another lady in the *peloton*.'

Peterson stared at the dromedary as it stood chewing some unidentifiable cud. The camel stared back, still working its rubbery jaws. Its brown eyes were huge and fathomless. There was wisdom in there, or stupidity, it was difficult to tell. Certainly mystery. If Peterson had been the sort of woman who worried about her looks, she would have been jealous of the camel's eyes, which were huge and dreamy. The beast's coat smelled, of course, clinkered as it was with dung of various colours and strengths.

While Peterson was staring, the beast suddenly changed its expression, spread its back legs, and began to pee. The steaming piss fell in a great torrent — and it fell and it fell and it fell, forming an immense pool in the doorway. The whole operation took a long age. Peterson could not believe the amount of liquid that came out. Finally the stream slowed to a dribble, then ceased altogether, the camel letting out a grunted sigh of satisfaction.

'Aw, Christ, look at that, will you?' cried Wynter, rolling on his side. 'What a stink.'

'Doesn't smell that bad,' Yorwarth said. 'Anyway, mate, I hear you're the one who's being put in charge of her, so the sergeant said.'

Yorwarth should have kept his mouth shut, because Crossman was descending the stairs at the time.

'No,' said the sergeant, 'that's your job, Yorwarth.'

'Why me?' cried the indignant private.

'Because you come from Australia.'

'What's that got to do with it?' the young man began scratching furiously at his eczema.

'Gwilliams has probably never seen a camel before, have you Gwilliams?'

'No, sergeant.'

'And Peterson and Wynter only know plough horses. Now, Australia has camels, I know that for a fact. Imports, perhaps, but definitely there. Therefore you are the most likely candidate for the job. You, Yorwarth, are the camel-rough-rider of this *peloton*. You will learn to handle the artillery. You will ride the beast. That's an order. Now,' Crossman went forward, just as the handling boy was moving the camel out of the doorway, 'what's her name? We can't keep referring to her as *it*, she might be offended. Camels, I am reliably informed, have rather vicious tempers. Don't turn your back on her, or she might take a chunk out of your neck.'

Yorwarth muttered, 'Now, he tells me.'

'Right,' Crossman said, turning to the Tartar boy, 'let's see who these two are, how old and who they belong to.'

Crossman spoke to the Tartar boy, who replied with the gravity of an elderly man. He told him the camel was three years of age, so far as he knew, and that her name was Vysehrad. He himself was nine and his name was Stikchuk but the British soldier-men had shortened it to Stik. His mother had lived in a village in the hills, until it had been burned down by the Russians when they retreated to Sebastopol. Now he and his mother lived in a shack at the back of Kadikoi. Stik said he was a proud man, his father had been a worker in the vineyards, but the vineyards had fallen into disuse and his father had gone to Yalta for work.

'The boy's name is Stik,' said Crossman to his men, 'and I want him treated well. No bullying — are you listening, Wynter? He's not here to look after you lot, he's here to look after the camel, whose name . . . ' They would never cope with Vysehrad. 'Whose name is Betsy. I want Betsy treated with every courtesy too. She is our gun carriage. Colonel Hawke wants us to assess Betsy with her cannon, and that's what we'll do.'

While he was talking with his men, Crossman saw Rupert Jarrard striding towards the hovel. He raised his hand to acknowledge a wave from the correspondent. Crossman noticed Jarrard was wearing his highly polished leather holster bearing a Navy Colt rather ostentatiously on his hip, as if he expected to use it at a moment's notice. The sergeant guessed this was probably to do with the presence of Campbell. No doubt the revolver was a sign to the revenge-seeking captain, to tell him that he would have no easy task if he challenged Jarrard to a duel. Jarrard's casual method of wearing the firearm proclaimed his proficiency with it.

When the American reached him, the pair shook hands and then went inside and up the stairs to be in private.

'Is that your camel?' asked Jarrard in amazement. 'Did you win him in a game of poker?'

'Very close,' replied Crossman, offering

Jarrard a seat on his cot, 'it was actually our friend Campbell who won the saddle-gun in a game of cards and brought it with him from India. The camel has been supplied to fit the saddle. We are to test the pair of them out together.'

'Rather you than me.'

Crossman lit his chibouque pipe and began puffing smoke.

'Well then Rupert, are you still avoiding Campbell?'

Jarrard grinned. 'I'm still holed up amongst the French. But, Jack, give me your congratulations, I'm deeply in love.'

Suddenly a pang went through Crossman. He was suspicious. Jarrard had been out riding a lot with Jane. Was it Jane to whom he was referring?

He said, stiffly, 'My best wishes, Rupert. Who is the lady?'

'Why, I have met the most . . . Wait, let me tell you from the beginning. Last week I went to a performance in that little theatre the French have set up. Not one of your bawdy shows, but a concert, with three violinists and a cello or two. I can't remember exactly. There was this lady violinist — I tell you, Jack, she played like an angel . . . '

All rancour gone, Crossman said flippantly, 'You are intimate with celestial musicians?'

'*String sonata number five, in E flat.* Rossini. You should have heard it, Jack — you should have seen her. She is a lovely creature, Monique, with exquisite hands — you have never seen such long slim fingers — and the way her wrist curved while she played — swans' necks don't come into it — and she was lost in her music, Jack. Lost in a wonderland of beautiful notes, majestic melodies. Her eyes were closed most of the time she was playing and swaying with the music, but when she opened them — it was like being kicked in the chest by a horse — it knocked all the breath out of me.'

'You have such a turn of phrase.'

'Laugh, Jack, laugh. I don't give a damn. I have found the woman who has at last put the word *marriage* into my vocabulary. Monique Foudre. Maybe you wouldn't approve of her, Jack. She's not from any grand European family. I guess you might say she's common, but I'm no Southern aristocrat myself.'

'You do me an injustice, Rupert. I have never considered breeding an essential asset. A little intellect, perhaps, and a few table manners. No freckles of course, you realize that the Fates oppose freckles, while blonde hair is *de rigueur*. Wynter is unaware of the fashion, having taken a wife to himself with dark hair, albeit streaked with grey. Mary is gold itself, but her table etiquette is wanting a little. You couldn't vouch that she would not steal the salt cellar from under your nose without a by-your-leave.'

'You're still making fun of me, Jack. Well, that's a discredit to you, you know. Monique is sweet and warm. She behaves impeccably at the table, and her voice is delightful. Not one of those harsh smoky voices you sometimes hear from French women. Lyrical is how I'd put her. In French of course — she doesn't have any English. I'm not great at French, but I'm learning fast. I call her the *imp*. She has an impish look about her.'

Crossman asked, 'What is she doing, here in the Crimea?'

'Entertaining the soldiers. The French are much better set up than you people, y'know. They've got everything over there.'

'Good for them.'

'Now, don't go all huffy on me, Jack. It's not your fault the British Army is a disorganized rabble. Now, what have you got to offer me?'

The two men were avidly interested in inventions. They competed with one another, in various ways, mostly by putting up inventors from their own or chosen nationality. Crossman was half-Scot, half-English — or so he liked to believe. Jarrard was all

American, with a touch of Swedish. Crossman believed that all the great inventors were Scots, with a few Italians and Frenchmen on the periphery, and the odd Englishman.

'Two men I haven't mentioned to you before — Cook and Wheatstone. You know we now have this telegraph link between the Crimea and our lords and masters back home? Well, the first of those was set up in 1839 I believe, running between Paddington and West Drayton in England. I understand it was the first use of electricity for long-distance communication.'

Jarrard took out a cheroot and lit it with deliberation, before saying, 'If it hadn't been for Benjamin Franklin, they wouldn't have had their electricity to use.'

'Nonsense, Rupert. Mr Franklin didn't *invent* or even discover electricity. It's true he invented the lightning conductor, but . . . '

'He explored the *nature* of electrical forces and furthered the advance of knowledge in static electricity.'

Jarrard's mouth was set in the way a donkey sets it jaw when it is going to be stubborn. Crossman realized he was on a hiding to nothing. He let the matter drop, even though he knew his sparring partner was blowing smoke rings. There was a lot of affection between the pair and Crossman knew that something was troubling his friend very deeply. What was more, he believed he knew what it was.

'Rupert, this business with Campbell. It wouldn't do anyone any good, you know, if you were to seek satisfaction.'

Jarrard drew a heavy sigh and waved away the smoke of his cheroot from the front of his face.

' 'Seek satisfaction.' What a quaint phrase that is. There's no satisfaction in killing a man. Even less in being killed by him. No, it wouldn't do any good and it would probably do a great deal of harm. He would be killed, for you know Jack, I am a deadshot — and I would either be incarcerated by the army or sent packing. In either case I wouldn't be able to do my job and would then be out of work. He would be dead and I would be jobless. There are others who would be affected of course. Campbell probably has a mother — we all have — and sisters perhaps. Maybe even a wife, though I can't imagine any woman marrying that popinjay. If he has brothers, they would come after me — they would do in the Americas. It's all of a piece.'

'Everything you say is true.'

'Yes, but Jack,' Jarrard dropped his cheroot and ground it out with the heel of his boot, 'in here,' he punched his own chest, 'I can't stand it. Campbell struts about the place defaming my name like the arrogant son-of-a-bitch he is, and I have to hear about it without flinching. I have to listen to some lisping French Hussar tell me they are calling me a coward. I don't like it, Jack. I don't like it one bit. It bothers me more than a tad, you know?'

'You are the better man, Rupert, we both know that.'

'I would like to put a hole in that man's forehead.'

'So would every Russian on the other side of the Inkerman ruins. In fact they would like to put holes in all of us, you included, probably. What I'm trying to say is that at any day, at any time, Captain Campbell may receive what you would like to give him. Why not wait a while and see if that happens, before you throw away your livelihood on a man who doesn't deserve to destroy you?'

Jarrard tapped Crossman's knee. 'You talk a lot of sense, Jack, but sense doesn't always help in these cases. Emotion. That's what counts. Pride, anger, hate, those sort of emotions.'

Crossman knew his friend was hurting badly, but he did believe it would do no good to challenge Campbell. Even were the captain to fall and nought said afterwards, there would be others to follow him. Such men, dicers and cardsharps, were strangely popular amongst the junior officers of regiments. Campbell was a handsome dashing man, charismatic in an arrogant sort of way, adored by the ladies, envied by many of his peers. The fact that there was very little between his ears except a cunning memory for the pips on a deck of cards did not diminish his stature in the eyes of his friends. An idle fop owning a wicked skill with weapons: this was the kind of man who was looked up to by the young subalterns and ensigns.

Jarrard left about midnight. Crossman then went down to see how they were coping with their latest recruits. Betsy had been taken to her bed by Stik, who was himself fast asleep on the very hay she was munching. It was a soft night, with soft stars. The guns were silent along the front. Now and again there was the crack of a musket, but the sound almost seemed a part of the tranquillity: full stops to sentences of calm, reminding everyone that, yes, it *was* a quiet balmy evening, and yes, they should be grateful for it. Death could be everywhere, but actually Creation was in progress, slowly changing the world and its wonders. Things were growing, transforming, mutating. A magnificent moon was rolling imperceptibly across the dark sky, into clouds like bushes, then out again the other side.

Crossman went to bed, stepping through the narrow lanes between the cots on the ground floor.

At around three o'clock he was awoken by an unholy row. Instinctively he reached for the pistol by his bed, having once been attacked in this very room by a Cossack assassin. However the noise was coming from below. He lit a candle quickly and ascertained that Major Lovelace was not in his bed. That much was a relief, for Crossman could hear Wynter's voice mouthing obscenities. He went to the top of the stairs.

'Wynter, shut up, or I'll have Gwilliams put you out.'

Wynter came to the foot of the stairs.

'It's her, sergeant,' he said. 'She's bin in the beds of other men.'

Crossman guessed that *her* was Mrs Wynter and prayed that the other beds were outside their own quarters.

Wynter continued. 'She's as drunk as a bishop's tart, sergeant, and I can smell it on her. If she an't bin in other's beds, how come she's got the money to buy gin, eh? I 'aven't given her nothing, so she an't got it from me. She's a strumpet, that's what she is. She don't know one bed from another and gets in where she pleases. What kind of wife is that for an honest man?'

Crossman half descended the stairs. Looking down into the room where an oil lamp was still sending out a dim light, he could see that Mary was in what looked to be a drunken sleep. Her blouse was awry and her skirt was rucked to her fat thighs, but she looked peaceful and happy.

Fortunately, Wynter's yelling had not woken any of the other soldiers. They could actually remain unconscious through a gun barrage. Like cats they would sleep through any sound except the one that was out of place, the sound that signified a threat. The clink of a Cossack's stirrup would have them up, or the snort of a Russian horse. But the noise of the guns, or Wynter's bawling, they were used to.

Crossman was beginning to tire of this badinage.

'Wynter, go to bed.'

'But she's a trollop, sergeant.'

'You knew that when you married her, man. Who else would have married *you*?'

'Sergeant, that's not fair.'

'No, but unfortunately it's true and you know it.'

Wynter shrugged: a gesture of helplessness. He looked down at his beloved. Her mouth was hanging open in a soft snore. She lay sprawled across the narrow cot. He heaved her to one side and then crawled on to the blanket next to her. Within a minute, he too was asleep, his arm draped around her broad shoulders. Soon the pair were snoring in harmony.

As Crossman stared down the lamplight caught the network of lash marks on Wynter's back, covered now in reddish-yellow scabs. Those streaks, those scars, would never completely go away. Wynter would have them for the rest of his life. He should have had medals to go with them, but the work the *peloton* did was not yet recognized by the authorities as being worthy of such rewards. Not that Wynter would have kept them for long: he would have sold them a week after they were presented.

Still, Crossman thought, they were quick enough to give the man a whipping when he had done wrong. It would not have hurt them much to have rewarded Wynter, and all the other members of the *peloton*, for doing their dangerous and unwholesome work for them. Such was the nature of large organizations. They expected utter loyalty, but gave little in return. They were made up of many individuals, most of whom were out for their own gains in terms of status and power. An army has many souls, of many shades and different colours. In a colony of ants each member works selflessly for the greater good. In a colony of humans any progress is through the advancement of individuals. The greater good comes along almost by accident when it falls into line with the desires of its leaders.

Later in the week Jane came to see Crossman, ostensibly to find out how Peterson was coping after her ordeal. She and Crossman went for a walk in a nearby orchard, out of sight of enquiring eyes. They were able to kiss hello and take each other's hands for a brief period.

'How are you, my dearest Jane?'

'I am well, Alexander.' She used his real name in private. 'If I looked a little peeked it's because Lavinia will keep me up late at night playing whist with her friends.'

'Oh, you don't looked peeked at all. You look positively lovely. A nonpareil in anyone's eyes. Look how rosy your cheeks are.'

She laughed. 'That's because I pinched them hard before I came to see you. But I'm sure my eyes lack lustre and my brow is dark.'

'I see nothing but stars and alabaster.'

She laughed again. 'Not very original, cousin, but it will do.' Her tone changed. 'How is Peterson? Has she recovered?'

'Physically, I believe so,' he replied, kicking at a fallen twig, 'but who knows what is in her mind, Jane. This is all my fault. I should never have allowed her to remain, once I found she was a woman. It was selfishness on my part. She is so very good with a rifle-musket and her skill has been very useful to me. It was wrong of me to exploit that.'

Jane almost snorted in a very unladylike manner. 'Alexander, she would not have it any other way. She would have hated you for revealing her secret to the authorities. So would they. What they are not supposed to know doesn't hurt them. And Peterson does love the army. I confess it is all very strange to me, but it is a fact.' Jane paused to reflect before adding, 'One would have thought that an extraordinary sharpshooter like Peterson should be a narrow-eyed, leathery man with a soul the colour of slate, whereas Peterson is a sort of — well, soft as a dumpling and with very little brittle character about her. She is an incongruity, Alex.'

'She is indeed. Talking of character, I hope she has the strength to weather the ordeal she went through. I cannot imagine what torture she's been through, but one hopes she has enough reserves . . . '

'I think you will find she is stronger than we believe her to be.'

That subject over, Jane asked how Betsy was faring.

'Never mind how she is coping with us,' replied Crossman, 'better to ask how we are coping with *her*. We managed to get the saddle and gun on her yesterday, but with a lot of fuss, and only for a moment or two. Did you know a camel can spit a wad some thirty yards? With a good deal of accuracy too. At least, Betsy can and I'm led to believe she represents the average dromedary in these parts. She struck Ali full in the back from that range, after he'd berated her for shucking off her saddle for the third time. I could see by the water in his eyes that the shot had stung him.

'And naturally, she bites, and won't get off her haunches when we want her to, or goes down on them when we don't want her to. She relieves herself at the most inappropriate times. She seems to be able to release a foul-smelling gas at will. When she curls back her lips and shows her long brown teeth she is most formidable and unapproachable.

'All in all she is a most uncooperative beast. Give me a horse anytime. I believe God made the camel, along with the stonefish and the stick insect, in order to provide the earth with absurdities. The camel is both comic and terrible — a product of whimsy and the ridiculous. It's going to take a lot of patience on our part to get her to do as we wish — and of course, added to all her other vagaries, she's female.'

Jane, very amused at all this, knew of course that the last few words were meant to provoke her and she didn't disappoint him.

'You obviously don't know females very well, Alex. For instance, you should know that it is not polite to speak of bodily functions in the presence of a lady — even those of domestic beasts. We are not supposed to know that such things occur. Actually females are not so complicated as men believe them to be, the fault lying with the fact that men are not very bright.'

Crossman was amused by her flippancy. He did enjoy her company. She was easy to speak with and seemed to have none of the swift mood swings of Lavinia Durham. He knew too that he was falling in love with her. Cousin Jane. Not really his cousin, of course, and surely he had loved her since she had been six? Perhaps he had better say something of that nature?

'Jane . . . '

'Hey!' came a loud voice.

They both looked up, startled, to see someone bounding through the trees towards them.

'Rupert!' muttered Crossman, heaving an impatient sigh. 'Impeccable timing, as usual.'

'Hello, Jack. Good day, Jane. How good to see you both.'

Jarrard stood there grinning, his face showing one or two marks. A cut above his left eye. A swelling on his cheekbone. A thick lip with a smear of blood on it. Clearly Jarrard had been in some sort of fracas and wished to be asked about it, because he simply stood before them, smiling, posing for admiration and comment.

'You've been fighting!' gasped Jane. 'Oh, Rupert!'

'Damn right I have, but with whom, eh Jack?' A wink followed this sentence and Crossman got it straight away.

'Campbell.'

'Exactly,' replied Jarrard with heavy satisfaction. 'I could stand it no longer, so I put myself in his way when he was walking to his mess tent. He of course challenged me — I couldn't very well challenge him, because I wanted the choice of weapons — and I told him it was to be fisticuffs. He looked surprised and asked if I would not prefer swords or pistols. No, says I, a good set of bare knuckles was all I needed.' Jarrard looked to the sky as if in praise of whoever lived there. 'It was the perfect answer, Jack. I wouldn't be in danger of killing him this way. In fact,' he rubbed his cheek, 'he wasn't an easy man to thrash. I've met easier. Caught me a good few times, but right prevailed . . . '

'Not *right*, Rupert. He was, after all, the injured party.'

'Never mind that. I knocked the damn wind out of that windbag and pummelled him around the head a fair bit. I blacked one of his eyes and I'm sure I broke his nose . . . '

Jane winced.

'And he finally went down and stayed down, much to the chagrin of his seconds. Oh, by the way, I borrowed your Lieutenant Pirce-Smith for my second. He didn't mind. I think he enjoyed it.'

Crossman heaved a sigh of relief this time. 'Well, at least that's out of the way, so long as he doesn't challenge you again.'

'He won't. I requested his word before we set to, that this would be the end of the affair. Reluctantly — for privately, Jack, I think he wanted to blow my head off — he agreed. I believe he thought he could break every bone in my body and thereby get his satisfaction that way. My bones are intact, my friends, and my spirit is soaring. If any of his fellow officers want the same sort of satisfaction, I'll happily oblige. I don't think they will though. Somehow a man like that loses his glitter when he's lying in the dust after a scrap. Different from being shot or run through with a sword. His reputation remains intact after a duel to the death. Sort of clean. But a man who's been knocked silly, his shirt ripped and his trousers muddied — well, the gloss goes off him. I don't think his friends will make any more of it.'

Jane growled like a lioness, 'How base you men are, sometimes. How can it make you feel good to know you've beaten a man senseless, Rupert? It may have been necessary, but you should still feel bad about it. You should be saying how unfortunate it has been and that you feel terrible. Men. I despair of you as a species, or a gender, or whatever it is that you are.'

'But he was calling me names, Jane. Everyone was talking. And I'd be a hypocrite if I came to Jack and told him I regretted the fight.'

'The word *gentlemen* is a misnomer. You are anything but gentle and you all remain boys of twelve years of age. I shall leave you now, to crow about your triumph. When you decide to return to civilized society, then I shall be glad of your company again.'

Jane strode off with a swish of skirts in a manner which delighted both the men who stood and watched her grand exit.

'She does that so well, doesn't she?' said Crossman, staring after her.

'They all do, Jack. They all do. Now, let me take you through it, blow by blow. If Pirce-Smith tells you otherwise, don't believe him. His version will be biased by the fact that it was a brother officer I pounded. Besides his vision was impeded by a fat French general, who happened to be passing by, and who stopped to watch the fun . . . '

Jarrard took Crossman through the fight from beginning to end, at the culmination of which Crossman was called to see that Betsy had at last accepted her gun-mounted saddle. A great cheer went up as Crossman and Jarrard approached to see that the miracle had been performed. Ali was looking pleased with himself. Yorwarth was looking worried, for the next stage was getting him up into the saddle. Stik was scowling, jealous of so many people taking an interest in his camel. Wynter, Gwilliams and Peterson were all looking smug, knowing they had not got to mount the beast. There was a festive air to the proceedings. Even Betsy was looking rather pleased with herself, obviously aware she was the centre of attraction.

'Right,' said Crossman, surveying the magnificent gleaming weapon that protruded from the saddle. 'Next we have to get

Yorwarth up there.'

'I told you, sergeant, I've never rode one of these beasts.'

'We're not expecting further miracles today, Yorwarth, and you can stop that scratching, your rash is not going to help you get out of this. If Betsy objects to you and shucks you off a few times, that's to be expected. Look, we'll put some hay down, to break your fall. It'll be as soft a landing as we can make it.'

'Oh, Lord,' muttered Yorwarth. 'If I break a leg . . . '

Stik ordered Betsy to kneel with a tap on her nose and a quiet word. The camel did as she was told. Yorwarth was then helped into the saddle. He sat there, a nervous wreck, his whole body shaking. Betsy was asked to rise. She did so, majestically. Yorwarth sat unsteadily in the saddle. In fact, to everyone's surprise, Betsy seemed quite happy to have him there. She simply stood and chewed and looked about her with those huge eyes, neither happy nor sad, but calm.

'Hey!' cried Yorwarth. 'I'm up.'

He took hold of the swivel gun and swung it in a sweeping arc, managing to strike Betsy's neck with the muzzle. Still she did not bolt or make any fuss. She was probably used to clouts from her handlers and thought it was one of those. It was all, you might say, satisfactory. Yorwarth proceeded to destroy several enemy defences with the gun, swinging it this way and that, and making firing noises with his mouth. His comrades ran around the static camel, pretending to return fire with their Enfields. Wynter told Yorwarth he had been shot through the head. Yorwarth replied that Wynter had been blasted to bits by canister just a moment before he had fired his weapon. It was all quite enjoyable, both to participate in and to watch. When they had finished their fun, Yorwarth was allowed to step down from the kneeling Betsy and they all went off to one of Ali's special lunches of brown rat stew, which he called 'steppe-rabbit meat' to ward off any squeamishness on the part of the British soldiers.

Crossman thought about the arc of the saddle gun. He loved inventors and inventions but rarely had the opportunity to do anything himself. Well, here was his chance. He borrowed some tools from a railway worker and fiddled with the gun, putting two stops on the swivel plate. Thus, when the gunner swung the weapon in future, it would only sweep through 340 degrees. It now stopped either side of Betsy's head, giving her 20 degrees of safety. Now if Yorwarth got overexcited he would not blow Betsy's head off by accident. Of course if the enemy were in front they would have to turn Betsy herself, but at least she would live to tell the tale.

He was standing by his handiwork, feeling very pleased with himself, when Jarrard called by.

'I would like you to meet Monique,' said the American. 'How about her next performance, on Tuesday? Look, why don't you bring Jane along. I'm sure she would enjoy a concert.'

'I'm obliged to you, Rupert. It would be good to get away from here for a few hours.'

'Great. Oh,' Jarrard reached into his coat and withdrew a crumpled envelope. 'Here's something for you, from Paris, France. One of the cellists was asking around for a Sergeant Jack Crossman of the 88th. When I said I knew you she handed me this. I hope it's not bad news.'

Jack frowned, taking the letter. He opened and read it in front of Jarrard, who waited patiently.

'It *is* bad news. I can tell by your expression.'

'Yes.' Crossman carefully folded the single sheet of paper, put it back in the envelope, and then pocketed it. 'Yes, it is. Very sad news. You'll recall I was once engaged to a

French lady, the niece of the owner of a vineyard north of here.'

'Lisette? I thought you were *still* engaged to her.'

'Well, technically, yes, but my letters have gone unanswered for several months now, so I thought she'd found someone else and was concerned about telling me.'

Jarrard raised his eyebrows. 'And that's what's happened?'

'No, no. This letter is from Lisette's uncle. Lisette died of consumption in Paris six months ago. The uncle wrote to me then, and once more besides, but the letters have obviously failed to reach me.'

'I am sorry to hear that, Jack. I recall you were quite in love with her, once upon a time.'

Crossman stared over the hard baked-mud ground towards the distant Fedioukine Hills. 'Yes, though it seems a lifetime ago. Time has such a strange quality about it, Rupert. A year at home — hunting, riding, shooting, fishing, walking the estates — studying, when I was younger — such a year passed by so very quickly. Spring followed winter, with summer right on its heels, and before I could take a breath, the apples were ripe and the leaves were falling from the trees. There, the seasons overtook one. Here they drag themselves along behind, wearing leaden boots. These last few months couldn't have passed more slowly.'

'I know — you want to kick July in the ass to shunt it on so that August can move up the tracks.'

'Something like that. Men crave immortality. Well then, the way to achieve it is to have a permanent war in dreary conditions. It seems we have been at Sebastopol forever already and it's been — well, yes, *under* a year. Incredible. So much has happened to me. So *little* has happened to the war. I have changed so very much and the war seems to be unchanging.'

'That's the nature of the beast, I guess. Look, Jack, I'm finding this conversation a little depressing. I came here walking on clouds. Can we cease with philosophizing and get back to happier moments?' He paused for a moment, then said, 'Oh, I'm sorry, I was forgetting. You've had bad news. Forgive me, Jack. I'm an insensitive bear at times.'

'No, it's me that's insensitive. I think that's due to the damn war, too. I feel very little. Sadness for a life lost, but I hardly knew Lisette. I mean, surely that's what marriage is about, getting to know the one you have fallen in love with? I should be devastated, inconsolable, but I'm not. I just feel a little emptier than before. These diseases that take our lives, they're rife amongst us, aren't they? How many dead British in this war so far, Rupert? From disease, I mean? Come on, you keep the figures for your paper.'

'My guess is around fifteen thousand. But look, Jack, I really have had enough of this moping. Buck up, boy. Climb out of the hole. I don't mind sympathizing with you over the loss of your Lisette, but I'm damned if I'm going to stand here mourning the British army. Does the letter say anything else?'

Crossman said, 'Yes. She's left me something. A small house in Paris. It was her grandmother's house, left to her in a will. I really don't deserve this, Rupert. I shall have to write to the uncle and tell him that someone in the family should have it.'

'Is the uncle rich?'

Crossman shrugged. 'He owns vineyards, here and in France. I suppose he has money.'

'Then keep the house. You'll only complicate things back there in Paris, France.'

Crossman nodded, thoughtfully. 'I'll consider it. Now, Rupert,' he said, cheering considerably, 'what is it with you Americans? Why do you always qualify Paris with France? There is only one Paris, surely?'

'No, the primary Paris is in Texas.'

'Oh, like the primary Sierra Nevadas are in

western America, I suppose? Those in Spain being the secondary ones.'

Jarrard grinned. 'You've got it.'

'We shall continue this discussion another time. Right now I've got to get the men ready for an inspection by Colonel Hawke. Sometimes he decides he ought to act like a real colonel and he descends on us with a strolling-cane under his arm and attempts to turn us into smart soldiers. Look at me.' Crossman's face was a weathered moon in the centre of a black forest of beard and wild hair. The uniform he was wearing was threadbare, dirty and of a strange brick colour. His crumpled forage cap sat upon the wild hair as if it belonged rather in his pocket. He was in truth, a mess. 'Will I ever become a proper soldier again? A well-turned out redcoat? I can't think it will ever happen. Colonel Hawke goes through the motions.'

Jarrard laughed. 'He'll be having parades next, with all six of you!'

'He does already. At least he lines us up, shortest on the right, tallest on the left, and then marches slowly along the ascending curve of heads, peering closely into each man's face and asking, 'How are you today, soldier?'

Jarrard was surprised. 'He asks that? An officer of a ranker?'

'He's one of a new breed, Rupert.'

'And what do they answer?'

'Always the same. 'Fine, sir, just fine.' Here you have Wynter, and others, moaning incessantly about the army, complaining night and day, and when they get the opportunity to air those moans and groans, what do they say? 'Fine, sir, just fine.' It's as if the world is run on rituals. One ritual is the moaning ritual, the other is the answering-an-officer's-enquiry ritual. The two seem to have nothing to do with one another. Simply rituals, never changing, always the same. The world is kept safe with rituals.'

'Litanies, you mean. The priest says 'Lord, have mercy upon us.' The congregation responds with, 'Christ, have mercy upon us.' The litany never changes. No one would think of changing it. They'll still be saying the same things ten thousand years from now. The language suffers from it.'

'But these litanies are like straws to a drowning man, Rupert.'

'Yes, there is safety in knowing exactly what the response will be, without fail.'

They were back where they started, so they parted and made a promise to meet later in the week, to attend the concert.

★ ★ ★

Despite the warmth of the evening, Crossman wore a Tartar's jacket over his coatee. Although he had always proclaimed that the ranks were just as worthy as the officers, the ingrained prejudices of his upbringing made him subconsciously wish to hide the fact that he was but a sergeant while in upper-class company. Most of the men, and the few women, who were attending the concert in the French camp were officers. Those who were not were generally serving those who were.

It irked Crossman that he had to hide his rank, but he did not want any incidents to spoil the evening. There was always the cavalry lieutenant (usually it was the junior officers who were the worst, creatures unsure of themselves, they being the parvenus of the army) who felt he ought to assert his superiority. Should one of them require a glass of beer, or wine, and seeing his sergeant's stripes order him to fetch one, he knew that in the company of Rupert and Jane he would tell that man to go to the very devil. This would of course cause a fuss and the evening would end there.

So he ensured that they sat to the side, not in the middle seats, and he had specifically requested that Jarrard should keep his voice moderate and his clapping modest. The

American was inclined to make a show of things. It was his wont to applaud with a very distinct and loud clapping of his rather large hands and yell 'Bravo' after every movement, even though he was aware one should wait to show one's appreciation for the performance once the whole piece was finished.

Love could not only be blind, but fairly brash too.

'Are you comfortable?' he asked Jane, for the wooden seats were not only hard, but rough to the touch. 'I could give you my jacket to sit on.'

He was relieved when she said yes and that his jacket was not necessary.

'That's good,' he replied. And it was good, for not only did he not want to take the jacket off for reasons already considered, he was also concerned that it might contain lice. Lice were not uncommon in the Crimea, and no doubt Jane had been bitten more than once since she had arrived, but he did not want the bites to come from any circus owned by him. 'What's the programme? Have you looked?'

Jane had been handed a piece of badly printed paper when she entered the open-air theatre — nothing more than an area roped-off and hung with hessian sacks, set with wooden benches — which told them of the delights to come.

'It's an evening of baroque,' she whispered. 'Do you approve?'

'Wholeheartedly,' he said with enthusiasm. He loved the music of the seventeenth and early eighteenth centuries. 'Is Purcell there?'

She smiled gently. 'In a performance by a French orchestra? I doubt it.' She looked again, then squealed in a delighted voice. 'Yes, yes, they have *Bess of Bedlam*. How wonderful. And pieces by Albinoni, Corelli and Charpentier. What a feast.'

Crossman was looking at a white shoulder, partially covered by a pashmina shawl. Jane's skin, that which he could see sweeping out of the shawl and into the lovely swan-neck, was delicate and scented. Her hair was pinned up, but some strands had come loose and coiled in the curve of her throat. There were no pearls or necklace of any kind. Simply a dimple there which he yearned to touch. He refrained, of course. The action would have been entirely inappropriate.

The rustle of her dress when she moved was one of the most exciting sounds he had heard in a long time and he found his heart was beating faster with every moment. Was it possible that a woman could do this to him, after all his escapades in the Crimea? It seemed so. It seemed that Jane, this fantastical-evening Jane, could send his blood racing round his body faster than an oncoming Cossack charge. He found himself murmuring poetry.

'Whereas in silks my Julia goes then, then (methinks) how sweetly flows, that liquefaction of her clothes.'

Jane immediately turned to him. 'What was that? Who is this 'Julia'?'

He became flustered. 'No one. That is, someone, but not known to me. It's from a poem by Robert Herrick. I — I was thinking of you, actually, and the sound your dress was making.'

She smiled. 'Oh, how — how sweet of you, Alexander. To be thinking of me, just because I'm sitting next to you.'

He laughed. 'Yes, it was a ludicrous thing to say, wasn't it? But it happened to be true. I have been thinking of you a lot, lately, pretend-cousin Jane. I think you know that.'

'I think I do.'

5

'There's Monique,' whispered Jarrard, as the musicians came out on to the stage. 'The second cellist.'

Crossman actually needed no pointer. Jarrard's earlier description fitted her perfectly. She was an elfin-like creature, diminutive, with darkish urchin-cut hair. Her face was small and heart-shaped, with large expressive eyes that twinkled when she looked in Jarrard's direction. To Crossman, she was the typical type of French girl — for girl she seemed, rather than woman — one would see in a village in southern France. One of those light-framed young women with an easy swinging walk, with no pretensions, no voluptuous movements such as a full-bodied Florentine or statuesque Andalucian might use. She was a sprite. A nymph. A girl with a quick and ready smile.

Crossman felt, just by looking at this young woman, that she could be easily hurt. She did not have a worldly air about her and any admirers she might have had previously would probably have been callow youths who did nothing more than blink from a distance.

She appeared as fresh, lovely, innocent and yet vulnerable as wild flowers in a Provence field. Crossman had no idea of Jarrard's previous relationships with women and he hoped the American was not going to play with this young lady. He hoped there was a streak of seriousness in his friend regarding Monique Foudre.

Jarrard, cigar protruding from his mouth, was clapping fit to rival the thunder of Thor. He was the only member of the audience to give the musicians a standing ovation *before* they had begun to play. Monique smiled shyly, a little embarrassed, Crossman thought. He tugged at Jarrard's coat, trying to get him to sit down. Jarrard finally did so, still clapping hard, with a dark look at Crossman.

While the musicians were tuning up a dog began to howl in a low voice. Everyone laughed. Crossman turned to see a black Labrador sitting by the heels of a British army captain. The dog's owner said, 'Lie down, boy,' curtly to the animal and the Labrador did as it was told, resting its head on its paws, without any further fuss.

'Quiet, Sabre,' said the captain. 'Good dog.'

It was then that Crossman noticed that the dog's owner was Captain Sterling Campbell. The captain suddenly turned and glared in their direction, except that he was looking at Jarrard rather than Crossman. The marks on the captain's face, like those on Jarrard's, had not yet disappeared. He looked quite ferocious and for a moment his eyes rested on Crossman, before switching again to the neck of his enemy, Rupert Jarrard.

Crossman whipped round quickly, his heart beating fast. Had the captain recognized him? It seemed doubtful. Crossman remembered he had been clean-shaven when he had played cards with Campbell. Now Crossman's face was covered in a big black beard. He and Campbell had passed each other just once in the street and there were soldiers aplenty in India and the Crimea. Hopefully the captain would fail to recognize him as the lieutenant he had once fleeced of a good deal of money.

Campbell was used to winning at cards. His main occupation, outside being an officer in the army, was gambling. He would no doubt remember those who had taken money *from* him, but those he had beaten would number in the hundreds.

A little later, once the music had begun, Crossman took a quick look behind him at Campbell, but the officer was no longer looking in his direction. His hand was down, stroking the neck of the dog while he listened to the music. There was a faraway look in Campbell's eyes. Crossman had seen that look on other men who had been to India. That exotic land of the Honourable East India Company seemed to capture the souls of all who trod her soil.

After the first performance, Jarrard predictably applauded like a maniac and yelled 'Bravo!' several times. Then he turned on Crossman and asked, 'What do you think, Jack? Eh?'

'I thought they played with great enthusiasm. How did you rate the performance, Cousin Jane?'

'Very fine!' replied Jane.

'I don't mean the performance, you weasel,' growled Jarrard at Crossman. 'You know I don't. What do you think of *Monique*? And anyway, she played like an angel. I can't think why she is not playing in the concert halls of cities like Prague, Salzburg or Vienna.'

'No doubt I shall meet her after the evening is over and I shall be able to give her a much fuller appraisal, but going by her looks she is an exceptionally pretty girl. How old is she, Rupert? Seventeen?'

'Eighteen,' replied the American. 'I know what you're thinking. You think I'm robbing the nursery.'

'No, I don't. But I do think she looks a little . . . '

'Naive? She's wiser than she appears, Jack. There's a good deal of maturity beneath that adorable face, believe me . . . '

The music had begun again, so they were not able to speak more on the subject. In fact they said nothing until Monique joined them later, at a table in the French canteen that had been set up to serve customers of the theatre. She immediately ordered herself a drink in a very firm, no-nonsense tone and then turned to smile at the company. Crossman was of course on his feet and after Jarrard had introduced them, murmured, '*Enchanté, mademoiselle.*'

Once the introductions had been made they continued in French, Jarrard a little behind the others, but still able to cope.

'So how long do you plan to stay in the holiday resort of the Crimea, Mademoiselle Foudre?' asked Jane, smiling.

'Oh, as long as the rest of the musicians, I suppose. We have no time limit, but of course the troops will tire of us sometime.'

'Do you not have venues to play at in France?'

Monique shrugged. 'We are not the best of musicians, unfortunately, and our services are not sought after.'

210

'Nonsense!' cried Jarrard. 'You play magnificently. I could hear the Gods sighing in envy every time your bow touched the strings.'

Monique laughed and nodded towards the American. 'The voice of love,' she said. 'How sweet to the ear, but my dear Rupert, unfortunately I am not so blind towards my own music. I play moderately well, as do the rest of my group, but we are not great masters or mistresses of our art. We do as well as we can. I am young. I hope to improve as time goes on, but I shall never be in great demand.'

Her pragmatism impressed Crossman. Jarrard was right. She was not as naive as she appeared. She had a good practical head on her shoulders.

Throughout the evening this young French woman continued to reinforce this view Crossman had now formed of her. She spoke with a wiser mouth than she at first appeared to own. By the time the evening came to an end Crossman was quite sure she would not let Jarrard toy with her: in fact Jack rather feared for his friend's feelings. In many ways Rupert was quite vulnerable and Monique, he was sure, would not throw in her lot with just any man. She appeared to be very fond of Jarrard, but she did not stare at him with adoring eyes, nor did she allow him to correct her when she felt she was in the right.

Monique began telling them an anecdote involving a Hungarian prince, when Crossman felt something sniffing his ankle. He peered down to see the black Labrador. It licked his hand when he reached down to push it away, fearful of looking around for its master. A voice behind called the animal to heel and thankfully the dog obeyed. Crossman felt a little fortunate that he was with Jarrard, whose presence prevented Campbell from coming up to their table to claim his hound. Crossman realized he was still in a cold sweat some few minutes later, after the dog had long since gone.

The following morning Crossman was up and about when Jarrard came to see him at the hovel.

'You approve?' asked the American.

'It's not for me to approve or disapprove, Rupert. I liked her. I liked her immensely. So did Jane. What are your intentions, if I may be bold enough to ask? Are they serious?'

'Absolutely. I am going to ask her to be my wife.'

'How do you think she will feel about your chosen profession? I mean, you are much like a soldier, Rupert. You follow the drum, if for different reasons. Will she mind you trotting off to a distant war every five minutes? Have you thought of that? It's not the kind of life every woman would want. Either she will have to forsake home and country in order to keep up with your global wanderings, or she will live the lonely life of a wife who waits at home for the occasional visits of her travelling husband.'

'Well, I've thought of that, Jack, and you see, she does roam around at the moment.'

'But she probably has no choice, if she wants to earn her living at playing her music. She may harbour a great desire to settle down in a little cottage with a white picket fence so that she may grow roses and vegetables and wave to her man from the window as he comes home in the evening. Lots of women do nurture this idea, you know, Rupert — false as it probably seems to you and I. Those who do not, and aspire to greater things, see themselves in a grand mansion overflowing with servants, with nothing to do all day but write billets-doux and plan the next ball. The husband does not feature so highly in this scenario, but he's there all the same, ready to change out of his muddy riding clothes in order to dine with her and her friends.'

'Lord, Jack, what pictures you paint,' cried Jarrard, his broad brow furrowing. 'I think I know women as well as you or any man, and what most of 'em want is love, pure and simple. They may hold those pictures in their heads, but they'll settle for anything when the time comes, so long as they get the man they fall in love with.'

'I hope you're right, for your own sake.'

Jarrard looked down at his highly-polished brown boots. 'So do I. So do I. I keep convincing myself, then fading away again. There's nothing so terrible, I'm told, as a disenchanted — no — a *dissatisfied* wife. They're the very devil to please. But I do want her, Jack, and I shall have her.'

'As you say, Rupert. I wish you well, you know I do. I just don't want you to make a mistake.'

That morning they were going out to test the camel gun. Jarrard had asked to go with him. He wanted to write a piece on their efforts.

'I can't see our own army investing in such a contraption, but the readers will be amused.'

'Amused?' said Private Yorwarth. 'Listen, Mr Jarrard, we ain't here to amuse. This is serious stuff, This is advanced warfare, so the sergeant told us. Battles have been won with these here progressive weapons. Gwilliams been asking around, ain't you Gwilliams? Tell

Mr Jarrard what you heard from those Turks you talked with the other night.'

Gwilliams and Jarrard did not get on and insulted each other behind each other's backs, but in public they were polite enough. Still Gwilliams could not get himself to copy Yorwarth's 'Mister' and dropped it for purposes of telling his stories.

'See here, Jarrard,' said Gwilliams, 'you know the word zumbooruck comes from Turkish? Well, that's a fact. It means a hornet or some such and it was a device that was around before gunpowder. In the old times zumboorucks was big crossbows mounted on camels and the twang of the thing sounded like a hornet, I guess — much like the word musket comes from mosquito — the whine of the musket ball and all.

'Anyways, they've been around for some time. Back there in the seventeen hundreds a Prince Bedar Bakht was killed by a shot from a zumbooruck gun in some battle down by a river, then damn me if his brother Walajah didn't meet the same end when he tried to avenge his older brother's death. Then just thirty years ago, in some place called Khorasan . . . '

'Near Afghanistan,' murmured Jarrard.

' . . . there was this Futah Allee Shah. Anyways, this fellah hated war, had a yellah streak I guess, and he come up against some zumboorucks, fell from his horse in a swoon of terror and got trampled on by his own cavalry, and I guess he got his, being a coward and all.'

'Interesting tales, Gwilliams.'

'There's more, but what I'm tryin' to say is, these here swivel guns on camels have been around long enough. If they wasn't no good they'd be on the trash heap. That makes sense, don't it?'

Crossman thought it did and supported Gwilliams.

'The fact that they're still in use, two centuries after they were invented — you did say two hundred years? — means they have a future. Ah, here's Betsy now . . . '

The camel, gun-mounted saddle in place, was being led by Stik, who was as sullen as ever. The boy's eyes rested on this group of soldiers with suspicion. What were they going to do to his camel today? He trusted none of them. Not even their leader, that man with three stripes. Stik would keep a wary eye open for any danger to his valuable beast and woe betide the man who caused it.

Crossman said, 'We need to take her away into some quiet place in the foothills, where we can experiment out of the way of prying eyes. We don't want the colonel's secret weapon to be common knowledge amongst the troops. There are too many spies in Kadikoi . . . '

'Sergeant Crossman's *peloton*, to name but a few,' said Jarrard.

They all trooped off north, up the Kadikoi road. Amongst many others they passed on the way a lady on a horse. She regarded them with some amusement. Jarrard doffed his hat, Crossman saluted.

'Good morning, Mrs Durham,' said Crossman in a very formal tone, aware that every man present knew that he had been this woman's most intimate lover within the last year. 'I hope the day finds you well?'

'Thank you, sergeant, I am very well. Good day to you, Mr Jarrard. And have you captured one of the enemy? How fierce the beast looks. I am all a-tremble just studying his formidable ordnance.' Betsy was quietly chewing away, her big doe eyes resting on nothing in particular. 'Does the dromedary fire the weapon himself or is he assisted by a soldier?'

Crossman was of course irritated by this banter, but he knew he would have to give it to her back in kind, or she would feel she had won points.

'My camel is very offended, Mrs Durham,

since she is of the female gender, not the male.'

'An Amazon? Great heavens, sergeant, you have your own Boadicea, leading you against the Russians. I am envious of her. You know I have always wished to be a soldier, but being a woman in a male-dominated world this has not been a possibility.' Lance-Corporal Peterson made herself small in the background. 'Yet here is a lady who has been recruited without regard to the fact that she is of the weaker sex. Yes, I am jealous.'

With that, Mrs Lavinia Durham rode away, leaving Crossman fuming with annoyance.

The worst was yet to come. They had to pass the encampment of the 93rd Foot, the Sutherland Highlanders. The jeers from the soldiers in kilts were more than even Wynter could bear and he almost came to blows with a private twice his size. In the middle of it all Crossman's friend, Sergeant-Major Jock McKintyre came out of his tent to see what all the noise was about, bawled at his men to 'get about army business' and then had his own few jocular comments to make about camels and their masters.

'Yer a few too short of a caravan,' said McKintyre. 'Ah could loan ye a wee goat or two, tae make it up!'

'Very funny, Jock,' replied Crossman.

'Aye, ah thocht so.' He laughed and then, as if noticing the glares directed at him, McKintyre's face took on a serious look. 'Och, ah'm sorry, Jack. Ah couldnae help mahsel'. See, what ye really wanted was advice as to yon other two, wasn't it? Well, they went that way,' he pointed up into the hills. 'If yer right quick ye'll catch 'em afore the noon.'

'Who are you talking about, Jock?' asked Crossman, wearily.

'Why, Jack, the other two Wise Men, following yonder bright star.'

'Sergeant,' said Wynter, 'I want to go home. Why are we all here? It only needs you and Yorwarth, don't it?'

They left Jock McKintyre and his troops chuckling away to themselves. Throughout any campaign such as this the Highlanders had had to weather the jibes associated with their kilts, being called 'ladies' and worse, and it did their Scottish hearts good to get in a few barbed arrows.

Once they found a shallow valley where they believed themselves to be alone, Crossman and his men made ready with Betsy and her armaments.

'Stik, make Betsy kneel. Now, Gwilliams and Wynter, load the gun with a round shot. We'll try a fistful of musket balls afterwards,

219

but I want to see how she reacts to a cannonball first. Get to it.'

Jarrard went and sat on a grassy knoll, took out his leather-covered notebook and rested it on his knee. Out of his other pocket came pen with nib protector and a bottle of ink which had an ingenious seal. It was a traveller's kit he always used.

'I hope someone will talk me through things, as they are done. I would greatly appreciate it,' said Jarrard.

Peterson, still very quiet since her ordeal with the Cossacks, went and sat beside him.

Ali, who had also said very little that morning, climbed to the crest of escarpment behind the knoll to stare out over the surrounding countryside. The Turk was ever on the watch for enemy cavalry, who roamed in packs in these parts. A hare started from right beneath his feet. Normally he might have whipped out one of his many pistols and tried his luck, but today he simply watched it run.

Down below serious work was in progress. The gun having been loaded, Yorwarth lit the portfire from a smouldering linstock and stuck it into a holder on the saddle.

Both Stik and Betsy regarded all this activity with mild anxiousness. Betsy kept turning her head to have a peek at what was going on. It was clear she did not like the smell of the raw gunpowder and the lighting of the portfire had her trying to get to her feet. These smells, not completely new to her but never so close before, were quite disturbing. She was aware she was carrying them on her person. The fragrances of frankincense or myrrh would have been fine: Betsy would have recognized them somewhere in her racial memory. But gunpowder and fire. Those were scents preceding something rather sudden and alarming.

'Right, into the saddle, Yorwarth.'

'I don't like this, sergeant. What if she bolts?'

'Stik will hold on to her reins.'

'He's a little-bitty boy. She'll drag him from here to kingdom come, sergeant. I don't like this at all.'

'Yorwarth, I'm ordering you. Get on the camel. You have nothing to worry about.'

Gwilliams said, 'He's yellah, just like that sultan fellah who got trampled to death.'

'You do it then!' challenged Yorwarth.

'It ain't my job,' replied Gwilliams. 'It's yourn.'

Yorwarth finally climbed into the saddle and Betsy then gathered her strength together and got laboriously to her feet. They splayed out a bit more than usual, with the extra weight. She stood there, calmly, while Yorwarth swung the gun back and forth, testing the trajectory and arc of fire. Crossman's restricting device seemed to work quite well. At least Betsy wouldn't get her head blown off that long curving neck.

'Wynter, you hold her tail,' said Crossman, feeling a little anxious himself now. 'Hold on to it tightly.'

'What if she kicks?' cried the put-upon private. 'She'll knock my guts out!'

'You just hold her steady. Gwilliams, you help Stik with the reins. That's it. Everyone ready? Right, Yorwarth, what are you going to aim to hit?'

'That small tree up there,' he pointed to a thorn tree halfway up the slope ahead. 'I'll go for the middle of the trunk.'

'Good man. Lay the gun then . . . '

Yorwarth did as he was told.

'Now, apply the portfire to the vent.'

The portfire was applied.

The gun fired. Betsy jerked sideways, but managed to remain on her feet. Though startled, she did not bolt. However the wet green wad she was chewing shot out of her mouth as if from a cannon and hit Gwilliams in the back of the neck. At the same time Betsy loosed her bowels and a steaming flow fell as a stinking waterfall down Wynter's legs and all over his boots. The shot from the gun hit a rock at the base of the target tree and ricocheted upwards, narrowly missing Ali, who was still surveying the scenery. It passed by his head an inch from his ear. The ball ended up imbedded in the hillside beyond.

'Wow!' cried Peterson, coming to life for the first time in weeks, 'That was really something, sergeant. Do it again!'

'Look at my boots!' wailed Wynter.

'Look at my shirt!' yelled Gwilliams.

Stik was thoroughly disgusted with the whole affair. He threw down the reins and went and sat next to Jarrard.

'Well,' Crossman said, trying to muster some enthusiasm, 'that wasn't as bad as we expected. And Yorwarth almost hit the target. Let's do it again, this time with canister . . . '

Over the course of the morning they fired the gun several times and things improved. Betsy managed to control her bowels and eventually became blasé about the explosions taking place on her hump. Yorwarth became more accurate with the brass weapon. The importance of it all gradually seeped through into Stik's imagination and he wanted a go with the gun, proving himself quite a capable shot with it. Gwilliams and Wynter cleaned themselves up with grass and water from a pool and even they began to see the funny side of the opening shot. Jarrard announced he had some very interesting copy which would have his readers in stitches.

By the time they were ready to go home, they were a fairly cheery bunch.

On their way back, the Bashi-Bazouk spotted a group of horsemen in a shallow depression to the north. With his spyglass he soon ascertained they were Russian Hussars, not more than a dozen of them.

'Are they in range, sergeant?' asked Yorwarth. 'Can I have a go?'

Peterson loaded her Enfield. 'We can all have a go, can't we, sergeant?'

The British were armed of course, with their rifle-muskets, and Crossman could see that any cavalry below would have to charge up the slope to reach them. First he made sure there were no other troops in the vicinity. He didn't want to fire on a dozen to find they were reinforced by a whole squadron hidden behind another ridge. After some time he was satisfied they were on their own and decided on action.

They would be able to pick the Russians out of their saddles with great ease, should the cavalry below decide to charge them. It was an opportunity too good to miss. He instructed Yorwarth to load the swivel with a ball, still keeping the riders in view. Just when

Yorwarth announced that he was 'Ready!' the Russians turned and began heading south towards Crossman's group, though it seemed from the casual way in which they held themselves that they were not preparing for a fight. They had simply changed direction at whim.

'There's someone down there!' said Peterson, pointing.

Peterson of the eagle eye.

Using his glass Crossman picked out a figure walking amongst the rocks. It was a man with a brace of game birds slung over his left shoulder and a hunting weapon in the crook of his right arm. He seemed unaware of the Hussars, being in a gully and out of their line of sight. Peering hard through the glasses Crossman was able to make out the walker's attire. He was wearing a shooting jacket and boots of a distinctive cut and cloth: clearly a British gentleman out bagging dinner for himself and his friends. There was an air of dreamy indifference about the way the man was walking, as if he believed he was on some country estate in his homeland and was thinking about coffee and biscuits after a morning's hunting.

The two parties — the hunter and the Hussars — were on a collision course. They were clearly unaware of each other's presence, the hunter being below the rise and walking parallel to it, the riders coming up the far side, ready to crest the hill. Suddenly Crossman saw the hunter's head jerk towards the ridge. He had finally heard the sound of horses' hooves. The lone man then looked about him quickly, found a boulder, and ducked behind it.

'Time to show your skill, Yorwarth,' said Crossman, the glass still imbedded in his left eye socket. 'Fire at will.'

Yorwarth asked in an unsteady voice, 'What's the target, sergeant?'

'Aim for the middle of those riders. Remember they are moving towards you, so allow for that, but not too much, they don't seem in any great hurry.'

The shot thundered by Betsy's ear.

Despite the fact that this intrepid beast had got used to explosions near or around her head that morning, there had been a long lull since the last shot had been fired. She jumped a good foot in the air, almost unseating Yorwarth. However, she did not project her wad and a mere dry fart came from the rear end, much to the relief of Ali who had forgotten the earlier incident and was standing close to her backside.

The ball landed in the middle of the Hussars, sending up a spray of rock splinters, earth and turf. None of the riders was hit, but they were clearly shocked, and one rider actually turned and galloped a hundred yards back the way he had come. Yorwarth loaded the swivel as quickly as his precarious position would allow. The riders were milling now, looking around them, seeking the source of the fire. A second ball was sent on its way. This time it hit a Hussar full in the chest, taking him out of his saddle and over the rump of a neighbouring mount. A corporal then saw where the shots were coming from and drew his sword to point with it.

'Let's have some sharpshooting here,' said Crossman to his riflemen. 'Find cover. Fire at will. Rupert, you may use my new Enfield, if you know how. Look after it, it's government property. I shall direct fire.'

The *peloton* did as told and began shooting down on the Hussars. However, the distance was very great and the rifles had little effect except to inform those below that they were facing a small arsenal. Yorwarth sent another ball on its way, but just before firing Betsy had sagged at the knees for some reason, and the shot was low. It struck the ground a short way behind the figure crouched under the boulder and that unfortunate man turned and shook a fist. Then he set himself again, with his shotgun pointing at the ridge, ready to shoot the first rider who showed his head.

'Don't do it!' murmured Crossman. 'They don't know you're there and it's better for you they remain in ignorance.'

The Russians remained indecisive, turning their horses this way and that, and then finally, as the shooting continued, they gathered up the dead Hussar, took his horse, and rode away. Crossman watched them go in great satisfaction. 'Betsy's first action,' he said to the others. 'The colonel will be delighted.' They let out a hoarse cheer.

The British gentleman came up to them as they descended. He stared at Betsy and Yorwarth with wide eyes, then turned his attention to Crossman.

'Sergeant!' he said, smiling weakly. 'What goes on here? You almost removed my head from my shoulders.'

'Sorry about that, sir. Our gun emplacement decided at that moment to genuflect. She is not yet used to the correct procedures of the RCA and is inclined to dip her head occasionally in search of fodder, even during an important action. We are endeavouring to correct this habit.'

'RCA?'

Crossman grinned. 'Royal Camel Artillery.'

His men laughed.

The hunter laughed too. He was in fact

Lieutenant Pirce-Smith, Crossman's immediate superior. Pirce-Smith, though a newcomer, was now Major Lovelace's right-hand man, a position Crossman would dearly have loved to fill, but being a ranker was not considered.

'The colonel's new secret weapon, sir. We call her Betsy and she punches like a prize fighter, don't you think? In case you're wondering, those were Russian Hussars on the other side the ridge. I was hoping you would not give yourself away, because we were too far to cause them much harm with our rifles. One of them was killed by a ball from our swivel.'

Pirce-Smith stared at the zumbooruck. 'A falconet,' he breathed. 'I never thought to see one here. They are all the thing in Aden and India of course. An uncle of mine once described one to me, while I was still a child playing soldiers, and I never forgot it. In fact I made one out of clay . . . ' He suddenly realized to whom he was talking and his tone changed from wonderment to sternness.

'Well done, sergeant. You saved my bacon there. I was just trying out one of my new Lefauchaux pinfires.' He showed an admiring group the shiny bluemetal shotgun with the dazzlingly polished stock.

The lieutenant now turned so that he was addressing Jarrard, the one man present who was a near equal to him in status and rank. The others could listen, if they wished, but they could not take part in a personal conversation with a commissioned officer.

'The weapons were most kindly given me by Major Lovelace who has graduated to Purdeys. I must say they are most superior, the Lefauchaux I mean.' He nodded towards the game birds strung over his shoulder. 'Snatched the little beggars right out of the air. Absolutely dead accurate. The kick is pretty fierce of course, but you've got to expect that, with Lefauchaux. One could reduce the charge, but then the balance suffers. These weapons are finely tuned and there is a recommended charge. Mr Jarrard, you must come with me and try them sometime,' the lieutenant added generously.

'Obliged,' replied Jarrard, keenly aware that his friend Crossman would have liked to be invited too, but also knowing it was an impossible situation with the British army. 'Any time.'

'We could come as beaters, sir,' interrupted Wynter. 'I was raised a boy on an Essex farm. I know how to organize a line of beaters.'

'I'm sure you do, Wynter,' Pirce-Smith replied. 'And I thank you most kindly for the offer. Sergeant,' he turned again to face Crossman, 'I am most truly grateful for that action back there. I feel sure I should have been overrun, if not for our friend Betsy here. I will be speaking with Colonel Hawke about it and recommending something in the way of a medal. I know you probably won't see one, being as we are, but the sentiment is there.'

'Thank you, sir. I believe my men acted with promptness and efficiency, and I'm justly proud of them.'

It was nothing much, in the way of exchanges, but it was significant. Crossman and Pirce-Smith had not begun their relationship with any great affection. In fact loathing and dislike were not far from the surface for quite a long time after their first meeting. A bridge had been crossed though and there was now a modicum of trust on both sides. Resentments, again on both sides for various reasons, had evaporated. They were not friends, nor could be, but they had reached an understanding with this little fracas in the hills, which in itself was nothing much in the way of military actions.

The lieutenant's eyes then roamed over the camel again, lingering on the magnificent saddle and its brass swivel.

'Exotic, to say the least. Beauty on the beast.'

The misquotation was an accident, but everyone present thought the lieutenant very clever. They all strolled back towards Balaclava, running the gauntlet of jeering Scotsmen again, but giving as good as they got. Back at the hovel, Betsy was relieved of her saddle and gun, and Stik was given a present of a silver coin by Lieutenant Pirce-Smith. The boy stared at this gift with wide disbelieving eyes, which were later turned on the lieutenant. Clearly Pirce-Smith had captured the heart of someone who would now die for him should the need arise in the future.

Later Crossman went to see the colonel, finding him in jubilant mood.

'By God, sergeant, this is good news. Lieutenant Pirce-Smith tells me the zum-booruck saved his life. I've already reported to our new commander in chief — oh, don't worry, he's not like the old one. I think he's quite in favour of our activities, to tell the truth. General Simpson wouldn't have been *my* choice, but then he's better than some. At least he listens to sense on occasion. I digress. I'm most pleased. Most pleased.'

'Thank you, sir.'

The colonel went to the window, looking out over the formless ground which stretched between him and the front.

'You know, sergeant, this war has already gone into legend back in Britain?'

'Sir?'

'The Light Brigade.' Hawke sighed. 'The loss of the Light Brigade was a sad and terrible thing to us here, to the army in general, but to the ordinary civilian in a Portsmouth street, or a square in Edinburgh, that awful charge was something glorious. Can you imagine it? We lost the best part of five regiments on that bloody field and they talk about it as if it were a victory . . .'

'I have never really understood cavalry, sir. I too abhor the loss, but as to whether the tactics were sound or not, I have no real idea. Of course, I listen to talk and it seems to me to be madness to charge the mouths of cannons.'

'Madness, absolute! Now the Heavies, they did precisely the right thing, scored a wonderful victory over the Russian cavalry, yet who remembers them? Are the Greys and the Royals spoken of in awe in the inns of Glasgow? No. Are the Inniskillings praised in small Irish villages? Not a jot. Nor do the heavy dragoons receive appreciation in the taverns of London. No one remembers how glorious, how successful our myopic General Scarlett was on that day. He led his men against superior forces and triumphed. Were we Romans we would be crowning his head with the laurel and parading him through streets of cheering citizens. Instead we quietly put him to one side with a pat on the back. I sometimes wonder if the British are the only nation who celebrate their defeats. We do seem to revel in it.'

'Perhaps it's because we have had so few of them?'

Calcutta Hawke swung round with an iron smile on his face.

'Now, sergeant, you're being partisan. No, I tell you what it is with this Light and Heavy thing. It's the *style*. People are interested in getting the job done, that's certain, but the style in which it's done is more important than the effectiveness. Light cavalry? Lots of dash and élan. Sets your heart racing to see those beautiful light horses at full gallop, their riders high in the saddle, sabres flashing in the sun. The Heavy cavalry is more disciplined, has a more serious way of going about its business. A heavy, plodding force that smashes through the enemy ranks using its sheer weight. Draught horses! They don't excite the popular imagination at all. The difference between the two is not just ingrained in the contempt they show for one another, but in their physical images. Who cares whether the Light Brigade failed, and failed miserably, and the Heavy Brigade prevailed, and with honour? No one but us.

You were there, sergeant. How did you feel?'

'Sick, on the one hand. Proud on the other.'

'There you are then. Now with our new zumbooruck squadron — for I plan to have one if this war goes on much longer — we shall go for racing dromedaries. They have them, you know, in Arabia. They race them bareback. I want our camels to excite the public imagination. We shall have gold and scarlet trappings on our saddles. Slim hammered-bronze swivels that gleam in the sun. We shall have riders and gunners dressed like zouaves: flamboyant, dashing, full of colour and zest! Can you see it, sergeant? We'll encourage a nickname and become as famous as Skinner's Horse in the Indian army. Hawke's Zumboorucks!'

Crossman stood there, nodding, wondering whether his colonel had been smoking too much of the local tobacco.

★　★　★

If Wynter had thought that being married would make his life less miserable he had soon been put right. He now spent much of his waking time prising Mary out of drinking huts and gambling tents. Not that she was ever unhappy to see him. She always greeted

235

him with a cheery note, telling him to come on in and join the fun. Usually, by the time he found her, he was so dispirited the anger had fled him. Once or twice he got into a fight when he found her on the knee of soldier or sutler, but soon realized that this could be a never-ending cycle, for the trouble with Mary was not the lure of infidelity — she actually did not care much for the act of lovemaking — but once she had a couple of drinks in her she was such an amiable person she wanted to hug the world. Occasionally she would bed a man for money, when Wynter refused to give her any, but even *he* did not find that too offensive, once she had explained the process to him. The men, she told him, were usually so drunk they paid their money without getting anything but a snooze on a different bed, or by the time they were sober they had forgotten what had happened and to whom. Since this was Wynter's own experience of visiting whores he believed every word she said.

However, it did grieve Wynter that Mary was seldom around and seemed quite happy to be without him. He felt she ought to be there to cook his meals and do small chores for him. After all, wasn't that what a wife was for? So he employed the son of a Chinese washerwoman, a fifty-year-old man everyone called Canton Joe, to root Mary out whenever he wanted her for something. Canton Joe charged a halfpenny a time, a farthing of which he gave to his sixty-five-year-old mother. Canton Joe's mother's laundry was just across the street, so Wynter simply had to yell, 'Joe!' at the top of his voice and the smiling toothless Lee Choeng Ho (Joe's real name) would come trotting across to the hovel in his wooden clogs.

'Joe!' called Wynter one morning, 'get over here you lazy Chink!'

Peterson took Wynter to task. 'Joe isn't lazy. It's you who's lazy. If you were a woman you'd be called a slut.'

'Well I an't a woman, am I?' growled Wynter. 'Ah, Joe,' the Chinese man in question had appeared in the doorway, 'fetch my Mary — udder one — for me, will you? She didn't come home last night.' Wynter tossed Joe a halfpenny, knowing Joe had to be paid first, not when he returned. Joe caught the coin deftly with his left hand and transferred it to his pocket in a trice.

'I go look-see for udder one.' Joe spoke China Coast pidgin and 'udder one' was anyone else who was not present. It could be quite confusing, as when Joe added, 'Udder one say udder one gone Jonnie Bread housie.' Which meant that someone had told Joe that

237

Mary had gone to a bawdy house called Jonnie Bread's. 'Master wait here.'

Canton Joe always told Wynter to wait there, even though Wynter had no intention of going anywhere. However this day Joe came back with some shocking news, which had Wynter rocking back on his heels. Joe was wringing his hands and his face had a tragic expression.

'Master Harry, udder one, she dead!'

Wynter sat there stunned for a moment. Predictably his first concern was with himself. 'Was it a catching disease?'

Joe shook his head, dumbly.

'Cholera then? The drink? Was it an accident?'

'No, Master Harry, she killed by udder one. Missie Mary, she murdered.'

Wynter jumped off his cot and Peterson, the only other member of the *peloton* in the room at the time, let out a gasp.

'Who did it?'

'Not know, Master Harry. Missie Mary, she go with udder one backside-housie. Udder one he hit missie with bottle, many time. Nobody hear. Nobody look-see him go. He go back window. You go now, Master Harry, look-see Jonnie Bread.'

Wynter dressed himself. Peterson watched him, not out of any interest, but because he looked so grim she was afraid he was going to do something stupid when he went out.

'I'll come with you,' she said, once he was ready.

'Suit yourself.'

The pair of them went to Jonnie Bread's hut. Jonnie was a lascar who had once cooked in the galleys of British naval vessels and was famous for the chapatis he cooked in a tandoori oven in front of his hut. Like most of the Crimean traders he also sold alcohol. He was at that moment washing the tin mugs he sold his arak in, the dirty water coming from a man-made pond just outside his back window. The pond had been dug some six months before as a deep square latrine, but had almost immediately filled with winter rain and was now a source of water for several sutlers' huts.

'Harry,' said Jonnie, wiping his hands on the dirty seaman's lammy he had worn for nearly seven years without washing it, 'sorry about your loss. It was me what found her, early on this mornin'. I would've sent somebody over to you, but there wasn't nobody with me till Canton Joe came.' Jonnie's English was near-perfect, having been on British sailing ships since he was a boy of twelve.

'Where is she now, Jonnie?' asked the

dispirited Wynter. 'Have they took her away?'

'No,' he nodded at a tiny back room. 'In there. I didn't come myself, see, because them what did it might've come back an' stole the body.'

'Them? I thought you said to Joe it was only one man.'

'It was, it was. That's just my way of speakin'. I didn't see exactly who, 'cause I was too busy with serving customers. You know what it's like in here, round about three in the morning — heaving — and the smoke so thick you can't see your hand in front of your face. I think I knew the door to the room had been opened, but I didn't see Mary or anyone with her.'

Wynter sighed. 'All right, Jonnie, it an't your fault.'

Wynter stuck his head round the doorjamb to peer at the body. Mary was sprawled over the end of the bed, half-naked, with her head touching the floor and her feet on a greasy strawmat pillow. Wynter was glad he could not see her face, but he was aware of a pool of blood under the bed. Her right arm dangled over the edge of the bed. There was a clump of hair in her fingers, gripped by bloodied fingernails. Wynter guessed that Mary had torn it from her attacker's scalp. It was dark curly hair, with a peppery-grey amongst it.

However, there were thousands of men from whose head that hair could have been taken, all within six miles. The clue, if Wynter thought of it as such, was no significant clue at all.

Wynter pulled back, saying to Peterson, 'You can have a look.'

'No,' she replied, emphatically. 'I don't need to.'

He shouted back, 'I didn't *need* to neither.' Then to Jonnie Bread, he added, 'You better report this. This an't nothin' to do with me, it's to do with you. You better tell the army Mary's been killed. I wasn't here so it can't be me. Where's the bottle?'

'What bottle?'

'Canton Joe said it was done with a bottle.'

'Oh, that?' said Jonnie. 'It's on the other side of the bed. You can have it if you want it, Harry.'

Harry didn't want it. He simply wished to know where it was. Wynter left, with Peterson stumbling along after him.

'Aren't you staying, to see what happens?'

'No I an't. They'll make too much of it, they always do. I'm after getting the bastard what did it to her.'

'And how are you going to do that?'

'By askin' questions, same as how you find out anything. Somebody saw her go in that room and they'll know who with. I'm goin' to find out, see, and when I do he'd better watch out.'

Sergeant Crossman was waiting back at the hovel for them. Both Wynter and Peterson were supposed to be on a training exercise and the sergeant was angry with them for not showing. However, once the circumstances had been explained to him, his anger turned to sympathy.

'Sorry to hear that, Wynter. You've not had a lot of luck lately. Poor Mary. She was a plucky woman, to fight with her attacker like that.'

'Oh, she was good at fightin', I can vouch for that. Sergeant, can I have some time off to ask a few coves some questions? I know who gets in Jonnie Bread's place at that time of the morning. Them as has got nothin' to hide won't mind answerin' a question or two. Them as do mind better watch out, 'cos I'll be wanting to know the reason.'

By the time Crossman got to Jonnie Bread's some soldiers had been for the body. They said they would bury her with the last week's cholera victims. Since the murder had not been witnessed no one was too concerned about catching the killer. There was a lot of speculation over certain individuals who were known to have ugly tempers when they were drunk, but that was about as far as anyone got. There had been one or two murders in the past which had gone unpunished, where the killer had not been obvious. There was no one to go picking around, looking for things that would lead to the killer's arrest and hanging. No one would have thought to do such a thing, except perhaps a relative or a close friend.

It was unfortunate for the killer that Wynter was the kind of man who knew who to ask and where to look for information. Before the morning was out Wynter had a good idea of who had killed his wife Mary. He went out, armed and dangerous, looking for the man. A search of the camp failed to unearth the person he was looking for, so when evening and darkness came around, Wynter went back to the hovel to see Crossman.

'I know who done it,' said Wynter, dramatically. 'It was Charlie Dobson.'

'Who is Charlie Dobson?' asked Crossman.

'Deck hand from the *Conquerer*, a frigate that went out last month. He should've been on it, but he was drunk as a pig and missed the tide. He's a big ugly brute. Nasty streak in 'im. Heavy bastard with a fist as big as my head. He's broken a few faces since he's been here, some of them whores from the tents. Don't matter to him who he hurts and who he don't. Who's goin' to help me look for the bastard tomorrow?'

'I'll come,' stated Gwilliams.

'Me too,' said Yorwarth.

Crossman shook his head. 'I'm not having my men roaming the Crimea, bent on drawing blood. Do you want to hang yourselves? You are not vigilantes, you are soldiers.'

'I might 'ave guessed *you* wouldn't come,' snarled Wynter.

'You're not listening. *No one* is going. I shall inform Major Lovelace of your suspicions, Wynter, and he will get someone to follow them up, but there will be no personal man hunt. You understand me?'

Wynter said, 'I thought you was one for justice?'

'I am.'

Crossman would not be moved. Even Peterson thought he was being unreasonable. When the sergeant had gone, Wynter said, 'I'll get Yusuf Ali on to him. The Turk will root him out. I know he's the sergeant's man, but he liked Mary. He'll find the bastard and when Ali goes out after a man's blood, that man had better be somewhere else.'

Ali was subsequently pulled aside when he came in that night. Given the story he went out again, straight away. Wynter was confident that before the morning Charlie Dobson would have a knife in his back. However, when the Bashi-Bazouk returned with the dawn, Wynter was informed that Charlie Dobson was nowhere to be found. He had vanished from the camp.

'Gone up into the hills,' muttered Wynter. 'Well he might. I'll catch up with him, you see if I don't. Killing my Mary like that. She wouldn't do harm to a fly, Mary wouldn't.'

Whether Wynter used the murder as an excuse to get drunk during the day or not, Crossman wasn't certain. However, he let it ride, warning the others not to indulge along with the grieving soldier. Wynter grew increasingly morose and maudlin, talking on and on about how much he had loved his Mary, and how much she had loved him. At first the others let him ramble on, hoping he would burn himself out before long, but when that did not happen the resentment set in. Peterson was quite scathing about Wynter's 'marriage' and how it seemed that all he cared about was getting Mary into bed. She said what Wynter wanted was a slave, not a wife, and there was good reason why Mary wandered most of the time.

'That's not fair,' cried Wynter. 'She took some of me pay, didn't she? I never hit her, did I? Model husband, I was.' His remarks gathered bitterness as they went. 'You don't know what it's like, bein' married, Peterson, so you can just shut your porthole, see. Married people, why they have a sort of secret life between 'em. You don't know how much I loved my Mary. You can never know. Only she and me knew.'

Peterson saw the sense in this, but she did point out that if it was all so cosily secret, why couldn't Wynter grieve in silence, and not drag the rest of the world into that pit of despair in which he loved to wallow.

'Well, I like that. I like that, oh yes sir. Comrades in arms, we're supposed to be. All together, helpin' each other. I hope you never end up in the workhouse, like my mum and dad,' he added, darkly. 'In there you have to stand by one another or you go mad and end up in Bedlam.'

After three days, during which Ali scoured the French, British and Sardinian lines, and failed to find Charlie Dobson, Wynter announced he was going into the hills to look for the miscreant.

'Don't try to stop me, sergeant,' he warned. He stared at Peterson. 'Even if you don't think I was good to Mary, you can't expect me to let her murderer get away, an' nothing done.' He armed himself with rifle and ammunition. 'If he's out there, I'll find him. I know those hills as well as Ali now. I know how to track a man. I'm goin' to find him and kill him dead as he made my Mary. She was like a little dove, she was, an' wouldn't have hurt no one. I'm going to put a ball in Dobson's black heart and if he pleads for mercy while I'm doing it I'll enjoy it the more.'

Crossman could sense that the other members of the *peloton* approved of this stance by Wynter. They had all liked Mary and the thought that her killer should be at liberty, possibly never being brought to justice, was something none of them could countenance. The sergeant was out of sorts, physically, having had a bout of dysentery. The general malaise which a prolonged war creates in a man's spirit had descended on him and a low state of morale was gnawing at him like a canker. He tried arguing with Wynter, but others interceded on the soldier's behalf, and Crossman found the whole pack united against him.

Finally he gave in. 'We'll all go, Wynter. But I need you to promise me you won't kill him. We need to bring him back alive. It's just possible he wasn't the one who killed Mary . . . '

'He was seen goin' into that room with

247

Mary by two men whose word I trust,' said Wynter, emphatically, 'an' he didn't come out again.'

'I grant you that is damning. But we still have to hear what he says for himself. There may be circumstances . . .'

'There an't no circumstances.' Wynter was firm. 'A man with a violent temper like that, full o' gin? Then he disappears off the face of the earth? He done the deed and he's goin' to pay the price. It'll be a mercy from me. A ball instead of the rope? Why that's a gift. But it'll make me feel better to be the one to do it. They won't let me haul on the rope, that's sure, so a ball is what it's goin' to be.'

Crossman nodded, but said to the others out of Wynter's hearing, 'If we catch this fellow, grab Wynter and hold him fast before he can shoot.'

As the whole *peloton* rode out he said privately to Ali, 'What I cannot understand is why no one heard her scream.'

Ali shook his head. 'Sergeant, you must go to Jonnie Bread's house in the night. There is much noise from happy soldiers, from women with the gin and brandy. Mary can scream loud, but no one take notice or stop to think much. Too many other women scream in front room, with laughter, with drink, with loving. Even if they hear, maybe they think the scream from Mary mean different reason?' He nodded, significantly. 'They just smile into each other's face and say, 'Lucky man, Charlie.''

'I understand,' Crossman said, sighing. For once he felt the general mood was against him and, feeling so low in spirit, he had no will to go against it. 'This business is ugly though. I could lose my stripes over this. But Wynter is right, I suppose. We can't let this man get away.'

They spent the rest of that day and much of the next two, searching the hills for signs of Charlie Dobson. They found nothing, though they ran into a large column of Russians in an area on the other side of the Chernaya River and had to ride like the blazes to save their skins. After this incident Crossman told Wynter the hunt would have to be abandoned. They returned to the hovel in Kadikoi to find Major Lovelace anxiously pacing the floor wondering 'where the hell' they were. Crossman explained the situation, thinking it was better to keep to the truth, but Lovelace was not sympathetic and told him he was running close to the edge of a cliff.

'I am aware of that, sir,' said Crossman, finding it rather unpleasant to be dressed down by the major, who, because of the nature of their work, was normally inclined to be amiable and lenient with his men. 'It won't happen again.'

'You better make damn sure of that, sergeant,' said the coldly furious Lovelace. 'Yours is a position of responsibility. We can't have these juvenile escapades. I appreciate Wynter's loss, but he'll have to bear it in a civilized manner. You've been too much in Jarrard's company. He's been talking about lynching parties, hasn't he? That's mob rule, sergeant, and it won't do for the Army of the East. Our work is already considered to be unsavoury in certain quarters. Don't give our enemies more ammunition than they have already.'

'I'm sorry, sir. It was stupid. I see it now. And Jarrard has had nothing to do with this. He doesn't even know of it.'

'I'm glad to hear it. I'm glad he's no fool . . .'

The major didn't add 'too' but he might just as well have done. Crossman was dismissed and went away with his tail between his legs. He went for a walk to cool his head. It was usual when a sergeant got a dressing-down from his superior officer to go and take it out on the men, where the fault more often than not actually lay. But this time the fault was wholly with the senior NCO and he could not vent his spleen on the lower ranks, having condoned the whole expedition, if only to keep the peace. It was rather a bitter potion to swallow, being in the wrong. Crossman was not used to it. Lovelace could never be a father-figure, being only a few years older than Crossman himself, but the major's fury had certainly brought back childhood memories of being severely criticized by his father for some infringement of household rules. They were ugly memories, of the young Alexander standing in the corner of the nursery, while his father berated him for speaking without being spoken to, or for running along the passageways, or for some other crime, equally heinous, which offended against the dignity of the Kirk household.

Later, Yusuf Ali came to him when there was no one else around.

'Sergeant,' said the loyal Turk, 'I was under window and hear the major speak to you. I never hear him speak to you this way before and it is of course not right for him to do so. You are our leader. You must have respect. This is not respectful. So, what must happen is this. The major will soon go into Sebastopol, to look at Russians, see what is happening. There is no reason why he should come back.'

Crossman, still smarting under the deserved ticking-off was only half-listening, but at some point he suddenly realized what the Bashi-Bazouk irregular was inferring. He looked at Ali sharply. Ali nodded, half-closing one eye, as if to say, 'The deed is as good as done.'

'No, no,' cried the panicking sergeant, gripping Ali by the shoulders. 'You must not do anything to Major Lovelace. He was right in what he did. I am, after all, a lowly sergeant.' Crossman actually realized this explanation was going to do no good in this case. He changed tack. 'You see, the major and I are good friends. We went to the same school. In England that makes him almost my brother. What he did was between the two of us for the sake of the men. Later we laughed about it. It was foolishness.'

This hastily cobbled-together story did not make the least bit of sense, but Crossman was desperate. He knew Ali was capable of anything if protecting his honour. The sergeant and he were family, therefore the sergeant's honour was inextricably entwined with his own. If someone offended against the dignity of the sergeant, they offended against Ali. Where such things were concerned, they were as one man, undivided. Anyone who treated the sergeant with contempt was spitting on the honour of Yusuf Ali and there could only be one answer to that.

'Foolishness?' repeated Ali, grasping at a word which might make some sort of sense. 'It was a joke?'

'Of course,' laughed Crossman. 'There was no malice in the major. We British soldiers, we have strange ways.'

Now this was something Ali *could* understand. At least, it was within his experience of the British. He had seen meetings between two Englishmen, or other British nationalities, who had not seen each other for some time. They seemed to insult one another with harsh language and ugly expressions for ten minutes, before breaking into a roaring laughter and then going off arm in arm together to a drinking tent.

Only a week ago he had witnessed two British sailors disembarking from different vessels and, on seeing each other, one yelled out in a nasty tone, 'Joe, you old bastard, where've you bin hiding that bald head of yourn? I an't seen that ugly fish-face for more'n two years now, give or take a long week.'

Whereupon the other replied in the most aggressive way, 'You dirty old walrus, Dan Spake, is that you under them greasy whiskers? What are you doin' in that rotten tub? Last time I saw you, you was crawlin' out of some tavern in Liverpool.'

Then, as they got closer, a wave of the hand in front of the nose and the words, 'By God, you stink worse'n a penguin's arse.'

'You an't no perfumed goddess, yourself.'

'Come and have an ale,' said the first sailor.

'Don't care if I do,' replied the other.

And off they had gone, after first punching each other on the chest once or twice, chuckling, and informing one another they were miserable old farts.

Ali said to Crossman. 'Yes, your ways are strange, but still I will watch the Lovelace. If I think he has treachery in his heart, I will cut it out. You and me, sergeant, we are men of honour.'

'Believe me, Ali, the major is of the same honour.'

Crossman parted from his Turkish comrade with some misgivings. It was going to be a while before Ali trusted Lovelace again, unless something happened to confirm what Crossman had told him. If Ali believed that Crossman was merely protecting his superior officer, which was indeed the case, then anything could happen.

Happily Lovelace came to Crossman the very next day and said, 'It's time you and I went out into the field together, sergeant. Get ready for a fox hunt tonight. Just you. I had intended to take Lieutenant Pirce-Smith, but he is otherwise engaged.'

It was the first time that Lovelace had asked Crossman out on a mission. Since Crossman had just been speaking with Pirce-Smith, unknown to the major, and that young lieutenant had bemoaned the fact that he was wallowing in idleness at that present time, Crossman could only deduce from this change of heart that the major was repenting his earlier anger. Crossman guessed that now Lovelace had taken time to cool a little and gather his thoughts he was regretting having given the dressing-down. He could not of course say so. His character as an officer and English gentleman forbade any intimacy of that sort. This gesture was much the same apology but without the words. Both men would understand what was behind it.

'I shall be ready, sir. Thank you.'

'Oh, don't thank me, sergeant,' replied the major, airily, 'I might be leading you to your death.'

Crossman went straight to Ali and told him the major had apologized.

Ali looked sceptical. 'He said sorry?'

'No, he invited me on a mission with him.'

'Ah, that is indeed an honour,' said Ali, his chest rising. 'When must we leave?'

'No — Ali — no, just me alone, I'm afraid. No one else.'

Ali looked taken aback. 'Just you?'

'Yes, but there is nothing sinister in this. He's not going to do away with me when we're out of sight of the army. I told you, the major and I are friends. He wishes to make it up to me.'

Ali stared at Crossman through narrow eyes, then gripped the sergeant by the shoulders with those thick, broad, strong hands. Having seen how the major operated in the field — if he took someone with him it was always a subaltern — this could mean only one thing to the Turk.

Crossman was startled to see tears welling in the corners of Ali's brown eyes. 'He is going to make you an officer,' said the Turk in a husky voice full of emotion. 'My sergeant is going to be an officer.'

Crossman did not want to crush his friend and guide by telling him that the major was going to do no such thing. He made up one of his white lies, to keep Ali happy.

'Perhaps — but after the war — it would — spoil the way we do things at the moment to make me an officer now.'

'Ah, yes, I understand.' Ali turned away, his voice still thick. 'I go to tell my wife. She will weep, I know. You are like a son to her.'

Since Crossman was probably only about five years her junior, this was another startling piece of news, but the sergeant felt things had been settled nicely and he let Ali go on his way.

6

Lovelace and Crossman slipped through a gully at the end of which they knew they would find a large drain. The drain, clogged in parts with debris, but passable, would lead them into a part of Sebastopol which had a stretch of wasteland fronting some gutted buildings. This part of the city had been heavily bombarded by the allies and consequently the tide of humanity had moved back from this beach of rubble.

Just before entering the drain, they passed a spot where Crossman paused to stare at the remains of a decomposed body jammed almost out of view between three standing stones. There must have been several such corpses littering the landscape, caught in crevices or holes, out of sight and mind. This was not a place frequented by either the Russians or the allies, the topography being too jagged and rugged for a group of any size to launch an attack. Incised by deep, narrow, winding natural passageways, between sharp-edged lips of rock, even a force the size of Goodlake's sharpshooters, a company, would have trouble scrambling around. The Russians themselves would be content with surveying the area from a distance, knowing of the difficulties it would present to any large attacking column.

'What is it?' asked Lovelace.

'Diodotus.'

Crossman was speaking of a young Greek spy they had used a short while back. The young man had been shot through the neck and spine, right here, in front of Crossman. According to a Russian officer called Tolstoy, to whom Crossman had been introduced by the Greek, Diodotus had been a promising poet. His talents had obviously gone with him now, to the afterlife. It raised the unavoidable question in Crossman's mind at the time, as to how many talented young lives had been lost, how many great works of art, books, statues, inventions, discoveries, would not now amaze the world of the living. Some Shakespeare, or Michelangelo, or Brunel may have had his legs shot from under him in this pointless war, robbing future generations of what should have been a priceless heritage.

'This is where he was killed?'

Crossman nodded. 'He dropped a dark lamp and we were caught in its bright flare.'

'You're lucky that isn't you then.'

'Just what I was thinking.'

They continued on their journey, leaving the rags on the bones of Diodotus to blow in the wind and the rain. Crossman and Lovelace set some small traps in the drain before leaving it. Not man-traps, but devices of twigs and thread. When they returned by the same route, something they usually tried to avoid, they would be warned if their entrance had been discovered. Unfortunately as the war progressed the holes in the enemy defences — be they ever so small — had mostly been closed. The spies and saboteurs were now down to a quarter of a dozen, which were jealously used.

They also left a dark lamp just inside the drain on the Sebastopol side, to use on their return.

Once in the streets of Sebastopol they made their way down to the harbour. It was Lovelace's contention that any signs of change would be found down there. The defences of the city were daily blasted, rebuilt, blasted again, but very little altered on the perimeter. In the town itself people just went about their normal daily chores, living their lives while war raged all around them (and occasionally fell on their heads). The waterfront was where the hustle and bustle of change took place.

The two men were dressed as sailors, a

disguise Crossman usually sought to avoid left to his own devices. He always felt his soft hands would give him away. However, Lovelace had pointed out to him that his hands were not what they used to be, having been hardened by almost two years of hard labour since leaving Britain. Crossman, inspecting the callused palms, agreed that he was not now the effete nobleman's son who had left the shores of his homeland to journey out into a cruel hard environment.

The pair entered a tavern fronting one of the main quays and Lovelace immediately caught the eye of a man who sat in a dark corner. Their contact was with some water-front workers. He excused himself after a few minutes, ordered some drinks from a serving woman while threading his way between rickety tables, and sat down with Lovelace and Crossman. He was a large man, in his late forties or early fifties, with a thick grizzled beard and a wicked scar under his right eye. His nostrils were like caverns and had their own forests sprouting through the openings. Crossman had to sit back in his chair to avoid a very strong halitosis problem.

For a moment the contact stared at Crossman, before raising his eyebrows at Lovelace.

'One of my men,' said Lovelace in Russian.

'Are they all so young?' growled the man in amusement. 'And so beautiful?'

He put his hand on Crossman's knee under the table and then smiled when Crossman jerked his leg out of reach.

'And so sensitive to the touch!'

His hand came down again, near the thigh, and clamped there like a steel vice. This time Crossman did not squirm away, knowing he might attract attention to himself and his companions. He bore the indignity by staring into the man's eyes with a steely glare, until the hand removed itself and was then on the tabletop, rolling tobacco for a foul-smelling pipe.

'Gregory, no games, please,' ordered Lovelace. 'We are here on serious business. What's happening at the moment?'

'Pah!' said Gregory, exhaling a stink into Lovelace's face.

Lovelace grimaced and hardened his words. 'If you continue this very dangerous exercise I shall not only stop your pay-ments . . .'

'Yes?' came the amused tone again.

'I will shoot you in the belly with this pistol I have under the table. I warned you when you started on my other man,' Crossman guessed this was Lieutenant Pirce-Smith, 'and it has to stop. You understand me,

Gregory. It has to stop, *now*.'

Sulkily, Gregory said, 'As you wish, but the other one, he was such a pretty young man, with skin so smooth and white. Beardless. Almost a woman, but not one, thank the stars. You are so lucky, sir, to have such men about you. A virtual harem. And you, Victor, a man with the power to order them to do as you wish, while I have to buy such favours.'

'To business, if you please.'

Gregory's expression changed, becoming very serious and businesslike. Lovelace had chosen a table apart from the others, near the window through which he could see people coming from the outside. Gregory spoke in a low voice, under the general hubbub in the room, pausing only to accept the drinks from the serving woman, a blowsy, dispirited, fair-haired female of no particular age. Once she had gone, Gregory nodded towards the window and the harbour beyond it.

'They are collecting boats,' he said, 'and plankings from the floors of warehouses. I think they mean to make a bridge, over the water, for the citizens and the army to run away quickly.'

Lovelace frowned. 'You mean an escape route?'

'That's what I mean, Victor.'

'We must not let that happen,' said

Lovelace, coldly. 'If you see such a bridge under construction, you must destroy it, do you understand, Gregory? Or inform me swiftly, so that I can do it. You will be paid well for any sabotage, you know that.'

'I understand, Victor. Now, something else. The army is going to do something, I don't know what. I think maybe a new attack? General Gortchakoff is doing this. I hear it from one of his house servants, a very close and amiable friend of mine. Big attack.'

'Where?'

'I don't know, this is the truth as it was confided to me. No one knows but Gortchakoff, and I do not sleep with him.' Gregory grinned into Crossman's face then he turned to Lovelace again. 'Victor, I think it might be Inkerman again. The British are weaker than the French, in numbers, so I think Inkerman. What do you think, Victor?'

'I think we must find out where the attack is coming, not guess.'

Gregory shrugged. 'Maybe Gortchakoff keep it in his head until the last minute? Maybe we never find out until it happens?'

'We must do our best, Gregory.'

'Of course. I always do my best.' He downed his drink with one sweep and swallow, then grimaced like someone taking a draught of nasty medicine. 'This vodka is the best I have ever tasted,' he said. 'Come, you, shiny-eyes. You drink this excellent vodka with your friend, Gregory.'

Lovelace nodded at Crossman. Crossman took the cracked glass of colourless alcohol and threw it back into his throat. It burned like blazes and his eyes watered. It was foul. He began coughing, violently, until Gregory got up and slapped him on the back several times with a hand like a meat platter, before turning to the rest of the tavern and saying, 'A young sailor boy with a throat like a baby finch. He thinks because he has grown this big rough beard that he can drink like a man.' There was laughter from the other tables and Gregory grinned, before ruffling Crossman's hair.

'We must leave now,' ordered Lovelace. 'Gregory. The purse is on my seat.'

The two British men stood up and began to leave. Gregory went back to his seat and reached under the table, to take the purse from Lovelace's chair. As Crossman passed the man, he bent down and yanked hard on the nose hair sprouting from Gregory's left nostril. Gregory yelled and jumped up, falling backwards off his chair. But before he could retaliate, Crossman was out on the street. Crossman felt enormous satisfaction, though he could see by Lovelace's expression that he was in for another ticking off.

'He humiliated me,' said Crossman, before the major could speak. 'I could not let that go without some return in kind.'

'This is not a game of tit-for-tat,' growled Lovelace. 'Gregory is a very good man, when it comes to our business. I have to cultivate my spies as I find them. They do not grow in flowerbeds. What men like Gregory do out of my sight is neither here nor there, nor of any interest to me.'

'He's a rafter rat. His preferences and practices are his own — I have a cousin in the same mould — a very witty and erudite cousin, whose company is a great delight to my mother — but this Gregory is a sewer rodent. You are my senior officer, but I will not tolerate being treated like a gamin. Even you can't expect that of me. Where did you find such a verminous creature?'

'Traitors and spies are found where you expect them to be found.' Lovelace sighed and his anger suddenly dissipated. 'I'm sorry, I should have warned you. You took it better than Pirce-Smith, I have to tell you. The lieutenant almost swooned when that hand clamped itself on his knee. It's a price we pay. Come on, we have another one to meet. Don't worry, this one is a woman. She won't grab.'

'And is your name really Victor?'

'Of course not,' replied Lovelace, 'but I hope to be one, at the end of this war.'

As they made their way through the drab streets, with its dreary-looking citizens and soldiery dragging their feet here and there, Crossman could not help but be aware of the low spirits of the inhabitants. They seemed to breathe defeat from every pore. Crossman felt a great empathy with the men and women of Sebastopol. Walking amongst them like this, he could sense their despair, see it in their eyes, feel it in their tread. They knew something dreadful was going to happen to them and their city of rubble and ruins, it was just a matter of when. Even should they be fortunate enough to escape the onslaught of that terrible foreign army which had ringed their walls for so long, raining death on them, they would become refugees, without homes and hope, their possessions in a handcart, their houses left to the conquerers. Rape and pillage was what they expected, if they remained. That's what conquering armies did. They became a barbarian horde for a short while, no matter they began as a civilized army. They took revenge on you for the audacity of defending yourself and your homeland.

'Why do you wish to blow up the bridge, if

they build it?' asked Crossman, as they walked down a deserted alley.

'Why? Because they must be seen to be physically *defeated*,' answered Lovelace, firmly. 'We cannot walk into an empty city. There has to be some reward, some satisfaction for the British government and glory for the army. Otherwise it will all be a great waste of time. A sense of elation is necessary. Imagine a prize fight where one of the fighters simply fails to come back after excusing himself in the middle of the milling. The whole event would fall flat.' His voice hardened. 'There must be no escape, no compromise of that sort. We have been fighting too long not to be given our just rewards for our tenacity and stamina.'

'But if lives are saved?'

'It's not about saving lives, it's about a satisfactory conclusion.'

Once again Crossman had been given an insight into the diamond-hard heart of his superior officer. Lovelace wanted not just an end, but a spectacular end to the war. He wanted not just to win, but to triumph. These were not goals which Crossman himself believed important. The object of the war, so far as he understood it, was to prevent Russia from expanding its influence and power. This object being achieved, what did it matter that the war ended with a fizz, rather than a bang? The regiments could go home having done their job without losing any more men.

'I know what you're thinking,' said Lovelace, 'but it really is necessary to prevent any other ambitious rulers trying to do the same. You stamp the fire out, thoroughly and with great show, in order to make a point.'

They were now again in a street with people, so the major stopped speaking English and went back to Russian.

Following Lovelace's eyes, Crossman stared down the street. It being a fine day there were one or two women in black garb sitting outside their houses, close to their front step, doing things with their hands — crochet, embroidery — in the manner of Mediterraneans. It seemed that those from the Black Sea had a similar culture. Lovelace was looking at one of these women. She was firmly-built, with a strong face and a heavy nose which age had not turned frail. Sitting on a wooden chair, she was plying thread through a piece of red cloth stretched over a circular frame, looking up occasionally to smile at passers-by. Some gave her a greeting, others did not.

Lovelace took Crossman by the arm and steered him back into the alley. They hurried along, away from the place.

'Was that not her?' asked Crossman.

'Yes it was, but the signal told me she was being watched.'

'Signal?'

'The red cloth. If all had been well, it would have been white.'

'Oh.'

'If we cannot meet with the woman our business here is done. It'll be nightfall in a couple of hours. Like Thomas Gray's ploughman, we must homeward plod our weary way.'

After darkness had fallen the pair made their retreat from Sebastopol the way they had come. On entering the drain they lit the dark lamp they had hidden there and in its single narrow beam found several of their traps had been sprung. Someone would be waiting for them on the other side of the gulley.

'Were we seen going in?' asked Crossman. 'Why not arrest us in the city?'

Lovelace murmured, 'Gregory, perhaps?'

'But did he know our route?'

'No, of course he didn't, did he? We must have been seen by some civilian or other and reported. They'll be waiting for us on the other side of the drain.'

Crossman said, 'Should we go back and try another exit?'

The sergeant, albeit only an NCO, was not used to deferring to another man. It had been a long time since he had asked for orders from a superior out on one of these fox hunts. He was used to leading and making the decisions himself. He waited as Lovelace deliberated. He knew that the major was running over the options in his mind, weighing up the possible consequences of turning back. There was an obvious one which occurred to Crossman and happily it was also in Lovelace's mind.

'They may have closed off our retreat by now. The door behind us is probably locked too. We have to go on.'

'They'll just blaze at us as we go out of the drain. We won't stand a chance.'

'My guess is that they will be curious,' said Lovelace. 'The human being is a curious beast, thank God. They may want at least one of us alive, to question us, find out what we were doing, hoping to discover our contacts. I think they'll hold back at first, hoping we'll walk unsuspectingly into their arms.' He checked his pistol grimly in the light of the dark lamp. 'Well, they won't take *me* alive. I — well — we've both undergone torture in their hands when they've been trying to extract information.'

Crossman certainly had: by a certain Major

Zinski. The Russian had been repaid in full by the sergeant and was now hopefully undergoing the tortures of the fires and demons of hell. However, Crossman had not been aware that Lovelace had also been through such an ordeal. When was that? He did not recall the officer ever having been missing for more than a week.

'What do you suggest, sir?'

'That we crawl out of the end of the drain as if we do not suspect anything, perhaps chattering quietly to one another, then make a quick dash for cover. It's fairly dark out there, but it's not long beyond twilight. We can still be seen enough to be targets. Can you picture the topography outside? There's a large standing stone to the left, about twenty yards from the end of the drain. I suggest we both run for it. You will go first . . . '

'You're the leader, sir.'

'Don't argue. You know better than that from your own experiences. You will go first. You have your pistol?'

Crossman's Tranter was already in his hand. He cocked it with the cocking trigger.

'Yes.'

'They may have stationed someone — perhaps more than one — behind that stone. You will shoot them before they shoot you. The stone is backed by a sheer face — the side of the gully. They can't get anyone beyond that, so if we make it, we'll have good cover and can't be overlooked. I am ready, sergeant. How about you?'

Crossman's heart was beating fast. 'Ready.'

'They believe they hold the winning cards. Let's trump them.'

The pair carried out their plan, whispering nonsense to each other as they crawled out of the drain, laughing quietly as if amused and greatly relieved to be beyond the confines of Sebastopol's defences. They then jumped to their feet and were off like gypsy lurchers, scrambling over the rough ground towards the standing stone. Flames flashed from muzzles and the thunder of small arms was loud around their ears in the confined space. Bullets whined and zipped, zinging from rocks and the odd stunted dwarf tree. Crossman ran full into a man who stepped from behind a boulder. Instinctively he pulled the trigger of his revolver and the unfortunate fellow took the shot full in the chest at point blank range. The man groaned and fell away, Crossman trampling over his body. Lovelace actually tripped on him, but managed somehow to keep his feet. Then the pair of them, only seconds after leaving the drain, were behind the tall stone, panting. Crossman fired two wild shots into the dark lanes and shadows of that stretch of evening between him and the drain, to deter anyone close by.

'Are you hit at all, sir?' he asked Lovelace.

He had to wait for the answer, for a fusillade of shots came out of various corners of the gully, smacking into the standing stone and the natural walls behind them.

'No, not hit. I'm a bit banged about, having run into a rather solid boulder. Fortunately I bounced. I may have broken my arm, but that is neither here nor there. What about you, sergeant?'

Crossman was now aware of a trickle of blood going down his arm and dripping out of the sleeve cuff.

'I think that man I killed had a knife or bayonet in his hand.'

'Are you badly hurt?'

'I — I don't think so. Blade went through my lower arm, I think. Yes, it's definitely tender. Lower left arm. But the flow isn't bad. I don't think it's an artery. I can dress it myself, if you'll keep the watch, sir.'

'I can certainly do that.'

There was another exchange of gunfire while Crossman dealt with his wound. It was not much more than a shallow cut, his shirt and coat protecting the area. Crossman took a strip of cloth he carried for the purpose out of his pocket and bound himself with it.

'What about your arm, sir?'

'That can wait.'

By this time the gunfire had died down to the occasional bark of a musket, or Lovelace's pistol cracking by his ear. This was pretty much the pattern of the whole night. When an early grey dawn came the Russians, a score of them by Crossman's reckoning, began to intensify their attacks again. The two Britons exchanged the odd shot or two with their enemy, wondering when the main assault would come and conserving their ammunition in order to deal with it as effectively as they could.

However, help was at hand. The fracas had been heard from the cemetery close to the Picket House Ravine. Some Rifle Brigade skirmishers had been despatched to investigate. These now engaged with the Russians scattered amongst the rocks. After a brief fight the Russians melted away towards their Strand Battery. The British riflemen themselves then drew back, being close enough to the Russian defences to be picked off by sharpshooters. Lovelace and Crossman now felt it safe enough to make their escape along a small ravine which would lead them back to the British Left Attack lines. On stepping back over the body of the Russian he had shot with his pistol, Crossman realized it was an officer. He paused for a moment to cut the soldier's scabbard from his belt and take the sword from his hand. Crossman's blood was on the blade. He wiped the length of steel on the corpse before returning the sword to its sheath.

'Trophy?' murmured Lovelace. His arm was now slung in his unbuttoned coat.

'It's for my brother,' replied Crossman. 'I wouldn't normally do this.'

'You don't need to apologize to me.'

'No, I know, but I feel foolish. It's a particularly handsome weapon, don't you think? James was sent home ill. It's just something . . . '

'Of course. I have brothers — and sisters.' The major seemed to reflect for a moment. 'A good too many of them.'

Crossman thought that a strange remark, but let it pass. Once they had reached a safe zone, Crossman inspected the blade. It was a magnificent weapon indeed.

'Seeing the light glinting on that edge,' said Lovelace, as they walked side by side, 'reminds me of the story of one of my brothers. Have you ever heard of Matthew Lovelace? No? Well, he's quite famous. He was in India with John Company, naturally. An Acting DC on the North-West Frontier, the Punjab. Not one of Henry Lawrence's

'Young Men' exactly, although he knew most of them and was known by them. One day he rode out alone from his district to look for a rather incorrigible bandit chief who was reported to be in one of the hill villages. By chance the first person he saw when he entered the village was the bandit chief himself. Matthew immediately ran him through and cut off his head. When he got back to his office he placed the head on a stool in the corner of the room, then invited all the chiefs of the area to come and see him, one by one. No one mentioned the head, but all saw, and knew the kind of man they were dealing with.'

'I heard that story,' said Crossman, 'from my father, but he said the man was Reynell Taylor — not your brother Matthew.'

Lovelace's jaw stiffened. 'Oh, he did, did he?'

'But he could be wrong of course — my father has been wrong about a lot of things.'

'The story comes second- or third-hand to me, too, so I will not stand upon my oath, but I feel sure it sounds like Matthew.'

Crossman realized the major was irritated, so he changed the subject to more pressing matters.

'Will we warn the French that there may be an attack?'

'Of course. My compatriot on the French side is a Captain Lefontaine — we exchange most information. Some, of course, I retain — and doubtless he does the same. Our interests do not always coincide.'

'This General Gortchakoff . . . '

'Who just happens to be another Russian Prince. Yes, what of him?'

'Is he a brilliant stategist or tactician?'

Lovelace let out an ironic laugh. 'There's only one man of any real brilliance in Sebastopol and that's Todleben. It would be a wonderful thing if princes were born genius generals but in fact very few of them are. Men like Wellington and Napoleon come from all walks of life, yet the governments of today still cling to the idea that nobility brings with it a kind of intrinsic knowledge of warfare. Alexander the Great was a prince, thus all princes, dukes, earls, barons, and so on must inherit his skills. These nobles keep making huge mistakes, but that doesn't prevent governments from appointing them to the very highest ranks in the world's armies.'

'It's an easy route, I suppose,' said Crossman. 'You don't know if a general is any good until you've tried him in the field. There's no other way. So do you try Tom, the blacksmith's son, or do you try Lord Fotheringale?'

'Exactly. But Lord Fotheringale having once failed, they try him again, and again, and again, hoping that breeding will out and the best has been trapped inside the noble head, just waiting for the right opportunity to burst forth in a blaze of glory . . . Ah, here we are, almost home.'

They had reached Kadikoi and both men were exhausted. Crossman could see in the day's light that Lovelace had bruises and scrapes down the right side of his face. He was indeed very 'banged about' and needed attention from a surgeon.

'There is one man I know very little about over there,' said Lovelace, as they approached the hovel. 'Gortchakoff will undoubtedly use General Liprandi — well, he is neither here nor there — but I'm supposing General Read is still around too. Read is something of an enigma to us. He could turn out to be a genius in battle, which wouldn't suit us at all. I prefer they should have old incompetent generals, like the ones we have.'

'Read? That doesn't sound like a Russian name.'

'It isn't. General Read has Scottish ancestory.'

Crossman stopped in his tracks. 'As I have,' he said, quietly.

'That doesn't automatically make the pair

of you brothers,' said Lovelace, smiling. 'We're all a great mix you know. I have, among other ancestors, Norwegians and Orkney Island fisherfolk.'

'Yes, but it seems most peculiar — a Russian general with a name like that.'

'A rose by any other,' Lovelace replied, cheerily, limping ahead of Crossman. 'Here, see if you can rustle up a couple of hot baths, sergeant ... ' They were back to their respective ranks again. 'I'll pay for 'em. That Albanian fellow in the hut where steam issues forth at all times of day? I'm sure he'll oblige. You know the man I mean? And get that wound dressed. I'm going to see a surgeon friend of mine who's expert with balms as well as a saw.'

Crossman did know the Albanian and went to make the arrangements after having his cut rebandaged. Major Lovelace joined him, his arm in a sling after having been set and splinted. He had indeed broken it, the bone having pierced the skin. Crossman felt guilty for not insisting that it be inspected while they were behind the standing stone. But the major was a law unto himself. If he had wanted it looked at, he would have asked. There was something of the martyr in Lovelace. It suited his image of himself to bear the pain of the injury without complaint, until it could be set and put in splints.

After his luxury bath, which must have cost Lovelace several days' pay, Crossman was visited by Rupert Jarrard. The pair of them sat in some chairs outside a sutler's hut and contemplated the siege railway. A sturdy set of mules were pulling a truck up the slope with apparent ease.

The American asked Crossman for the inside story on the 'raid' he had just carried out, hinting (untruthfully) that he already knew a great deal. Crossman normally gave his friend some sketchy details, which the correspondent would fill out in his own way. No real names would be used in any case and Jarrard had the knack of the novelist, in being able to dramatize a situation well for his readers.

But this time the sergeant had to say no to his friend, since he had not been the senior officer on the expedition.

'In any case there's no great excitement in the content,' Crossman said. 'Leastways, not in the actual fox hunt. Getting back, the last few yards, was a trouble, but there are such skirmishes amongst the picquets every day.'

'I appreciate your problem,' replied Jarrard. 'I understand you went with Major Lovelace? This time I shan't press you, Jack. Say, have you asked that lovely lady to marry you yet?

Now that you're off the hook with the earlier one, the French farm girl.'

'You make me sound like some evil lecher, Rupert, grabbing at every woman who comes my way. And 'off the hook' is not a phrase I would use myself in the circumstances. I do not believe fisherman's parlance appropriate. However, I take it you mean Jane? No, I have not declared my interest. How can I? I'm a sergeant in the infantry.'

'People still worry about such things in England?' said Jarrard, sounding genuinely surprised. 'I know cavalrymen are dashing and all that, but a good marching regiment, fifes and drums going, has its glorious side too. Listen, you've got that wound at the moment. Women love men with wounds. It brings out the sentimental side in them. They often say yes to a pale soldier draped over a chair or bed, when that same man wouldn't hold any interest for them if he was robust and hearty.'

Crossman smiled, amused as usual by the American's banter. 'It's not the regiment, it's the rank, and well you know it.'

Jarrard sighed. 'Well, I have to say I'm still disappointed. We don't have a classless society back home either, but at least it's based on money and not some fanciful notion of bloodline and breeding. There's some reason for a girl with money not marrying a dirt farmer or drifter. But to worry about breeding! Hell, she's not going to produce street urchins just because her father's a lord and yours is only a baronet.'

'Her father's not a lord — but I take your point, Rupert.'

'I take it you'd be poor whether you were a sergeant in the infantry or a captain of dragoons, Jack.'

'Probably worse off as the captain, having to maintain all the accoutrements associated with being a cavalry officer. Being the younger son of an aristocrat is much the same as being the younger son of a blacksmith. I inherit nothing. The army or the church, that's the choice of the later sibling. Scratch out a living from miserly parishioners, or claw in pennies from the paymaster.'

'Your father doesn't give you an allowance?'

'The estates are in a bad way and I doubt he could afford to, even if we were on better terms. As it is, he'd rather see me starve.'

'So,' said Jarrard, as Crossman lit up his chibouque and took a long pull on a Turkish blend, 'what's to stop you and Jane?'

'Oh, God, Rupert. Do you think she could share a space six feet by three in the barracks, with merely a blanket to separate our end of the room from that of the men? It's unthinkable — a different life entirely. No, no. Jane is a lady . . . '

Jane Mulinder was indeed a lady, whose father owned practically the whole of Derbyshire, give or take a few worthless pockets of bottom land belonging to the queen. Her looks were not unprepossessing — at least, Crossman was possessed by them. And Jarrard himself had been captivated enough to go out riding with Jane as often as time would allow. If her looks were unfashionable, no one could deny her dark beauty. The times demanded golden-haired wives with skins of ivory, but Crossman was not a great man for following fashion to the extent that it could rule over the preferences of his heart. With some aristocrats, this could well be the case, and they would suffer for it eventually. He found her looks exquisite, even if her hair was jet black and her skin less than pale. He found her spirit indomitable. She had been jilted yet she faced the music back in England and only later had taken a dangerous voyage to a dangerous land to find herself again. He found her personality extraordinary! Why only the other day . . .

'Jack, are you listening to me? You've gone off into one of your reveries again. What is it this time? Steam engines again?'

'Good God, no,' said Crossman, pulling himself back to the real time and place. 'No, no, I was actually thinking of Jane.'

'Good thing too. Damn it man, she turned me down you know.'

This was enough to jolt Crossman upright in his chair. The long-stemmed pipe fell from his mouth to the ground. He picked it up quickly, ascertained that the stem was still intact, then rounded on his friend.

'You asked Jane to marry you?'

'Damn right. She's a lovely woman. Why wouldn't I?'

'Even though you knew — you knew — about my attachment — my *strong* attachment to her?'

'Hell, Jack, this is *love* you're talking about, not some horse we both want to buy. I wasn't going to regret something my whole life simply because you saw her first. No, no, Jack — love and war, love and war, fellah. Had you been married, or engaged, I might have thought twice. But you haven't even told her you love her yet, Jack.'

'How do you know I haven't?' said Crossman with an accusing look.

'She told me. I was her confidant. Her friend. She talked to me about everything, especially you. She said she couldn't talk with Lavinia Durham about you, because it would

285

all get back to you. So, she talked with me, and we grew fond of each other in the process. Not fond enough for me, obviously, because I wanted to make her my wife, and she declined, very nicely thank you, but she declined. Hell and damnation, Jack, I certainly wouldn't have let the fact that I'm no wealthy aristocrat hold me back, either. I just piled in there with my proposal and got my butt kicked for it. You should do the same. I hope you get yours kicked too. It would give me infinite satisfaction to have you suffer as I did. It damn well hurts, friend — it hurts just about everywhere — pride, spirit, heart, guts, head — yep, just about everywhere you can think of, it's damn-well painful. I would like you to join me in my little hell, just for the company. It would make me feel better. Wasn't it one of the Greek philosophers who said miserable people liked to see others more miserable than they were themselves?'

Crossman stared at his good companion. 'You certainly believe in honesty, I'll give you that, Jarrard. What about Monique? Are you not in love with her then?'

'Oh, yes *now*. But give me the choice again, and well, I just don't know, Jack. If I had detected just a little wavering in Jane, well — it's all water under the bridge now. Monique is delightful and she adores me.

Thinks I'm king of the wild frontier. That's hard to resist. And you've known Jane, for how long? Six hundred years? How could I even think I stood a chance against that sort of history? You British genteel types, you meet in the cradle. An outsider doesn't get a look in.'

'You leave me breathless, Rupert. I don't know what to say. I suppose I should start by saying, hard luck old chap. I won't say better luck next time. I'm astonished though. Going behind my back like that. You could have come to me like a gentleman and said, 'Jack, I'm going to ask Jane to be my wife. I thought it best to inform you first, since you have a personal interest.' That's what a British officer and a gentleman would have done.'

'Well, good luck to British officers and gentlemen. I'll be damned if I'll ask *anyone's* permission to marry the woman of my choice, even if he does think he's my best friend. What would you have said? You'd have made up some cock-and-bull story about how you and Jane had pledged a lifetime's devotion to each other in the nursery. Or more likely have called me out. Yep, that's what you would have done. Challenged me. Nope, that's not the way Rupert Jarrard does things. He goes out and gets, *then* tells his best friend.'

'Typical.'

'You would have been the first to know — afterwards.'

'How thoughtful.'

'That's me — heart of gold.'

Jarrard lit a cigar and they sat there, side by side, not looking at one another for about ten minutes, puffing away.

Finally, Crossman broke the silence by pointing at the railway with his chibouque and asking, 'When do you think the first locomotive will get here? I've heard they're considering a Wilson tank locomotive 0-6-0. They use them in the collieries up in the North of England, you know. Supposed to be very reliable. We will get new models, of course.'

'My information, which comes reliably from Russell, is that you're going to get a second-hand engine from a company called St Helens Railway. Built by Jones, Turner and Evans. A tender locomotive with an 0-4-0 wheel arrangement.'

'Really? Well, Billy knows best, I suppose. Shame, it would have been splendid to see a shiny new engine here. I'm hoping they'll ask for volunteers to maintain them. Do you suppose they will bring their own engineers out from Britain?'

'Without a doubt. You might try asking though.'

Colonel Hawke sent for Crossman shortly after the sergeant's meeting with his friend. Crossman entered the room and found Hawke talking with none other than Captain Sterling Campbell. Crossman could have sunk into the floor. Instead he saluted and stood to attention, waiting to be addressed by his superior officer. In fact Campbell merely glanced at him, told the colonel he would see him later, and then left. Crossman thanked God that Wellington had stated the common soldier was scum, thus giving men like Campbell a good reason not to pay any attention to men like him. Crossman was sure that some officers did not even look into the faces of their men, regarding them as automatons, there for the sole purpose of drilling and parading for show, and leading into battle for glory.

Hawke was of a different mould. He saw the creatures behind the uniforms and knew their worth. Crossman had been told by Lovelace that Hawke had a high regard for him, which naturally raised the colonel very high in the sergeant's eyes. Hawke actually asked for Crossman's opinion at times: something staff officers did not even do of regiment officers. Had Crossman been an officer himself he had no doubt Colonel Hawke would have acted as his mentor and patron. One only had a glittering career in the army through preferment. Talent was needed, of course, but you could have all the talent in the world and still wither in some dusty corner of the organization. To become a high flier, someone who was swiftly moved into the best jobs, someone promoted rapidly up the ladder, someone in the right place at the right time, one needed a help from someone in power.

'Ah, Mr Fancy Jack,' said the colonel, shuffling some papers on his makeshift desk. 'Well done on the Sebastopol thing. How's your arm?'

'Healing quite quickly, thank you, sir.'

'And the major's arm?'

'I haven't seen the major for a while, but it looked well enough in its sling the last time we were together.'

Hawke chuckled. 'How is it that you copy his fashion, sergeant? If the major had broken his leg I suppose you would have limped in here this morning, eh? Never mind. To business. We have to discuss this impending attack by the Russians. I want my falconet, my zumbooruck right there in the middle of it all. A good chance for you to assess the camel in a real action.'

'We have already . . . '

'Oh, I know, I know, but that was just a

skirmish. This looks like being another Alma or Inkerman. What say? You don't have to charge the enemy of course. You can stay on the fringes, shoot at 'em from the edge, but keep moving about. A camel is a large target.'

'I was about to say that, sir. A very large target, sticking up out of the mass. We'll be very tempting for the Russian gunners.'

'That's why I say you've got to be nippy, keep running around. Fire and run, fire and run. That's the idea. How are your men? All holding up well? What about that Canadian? Useful to you?'

Crossman was certain that Gwilliams was an American, but the colonel had got it into his head that the British connection was strong.

'He works well. He's not an unintelligent man, either. Self-educated I believe, having access to worthy books at one time.'

The colonel nodded. 'Ah, worthy books! Not that they have ever interested me. Can't seem to sit still long enough to read. Rather be in the saddle, or out walking with a dog and a sporting gun . . . ' Crossman felt this was the colonel's image of how he would like to be, not how he was. In fact Crossman had often seen Hawke with that formidable nose between the pages of some tome or document. 'So, Gwilliams settled. Yorwarth?

Has he had that horrible jaw fixed yet?'

'The jaw is as fixed as it'll ever be, sir, but now it's a skin complaint.'

'Never up to the mark, is he? Peterson? Recovered from that ordeal? Not pleasant, to be tortured.'

'Fine, sir.' They both avoided the use of gender. 'Still scars there, inside of course, but otherwise . . . '

'And the damnable Wynter? I understand Yusuf Ali keeps him in check while you're not around. Nasty, that business over his wife. I would have it thoroughly looked into, but I'm told that the perpetrator is known to you and that you have put the word about. You shouldn't have gone off on that goose chase, of course, but you already know that. I want no precursory justice, mark you. If you find the man, hand him over to the proper authorities for them to deal with. That's the right thing to do. A firing squad or an official piece of hemp, not a peremptory hanging.'

'Of course, sir. I hope you know me better.'

'Indeed, but one likes to hear it from the horse's mouth. Well, I think that's all, sergeant. Get out there and practise a little more with the camel. She's a fine beast, isn't she? What do you call her?'

'Betsy.'

Hawke's face clouded a little. 'Hummph.

Not quite a warrior's name. You might have given her something stronger.'

'We did think of Boadicea but found it a bit of a mouthful.'

'Yes, well — what about Diana?' said the colonel, brightly. 'No, huntress, ain't she, not a warrior? I know, Athena. Athena the Greek goddess of war.' He slammed his right fist into his left palm. 'By Jove, there's a name to conjure with, sir! Athena.'

Crossman coughed into his own fist. 'That's just it, sir. Greek. You know Ali will sulk for hours if we give her a Greek name. The Turks and their historic enmity with the Greeks? Besides, quite honestly we think Betsy has got used to her name. It's not Joan of Arc . . . '

'Thank God,' said Hawke, having his own historical enmities. 'We don't want anything French.'

' . . . but she does respond to it.'

'Oh, well, for field purposes we'll leave her with Betsy, but if I have to put it in some official paper, it'll need to be changed to a name with a bit of blood and fire about it. *Banshee*, something like that. That'd go down well with your regiment, sergeant, being Irish.'

Crossman left the colonel running through a variety of female names with 'edge' to them.

Ali was waiting for him when he got back and was naturally disappointed not to see some sign that Crossman had received his commission.

'I think he make you an officer,' growled the Turk. 'He should make you the ensign.'

'It won't happen, old friend,' said Crossman. 'Believe me. Things like that are so very rare in the British army. Now you irregulars, you Bashi-Bazouks, you have no need of officers. Every one of you is a chief. Every one of you is a general. Now that's the kind of army I like.'

In trying to change the subject he had opened a can of worms. Ali's eyes lit up.

'When this war is finished — soon — then you leave this pretty-jacket army and its red sleeves. You join with us, the Bashi-Bazouks! My general he makes you a grand officer straight away. You will have gold curtains, here on the shoulders,' he waggled his fingers over the top of his arm. Then he half-closed one eye as he imparted a confidence. 'Me, I know people. My cousin's cousin on my mother's side is a boyar — you know what is a boyar? — a very important citizen in Turkey. This boyar has the ear of a kneses, a village chieftain, who knows the head-horseman who looks after the stables of none other than Ismail Pasha himself! Ismail Pasha is very fond of his head-horseman. His head-horseman is very important to him.'

Preferment! Crossman was being offered a position in an irregular cavalry force, where he would have a mentor and patron. Advancement would be swift. All he had to do was leave the British army and join with a vagabond gang of wild irregulars. How easy it all was, when you knew someone who knew someone.

'In that case, Ali, why are you not a general?'

'Ah, me?' cried the Turk, who was the very image of the round, genial uncle who arrived with gifts for the children on Christmas day. 'I have not the countenance. You! You have the countenance of an officer. Tall, thin, with the hard eye. You would wear an officer's sword with great presence. Men would tremble before you. You have great contempt, great *arrogance*. I have not the proper arrogance, only a humble pride and a fierce honour, which are not enough to make for a good officer in the Turkish Army, for every Bashi-Bazouk has these noble but common traits. No, Ali would be proud to bow before you. We would fight together as brothers, against the enemies of Turkey and England.'

Crossman was flattered, of course, by this impossible dream. He didn't exactly care for the idea that he presented himself as *arrogant*, and hoped that it was Ali's poor use of English that was at fault here. But it was quite romantic, to picture himself as a son of the saddle, riding some terrifyingly wild horse into battle alongside his companion. What a colourful picture it made. Why, Jane would swoon with delight, wouldn't she?

The irony of the situation amused Crossman. He and Ali spent that night out in the hills, under the stars, the smell of woodsmoke in their nostrils. Ali was indeed a great friend to him and he would miss the man once this war was over. There was little chance they would meet again, afterwards, unless Crossman ever reached a position where he could send for Ali and use him in some capacity or another. Or the reverse, which seemed even more unlikely. Ali was a rough and ready warrior, eager for action, even though there were more grey hairs on his head than dark ones.

Over the next two weeks Crossman and his men went out with Betsy and practised with the swivel gun. Various charges and types of ammunition were used and Betsy had begun to take it all with great aplomb. The blast of the cannon close to her ear bothered her very little now. Firing from the back of a dromedary was similar to firing from the deck of a ship. A naval gunner would have better known what to do than Yorwarth did, for Betsy dipped and swayed, even when she was standing relatively still. She was actually worse than a ship's deck, for at least the swell or waves had some sort of rhythm and pattern to them, and could be seen coming, whereas Betsy was completely unpredictable. A shot with a judged low trajectory sometimes finished going almost vertical. 'Firing at the moon,' Wynter called it.

In his spare time, which because of the nature of his duties was considerable compared with other sergeants of line regiments, he walked and talked with Jane Mulinder. The pair had to be discreet because it would have aroused great indignation if they were seen by Crossman's superiors. Jane would not have minded, but Crossman would have. There would have been awkward questions, which would have involved revealing private matters. A gentleman's 'private matters' were guarded with great jealousy, even in the less reserved atmosphere of a war front. Crossman indeed had a great horror of being open to view by all. His family, his old friends, his former life: these were taboo subjects, even to someone like Jarrard. The walls had to stay up, the gates closed, and therefore his courting of Jane — for that was what it was, he had now admitted to himself — had to be secret. They would meet under an elderly broken tree, leafless even in the summer, down by a brook where the water trickled over smooth stones.

'How is your father?' Crossman asked one balmy evening. 'Is he well?'

'Would you wish him not to be?' she said, teasing.

'Of course not.' Crossman recalled a genial old gentleman who had fathered his children late in life, his youth and earlier energy having gone into managing his vast estates. 'I have a very high regard for your father. I know he doesn't think much of me. He believes me a bad son.'

'You know he thought you the very worst scamp for deserting your own father's household? 'Running wild,' he called it. Since very little news came back, except for the fact that you had absconded, he believed you had run up debts or something, and had left your father to deal with them. 'Younger sons,' I remember him growling, 'they are the very devil when it comes to gambling and frittering away money on fashion. I suppose the boy had several hacks, did not go short on servants while in town, and stayed at the very best hotels?''

'I never did,' protested Crossman in a high

voice. 'I was very frugal.'

'Well, Father wasn't aware of that.'

'He was ready to believe the worst of me?'

'Of course. He is an elderly man. Men become rigid in their views when they reach a certain age. My younger brother spent a fortune without Father's knowledge, until the day when Father had to settle for him. So, when he heard that your father was dashing around the countryside, looking for you, he naturally assumed you had done something of which you were ashamed and that you were hiding from everyone. He might have added some indiscretion with a lady, except that I nipped that idea in the bud. I was quite prepared to believe you had been outrageously extravagant, but I could not countenance the possibility that you were a libertine.'

'Why not? Why not a rake?'

Jane smiled and took his hand. 'That would not have suited my dreams at the time.'

'But, you were prepared to consider me a waster!'

'Oh, young immature ladies don't mind things like that in their men. It makes them less stuffy. We think we can cure you of such ills, with love and great affection. Why do you think women marry drinkers and gamblers? Because they don't mind drunks and gamesters? Of course not, they marry them because they think they are the one woman in the world who can change this man's lifestyle.' Jane's voice dropped a little. 'I know that is all stuff and nonsense now, of course. You can't change a man, once he is set in his mould. Not without great passions and upheavals of both spirits, which the relationship cannot always survive.'

'Well, I hope you don't consider me too boring when I tell you I dislike cards and only drink on social occasions.'

She smiled again, shaking her head, but then became more serious once again.

'No, you are no waster, and I hope no Don Juan, though I feel you are overfond of female company.' This much was true and he looked away from her eyes for a few telling seconds. 'I am also sure though that you are at heart an honourable man and able to withstand temptation, if that sense of honour comes near to danger. No, you are not boring, Alex. Not at all. If anything, I fear the other extreme. You seek excitement. You seek glory. That could be as fatal for any woman as drink or gambling. The paths of glory lead but to the grave and no lady wishes for early widowhood.'

'Strange. You are the second person in the last few weeks to quote Thomas Gray to me. I might dispute your last remark. There are some who having wed old men for their wealth, cannot wait for such a state, but I do not wish to get into an argument over that cynical thought. I would argue, however, against the idea that I go chasing after glory. I am a quiet man. Were I raised anything but a Scottish Presbyterian I would be a follower of the teachings of George Fox.'

'You, a Quaker? Never, Alexander. You were born to hold a sword in your hand, I'm afraid. Why did you join the army? To escape your father? No. There were other professions you might have chosen. The church for one. If you are such a peaceful man you would have moved into a peaceful profession and not followed the path of the warrior. I fear for you, because you do not like to maim and kill. That's what a soldier does and you abhor it, but you can't follow the drum and not fight. There must be a constant war going on inside you, a great tension that threatens to tear you apart, because you love most things martial, but not war.'

He stared at her. 'You must think me a shallow creature?'

'No, you are complex, that is all. Most of us are. If you were shallow you would love the army because it's a safe place, where the lines of order and discipline are well defined. But it isn't that, with you. It may be with some men, but not you. With you it's more complicated. There are many men who do not join the army because they wish to kill and maim. The most common reason is security. It is a job and nothing more. Some join because they like to ride fast horses, dressed in a dashing uniform. Some to escape an ordinary life. None of these apply to you, I think . . . '

'You told me I seek glory.'

'Glory and excitement. The glory for your own sense of well-being and worth, which have been stripped from you by your father. The excitement? Well, I think you find that in travel and foreign cultures, meeting strange peoples. I know this because I feel it too.'

He smiled at her now. 'I could become a missionary. That would do it all just as well.'

'You could, if you believed, as missionaries do, that people the world over need to become Presbyterians or perish in the fires of hell. No, Alex, I'm not sure of the *exact* reasons why you feel a need to be soldier. If I did, perhaps I could help you to renounce the life. Can you visualize yourself in any other profession? Why, sir, you renounced the landed gentry in order to become an ordinary foot soldier! The attraction was as strong as that!'

'True. I threw away comfort and status for

these now rather battered marching boots.'

'Therefore you must go for a soldier, or wither and die.'

He accepted her judgement. 'There must be other men like me?'

'Many. They are legion. The army is full of them. I just wonder whether — whether I . . . ' She stopped, realizing that she was about to say something which would leave her vulnerable.

He rescued her, gallantly. 'Whether you would wish to be good friends with one?'

'Precisely,' she breathed, grateful for the lesser charge.

The balmy evening was coming in. A mellow redness filled the western sky which washed into the smoky regions of high cirrus clouds. There were bats out now, diving for insects around the old tree. Bird calls could be heard amongst the scattered stones and clumps of trees. For once the cannons on the lines were silent. A sporting gun was being used, somewhere in the hills, but its hollow-sounding reports were more comforting than alarming. Perhaps that was Lovelace and Pirce-Smith, out bagging game birds? And a church bell was tolling, a long way off. It had none of the melodic notes of English bells ringing the changes, having a rather metallic tone, but it was doing its best to sound hopeful. Dogs barked, in the camp below, and the smell of stabled horses was heavy in the air.

There seemed to be a harmony about it all, which belied the general situation. It was difficult for Crossman to believe that men were desperately ill, even dying, not so very far away. There was still the spectre of cholera haunting the soldiery. Respiratory diseases, stomach complaints, and various other illnesses were carrying men off all the time. The surgeons and physicians did what they could, which was very little. Camp-following apothecaries and vendors of herbal cures, not to say purveyors of old wives's lore with their dead mice to hang round necks, and their black toads to put in sleeping socks, were all making a good living in the camps. The angel of death also visited, though less seldom than in her guise of sickness, in the form of lead and steel. There were skirmishes, little battles, still going on, even when the howitzers and mortars were silent. And of course, the omnipresent sharpshooter kept his toll mounting, day by day.

'You are thinking very hard,' said Jane. 'I can see the ploughman's furrows on your brow.'

'Oh. I was just — just being thankful for this lovely evening. A warrior appreciates beauty too, you know.' He might have added, *which is one of the reasons why you attract me so much*, but failed at the first fence.

'I must be getting back. Lavinia will be concerned for me.'

He snorted at the mention of Mrs Durham's name. 'Lavinia! Now there's a warrior for you. Had she been born a man she would be a general by now.'

'Had she been born a man,' repeated Jane, 'she would be dead, for she would surely have been at the front of the Light Brigade's charge on the Russian cannons. I accused you of seeking glory, which disturbed you. Had I accused Lavinia of the same, she would have considered it a compliment. My dear and precious friend Mrs Lavinia Durham is as excited by a battle as some women on being invited to a ball at the royal palace. She would rather watch a fight than dance a waltz, that much is certain. I love her dearly and do not mind speaking of her faults thus, for she does not regard them as faults at all, but considers them merits.'

Crossman agreed. 'She is beloved of the troops. They may quake before they go out to face the guns, but they are proud too, of doing their duty. If she does not tell them all personally that she thinks them heroes, her shining eyes after a battle reveal the feelings in her breast. I swear that many of them come off the battlefield and take a detour, just to get some praise from those eyes. Every war should have a Lavinia Durham. The men need to be praised. Lord knows they had little enough of it from Lord Raglan, though I'm sure their own colonels gave them their due.'

'Well, we have a new commander in chief now.'

'Not much better than the old one, I'm told,' said Crossman. 'I wonder if it is possible to get a good commander simply by appointing greybeards. Nelson and Wellington were not above middle age when they commanded over navy and army. For my money Sir Colin Campbell stands head and shoulders above the old men they keep sending us.'

And that was the problem, he thought, as the pair of them made their way down the slopes to the settlement below. The old men did not know when to step aside. His namesake, Alexander the Great, was barely out of his knee-breeches when he led his men to glory. Julius Caesar had earned many of his laurel wreaths by his thirties. On his forty-forth birthday an ambitious Mongol horse-warrior had defeated all his enemies and had proclaimed himself Genghis Khan, or 'Emperor of All'. Crossman did not know how old Tamerlane had been, when *his* Mongols destroyed most of central Asia, but he would wager the man had not been in his dotage. Rodrigo Diaz de Vivar, otherwise known as El Cid, was in his fourth decade when he defeated the Moors. Napoleon of course, damn his Corsican soul, had been in his twenties when he took the French army from the brink of defeat against the Austrians, to the first of many such victories under his generalship.

'Yet they keep sending us these doddery old clerks who cannot make a decision as to whether their breakfast eggs should be hard or soft.'

'I do beg your pardon?' said Jane, with an amused smile.

'Oh, sorry, was I speaking out loud? It was but a thought, really.'

'You often do. It's a good job you don't harbour any dark secrets. I should soon learn them all, Alexander.'

He laughed at that, linking arms with her to prevent her falling in the darkness, as they descended to the lights below.

7

Wynter had been sent with a message to Colonel Hawke just before dawn. He had left in a mood of thunder, having been woken from his sleep by Major Lovelace. There was not a lot of enjoyment stumbling over the dark ground at the rag end of the night and those who were awake could hear Wynter's grumbling until he was out of earshot.

Crossman rose from his bed as Lovelace fell into his. The sergeant went to the window and stared out over the unkempt terrain beyond Kadikoi village. The line of sight was broken by a mountain village called Karani. It was here, in April, that the Sardinian army had assembled: 15,000 of them, under General La Marmora. The Sardinians had settled in well, bothering no one, taking on their duties with little fuss. Alongside the British they looked fresh and smart. The British infantry were quite jealous of the Sardinian hats: broad-brimmed, with a sweeping feather and reminiscent of those of the Royalist cavaliers during the English Civil War. Dashing was the word that was used.

The landscape was bleak at this time of the

morning. It had rained during the night and as the light began to reveal the world in all its lack of glory Crossman could see how damp and depressing it all was. Animals were standing, shivering, four-square on their limbs: a cluster of horses in a corral, a solitary mule in a paddock, one or two camels wandering around mindlessly. Flapping tents dripped on a dull muddy earth. A tattered flag flapped in a desultory fashion from a home-made flag pole outside a colonel's residence. The sentry by his door was fast asleep on his feet, his rifle-musket used as a prop to keep him from falling flat on his face. A drunk, possibly a sailor, was curled up on a wooden step, the door closed firmly against him. Near to him a dog was labouring, chewing at the grey bone of some unidentifiable animal.

A troop of dragoons passed under the window, going out for some early morning exercise, their bridle rings and stirrups clinking. Some of the troopers appeared to be half asleep, though they were sitting tall in the saddle, looking quite smart in their tight uniforms. Here was another point of envy: irregulars all seemed to have loose, easy clothing, while regular soldiers were constricted by theirs.

'Come the revolution,' muttered Crossman, 'it will all change.'

Then he remembered, the French had had their revolution, and bloody and horrible it had been. Yet here they were, still in their shiny, tight uniforms, and their uncomfortable helmets, much the same as the British, whose kings and queens still slept safe in their beds.

It was a Wynter in a very different mood who came running back to the hovel with a message which he delivered with breathless speed. Crossman could hear everything from the room above.

'They've attacked — the Russians. Down by the Chernaya. We've to get Betsy and go off to drive 'em back.'

Peterson's sarcasm came naturally. 'Oh, right, the six of us will just march down there. Just the sight of us will be enough for the Russian army to take to their heels.'

'No, you nanny goat. Us, the Frogs and the Sardines.'

He seemed pleased at being clever enough to keep his references within the natural world.

Crossman came down the stairs, just as Peterson's incredulous question was being asked. He was aware that the French force on the Fedioukine Hills was around 18,000 men and nearly fifty guns. The Sardinians were on Mount Hasfort, 10,000 of them, with thirty-five guns, or thereabouts. There was also cavalry and horse artillery to support them. The British presence in that area was a single cavalry division under General Scarlett, the hero of the Heavy Brigade charge at Balaclava. No, he was wrong, there were other British soldiers in the area, or could be. The Reserve Artillery could be on the scene quite quickly.

'Who sent you, Wynter?'

'One of Colonel Hawke's men, sergeant. Told me to come and get you, and the rest of us. Said Lieutenant Percy-Smudge will meet us at the front.' Wynter looked keenly at Crossman, wondering if he would bite on the insolence. Crossman however was not going to play games at such a time. Pirce-Smith was old enough to be able to protect his own name. Wynter continued with, 'I've already sent for Stik and Betsy. They're comin' soon as the old girl's saddled and gunned. Stik's got a couple of his chums workin' with him. She's in a bad temper this morning, but Stik's takin' no nonsense.'

Crossman was as duly impressed by this forethought on the part of Wynter as he was expected to be.

'Well done, Wynter. You did the right thing. We'll get that stripe back for you one day.'

'Thanks, sergeant.'

'Did the colonel's man give you any idea of the size of the attack?'

'Said there was two divisions comin' against the Frogs and two against the Sardines. There may be more waitin' in the wings, he said. It's our chance to try out our secret weapon, he said, to drive the Ruskies back. He reckons Betsy will scare the pickled cabbage out of them.'

'You'd better go upstairs and tell the major what's happening. Did you get a reply to his message?'

'Couldn't, sergeant. The colonel weren't there. He was gone somewhere. His man wouldn't say.'

'All right then, up you go.'

Wynter rushed up the stone stairs, all his bad feelings for the major having evaporated with the excitement of the attack.

Crossman said to the others. 'Well, are you ready? Gwilliams?'

'Yes, sergeant. Ready and willin', if a mite unsure about being able. I've got this notion that Betsy will make a clear target on a hilltop, and they'll shoot her off it in a second. I can see them licking their fingers and wetting the sights on their weapons, soon as Betsy steps up. Unmissable, I reckon. I don't figure we'll last long.'

'Me neither,' Peterson chipped in. 'I don't

think Yorwarth's going to need to worry about his bad skin much longer. He won't have a skin by eight o'clock. None of us will.'

'Well, there's a cheery bunch for you,' chirped Major Lovelace, coming down the stairs ahead of Wynter. 'Just do your best. No one says you've got to be amongst the Forlorn Hope. In fact I would stay away from the bulk of the army. Work around the fringes. I'd like to come with you, but I'm ragged with lack of sleep. If I were you I'd make for the Traktir Bridge, over the Chernaya. That'll be the Russian objective, if I'm not mistaken. Well, good luck.'

Stik and Betsy arrived just a short while later. They set off at a fast pace for the bridge over the River Chernaya. The closer they got the louder were the sounds of battle. Betsy seemed to have got over her early morning grumps, but the noise of the guns began to make her edgy. Twice she stopped, like a mule, and refused to go on until Stik fed her with sugar lumps and whispered into her ear. Yorwarth sat behind the hump, looking awkward and vulnerable on the swaying beast. One could tell by his expression that he was not the happiest of men.

By the time they reached the battleground there had been a rather rash and impetuous attack by the Russians on the French breastworks. Some of the Russian infantry had crossed the river but an aqueduct impeded their further advance. Such were the vagaries of war that a structure possibly built by some ancient civilization should turn a contemporary battle. If it did not save the French from being overrun, it certainly assisted in their counterattack. There was a Tartar goatboy, sitting on top of the aqueduct, his legs dangling over the edge as if he were idly contemplating nature, rather than witnessing a battle on which the fate of nations depended. Certainly he had a marvellous view of the death and destruction, the mayhem and smoke of war, going on around him. He seemed rather indifferent to the fact that the French began to push the Russians back from whence they came. It was as if the fighting were somehow quite unconnected with him. He was a disinterested spectator.

Crossman and his *peloton* were just in time to see the French make a bayonet charge to drive the Russians back across the river in great confusion. The light was coming down sharply now, flashing on the forest of bayonets wielded by blue soldiers. Everywhere was the glint and glitter of shiny metal, like evanescent stars upon the ground. There was a dull boom following in the wake of a shrill whistling, as a missile went over the heads of the *peloton*. Crossman looked keenly through his glass and found a Russian light battery to the east. However, after that one shot at the zumbooruck, the light battery was attacked by some allied thirty-two-pounders and forced to retire. The Russian heavy artillery seemed to be outside the range of the allied guns however, for it continued to throw its weight around.

'Pity we haven't got a long-barrelled eighteen-pounder, instead of this small swivel,' said Crossman to Ali, who had been sent to join them by Major Lovelace. 'An eighteen would reach those Russian guns.'

'I think Betsy would make the complaint,' said Ali. 'The recoil would throw her on her back.'

'Of course it would, but I can wish.'

The air was full of the shrieks of wounded men, as desperate struggles took place on the water's edge. Musket and cannon were blasting out into the mild morning. Balls, large and small, were flying everywhere. Mortar and howitzer shells burst in the sky as rockets fizzed through the flying shrapnel. Yells and shouts added to the cacophony. Urgent bugles sounded, drummers drummed out advances and retreats. The heaving waves of men, flowing back and forth, the sweet smell of blood in the breeze, the harsh odour of spent and burning gunpowder, the clashing of metal on metal, the grunts, the groans, the moans, the screams of wounded and dying horses.

All this served to make Betsy less than happy with her first real action, her first proper battle. It happened then that a battalion of Piedmontese advanced on the Russians in good order. The Sardinians appeared to march as if on parade, supported by a company of Sardinian Bersaglieri. This assault was making inroads into the Russians, though the soldiers were tripping over scaling ladders left by the enemy.

Then one of several Russian ammunition wagons exploded.

Betsy immediately defecated to illustrate the fact that she was concerned by the situation. It seemed that she was aware she was going to make a clear target for the enemy, for she went down on all fours and refused to get off her knees, remaining hunched into the landscape. They did their best to get her to her feet, Stik helping them against his better judgement. She was adamant. Now she was down, she was going to stay down, and let those whizz-bangs go over her head, not through it. To emphasize her stand she bit Gwilliams on the shoulder and spat a wad into Ali's face.

When Peterson tried to lift her by her tail she rewarded the soldier with an enormous fart that would have lifted an oak from its roots.

Finally, they gave up, and let her be.

'Sergeant!' cried Yorwarth. 'Can I get off?'

Crossman shook his head. 'No, if we can't get her to stand up again, then you'll have to fire the swivel from there. Stik? Will she not rise? What's the matter with her? Is she afraid?'

'Camel is afraid, Stik is afraid,' said the boy. 'Can we go back now, sergeant?'

'No, we must do what we came to do,' said Crossman, firmly. 'We are soldiers and this is what soldiers do.'

'I am no soldier,' said Stik, stubbornly. 'My camel is no soldier.'

'You are being paid by the army and you will do the army's work.'

'Not very much,' argued Peterson for the boy. 'A pittance really.'

'We're all being paid a pittance,' Gwilliams argued. 'A few English pence.'

'Peterson, Gwilliams,' said the frustrated Crossman, 'I could do without your intervention.'

While they were thus talking a small boy came running up the slope dragging a drum behind him. He was in a French uniform. His eyes were like coins and there was clearly terror in his head and heart. He tried to rush by Crossman who reached out and grasped his collar. The boy struggled, kicking and scratching, until Crossman lifted him off his feet, drum and all. He stared into the child's face.

'Where are you off to?' Crossman asked him in French.

The child wriggled some more, then gave up, hanging limply from the sergeant's grip. He burst into a fit of sobbing, wiping his eyes on his left sleeve.

'I don't want to fight,' he said. 'My drum major is — is . . . '

'Has he been killed?'

'Yes.' The boy turned his head, awkwardly, looking back down the slope. 'He — he fell. I looked and there was blood on his chest. I must go now, back to the camp.'

He seemed calmer and Crossman set him on his feet. The boy immediately reached up and grasped Crossman by his beard, not so that it hurt, but firmly. It was obviously a gesture of affection, for the boy continued to hold on to it, even when Crossman gently pulled back with his head.

'Why are you doing that, boy?' he asked.

'I — I do this with my grandfather.'

'I am not your grandfather.' But he could see that it gave the child some sort of

318

comfort, so he stood there and allowed it. The *peloton* chuckled, not knowing what was being said, but clearly enjoying the sergeant's embarrassment.

Crossman went down to the boy's level, still being held by his beard, and looked into the child's eyes.

'How old are you?'

'Eleven, sir.'

'Where are your from?'

'From my parents' village.'

Crossman nodded. 'And where is that?'

'Near the great port of Calais,' said the boy with some pride in his voice.

'Then we are practically neighbours, for I live just across the water, on the other side of La Manche. Listen, child — what is your name?'

'Emile, sir.'

'Listen, Emile, if you run from the battle it is called 'deserting' and they might shoot you for it. Do you understand? You must go back down there . . . ' Panic showed in the child's face, but Crossman, despite the agony of feeling he had in his chest, knew that the drummer boy had to do his duty or face punishment. There was no other way but the army way. Some kind colonel might understand, but there were plenty who would not. 'You must go back down there and help with the wounded. Take off your drum and if the Russians come, then you can run, but if your soldiers are forcing them back you must tend to those who have fallen. Stay at the back, no one will fault you for that, but you must not run away.'

'Yes, sir.' The child made no attempt to let go of Crossman's beard.

'Emile, I can see great courage in your eyes. You are a soldier, aren't you? One of the brave French army?'

'Oh, yes sir!'

'I can see that. Well then, Emile, off you go, back down to that place over there — see — where your bandsmen are taking the wounded. Go down there and give some water to the men sitting on the ground. That would be a very brave thing to do, wouldn't it?'

The beard was relinquished at last. 'Yes, sir.'

'Go then. Take your drum.'

The boy trotted off, down the slope, the trailing drum banging on the ground behind him. Crossman saw Emile reach the spot where the wounded were being gathered and the surgeons were striding about. He unhitched his drum and ran to where a bugler was handing out water bottles. Taking one he hastened to a man whose right arm was missing. The wounded man drank the water, apparently grateful. Emile looked up and waved. Crossman waved back, gravely, his amused men smiling at him the whole while.

At that moment Mrs Durham rode up, her face alight. The contrast between the expression on her face and the one that had been on the French boy's face was remarkable. Hers was full of joy, while his had been an overwhelming fear. One would have thought Mrs Lavinia Durham had been informed that a flock of pink flamingos had descended on the River Chernaya bearing humming birds on their backs and that she was a great ornithologist, amazed at the sight. What was amazing her, exciting her, bringing her lovely features alive, was the sight of hostile conflict between two colourful European armies. The lady revelled in it. Her normally cream complexion was bright with heightened hues and her eyes shone. In an unnatural voice she asked who was winning, where were the British cavalry, the darlings of her heart, and had they charged the enemy yet?

At that precise moment however Crossman's attention was taken by a movement below. Several Russian columns, a whole division by the look of it, detached itself from the attack on Mount Hasfort and the Sardinians and turned towards the French. A brigade of Russian infantry then managed to ford the river and assaulted the right flank of the French position, beating them back and this time the aqueduct presented no barrier to them. The French began to suffer badly, much to the chagrin of the British lady watching from the top of the slope above them. Crossman was pleased to see that Emile had sensibly stayed with the bandsmen, who were off to the rear left and not in any great danger at that moment, the attack coming from the right of the line.

'Oh, oh,' cried Lavinia Durham. 'Are you to do something to help them, sergeant? Fire on the enemy. Help our brave comrades in arms.'

'Yes general,' replied Crossman through gritted teeth. 'Yorwarth, you heard the commander in chief. Fire at the enemy.'

With Betsy still determined to remain on her knees, Yorwarth fired a ball down amongst the Russians. No one saw it strike. Betsy remained remarkably calm. Ali reloaded and Yorwarth fired another. This time it struck a body of infantry and a space appeared in a Russian column. A cheer went up from the *peloton*. Crossman nodded, approvingly.

'That's the stuff, Yorwarth. Give them another one.'

'I think we're making an impact on the battle,' said Yorwarth, after a few more like it. 'See, they're retreating, sergeant.'

The Russians were going back, but it was not Betsy's artillery that was responsible of course. The Sardinians were now descending from Mount Hasfort and were attacking the Russians with fierce courage and great vigour, driving into the enemy flank and forcing the broken column back across the river again. This action by the Sardinians seemed to infuriate the Russian generals, and they renewed their attacks on the Fedioukine Hills, where a terrible slaughter began in earnest.

'Help them, help them!' cried Lavinia Durham.

'Madam,' said Crossman, taking the reins of her horse, 'if you do not retire immediately and ride off from here, out of danger, I shall be forced to order one of my men to drag you away.'

'Oh — you would not. You could not, Alex. You owe me much, you know, and I'm sure you would not insist on my going if you knew how I feel about supporting our troops.'

'I certainly would and shall, if you do not gallop out of range of those musket balls immediately.'

Indeed, there were shots almost reaching

them now, dropping amongst the grasses just in front. Most of them were spent by the time they fell to earth, but just the same Crossman had a horror of Lavinia being hit. It would do his career no good at all to have to tell Captain Bertie Durham that his wife had been wounded or killed within an arm's reach of an infantry sergeant. Bertie would not understand at all when told that Lavinia Durham was not in the habit of taking notice of ex-lovers, gentlemen such as Alexander Kirk, alias Sergeant Jack Crossman, and in fact used her hold over them to get what she wanted at times like these.

'Sergeant,' she cried, imperiously, 'you have no authority . . . '

'Gwilliams, get rid of the woman,' snarled Crossman, having had enough of her now. 'I don't care how you do it.'

Lavinia Durham gave out a little gasp, wheeled her horse, and rode away in great indignation.

Thus 'rid of the woman' Crossman could now concentrate on the ebb and flow of the battle. He could now see the British cavalry, one troop of which had detached itself, fire a few half-hearted shots at the enemy, then retired again. The Russians were now having a bad time of it and began to retreat in some confusion. This seemed to be the signal which

Betsy was awaiting. She rose to her feet and began to advance, with an excited Yorwarth firing from her hump. The others walked behind, guarding her flanks against any attack from splinter groups of the Russian army. Soon she had reached the water's edge, only to wade in up to her belly. In the middle of the river, about four feet deep at that particular crossing, she planted herself. Shots began to splash around her on the surface, but she was not deterred. She continued to hold her central position, while Yorwarth employed the gun to some effect.

The field was littered with dead and dying Russians. It was indeed a carnage. Prince Gortchakoff's attempt at breaking through had failed and he and his troops retired to the wooded heights where the allied cavalry could not get at them.

'Well, I reckon Betsy showed them Russ a thing or two,' said Gwilliams, as the *peloton* made its way back to Kadikoi, feeling pleased with themselves. 'Once she stood up, she showed 'em, all right.'

'I bet Colonel Hawke is going to be happy with us,' said Peterson. 'I shouldn't wonder, anyway.'

Crossman was summoned to the colonel's office the very next day. The sergeant got himself up as smart as possible under the circumstances and went along expecting some high praise for the morning's work, having already sent a written report to the colonel. He did not exactly approve of Hawke's desire to further his ambitions through a camel, but was quite willing to take any merit for his actions in that direction.

The colonel looked up as he entered and Crossman felt himself under a distinctly chilly gaze. He was puzzled by this, but considered the colonel had other things on his mind, besides Betsy. Hawke was responsible for any number of subversive actions and it only took one to go wrong for him to be answering awkward questions. The colonel then turned his attention to his desk top and proceeded to shuffle through papers, until it became impossible for Crossman not to open the conversation.

'What were the casualties yesterday, colonel?' asked Crossman. 'If you don't mind me asking.'

'Casualties? Oh, the figures,' said the colonel, vaguely. 'I'm told the Russians lost eight thousand men.'

'And our side?'

'Our side? You mean the French? Over a thousand, maybe more. The Sardinians lost only two hundred and fifty.' The colonel looked up again now. 'All in all the Russians were repulsed with vigour, I believe. General Pélissier regards it as a victory for the allies. I'm sure he's right. And you did very well, sergeant, by all accounts. Good work.'

'Thank you, sir.'

'Unfortunately,' the colonel now looked away again, 'something has come to my notice which disturbs me greatly. I am disappointed in you, sergeant, but unless you can offer me a reasonable explanation I shall have to take those stripes away from you.'

'Sir?' Crossman was stunned.

'I'm demoting you to private, Crossman.'

'I — I don't understand.'

Hawke rose to his feet and paced the back of the room, his hands clasped behind his back.

'You know a Captain Campbell of the 93rd?'

Crossman felt his stomach descend to his boots. His sins had caught up with him at last. Did he ever think he could get away with it? Some men would have, but not he. Even as a child his misdemeanours found him out.

'Yes — yes, I know him.'

'You impersonated an officer in order to play him at cards?'

At least it seemed that the abduction was not being put down to him, which was one good thing. For that he would have been flogged, at the very least. In point of fact he had had no hand in that plot. Still, his mind was in a whirl. He felt sick to the pit of his stomach. To lose his stripes! They were not much, it was true, in the grand scheme of things. He was no general. But they had been hard won. It would take years now, to get them back again, if ever he managed it!

'I am guilty, colonel. May I explain?'

'If you will,' said the colonel, eagerly. 'I dislike this situation intensely.'

'It will probably make no difference, in the end, because I did indeed put on the uniform of a lieutenant and pose as another man. My brother was a lieutenant in the 93rd at the time . . . '

The colonel snatched at this eagerly. 'You wore your brother's uniform? You were in expectation of purchasing your commission? To see how it would be if ever you were promoted?'

'No, sir, I did not. I wore the uniform of another man in order to win back the fortune my brother had lost to Captain Campbell at cards. I'm sure you must be aware that the captain is a gambler, sir? My older brother is unfortunately very gullible — a good man, but easily influenced — and Captain Campbell took advantage of that fact.'

Hawke's face became very grim. 'You are

accusing Campbell of cheating?'

'No, I am not. I am accusing him of drawing raw players to his table and fleecing them without regard to the damage he causes. Captain Campbell is no doubt a very skilful player, a man with great experience at cards and one on whom Lady Fortune smiles much of the time. I put it down to talent and good luck on his part, having no evidence of any deviousness. Yet men like him are not without guilt, for they ruin others without troubling their conscience. It was not my brother's money to lose, not yet, my father still being alive and well. I knew the captain would not play a lowly sergeant at cards, so I put on an officer's uniform.'

Hawke shook his head, sadly. 'What a pity the man is not a cheat. That would have been something to use in our favour. But there is no law which states an officer may not play at cards, whereas there is certainly one which prevents a sergeant from impersonating a lieutenant.'

'I would be wrong to accuse him.'

'Of course, of course. Oh, sergeant. I had such high hopes for you — for both of us.'

'I am very sorry, sir. The incident happened while General Buller was still here. No blame can be attached to you.' Crossman was so distressed he could not speak without a catch in his voice. The colonel could see how he had plunged his protégé into despair and therefore forgave him for what he said next. 'I must ask you, sir, whether you have the authority to take my stripes from me?'

'You mean because you are officially of the 88th Foot? The colonel of the Connaught Rangers has given me power over your career, Crossman. Would you rather the demotion came from him? I am quite willing to hand the matter over to him, if you prefer. The outcome will be no different I can assure you. Perhaps he would require a more severe punishment. It would still be an ill wind, if coming from a different quarter.' The colonel's tone was not unkind.

'I am happy for it to be handled by you, sir.'

Hawke sighed, deeply. He picked up a bunch of papers and then dumped them back down on the desk again.

'The problem we have now, is how to proceed with your *peloton*. Who is to take charge? I am reluctant to bring in another sergeant. It would not do at this stage. He would not fit. Yet, there does not seem to be anyone in the *peloton* at the moment who would be worthy of a sergeant's stripes, or indeed, who could lead the group as well as you have done. Yet we must have someone in charge.'

'What — what about the lieutenant, sir?'

'I have offered the position to Lieutenant Pirce-Smith, but he has declined. Of course, I could order him, but I am loath to do so. I prefer to have men about me who take to their tasks willingly. This is not a line regiment, this is clandestine work.'

Crossman's mind was in a whirl, but he was puzzled by this behaviour on the part of Lieutenant Pirce-Smith. Even in his distress he felt irked by this rejection. It added to his bitterness.

'May I enquire as to the reason for the lieutenant's refusal to take over my *peloton?*'

The reply was enough to shock Crossman into remorse.

'The lieutenant believes you are the best, possibly the only man for the job, Crossman. He argued vehemently that we should keep you in your post. I would be inclined to do so if Campbell were not so influential. He has one cousin in parliament and another in the admiralty, both with loud voices. My hands are forced. I can assure you that you would have received a much more severe punishment — a flogging, or even a term in the stockade would not be excessive for such a crime — had I not used my *own* influence in

331

the matter. But your stripes are forfeit, and must remain so. Of course, if in the future you should do some great deed, demanding that we restore you to your rightful position, then those voices might grow a little quieter.'

'I fully understand, colonel.'

Hawke, normally a man of iron features, softened for a moment before Crossman's eyes.

'It's hard, Crossman. Very hard. I can see your misery and it touches me. However, you are a tough soldier. You can bear this. There may be a battle coming soon. If you were to distinguish yourself . . . ?'

'Yes, sir. Thank you, sir. With regard to our present situation, may I suggest that Yusuf Ali takes command?'

'A Turk — over British soldiers? It would be unusual.'

'He is used to command.'

'I will consider it. Tell your men I will inform them later this morning what is to be done.'

'Yes, sir.'

'That will be all, serg . . . soldier.'

Once outside, Crossman gulped down air. A hot sun beat on his head from above. He felt giddy and weak. The shame of it! His father would be mortified. Bad enough to have a son who was merely a sergeant

— appalling to have him stripped of that lowly rank for a misdemeanour.

And now there was the *peloton* to face. How Wynter would crow! Yet the news had to be broken. And Crossman was the one who had to do it.

Crossman trudged back towards the hovel at Kadikoi. His legs felt as if they contained plumbum. His heart was leaden too. For some reason his body ached, physically, as if he had sustained a beating. He guessed this was the result of the shock of the bad news. What a terrible thing! Yet he had known the risks, when he had donned that uniform. Campbell had at last recognized him. It was just like the man to demand his pound of flesh, even though he had beaten Crossman that night and taken a sizeable amount of silver coins from him: prize money earned in a raid against the Cossacks. It was certain that he would not return the money, even though his *principles* had spurred him to take the stripes from the sergeant's arm. The captain was a double winner, humbling his opponent twice over. Campbell was the worst kind of officer. One who used the service as an arena in which to play his own games. Still, Crossman had ventured his arm and the consequences had finally caught up with him.

Gathering his strength together, he went

through the doorway of the hovel, to give the news to his *peloton*.

Once he had delivered it, he sat on the edge of Yorwarth's cot and stared at the floor. As he had expected there was silence for a while. The *peloton* needed time to take it all in. They stood or sat around the room and hardly a breath could be heard. Finally it was Peterson who spoke.

'You mean, you're the same as us now?'

'Not the same as you, Peterson — as a lance-corporal you outrank me.'

He felt utterly depressed. There was nothing any of them could say to lift him at that moment. Gwilliams said as far as he was concerned Crossman was still the leader and what did a set of stripes matter. Ali merely shrugged and spat through the doorway, signifying that he agreed with Gwilliams. Yorwarth began scratching his eczema, muttering something like, 'The army giveth and the army taketh away.' Wynter said nothing at all. Instead he reached under his cot and took out his knapsack. He removed something from the knapsack and walked over to Crossman, tossing the item on the blanket beside the ex-sergeant. It was a pocket-knife.

'You'll need somethin' to cut them stitches, when you take off the stripes,' said Wynter.

'Then after you've done it, I'll see you outside, behind the lean-to.'

'Oh for the Lord's sake, Wynter!' exclaimed Peterson. 'You've got the brains of a donkey.'

'You watch it too, hoyden. You an't got the sergeant to protect you now.'

'No,' said Yorwarth, quietly, 'but she's got me, pom. I'll stand up for her, when you like.'

Yorwarth was younger and less worldly than Wynter, but he was a lot bigger and stronger. Yorwarth had been raised on Australian sheep farms and had worked with heavy horses all his life and his forearms were thick and meaty. Wynter had always known that Yorwarth would make a formidable opponent in a bout of bare-fist fighting.

'I got no argument with you, Yorwarth. My beef is with this toffee-nosed toad here. He had me flogged.'

'That's a lie, Wynter,' said Crossman, finding these barrack-room politics sordid and dreary, 'and you know it.'

Crossman looked up into the mean, hard eyes of Harry Wynter. Son of an Essex farmer, Wynter was a forest bodger by trade, and wiry strong. He clearly felt there were several scores to settle. Sizing him up and down, for the first time assessing Wynter's ability to fight with his fists, Crossman saw a grim lean man with knotted muscles. The sort of man who could punch hard and fast, but with little weight behind the blows. Wynter relied on pummelling his opponent into submission within a few minutes, his arms going like steam-engine pistons, his small but flint-hard fists causing specific damage to the eyes, kidneys and genitals. He knew where to aim and did not stop raining hits until his adversary was on the ground, where he proceeded to kick him into unconsciousness if the those around let him.

Crossman on the other hand had had very little experience at bare-fist fighting. He was not like Jarrard, who had punched his way through school and beyond. He was not a man like Lovelace, who was a keen boxer. At Harrow the bullies had left him alone because of his ability with the fencing foil and the universal admiration that came from such a skill. He had not the temperament to raise his blood to fighting heat within seconds, as some men had, and found himself talking rather than fighting when it came to the point. He could count the number of serious fistfights he had been forced into on two fingers. One he had been left on the floor with a black eye, the other he had been the one still standing. They had been brief, confused affairs. Both had left him feeling flat.

'Wynter, I have not the spirit at the moment to thrash you. It would give me no satisfaction whatsoever to knock your head from your shoulders. Choose a better time. I have just lost something which took me a great deal of time and effort to gain. I have not the heart to mill it with some idiot behind the lean-to.'

Wynter sneered and kicked Crossman's foot. 'Scared, eh?'

Ali walked across the room and was about to slap Wynter's face with his large open hand, when Crossman said, 'No — no. The man feels he has a grievance.' Raising anger from cold had always been Crossman's problem in these cases, but there is nothing like a violent blow to stir a man's blood and heat it to boiling point. 'Wynter, do not kick me again, ever. If you do, I shall be forced to give you satisfaction.'

Wynter stepped back, he believed out of reach, and spat at him. The gobbet struck Crossman's brow. Crossman flash-fired and was on his feet in an instant. The ex-sergeant was almost a head taller than the other soldier and his reach was consequently long. He delivered a facer that sent the unprepared Wynter reeling backwards across the floor. The punch was a snake-like strike with a good deal of shoulder behind it. Wynter had

337

not been prepared for the speed of the blow and had taken the fist plumb in the centre of his features. His nose split and splayed. Blood gushed forth. He found himself broken, dazed and confused, lying in the doorway of the hovel as Lieutenant Pirce-Smith arrived. The lieutenant stepped over Wynter, looking down with mild interest as the groggy soldier tried to shake his head free of pain.

'Old scores being settled, I see,' said Pirce-Smith. That was all he spoke on the matter. He then addressed Crossman and the room in general. 'Crossman, I am sorry to hear about your problems. You have done good work in the past. I hope things improve for you in the future. Now, as for the leadership of this *peloton*, Colonel Hawke has asked me take over. I must admit I was reluctant at first, but on reflection — remembering the good work we have done together — I decided to accept the colonel's offer. Crossman, you will remove your bedding from Captain Lovelace's room. I shall be sleeping there in future. You will join the other men, down here. I acknowledge there's not a great deal of room, but you will make space for the extra man. Any questions?'

'When are we going out again, sir?' asked Crossman.

'As soon as I receive instructions from

Colonel Hawke,' came the reply. The officer realized that Crossman, in his spiritual agony, needed to be doing something. It was better to be out in the field than moping around the barracks. 'There will be a kit inspection at three o'clock this afternoon. I shall be the inspecting officer. Who's the senior rank here now?'

Everyone looked at Peterson, who went bright pink.

'Corporal Peterson, you are responsible for getting the men into a state of readiness for my inspection. That will be all.'

Wynter was standing, leaning against the doorjamb, holding his nose. Pirce-Smith glanced at him as he passed, saying, 'Clean the claret from your shirt, Wynter, before this afternoon.'

'Oh, yes, sir, thank you, sir,' muttered Wynter when the lieutenant was out of earshot. 'Never mind I'm bloody injured.' He glared at Crossman. 'My nose is broke. It hurts like buggery, you bastard.'

Crossman said nothing to him, not even looking up, but Peterson remarked, 'You brought it on yourself, Wynter. And see here, if you disrupt my *peloton* again, I'll have you on report. I don't care if they flog you again. I'd like it. I think you're a bloody pig.'

Wynter's eyes went wide and round. '*Your peloton?*'

'That's right, I'm the senior non-commissioned officer here and you'll do what I say or I'll report you to Lieutenant Pirce-Smith for disobedience and insolence in the face of duty. See, if you'd have had the sense of a mole you'd have kept your stripe and you'd have been the one in charge. Instead it's me who's the heavy horse here now and you'll do as you're told like any soldier. I've a good mind to request you go back to the trenches with the rest of the regiment, and we'll get someone who appreciates the advantages of being with us.'

'How about I tell our brigade commander that you're a woman?' said Wynter. 'How long would you be in charge then?'

Ali said softly, 'You do that, Wynter, and I cut your throat.'

The threat was not an idle one. Wynter looked around him at the other men, whose glares told him all he needed to know.

'Blood and fuckin' custard!' he cried, taking off his shirt and flinging it on to his bed in a great temper. 'I'm a widower, I am. No one ever feels sorry for me. He just lost a few stripes. I lost my wife. You bastards. I'll get even one day, you see if I don't. I'll burn the fuckin' lot of you in your beds.'

'The trenches!' warned Peterson, grimly. And as if she had been a leader all her life, 'I shall have to recommend it to the officer, if you don't follow discipline.'

Wynter stormed outside, barechested. They heard him at a nearby horse trough, splashing, presumably washing his bloodied face. When he came back he had calmed down a little. He swept the room with a contemptuous glare and then settled on his cot to sew a hole in his shirt. In the meantime Crossman fetched his kit from the upstairs room and found himself a place on the floor, by the old stove. The stove was not used in the summer, even for cooking, which was best done outside where the breeze could take the smoke and heat away. Once winter came around again, if they were still here, he would have to find a new place to bed down.

Gwilliams came to him and said quietly, 'You can have my bed, sergeant.'

'Call me by my name, now, Gwilliams. I thank you, but this will be fine.' He placed his belongings at the bottom of the blanket. 'I suppose I'd better get the pipe clay out . . . '

The men, and one woman, spent the evening cleaning their kit. As always they paid particular attention to their weapons. Wynter remained silent throughout. At half-past ten Major Lovelace entered the hovel. He went straight upstairs without glancing at Crossman. A short time later he called down and requested Crossman's presence. The ex-sergeant climbed the stairs, dreading the meeting. It was not that Lovelace would be censorious, but Crossman dreaded any show of sympathy. He wanted to be left alone with his misery and he had expected Lovelace to understand that. They were both from the same kind of background. Men of their stamp had an unreasonable pride, a great horror of appearing to demand pity.

He need not have worried. Any sympathy Lovelace felt was hidden beneath a layer of reserve as formidable as any suit of armour. He motioned Crossman to stand at ease.

'The colonel has of course appraised me of the situation. How do you feel about Lieutenant Pirce-Smith assuming command of your rangers?'

'The lieutenant is a very good man, sir. I had not thought so at first, but I was wrong.'

'I'm glad you think that. I think it too. Have you cleared out your kit? Yes, I see you have. This must be greatly annoying for you, but as the lieutenant said, this has nothing to do with your ability as a soldier. I shall remember that and I hope you will too. It may or may not be of some consolation to learn that I would have done exactly the same thing in your place. Family first was always the Lovelace motto. One doesn't leave one's brother to the sharks. That will be all, Crossman.'

'Yes, sir. Thank you, sir.'

He descended the stairs with a feeling of great relief. The major had come close to saying he was sorry, but he had not actually uttered the words.

Crossman bedded down early. Gwilliams and Yorwarth sat up late, talking in low voices to one another. Wynter went out, but came back before midnight, knowing that he needed a clear head for the morning inspection. Peterson went round and studied the state of her kingdom before going to bed herself. Yusuf Ali had gone out early. Crossman was fearful the Turk might try to settle accounts with Campbell, but he could not control the Bashi-Bazouk's every waking minute.

One thing Crossman was good at was sleeping. Even in his darkest hours he had always been able to put his head down and enter the realms of the unconscious. There was the misery of waking, of course, but at least he was not raggedly overtired. Everyone was up at dawn, laying out their kit. Peterson, aware that she needed to be seen to be fair, especially by Wynter, ordered Crossman to go out for the water. Crossman took the small barrel they used to store their water and, under a smirk from Wynter, went out and fetched the water from a nearby tank. While he was filling the barrel there was a commotion outside Jonnie Bread's. It took but a few seconds to go and investigate. When he returned he had some news for Wynter.

'Wynter?' Crossman said, after humping the barrel across the room and placing it near the stair well. 'I've got something to tell you.'

Wynter stood and squared his shoulders, thinking they were going to finish the fight started the previous evening.

'What?'

'I'm happy to inform you that they've found Charlie Dobson.'

Wynter's eyes widened. He snatched his gleaming bayonet from his blanket, where he had been polishing the blade.

'Where is he?'

'You wouldn't recognize him,' said Crossman, 'but Jonnie Bread assures me that it is Dobson. He recognizes Dobson's waistcoat. The corpse is bloated and horrible to view, but if you wish you can go and see it. They fished it out of the waterhole at the back of Jonnie's place just ten minutes ago. You may recall the water was getting low in the hole?

Well it became low enough to reveal the drowned body.'

Wynter shook his head. 'How did it stay down?'

'Apparently the man had weapons all over him, just as Ali does. Knives, pistols, a remarkable amount of ammunition. Charlie Dobson was a walking arsenal. A weighty fellow with all that iron on him. He must have struck and killed your wife. Afterwards, realizing what he had done he leapt through the back window and made off into the night, running straight into the waterhole. Like most of our sailors, he probably couldn't swim, and if the stories are correct, he was drunk. No one will ever know for certain what happened, but if he gave any cries they were not heard — not surprising considering the amount of noise that issues from Jonnie Bread's establishment in the early hours.'

'Dead,' said Wynter, lost in amazement. 'Dead an' no chance of me takin' his life a second time.'

'You will have to be satisfied that your revenge was carried out by the elements, Wynter, and be glad you avoid the gallows yourself.'

'He was a murderer, sure.'

'But not a tried and convicted one, and you are no paid state executioner, Harry.'

A look of indignation came over Wynter's face.

'Here,' he cried, 'who said you could call me Harry?'

'I can call you what I like now that I'm no longer a sergeant, Harry boy. Providing it's not insulting of course, otherwise we'd have to go to the fists again, wouldn't we? I take it you're not insulted by your Christian name?'

'No, o' course I an't.'

'Well, then — and feel free to call me Jack whenever you like.'

Crossman's delivery was so nonchalant and casual that he caught Wynter off guard. Wynter was looking for the catch the whole time. When he saw there was none, the humour of the situation finally got through to the Essex farm boy. Wynter suddenly grinned and nodded at Crossman.

'He's a card, eh? What? I'll be buggered if he an't. Now look, I'm off out to see Charlie. I want to poke him with a stick to make sure he's dead. Bloated, eh? I want to make him wobble like a jelly on a plate. Anyone want to come and watch?'

'I'll come,' said Yorwarth. 'I've never seen a man drowned away.'

The pair of them left, quickly, for the inspection was due in a short time.

'Ghouls, the pair of them,' muttered

Crossman. 'You think he would be satisfied with knowing his wife's killer has met his just end. But no, he needs to sate his lust.'

The gruesome pair made it back just in time for the inspection, which was thankfully just a formality. Pirce-Smith had to mark the beginning of his leadership in some way and this was as good as any. No one was brought to task, but they had to stand and listen to a little speech, about how things would be different now, not better, not worse, simply different, there being another man in charge. They listened politely, as one would to a vicar's sermon, the words going in one ear and out of the other. Once it was all over, Pirce-Smith ordered Yorwarth and Wynter to collect his kit and carry it upstairs for him. After this had been done and the officer was left to do his unpacking, Wynter and Yorwarth regaled the barrack room with the details of the drowned man.

'You could 'ave rolled him to his grave,' said Wynter, 'like a bloody great bladder full of piss. He sort of sloshed and wobbled when you kicked him, squirtin' out of his mouth and nose. You should have seen Jonnie's face. I mean, he's bin drinkin' the water all that time — 'is customers too! Bin making stews and soups, as well as bev'ridges. They've been havin' Charlie Dobson for supper every night.'

Peterson's face twisted into a mask.

'I don't need to listen to this.'

Yorwarth's description of the corpse was nothing short of gruesome, he described the exact pallor of the skin, the spongy consistency of the flesh, the way the teeth fell out of its mouth when Wynter prised open the jaws with his poking stick. It was a sight Yorwarth would never forget. Something to tell his grandkiddies, God willing he had some, one day in a long future.

'I'm sure your grandchildren will thank you for it,' Crossman said, 'when they wake screaming from their nightmares.'

Later that day, Crossman's duties left him free to visit Jane. He went to see her determined to get the ugly news over with. Things were actually no worse than they ever had been, since a sergeant is no more able to ask for the hand of a lady than a private. However, he had *felt* a little more worthy of her attention when the stripes were on his arm. He looked at the patch where one set had been. The cloth had been protected and was much newer, the redness of the colour stark against the rest of the faded sleeve. She could not fail to notice they had gone, the moment she set eyes on him. He need say nothing, but simply stand there.

As fortune would have it, when he knocked on the door of the hut which she shared with Lavinia Durham and her husband, it was the married lady who answered. Lavinia smiled into his face.

'Why Alex, that is to say, Jack. Do you call for Jane? She has presently gone to Vanity Fair, but will return shortly.'

Crossman stood there, waiting for the comment which never came. When he gave no reply to Lavinia's question, a puzzled frown crossed her brow. They remained staring at one another for a moment, then she invited Crossman in, stepping aside to let him enter.

'Is your husband not at home?'

'No, he is out doing something with his stores. You have no need of concern. He will be away until late this evening. You know how I approve of this match between you and Jane. I must do all I can to nurture it. Jane tells me you are a slow top, but I convinced her that you would eventually come up to scratch. My mother always said . . . '

'Damn your mother,' said an anguished Crossman, irritated beyond reason by this chatter, 'I've been stripped of my rank, Lavinia!'

Her face lost its colour for a moment, but it soon returned.

'Dear Alex, I am sorry, but it was not much to lose, was it?'

'It meant a great deal to me.'

She stared at the bare patch on his right sleeve, noticing it for the very first time. 'I know, and I never understood why, but then I am only a woman. These things are beyond the ken of mere females. Bertie forever grieves that he will never make colonel. I am happy to be the wife of a captain, for colonels are never at home, having responsibilities which take them abroad at all hours. This does not trouble me at the moment, but it will once we begin a family — but you are about to be vexed with me again, I can see it in your eyes. Dear Alex, I am truly sorry, but you know it will make no difference to the way Jane feels. It is you she loves, not Sergeant Crossman of the 88th Connaught Rangers.'

He relaxed a little, entering the hut and, managing to feel wicked, sat down in Bertie's favourite chair. In truth it was only a rattanwork chair and coming to pieces at that. He took off his forage cap and fanned his face with it.

'I'm sorry, Lavinia. I should not have snapped. It really is neither here nor there, is

350

it? I have lost my rank and there's an end to it. One of the consequences of having done so is the fact that I shall not be as free as I was. As leader of the *peloton*, I was able to manage my own time. Now my time will be managed for me. I shall be able to get away, on the odd occasion, but there is an officer above me to please now.'

Lavinia was wearing an incredibly white dress. She looked obscenely pure and Crossman was at a loss to know how she managed to look like an alabaster goddess in a place where filth was ubiquitous. It seemed wrong somehow. She appeared to cross the room on castors, her feet out of sight beneath the hem of the dress. Reaching his chair she stood beside it, her hand on his shoulder, in a gesture of comfort.

'Surely you had officers to please before now?'

'That's true, but to a great extent I was my own general. That's all finished. I am at the beck and call of everyone in the army, except another private like myself. I am the lowest of the low.'

It was at this moment that Jane entered the room with an urchin in tow. Unlike Lavinia, Jane was wearing a dark red dress that was splattered with mud almost to the knee. Her hair was in slight disarray, but her expression was composed. To Crossman, she had never been more beautiful. Jane Mulinder stopped short however, on seeing her two friends in a scene of intimacy: the man sitting in the chair as if he owned the establishment, the other with a proprietorial hand on his shoulder. From her expression they could both tell she was unnerved. She seemed to recover almost immediately and spoke in a bright voice, as if she believed the world were full of nothing but sweet innocence.

'What a perfect tableau! The brother returned home from the distant war, and the fond sister, her anxious wait over. What a picture you make. What is it that you are doing?'

'I rather thought we looked like the wayward woman and the rake,' said the mischievous Lavinia. 'I was making love to him, my dear.'

Jane's face turned to stone, then she laughed and said, 'You're bamming me — no, please, what is it? Something has happened, hasn't it?'

The urchin, a child of some eight years, grimy from head to toe, hair stiff with dirt, was still firmly gripped by the collar. He saw fit to speak up now that there was a short lull in the speeches.

'I don' wanna learn no numbers!'

'Who's this gentleman?' asked Lavinia. 'Did he try to steal your purse?'

'No,' said Jane, somehow managing to remove her hat and place it on a stand without letting go of the wriggling boy. 'This is Edward. His mother is Private McGurk's wife and this is their darling child. She asked me if I would teach him to read and write, there being no literacy in the family to date. I promised I would stuff the child with knowledge. You will of course help me, Lavinia, I know you will.'

'Will I? Don't set him down anywhere, Jane dear, he might infest the room. Can we do the schooling outside do you think?'

'Don't be prissy, Lavinia. Now, stand there young man and don't move. If you attempt to run I shall send Sergeant Crossman after you. He will shoot you down like a cur. Sergeant Crossman has no mercy in his soul. He has killed a thousand Cossacks and scoffs that he will have a thousand more before he leaves the Crimea. A boy like you would make a good running target — excellent practise for killing Cossacks.'

'Jane,' said Crossman, 'come here. I have some grave news.'

She let go of the boy and stared now, into his face, seeing the seriousness of the

353

expression. Edward remained where he was, unmoving, cowed by this tall man who now rose from his chair in the dark corner. He was like a wild creature caught among all-powerful hunters. He seemed to sense that the dark unknown world of adult fears was about to be unleashed in the room, and he shivered in his shoes.

'Oh?' cried Jane. 'Is someone dead? Your father? My father? Who is it, Alexander? Tell me.'

'No one is dead, Jane. Please, sit down, you look as if you are in a swoon. The news is that I have lost my sergeantcy. I have been stripped of my rank. I am so sorry to be bringing you this news, but I have shamed myself and my regiment by impersonating an officer, and now I am suffering the consequences.'

'What?' cried Jane in an astonished voice.

'You heard him, Jane,' said Lavinia. 'He has disgraced himself.'

'And have lost my rank.'

Jane said, 'But it is such a little thing . . . ' But she then saw Lavinia gesturing wildly from behind Crossman's back, and added, 'though I can see it would be important to you, Alexander.'

'Yes, yes it was.'

'Is there nothing to be done?'

He considered. 'No, I am guilty of the crime, for crime it was, and therefore must accept my punishment. I am back to being a private soldier, with no rank. It will take some time to claw my way back up again, but I must do it. There is one way . . . '

Lavinia stepped forward, her face drained of colour.

'No — not that, Alexander. Never that.'

Her voice was so full of passion it upset the young boy, who suddenly blurted out in fright, 'I shall learn my numbers, if you please, then go home to my ma.'

Crossman said, 'The child thinks this a madhouse. Come, we shall say no more about my problems. I had not meant it to turn into such a circus in any case. I hoped to find Jane alone, Jane could have passed the news on to you, Lavinia, and there would have been no need for all these theatricals. I'd better get back to the barracks. There'll be work to do. Our new officer is keen on cleaning things.' He stood up.

Jane said, fiercely, 'Not before you tell me what has frightened Lavinia.'

Lavinia said, 'He means to join the Forlorn Hope.'

Jane's voice was like that of a startled bird flying from a hedgerow. 'Forlorn Hope? What is that? Some kind of eastern religion?'

The ex-sergeant smiled, in spite of his spiritual agony.

'The Forlorn Hope,' explained Crossman, 'is a band of men who are the vanguard of an assault.'

'But surely if at the forefront they are slaughtered?'

'Well, yes, but those who survive,' he explained, gently, 'are automatically promoted.'

'The reason they are promoted,' broke in Lavinia, 'is because there are so few of them left, if any at all, it costs the army very little in the end.'

Jane said, 'Promise me, Alexander, that you will do no such thing. You will not join this band of sacrificed men. Those sergeant's stripes might have meant a great deal to you, but they surely are not worth throwing away your life.' Her voice went very low. 'I would be greatly disappointed in you, my dear, if you could not find it in yourself to consider my wish. If you have any regard for me, if you have any admiration for me at all, you will dismiss this thought from your mind.'

Edward sniggered. Lavinia silenced him with a glare.

'Lord Almighty!' Crossman cried, greatly exasperated. 'All right, Jane. I promise I will not join the Forlorn Hope. I'm not sure I was going to do so in the first place. It was just a consideration — but — but it is out my head, never to enter again. I shall probably die on the battlefield without bothering to join the damn vanguard, so it won't make a deal of difference will it. Good morning to you, ladies. I must away.'

He marched from the room with all the dignity he could muster, knowing he had been outmanoeuvred more than once in this world of petticoats. It was ever the same when the two women banded together against him. He tried to hold out against fearful odds, but eventually lost dismally. He had been thinking of joining the Forlorn Hope, but that option had now been torn from him by a promise. It gave him some amusement, for he needed to turn his head to lighter things, to imagine how Bertie fared in that household. The poor wretch must have been a walking shadow of a man. Bertie Durham had not been a great deal before marrying Lavinia, Crossman imagined, but since then he must have been turned into a shade that simply wafted from room to room.

He said as much to Jarrard, who called two days later to find his friend in the same terrible straits.

'Oh, I don't know, Jack. Men like Bertie

Durham are so dense it washes over them and they don't even get wet. I've seen men like that. They say 'Yes, dear,' and 'No, dear,' without even hearing the question, consciously. Listen, you know how something becomes so automatic you don't even have to think about it. Like riding a horse, for example. Well, that's how the Berties of this world operate. Their wife's words bypass their brain, trigger the right responses in their throat, without the man ever having to pay attention or think about the answer.'

'That sounds very cynical, Rupert.'

'It's a universal truth, my friend. That's why I never married. Probably never will.'

Crossman's eyebrows rose a fraction. 'What about Monique?'

'I might make the exception there. Who knows? So, what are you going to do? Ride it out?'

'Got to. No choice, is there?'

'You could leave the army, as soon as you are able to.'

'Not an option for me. I'm a soldier, Rupert, you know that.'

'A warrior through and through, eh?'

Crossman shook his head. 'No, a *soldier*. For me a warrior is someone who chases war. I do not pursue it, I simply do my duty when it is there to be done.'

Jarrard laughed. 'Jeez, you British are so stiff. If I pushed you over I swear you'd shatter, Jack. All right, a soldier then. We've had this conversation before. A damn contrariety if you ask me. Well, I shall leave you, friend, to wallow in your misery. When you feel like getting promoted to a civilian, please call on my help. I am only too willing to elevate men of your stamp to the station and status they deserve.' He paused in his stride for a moment, reflecting on what he had just said, and added, 'Some admirable alliteration in that statement! Walt Whitman, eat your heart out.'

With that the newspaper man got up and went about his civilian business.

8

It was that last magical hour before sunset, when the world is suspended in a kind of rosy peace. No guns were firing and men and women were going about their lawful business, if not staring dreamily into the red sky, doing small mundane tasks which occupied their hands but not their minds. Their thoughts, for the most part, were on the future. The soldiers and their wives were dreaming of their homegoing: seeing their families and friends. The sutlers were beginning to look around for another war in which to make a profit: this one would soon be over and then where would the money come from? The local people were thinking how wonderful it was going to be, once the several armies all packed their bags and returned from whence they had come.

Crossman was sitting on the edge of the stool, cleaning his Tranter revolver. He had the weapon in bits on a piece of cloth covering his lap. Having run out of gun oil he had purchased a bottle of watchmaker's oil from one of the sutlers. It was too thin, really, but better than nothing at all. There was a certain amount of pleasure in seeing the bluemetal pistol pieces laid out before him, gleaming with the oil. What most men liked about engines and tools of any kind was the way the parts had been precisely machined to fit into each other. How artistic it all was that the double trigger mechanisms of the Tranter, with their springs and levers, should come together so well and perform in just the way they should. Metal wears and weapons jam, but in the main they were as wonderful as a steam engine in their mechanical movements.

Weapons of course, were designed to kill. But that was only their purpose. One could admire the workmanship, the composition, the performance of a machine, while abhorring its *raison d'être*. A wagon carrying malefactors to the gallows has a horrible task to perform, but the design of the wagon itself may be admired while disassociating it from its purpose.

The only other stool in the room was being used by Gwilliams, who was trimming everyone's beards and hair. He was after all a barber and bone-setter by profession, as he never tired of telling his comrades. The floor was littered with hair of different shades and coarseness. It made for soft treading when crossing the floor.

'Sit still, Peterson. How can I do your

361

bangs if you don't keep your head still?'

'Bangs? I don't want any bangs.'

'He means your fringe,' said Crossman, without looking up. 'It's the North American parlance. And may I make a suggestion? Let Gwilliams cut it really short. You're starting to look like a girl.'

Peterson scowled at him. Crossman continued to study her without her being aware of it, not because of the scowl, but because of her pallor. Of late he had noticed that Peterson was looking quite unwell, especially around the eyes. The previous evening he had observed her going out of the hovel with Gwilliams. At the time Crossman felt there was something conspiratorial about this meeting. He had seen others approach Gwilliams in the same manner and knew the reason for it. When Ali was not around, or the complaint was a delicate one that they did not wish to share with the bluff Turk, the soldiers went to Gwilliams. Being a 'bone man' he set himself up and earned pennies as an adviser and curer of common ailments. Crossman deduced Peterson was unwell and was seeking the advice of Gwilliams. While Crossman trusted Gwilliams on many things, he did not consider he was even close to possessing the knowledge of a physician or even a regiment surgeon and this worried him. A quack was a harmless enough person, unless asked to deal with a serious complaint. Then he became a menace. Crossman decided to intervene.

When Gwilliams had finished with Peterson's hair, Crossman asked to see the North American outside. It was clear that everyone, even Gwilliams himself, thought Crossman was going to consult on some malady or other. However, when they were out of earshot of the others, Crossman asked him bluntly, 'Is Peterson pregnant?'

Gwilliams looked quite shocked. 'Why are you askin' me that?'

'She doesn't look well. I thought perhaps that the rape . . . '

'Ah, I see,' said Gwilliams, catching on. 'Well, you've got the culprits all right, but she ain't with child. She's got a pox.'

It was Crossman's turn to be shocked. 'She has a venereal disease?'

Gwilliams nodded. 'Must 'ave caught it from one of them Ruskies. It don't seem one of the serious kind. I gave her some stuff I make. She's got a burnin' at the moment, but that'll go away.'

So that was it! 'Thank you, Gwilliams.'

'You're welcome.'

Crossman went inside again. He sat down beside Peterson on her cot. She glanced up at him, surprised, then saw Gwilliams entering shortly afterwards. A quick look at Gwilliams told her that confidentiality, even less sacred with an unqualified healer than a real medical practitioner, was now broken. She blushed to the roots of her hair. She then concentrated on cleaning the mud from her boots, hunching into herself, pretending Crossman was not there.

'It isn't your fault,' he said, quietly. 'Go and see the surgeon, tomorrow.'

'If I do that, it'll be all up with me, won't it?'

'Despite what Gwilliams says, the problem might get worse. Better to be discovered for a woman and thrown out of the army than to suffer lasting injury.'

'I don't want to leave the army. Not yet. It'll be all right. I feel better now. Bloody Wynter has had it lots of times. He keeps catching it over and over. He's not dropped dead yet.'

Crossman said, 'No, but you've got to wonder about the state of his brains, haven't you?'

Peterson giggled, despite herself. 'Yes, you have. Addled eggs. But Gwilliams has given me powders and ointment. He said he used to work for an apothecary. Some of the stuff I swallow, some I — I put on.'

'Don't get them mixed up.'

She giggled again. 'I won't, sergeant.'

'I'm no longer that.'

'I can't call you anything else. That's how I know you.'

Crossman accepted this without further comment, but felt he ought to ask a final question.

'Are you sure you trust Gwilliams to know what he's doing?'

'When it first happened, I went to see Mrs Seacole, but she was away in the French camp. So I settled for Gwilliams. But she came back yesterday. I showed her what Gwilliams gave me and she said mostly it was all right. She said she would have gave me similar and that it works on the sailors. They're the worst, you know. Wynter got it once from wearing a dead sailor's trousers. He told me.'

'Did he now? Mrs Seacole, eh? Well certainly that lady knows what she's doing. I'm glad you got a second opinion. Never trust just one man's word.'

Her face went red and hot for a moment and in a vehement outburst she said, 'I'll never trust *any* man — not ever. They're filthy animals, every one.' She paused for a moment in embarrassment, then added, 'Excepting you, sergeant.'

Crossman went back to cleaning his kit, a little disconcerted by Peterson's plight. There was not much else he could do to help her though. All he had was advice. If she did not need that, then he had little more he could offer. He was glad to hear that she had visited Mrs Seacole. If there was one person who was more knowledgeable than even the regiment surgeons it was Mary Seacole. He would have trusted the West Indian lady with his own complaints, had he any that he could not deal with himself.

Lieutenant Pirce-Smith descended the stairs and looked about him approvingly.

'Very smart. Just because we're allowed beards does not mean we have to look like raggle-taggle ratcatchers, does it?'

'Beggin' your pardon, sir,' said Wynter, 'but I thought we was supposed to look like Tartars, who don't go about makin' themselves look neat and tidy.'

'Wynter, I could put any Tartar on the peninsula alongside you even now and I guarantee he would look a Sunday best.'

Pirce-Smith was beginning to get the measure of Wynter. It was the kind of answer Crossman would have given the private. Crossman felt rather piqued that the officer had taken over so smoothly and easily. This had been *his peloton*. He had spent over a year building it into the cohesive unit it was today, and now had to watch someone else reap the benefits. The army, like all huge organizations, had no conscience. It was not fair, never had been fair, and never would be. You had to accept that fact or perish in a well of bitterness. The wrong people were always promoted, the right people either got killed or were passed over. Injustices not only happened, they were built into the system.

Wynter's reply to his commanding officer was to take off his shirt and turn his back on the room. He pretended to do some task, noisily, so that it drew attention to his presence. In this way he displayed the flogging scars on his back, obscenely, as a man who has lost his leg might display his stump, to make others feel uncomfortable and even guilty. Wynter was a master at dumb insolence. If Pirce-Smith now accused him of such, he would turn with a look of innocent surprise and say, 'Who, sir? Me, sir? No, sir.' Sometimes Crossman felt like boxing the soldier's ears, shaking him roughly, and telling him to grow into a man.

'There you are — done!' said Gwilliams, removing the towel from around Yorwarth's neck with a flourish. 'Now, how about you, sir?' He asked the lieutenant. 'Care for a trim yourself.'

Pirce-Smith said, 'Yes, I think I will, Gwilliams. What do you charge?'

'Two British pennies to you, sir.'

Pirce-Smith sat on the stool. He removed his revolver which was stuck in his sash, and then his coatee with its extravagant heavy gold epaulettes. There he waited for the scissors to descend on his dark curly hair, which hung from his head in a floppy foppish manner.

'We say tuppence, but then you are a North American. Please leave the sidewhiskers, Gwilliams, I have nurtured them from infants.'

Yes, how easily the officer now fitted in. He was, perhaps, even less starchy than Crossman himself, who could be a snob at times. A genteel sergeant will protect his birth status with more vigour than a man who has not dropped his former station in life.

Peterson fingered the epaulettes with envy in her eyes. 'How much would these cost, sir, when you bought them?'

'A sultan's ransom, Peterson. Don't ask me the particular sum, for it makes me weep to think on it. I had much rather spent the money on a good horse, but there you have it.'

Crossman asked, 'Sir, are we going out in the morning?'

'Yes, we are, Crossman. It is what I came down to tell you all.'

'Spiking guns?' asked Yorwarth, hopefully. This would mean it would be a quick raid, there and back in a night, and then further rest.

'No, not this time. An ambuscade. Supplies have been landed on a beach to the north and are now kept in a cave. The navy managed to sink the vessel that landed them, but our sources tell us they are about to be collected by a party of Russians. It's our job to prevent those supplies from reaching Sebastopol. We will not be mounted. I'm hoping to use some steep escarpments that will not favour horses. Our escape on foot along goat tracks will be surer and swifter in such topography. Their cavalry will not be able to run us down in such country.'

'Ambuscade?' repeated Peterson. 'What's one of them?'

Gwilliams said, clipping away at the locks, 'It's officer talk for an *ambush*.'

'What Gwilliams says is correct,' remarked Pirce-Smith, 'except that others besides commissioned officers use the word. You will all be ready to leave in the morning, just before dawn, dressed in your Tartar disguises. Corporal Peterson, you are responsible for raising everyone from their beds. If Wynter gives you any trouble, please refer him to me.'

'Wha . . . why, that's a gross unfairness, sir,' cried Wynter. 'I'm a great respecter of rank, I am.'

'Glad to hear it.' Pirce-Smith swept off the towel and inspected himself in the shard of mirror which Gwilliams proudly held up before him. He turned this way and that. 'Not bad, Gwilliams. You know your work. I shall not be afraid to leave myself in your hands now, should I dislocate a bone. I'm sure it will be returned to the correct socket.'

'I know my trades.'

'I'm certain of that. Right, primed and ready, the rest of you!' There was even an attempt at humour. 'If I should not wake, please leave without me.'

The lieutenant went back upstairs. Wynter and the others kept their voices low, not because they were saying anything untoward, but it just did not seem right that their private conversation should be eavesdropped by an officer. What they said in the barrack room was theirs and theirs alone.

Peterson stroked her new Enfield lovingly. 'I'm going to ambuscade them Russians like they've never been ambuscaded before,' she said. Crossman could see, not surprisingly, there was still a great vengeance in her heart for the rape she had suffered. Whereas before she had shot them with indifference, now there was hatred accompanying the bullet. It was not a state of mind which boded well for the soldier. Her innocence had gone and she was going to put lead into the heads and bellies of those who had taken it from her.

Crossman himself had his own grief to contend with. It was not as devastating or destructive as that which Peterson had to bear, but it gnawed at his spirit none the less. He felt hopeless. How was he ever going to get back to his old self? Had he still been part of the line regiment, the 88th, he would not have felt the removal of his stripes so keenly. But in this new work of espionage and sabotage, an NCO had many privileges and a great deal more status. He had been able to converse with colonels, hobnob with majors, cock a snoot at lieutenants. Now he was a common soldier they turned their shoulder to him, were not interested in his opinions on how to go about a difficult task in the field. He had never felt quite so rejected since he had been a child in his father's house. It was difficult to keep the bile from rising, the bitterness from eating into his soul like self-generated acid.

The following morning Ali shook Crossman gently awake and the pair of them prepared the fire and a cooked breakfast.

Once they were out on patrol there would be little opportunity to make hot food. Others rose afterwards, drawn awake by the pleasant smell of cooking, and stumbled out with metal plate in hand. Wynter was one of the first. He gobbled his breakfast down without a thank you and then went back to his cot until Lieutenant Pirce-Smith descended upon the fold.

'What's this? Breakfast? How jolly,' said the officer, clearly pleased. 'You men know how to look after your stomachs, I'll give you that.'

He ate with them, chatting the whole while, quite at ease now amongst the ranks. It had not always been so and Crossman had had a difficult time with him in the beginning. But the officer had learned to bend, unlike his predecessor, who had always remained aloof. That particular lieutenant had died gallantly on the battlefield, clad not in a uniform but in a civilian suit, at Inkerman. They did not miss him, though they acknowledged he was a soldier. Pirce-Smith was preferable, most of the time, and had learned more in a shorter space.

'Up and on our way, men,' said Pirce-Smith, pulling on a bulging haversack. 'The war beckons.'

They did not so much march out of camp as sort of amble out, dragging their tails behind them. On the way they had to pass the 93rd, who were rising with the dawn. Crossman saw Jock McIntyre and tried to hide his face, but the bluff Scot would have none of it.

'Jack, ye scoundrel. Ah heard. Dinna fash yersel' laddie, ye'll get right back there soon enough.'

Crossman waved an acknowledgement, managing a grin, though how he forced it on to his face he knew not. He did not see Campbell anywhere around, for which he was grateful. Whether the captain would have smirked, or scoffed, or simply remained silently aloof, Crossman would have withered in his skin had the man been there. He hoped he would never see Captain Sterling Campbell ever again. In fact if the said captain had been blown away by a Russian cannon, Crossman would have kissed the gunner, not his daughter, his feelings were so intense.

They passed too, a mournful-looking Betsy, with her gunsaddle somewhere else, probably in Hawke's office. She was tethered to a stake in the ground and was chewing thoughtfully and watchfully as her former companions trudged by her. Stik came out, from behind a wall. He too stared at the group, then called, 'Sergeant?' Crossman looked up, instinctively. Then seeing Wynter's scornful eyes on him, he turned away again, feeling bereft. They left the pair still staring after them as they climbed the slopes, bound for an encounter with the enemy.

'I'll wager your arms feel lighter, Crossman,' murmured Wynter. 'You can swing 'em freely now, without all that weight.'

Wynter was enjoying himself. Crossman did not flinch or blink an eye under this jeering. In fact he ignored Wynter completely and began talking to Peterson about the Enfield.

'Still rather have your Minnie back?'

'No,' smiled Peterson, 'but there's not much between them.'

Wynter shut up after a while, when he realized that his taunts were falling on deaf ears.

The day opened up pleasantly, with small finches flocking from bush to bush, and hidden songbirds heralding the morning. There were butterflies too, clustered around a small group of shrubs. They flew out of the shade into the sunlight, flashing their bright colours, then back again quickly as if the sun would singe their wings. It was not a world of black powder and sharp steel, this hinterland. It was a quiet place, a place of stony tracks leading to grassy uplands. The war was nestling down below somewhere, as a town nestles in the crook of a valley. Most of the men, and the woman, were happy to leave its squalor behind them. Wynter was perhaps the only one who saw little difference between what they had left and where they were now. All foreign terrain was alike to him.

They walked all morning, pausing only to drink and eat. The fare on the march was salt beef, pork and apples. The officer had the largest load to carry on his back, something which had Crossman wondering. Pirce-Smith and Ali took turns at carrying it. It was clearly quite heavy and Crossman guessed there were probably explosives in there. He cursed at the bulkiness of his own pack at times, which was a great deal smaller. Besides food and water, each man was carrying two hundred rounds of ammunition in their belts, the weight of which caused chafing and consequent soreness at the hips. That, and the weapons beside, brought the pace down. Crossman was just glad it was summer and they were not clothed as they had been in the winter. As it was, they sweated as they toiled up the slopes, their thirst raging in their throats at times.

At noon they stopped in the shade of an overhang. Lieutenant Pirce-Smith ordered them to check their weapons while they were resting, to ensure no dust or grit had entered the barrels while on the march. If anyone thought this a fussy command, they did not say so, not even Gwilliams or Ali. The lieutenant himself took the sentry duty while this order was being carried out, after which Peterson took over from the officer on a high place with a good vista.

Pirce-Smith made a point of checking his own weapon, then asked Crossman to accompany him down to the shade of a fig tree.

'Private Crossman,' said the lieutenant, when they were out of earshot of the others, 'I should like to ask you your opinion on this ambush. What concerns me is that the Russians may create an uncommon situation. I would be grateful for the knowledge of whether this has happened to you in the past.'

Crossman gritted his teeth on hearing his present rank used so clearly and definitely. It seemed to him that Pirce-Smith was milking his experience, which had been hard-learned. This irked him and he snapped out a rather irritated, 'What do you mean, uncommon?'

Pirce-Smith's expression hardened. 'I would change that tone if we are to flourish together in the same environment, private.'

'I'm sorry, sir. Could you please elucidate?'

'I mean in your experience have they ever set traps? I don't mean specifically for you and your men. I mean, have they ever been wise enough to split their numbers?'

Crossman was still annoyed, but he hid it successfully. 'I see. You mean do they follow main force with a secondary force, or forces, within hailing distance. So that if the supply column is attacked they can call for assistance and thus trap the would-be trappers.'

'Something like that. Along those lines of thought.'

'It's only happened once and I'm inclined to think that it was more by accident than design.'

'Would you care to describe the event to me, so that I can form my own opinion?'

'Certainly, sir. We were part of a larger sortie out on the Woronzoff Road and once we had opened fire on the enemy we were attacked on our flanks by two more parties of Russians.'

'Was it a disaster?'

'We lost a sergeant and five privates from the 88th. On our retreat they fell into a disused sap of which we had no prior knowledge, even though it was one of ours. The Russian cavalry made great sport with their lances and swords. I saw the sergeant cleaved in two, down to the waist, by a single stroke from a heavy cavalryman. He had fought bravely to that point. There was little we could do to help the men, except fire on the cavalry from a distance. Three, I think, of those who had fallen into the trench recovered their muskets and gave fire, but were attacked in force before they had time to reload. Oh, yes, I recall a private was beheaded. After he had been stuck several times with lances he crawled out of the sap and ran in a hapless fashion, unfortunately away from our position. The final stroke was actually a mercy for you could see the man was out of his mind with fear and pain.'

'But you are inclined to think this counter-ambuscade was not planned but was simply happenchance.'

'That is my opinion, sir.'

Pirce-Smith looked satisfied and nodded. 'Good, we are too small a group to split into anything smaller.' He paused for a moment before adding, 'You looked disturbed during the retelling of that account. Was it regrettable?'

'Yes — yes it was. I was not proud to be part of it. Our retreat was more of a rout than an ordered withdrawal. We should have been close enough to save those men. In fact if we had *all* leapt into the trench, we would have had a good defensive position. Instead we rushed on, not realizing that we had lost them.'

'Were you in command of the sortie?'

'No, sir, I was not. My *peloton* was simply attached to the larger group for the purposes of the raid.'

'Then the fault was not yours. I know, I know, it is still galling to be a member of a bungled operation, but the greater blame lay elsewhere. Thank you for being so frank with me, Private Crossman. Please rejoin the rest of the men now.'

How that rankled! Private. He could not get used to it. It was like a sharp pointed tool of torture, probing him. The lieutenant, in using it, was simply following protocol, but still Pirce-Smith used it with too much satisfaction in his voice. The two had had their differences in the past. At one time Pirce-Smith had sought some kind of punishment for Crossman, when as a sergeant he had assumed command of a patrol sent out to bring deserters to justice, with no deference to the lieutenant's rank. However, Crossman hoped that would all be in the past.

Crossman had a relatively undisturbed night, apart from the interference of a persistent owl. He had never quite understood why owls hooted — or screeched — when they were supposed to be silent hunters. If it was to attract female owls, why not do that out of hunting hours? If it was to warn other owls away from their territory, surely they would warn every living creature — mouse, vole, rat, whatever — within the range of the hoot. The vagaries of the natural world were beyond him. Engines were reliable and understood, but animals were unpredictable.

He woke to find that Yorwarth, because the scratching of his eczema had disturbed the lieutenant, had been sent for water. It got him out of sight and mind while the rest of them struck camp. They were about ready to march when they heard the sound of Yorwarth yelling to the accompaniment of empty canteens drumming together. Yorwarth was obviously running back without having filled them. The scenery around the *peloton* was of sloping broken rocky ground studded with bushes, some of them thorny, and everyone peered down to see where Yorwarth would emerge. He came from behind a bush down to the left of their position. It appeared to Crossman that the air was full of a black cloud of canister or grapeshot. He went down on one knee, rifle-musket at the ready, wondering why they had not heard the sound of guns.

It took but a half-second to realize how foolish had been his first observation. From that point on the whole episode took on a kind of unnatural motion. The sound of a swarm of angry bees could now be plainly heard by everyone. There were tens of thousands of them. Yorwarth was waving his arms, slapping at the black flecks which kept pace with him, surrounding his head. The vanguard of the bees, ahead of Yorwarth, then began stinging the dumbfounded watchers. Without waiting any longer everyone turned and began running blindly away from the oncoming swarm, Yorwarth's alarming screams in their ears.

Crossman had been brought up on estates where he had been left in the care of gardeners, while his stepmother cut flowers for her tables. He had chatted with them for hours, gardeners having funds of folklore with which to entertain young gentlemen. He now recalled, as he rushed desperately away from the attacking bees, that in the absence of a building to hide in, one should run through bushes and foliage, to impede and break up the flight of the swarm. This he did now, with remarkable alacrity. He stopped only when he was about 250 yards from the original camp site with the vague recollection that bees, however angry, will only chase their victims for around fifty or so yards. These bees had pursued him for a lot further than that and seeing several still clinging to his shirt he realized they were not ordinary bees. They were much larger, seemingly much fiercer, and left an enormous sting behind.

First he swatted and brushed away those bees still on his person. Then he plucked two or three stingers from the backs of his hands, the extremities which had suffered the most. Looking back up the slope, he could see none of his companions. He would not blame them if he they were still running, halfway back to Balaclava! After a while he felt he ought to go back up the slope, though the stings were extremely painful and swellings had appeared. One was on his neck and was agony. He felt that a second Adam's apple had appeared alongside the real one.

It took great strength of will to return to the spot where they had left some of the equipment.

It was deserted. Crossman stared about him. After a while he heard a low groan and on investigating found Yorwarth collapsed under a bush. The soldier was in an appalling state. It was difficult to recognize him as a human being, let alone as Yorwarth. From somewhere beneath the lumps and bumps a voice moaned incessantly. Yorwarth seemed to have difficulty in breathing: under the moaning was a rattling sound. His throat and neck were so swollen they were of a hideous size.

The others were drifting back now, all showing injuries from the bees, some of which were still in the district. Wynter made it his duty to kill as many of the insects as possible, while the rest crowded around the unfortunate Yorwarth. Ali made a tube out of some stiff leather and forced it into the mouth and partly down the throat of Yorwarth to try to assist his breathing. It was not very successful. Within a very short time Yorwarth had ceased to take in air and was dead.

'He can't be gone!' cried a distressed Peterson, the most ailing of those who remained. 'Not just from *bees*.'

It did indeed seem incongruous, that someone who had survived months in a war where terminal disease was rife and death from the enemy ever-present, should succumb to the stings of an insect. It did not seem right to any of them. They stood over the corpse and shook their heads, more upset at that moment by the manner of the death, by the trivial nature of the killers, than the loss of their comrade. A pack of starving wolves, yes. A crazed bear, acceptable. But a bunch of bees? No, that did not seem fair at all. God was being absurd. Yorwarth was only seventeen. An awkward boy in a war far from his homeland. It did not seem right.

'We must move on,' said Pirce-Smith. 'Cover the body with stones. We shall have to collect it on our return journey.'

They did as they were ordered in a kind of dream. Some of them were now beginning to feel the effects of the stings themselves. Worst among them was Peterson, who had begun shivering and shaking in a most alarming manner. When the shaking turned to full convulsions, Pirce-Smith made camp again. The group remained there the rest of the day and the next night. Ali did what he could to relieve the symptoms suffered by Peterson, with compresses and herbal remedies. Some of the others felt ill too, but not to the same extent as Peterson. By morning she had recovered somewhat. She was able, shakily, to take food and water.

Pirce-Smith wanted to press on, but realized with the loss of one man, and their prime sharpshooter temporarily out of action, it was best to gather strength before attempting a hard march. There was a time factor, but they had set out with plenty of leeway, wanting to be in the area of the ambush well before the Russian supply caravan arrived. However they were using up that leeway rapidly.

At noon he had them on their feet and back on the trail. Thereafter they had frequent stops, but at least they were heading in the right direction.

That night they camped in a grove of olives. There was little talk amongst them. In the morning Crossman went for the water. His officer woke and followed him down to the beck. There the two men had a private conversation, out of earshot of the rest of the men.

Pirce-Smith said, 'That was a bad business, back there with the bees. You had told me a little story, just prior to that incident, in which I fondly imagined myself doing the right thing, instinctively. You said your retreat from your sortie was more of a rout. I felt rather superior when you told me that. I told myself at the time that I would never panic and run, no matter what my commander did. Well, I was wrong. I just panicked and ran.'

'It was a very uncommon situation, sir. One probably only gets attacked by deadly bees once in a lifetime.'

'Still, I should be prepared for the unusual. I was not. I did what I said I would never do. It was unforgivable. Now a man is dead . . . '

'We could not have saved him, had we stayed to face the bees.'

'Perhaps not. I don't know.' The officer was quite remorseful. 'Nothing to be done now, of course. It's over. I don't know what the colonel will say.'

'Sir, he will tell you that he would have done the same thing in the same circumstances. The greatest hero in the world cannot stand and face an unstoppable force. I too am horrified that I ran. But when I stop to think about it, what else was there to do? We have no protection against a swarm of bees, no weapons to destroy them with before they kill us, nowhere to hide. I was told by my gardeners as a child that even if one jumps into a pond and submerses oneself, the bees will still be there waiting when one surfaces. Their advice — and they are country people who know country ways — was to run. The only way to avoid being stung is to get out of the bees' territory. Run. That's what we did.'

'It still seems cowardly. How is Peterson, by the by? Is the corporal getting any better?'

Pirce-Smith somehow managed to speak about Peterson without bringing gender into the sentence.

'See for yourself, sir. She's pale, but recovering. I think she'll be all right. How about you? You were stung several times too.'

'Once I'd emptied the contents of my stomach, quietly behind a boulder, I felt much revived.' He touched one of his swellings. 'I was fortunate enough not to get stung on the throat or mouth, which was the method by which they killed Yorwarth so swiftly. Would that we pursued our ends in this war with as much skill and determination.'

Crossman did not like to point out that bees had no real method. They were not a thinking enemy, but an instinctive one. Pirce-Smith spoke as if the insects deliberately set out to kill Yorwarth and the schemes their generals had devised had met with planned success. Surely they had no strategy or tactics? They simply descended like barbarian hordes on those who dared to invade the regions under their protection.

'I think you did all you could, sir. I would have no further thoughts on the subject.'

Pirce-Smith was silent for a while, looking out over the arid landscape, with its dry grasses and brittle shrubs. It seemed he wanted more from the private, but was reluctant to pursue it. Finally, when the silence had gone on so long that Crossman felt he should either be dismissed or given further instructions, the lieutenant turned to him again. Pirce-Smith spoke in a choked voice, emotion buried deeply within it.

'I came to the Crimea to prove something,'

he said. 'I have a feeling you did too. My father spent some time in India and he told me stories — you must have heard them too,' he seemed determined to pull Crossman into the boat with him in this soul-searching exercise, 'of Henry Lawrence's 'young men'. John Nicholson, Edwardes, Neville Chamberlain, Harry Lumsden, Hodson, Taylor, Abbott and Henry Daly. I know all the names by heart. They went to India barely out of the schoolroom and forged a place in history for themselves on the North-West Frontier. The Punjab, Afghanistan and Kashmir. They did it — are still doing it — with their intellect, their courage and with force of arms. Forming armies from native troops, conquering the Sikh empire, taming the wildest of the Afghan tribes and enriching the East India Company.

'I joined the army to be like them. Theirs was — and probably still is — a powerful experience. They are legends amongst those whom they lead and rule, let alone back in their homeland. I yearn to follow in their wake, to prove my metal in the way that they have proved theirs. They are living gods. Some say John Nicholson cannot be killed. He has walked into fire and lightning storm a number of times and has come out unscathed. He has killed more men than I have shaken hands with.' He paused and gave a wry smile. 'Now, I know that histories are exaggerated, coming out of the Indian subcontinent, a place of mystical happenings, of phantastical occurrences, but a great deal is true. My father as a missionary bore witness to many of the deeds performed out there.'

Crossman said mildly, 'If you wished to follow in the footsteps of Nicholson and his band of brothers, why did you not go to India?'

A cloud crossed the lieutenant's face. 'Because they are there, they have done it. I need to whet my blade in some new untrammelled territory.' It was almost as if he resented the fact that Lawrence's young men had got there before him, leaving him no new territories to open up and stamp his name in their dust. He sighed, looking about it. 'Sadly this is not the place. Somewhere like Africa, perhaps? Or China? But, enough talk, we had better get back to the rest of the men.'

He stood up then, abruptly, and strutted back to where the others were resting, leaving Crossman to follow on behind. When he had first drawn Crossman away, it was as if he wanted his opinion on his career as a warrior so far, but had then realized, halfway through the revelations on his desires, that he was not speaking to an equal. In losing his sergeantcy Fancy Jack Crossman had lost some of his flair, and with it his force of personality. He did not feel this in himself, but others felt it for him, and acted accordingly. The lieutenant had wanted the approbation and approval of the old Crossman, not the new one.

He had taken Crossman aside because like certain inexperienced commanders he needed reassurance when something had gone wrong — an unnecessary death of one of his men — and sought it from his next in command. He needed to know he had done the right thing and would not face criticism on return to headquarters. Peterson was actually the next in line for the throne out here in the wilderness, but had so little charisma the lieutenant would have died rather than open himself to her. Besides, she was a woman, and women approved of many things which Pirce-Smith found horrifying: things like humility and turning the other cheek. Crossman, at least, was from a genteel family, had a major for a father and a lieutenant for a brother, even if he was not an officer himself.

But actually Crossman was still too steeped in his own troubles to want to lift the lieutenant and reassure him of his worth.

'Men,' said Pirce-Smith, having shed his revelations and was now the hard-shelled, confident lieutenant again, 'gather round.'

They gathered to hear the wisdom.

'The day after tomorrow we need to be in position to attack. It will mean a forced march. Peterson, are you still fatigued?'

'No, sir. Fit.'

'Good. We have lost some time, but we shall make it up. On your feet now. Do not halt until I halt. Keep up with my pace. Do not ask me to slow. Do not request rest stops, for there will be none. You will eat on the march, drink on the march, and save your breath for the coming fight. I want no stragglers. Keep the line tight. Any questions?'

There were none.

'Right, follow me.'

The officer strode out and the soldiers followed, Ali taking up the rear as usual, to prod any slow tops. The ground was rough and covered in stones. It was hard going. True to his spirit, Pirce-Smith forced a very fast pace, his eyes fixed on a point three feet in front of him. Boots trod the trail, making the only sounds. Occasionally they crushed herbs, sending up a refreshing aroma to the nostrils of the soldiers. Startled birds flew out of rocky crops. Hares came out of forms and dashed across their path. On they tramped, following the young officer who was desperate to make his mark on the world.

By noon they had been walking for five hours. The big pack had been passed around. Even Peterson had taken a turn. Most of them were beginning to shake at the legs, for the pace had indeed been fast, though it had slowed a little in the last hour. Still Pirce-Smith showed no signs of halting for a rest. No one asked him to. It was not that the likes of Wynter were afraid to ask. It was that no one wanted to show himself to be weak. If the lace-collared son of a clergyman could march forever, so could they! To give him the satisfaction of knowing he was tougher than his own soldiers would be monstrous. Each one of them was going to march until their blisters burst and their boots were full of blood. If the man kept going for another five hours, they would be with him.

'I need a bush,' said Gwilliams, after another hour. 'I have a flock of finches up my ass.'

'You need to rest?' enquired the officer, without pausing in his stride. 'I told you, no requests.'

'I need a shit, is what I need. Fuck your rest, sir! I can piss on the march, but I sure as hell ain't gonna drop my pants and crap down my legs.'

The request was reasonable and Pirce-Smith knew it. He had been defeated by bodily functions. He had wanted to report to Hawke that they had marched from dawn to dusk without a break. When he thought about it, it was a miracle the men had come so far without a toilet stop, for most of them were verging on dysentery.

'Fall out,' he ordered. 'Ten minutes, only.'

'As long as it takes,' corrected Gwilliams, who was as mad as anyone that the stop had to be made. 'Two minutes or half an hour. You can't slam your asshole shut, much as you want to.'

Most of them went off into the bushes. Pirce-Smith included. Once the subject had been mentioned, it triggered responses in all of them. Only Ali remained. He had the retention powers of a saint. He would burst before admitting he was as frail as other men.

The air was heavy with odour and at first the men were glad to be back on the march. As with all stops though, this one had caused muscles to stiffen and joints to lock. Crossman knew that he was not alone in finding it hard to get his legs moving again. It was as if there were sand in every socket, grinding his bones. While he had not been well-oiled before, he had at least had the benefit of perpetual motion and a mind which had been elsewhere. Now he was aware of his pain. The hypnotic state of a rhythmic march had been broken. Weariness flooded in. Crossman was worried about Peterson. Her pallor had turned very grey and there were dark shadows around her eyes and at the corners of her mouth. Crossman wondered whether to say something to Pirce-Smith about her condition, but could not shake off the feeling that the lieutenant would be less than sympathetic.

By three o'clock in the afternoon the line was strung out and the walk ragged. Peterson had to be continually prodded by the Turk at the back, to keep her putting one foot in front of another. Crossman knew her mind and realized it was important to her that she was not the first to halt, or the fact of her gender would be called into question.

Inevitably, it was Wynter who cried enough.

'Sir! Sir! I've lost my boot.'

They all stopped, turned in great fatigue, to see that Wynter had indeed lost his footwear. It was lying on the trail three yards behind him. A trick, Crossman had no doubt. Wynter had somehow surreptitiously untied his laces, or allowed them to untie, and slipped his foot out of the boot. There it lay though, without a foot to fill it. They all stared, glad of that boot, knowing the march would not continue once it had been halted a second time. Not for an hour or two at least.

'Can I get my boot, sir?'

'Damn your boot.'

'Yes, sir, it should go straight to hell, as you say, sir.'

'Do not try my patience, Wynter, or you will be flogged here and now.'

Wynter could see the officer was not playing games.

'No, sir, sorry. Shall I put it on again?' He retrieved it and tried to force his foot into it. 'Swollen. It won't go on. Not yet. Can I bathe my feet, sir? In some cool water. Maybe then . . . '

'We will rest,' said Pirce-Smith, almost weeping with frustration, knowing they had the worst of the march behind them and had only a few hours to reach what would have been more than just a modest feat of stamina and endurance. But mid-afternoon was really nothing much to bleat about. Dusk without a proper halt had been his aim: now it was out of the question. 'We shall remain here for two hours and then press on into the evening.'

The soldiers sank to their bottoms. Water was passed round, and chews of salt pork and beef. Most of the group stared fixedly in front of them as they ate and drank. Peterson fell asleep sitting up, halfway through pulling off her right sock. She still gripped the toe of the blood-soaked item while she snored softly to herself, bent over with her head touching her knees. Her other foot was still clad and was undoubtedly painful, but not enough to wake her. No one blamed her. Others felt as if they could sleep for a week.

After two hours though, Pirce-Smith had them on their feet and ready to go again. In truth Crossman felt refreshed enough to put one leg in front of the other and get the rhythm going again. He was aware that time was short and had it been him in charge of the *peloton* he would have forced the pace just as the lieutenant was doing. Whether he would have given them regular short rests was another matter, but it was all a question of whose theory one followed. Some experts said that breaks were bad on a long march, others thought them necessary. Crossman would have judged the mood and his own feelings at the time, and would have acted accordingly. He might have followed the same course as Pirce-Smith.

Gwilliams fell in beside him, as he trudged along.

'Feels like the March of the Ten Thousand, don't it?' said Gwilliams.

Crossman was completely thrown. 'Explain your meaning.'

'You know, the lost army of the Greeks? Folks led by a general called Xenophon — leastways, he weren't a general at the outset — had no rank at all, but put himself up, as a volunteer general. Ten thousand men, all lost in the wildernesses of Asia Minor country, led by a man who didn't know where the hell he was going. You know the story.'

As usual, Crossman was impressed by the North American's book-learned knowledge of the Ancient World. Gwilliams had lived with a 'preacher man' as a child and had access to the man's library. He had gathered in knowledge 'by the cart load' simply by burying himself in densely written tomes, day after day. He came out with the most donnish references, some of which Crossman was aware of, but often so obscure as to be opaque to him. The trouble was, Gwilliams thought everyone knew these things, especially high-hats like Crossman, and he always expected an informed response.

'I'm not sure I do,' Crossman replied, stumbling and then recovering his feet on the path in the fading light. 'I did study Greek of course, and there is a vague recollection in my mind about an author, a Xenophon. Did he not write a work entitled, *A History of my Times*.'

'That's the same fellah. Well, it happened

like this — during one of the wars between the Greeks and the Persians — round 400 BC I recall — there was some fracas on the Asian shore. An army of Greeks got pushed inland, on the retreat, and got 'emselves lost. Ten thousand warriors with no idea where they was, where they was going and how they was going to get back. What's more, all their commanders — five generals and their captains — had been lured away by Persian promises of a truce. Persian commander chopped down the captains and took the generals to the Persian court, where they was put to death, immediate.

'So, here was this lost army with no ranking officer to take charge. Some queer puzzle, eh? Well, this fellah called Xenophon, just a common soldier, he volunteered to lead 'em out of it. Said he'd do his best for 'em, no matter what. This Xenophon led them on a march through wild places, over uncouth mountains, unobliging rivers, without guides or officers, through lands of barbarous tribes which they had to defeat, messed with at all times by the damn Persians, who tagged along behind and picked off stragglers. I tell you brother they had a time of it, them old Greeks in that walk through wild country. Months of it. Seasons of it. Attacked by any number of hostile savage hillmen, who could defend narrow passes in the fastnesses of the mountains like nobody's business, who rolled down rocky masses on Greek heads to crush 'em when they came up, and rolled down boulders on top of 'em when they went down the other side. They was cold, starving, and lost a deal of men on the way.'

Crossman, entirely envious of a man who had gone from private to general just like that, said, 'Now that you tell the tale, I do remember my Greek master giving us the same, but in a much drier manner, and we having to decline verbs and search for gerunds at the same time, it probably went in one ear and out of the other. Look, I feel our little march is but a Sunday jaunt, a stroll in the park in comparison — but I hope your story has a happy ending. Otherwise it will all be lost on me. I cannot bear it if it has a miserable end. I feel for those poor Greeks sorely.'

'Most certain it ends well,' continued the North American. 'This General Xenophon in the end led 'em to the sea. Once they got to the ocean, they felt they was halfway home. There was Greek colonies on the coast and they got friendly help. I tell you,' said Gwilliams, 'I admire them Greeks. They did things like that. They wasn't even professional soldiers, like you and the lieutenant, not mostly. No, they was shopkeepers and tradesmen and scholars and such. Militia. Called to arms by their city, they put on armour and marched out to war, just for the sheer hell and duty of protecting their homes and families. Now me, I got Greek blood in me somewheres, that's for sure.'

'You certainly have the dark colouring and olive complexion — but what about the auburn beard?'

'That's another part of me. Viking, maybe, mixed with a bit of Anglo-Saxon. It's the Greek part that comes out at times like this, you understand. Goes straight to my feet. Now the Romans knew how to march, but they used good roads to do it on. There was no straight roads for the Greeks. They just up and tramped over rough ground, like we're doing now.'

'Is there any Roman in you, do you think?'

Gwilliams nodded, vigorously. 'Why not? They was around too. Roman, Greek, Viking, you name it.'

There is nothing better to cheer a miserable man than a story about men who had a harder time of it and came out of it all with a hand of trumps. Also, for Crossman, there was the vague feeling of letting the Fates deal with the problem of his demotion. Somehow Gwilliams, in his story meant to make them feel better about their march, had incorporated a tale about a common soldier who rose to general rank at a stroke. Although Crossman could not envisage himself being quite so fortunate, there was always the possibility that a situation would arise where he was put in command again. While he would not wish his present commander any harm, officers were killed in a war, and vacancies appeared. Peterson was in no state of health to take command, which would fall naturally on the head of someone who had held that position previously.

Of course, Pirce-Smith could survive the war and Crossman could be killed. That would be all right too, he thought with morbid satisfaction. At least he would not have to face going home to England as a common soldier. He would not have to endure the thought of Jane in some other man's arms, he himself being a totally unworthy suitor. Yes, being dead, being killed in some glorious action, had its merits.

By marching on, into the night, Pirce-Smith had risked injury to himself or one of his soldiers. But at around two o'clock in the morning they were at the gorge where they intended to attack the Russian supply column. Pirce-Smith peered about him, hoping to see some sign in the moonlight

401

which would tell him that the Russians had not already gone through. Of course there was nothing, which annoyed him. He spoke roughly to his *peloton*, told them to get some rest, and then lay himself down on a blanket to ease the night away. He had actually no need to ask his soldiers to bed down. They had sunk to the floor where they stood and were, most of them, fast asleep. Only Ali remained awake, determined to keep guard until morning, just in case the Russians came early. There was also, of course, the possibility that the whole thing was a trap. They were relying on information out of Sebastopol, from spies with doubtful loyalties, and the Turk was leaving nothing to chance.

At five o'clock, Ali woke Crossman and asked him to take over the sentry duty. The Turk had hoped to get through the night but found himself so exhausted he could not prevent himself from dropping off. Crossman wrenched himself from a deep and ragged sleep to a muzzy awareness. He nodded in answer to Ali's question and got up slowly to splash water on his face. After about thirty minutes he managed to shed the desire to lay down his head again. There he sat, blanket around his shoulders and musket in his lap, until seven o'clock. He woke the lieutenant at this point, hoping to get himself at least another hour in bed.

'What is it?' muttered Pirce-Smith, irritably. 'I was sleeping.'

'I know, sir. We forgot to post a sentry last night.'

Instantly the officer was sitting up and rubbing his face. He looked at Crossman in alarm. 'You mean *I* forgot.'

'No, we all forgot. All except Yusuf Ali. He stayed up half the night and then handed over to me, but I'm afraid I can't keep my eyes open any longer. I woke you because I do not want to usurp your command. I felt it better to inform you of the situation, then let you decide who to wake, if anyone. I must lay my head down.'

'Yes, of course you must, Private Crossman. You must be exhausted. Go to it. I'll sort it out now.'

'Yes, sir. Thank you.'

'No — thank you.'

Crossman knew no more until he was being roughly woken himself by a delighted Wynter.

'Come on! The officer wants us. Told me to get you up.'

'Did you kick me then?' growled Crossman.

'Eh? I — it was an accident.'

'The next time you kick me I'll break your leg.'

Wynter scowled. 'Don't you threaten me. Anyways, the officer wants us. He's up there.'

Crossman took out an old fob watch he kept in his pocket. It told him the time was now ten a.m. Above him the lieutenant was holding a council of war. He joined the other men who were eating and drinking at the same time as listening.

'We will go, three of us to each side of the gorge,' Pirce-Smith was saying. 'Crossman, Peterson and Yusuf Ali on this side — Wynter, myself and Gwilliams on the other. When the column comes through you will open fire only on my signal. Now, the signal,' he looked about him. 'Who amongst my team can give a shrill whistle?'

'Me sir,' said Wynter, pursing his lips for a demonstration. Ali immediately clamped his hand over the soldier's mouth.

'Not now, you idiot,' snarled Pirce-Smith. 'They might be in earshot. When I tell you.' He turned back to Crossman and the others. 'When you hear Wynter's whistle, you will open fire. Every shot must hit a man, you understand? Once the ambush has begun, Yusuf Ali will go to a high point. He will take this bugle,' Pirce-Smith produced the instrument with a great flourish, 'and use it as if rallying a whole company. He will then let off two or three gunpowder charges, to simulate the sound of guns being used and to send rockfalls down on to the heads of the enemy. This will add confusion to their ranks. They will think we have many more men up here, plus cannon, and they will panic and hopefully run. Peterson, it will be your job to kill the horses drawing the wagon, or wagons. Now don't give me that look — if you can kill a man, you can kill a horse.'

'So that's what was in the big pack,' said Wynter, rubbing the strap marks on his shoulders. 'We puzzled on it.'

'Now you know. Bugle and gunpowder. There you have it.'

Crossman thought the plan a little too elaborate, but then he was not in charge. It had a certain amount of audacity, which he appreciated. And he was aware that they were high up, out of reach of cavalry. Any men that were sent after them would have to climb a precipitous cliff, exposed to fire the whole journey, and then pull themselves over the top. Without a great number of men it would be suicide. The Russian officers were quite capable of sending their men on suicidal attacks, but Crossman felt that the strong possibility of failure in this case would be enough to deter them.

He knew Pirce-Smith's eyes were on him at that moment, trying to gauge his reaction without having to ask for it. Crossman tried to look as if he approved, which he did, in principle. However, it was impossible for the lieutenant to openly ask his opinion, so nothing was actually said.

After that they split into their two separate groups. Pirce-Smith, Gwilliams and Wynter made the hazardous climb down the cliff, then up the other side, while Ali kept watch for the enemy column. Once they were in position on the far side a handkerchief was fluttered. They settled down into natural sangars, to await the first sign of the Russians. Peterson was saying to him, 'I hope there's silver or gold. You remember we got that prize money waiting for us? What we took from another Russian column? I'm going to spend that, when I get home. I'm going to buy a carpenter's shop and depend on my own living!'

'Good for you, Peterson, but let's get the war over with first.'

Crossman's money would not be waiting for him. He had spent his at the card table with Campbell. Illegally of course. Any prize money earned by the *peloton* was being withheld until the war was over. Any man who deserted would lose his prize. Any man who thought he was rich enough to refuse duty would have it confiscated. It was that simple. Only those who did their duty, who survived the war and were discharged honourably from the army, would be permitted to collect.

'How are you feeling?' Crossman asked the woman soldier. 'You look a little better than yesterday.'

'Sore,' she muttered, 'and a bit feverish, sergeant. But I prefer you don't say anything to the lieutenant.'

There was no time to answer her, for at that moment sounds were heard coming from the end of the gorge. At first it was the snuffling of horses, and grinding of cart wheels on the stony ground. Then the muffled low tones of speech. Ali tapped Crossman's arm and pointed. A supply column was coming into view, moving slowly into the hazy distant end of the gorge. It was led by a troop of cavalry: dragoons with rifles slung over their right shoulders. Crossman was delighted to see that the rifles were encased in waterproof covers. Clearly the Russians were not expecting an ambush or those weapons would have shed their coats. However, just as Crossman was feeling pleased with the situation, he realized that the dragoons kept coming, and coming, and coming. There were many more of them than a few supply wagons justified.

Then the wagons themselves appeared, mostly arabas drawn by oxen, with Tartars at the reins. There were some lighter carts, but these were pulled by horses and driven by Russian soldiers in uniform. These were full of infantry who, Crossman noted with chagrin, had muskets which were not encased in waterproof covers. The wagon train itself was much longer, much larger than expected. It stretched back a long way and was followed again by a sizeable body of dragoons.

'Too many,' muttered Ali.

Crossman whispered, 'You're right, Ali, far too many. We can never take this number.'

The jangle and jingle of horse metal got closer and closer. Soon they were gazing down on Russian helmets and caps. Crossman looked anxiously across the divide, at his commanding officer's position on the far side. No shrill whistle was forthcoming from the lips of Wynter. Surely there would be none? It was suicide to attack such a huge force of heavily armed soldiers with just six men. Pirce-Smith, eager as he was to make his mark, would not force this issue.

Ali, who had been ready to dash up the mountain with the bugle and set off the gunpowder charges, now relaxed. Clearly, he believed the lieutenant would abort the mission. Peterson, however, looked agitated.

She kept staring across the gorge, her face screwed into a waspish expression. She kept adjusting her position in a jerky, unpredictable fashion, as if irritated by the lack of action from her superiors.

'Calm down, Peterson,' whispered Crossman, 'I don't think anything is going to happen.'

She shot him a nasty look and replied in a loud voice, 'Don't tell me to calm down. I'm the senior rank here. It's me who's lance-corporal, not you.'

Crossman stared down at the troops below, but fortunately the noise of the column was great enough to drown Peterson's voice. None of them appeared to have heard her. He then turned back to her, seeing a dangerous look in her eyes. Something had turned in her head. She did not look rational. She was again looking over at her commanding officer's position. 'What is he waiting for?' she hissed. 'They'll be gone through before we get chance to hit them.'

There was no whistle forthcoming from the other side. It was clear now that Pirce-Smith intended to let the Russians go. Crossman was relieved, but there was still the problem of Peterson. He was several yards from her. Ali was closer. He caught the Turk's eyes and motioned with his head towards the woman soldier. Ali nodded. He too was a few yards from her but he was closer than Crossman. He started towards her, crawling on all fours, like a spider going at its prey.

Too late. Peterson's shot rang out and a dragoon officer was flung from his horse by the impact of the ball as it struck his head.

'Dirty bastards,' she shrieked, reloading even as she was berating those she saw as responsible for her condition. 'I'll show *you*.'

For a short moment there was no reaction from the Russians below. They appeared shocked and stunned. Then shots came from Pirce-Smith's side of the gorge. Clearly there was nothing for it now but to kill as many of those below as they could. Ali rushed up the hill. The sound of the bugle came a minute later, just as the Russians were gathering themselves and returning fire. Already eight or nine of their number lay dead or wounded in the dust. Others sought cover but there was little to be had on the floor of the gully. Explosions came from above, which precipitated landslips, sending tons of rock cascading down upon the dragoons and infantrymen below. Horses were whinnying and fighting for space. Some of the wagons continued to rumble on, towards the other end of the gorge. Others, those containing men, remained.

Peterson shot first one driver, then another fifteen seconds later, as if only now that she had created havoc remembering what her orders had been. The sporadic enfilading fire was having its effect on those below. Russians were going down one after another. For a minute or two, as Crossman fired, reloaded, fired again, he had the feeling that they might bluff the Russians into a retreat. Certainly one or two of them were panicking, riders forcing their horses between wagon and boulder, in order to gallop their mounts out of range of the deadly accurate fire.

But the superior numbers of the Russians soon changed the tide of the battle. A blistering return fire from the infantry, who had turned over one or two wagons to use as protection, smashed into the rocks as a storm of iron. And once the dragoons had unsheathed their rifles, they too added to the black blizzard of musket balls flying up at the ambushers. Soon the attackers were unable to lift their heads for fear of having them shot off. The air was full of whining, whispering bullets.

Russians began to scale the escarpments on either side of the gorge. It was time for the *peloton* to vacate their position and make their escape.

Peterson began to crawl away from her

411

position. Crossman followed. Ali was waiting for them a little further up the slope. Fortunately there was an overhang which protected the three soldiers from the worst of the counter-attack. They were able to scramble away along a goat track and into the uplands beyond the narrow gorge. There was little point in waiting for the others, on the far side of the gully. Speed was essential if they were to escape death or capture. Finally, when they were out of sight and range of the Russians, they began to run, leaping over boulders, fallen trees, and away into the hinterland.

Peterson soon had to be half-dragged, half-assisted to keep up with the two men. Her breath was laboured and she was sobbing, though Crossman felt it was with rage rather than sorrow. When the three finally halted and had gathered breath, some distance from the gorge, he turned on her and cried, 'What the hell were you doing?'

She looked sullen. 'We were supposed to ambush them.'

'You were *supposed* to wait for the lieutenant's signal.'

'I thought I heard Wynter's whistle,' she said, her sour expression changing to a canny look. 'I'm sure I did.'

'You are liar, Peterson,' growled Ali. 'There

was no whistle. What, you think we are deaf? There was no signal. You break orders. They flog you for this.'

'If it wasn't a whistle, then it was a cart wheel squeaking. I heard something, that's why I fired. Why do you think I fired?'

'You fired,' Crossman said, 'because you didn't want the operation aborted. You wanted to kill Russians. I was there, Peterson. So was Ali. We know what you were doing. It does you no credit.'

'Credit,' she spat at him, her face twisting and growing dark with hate. 'What credit was it to them who made me dirty? They did things to me, sergeant, and now they've left me with something vile in my body. Something they put there. A horrible disease. They put it there. I'll kill as many of them as I can, whenever I see them. I'm telling you, sergeant, you mustn't trust me anymore. I'll blow holes in them until there's none of them left. They fouled me up. Well, I'll foul them up now. I'll shoot them down like curs until there's no more left to shoot.'

'I understand how you feel, and you're not wrong to feel it, but you can't endanger the rest of us with your vendetta. A soldier obeys orders, Peterson, because there're other lives at stake besides his own. When we get back you will report to a surgeon. If it means you will be thrown out of the army, so be it. If you won't go, I shall drag you there myself.' He placed a hand on her shoulder and his voice grew quieter and more gentle. 'You're a very brave woman. I am proud to have known you. But you have become unpredictable and dangerous to the rest of the *peloton*. I have to do this thing, even though I regard you as one of the best soldiers I have ever been fortunate to command.'

She looked up with a miserable expression.

'Am I still your friend, sergeant? Even though I've done wrong?'

He knelt down and gripped her by the shoulders.

'Ever and always, Peterson.'

'Mine too,' said Ali, gruffly. 'Always I am jealous of your shooting, but I put this aside to say I am your very good friend, like the sergeant.'

She began weeping openly now.

'I hope the others make it back all right,' she said.

'They'll be fine,' replied Crossman, but not at all convinced by his own words. 'They're soldiers. They're 88th. They'll make it.'

9

Crossman, Ali and Peterson made it back to British lines. Later the other three came in, looking harrowed and weary from running. All of them, against the odds, had made it back alive. Ali immediately went off on a borrowed mule, to retrieve the body of Yorwarth. Peterson, wishing to pre-empt the trouble that was about to descend upon her head, went off to find a surgeon or physician. Before she left, Crossman said to her, 'It would be advisable to be seen by someone sympathetic. There was a Dr Barry I met several months ago, who seemed a gentle sort of man . . . '

There were some roughly built stables used as a small hospital for the walking wounded in the north of Kadikoi. Peterson walked over hard rutted ground to this establishment and entered timidly. It was stifling inside. There were one or two sick soldiers, stripped to the waist, sitting or lying on beds. Impassive and vacant they did not look at her. The light was poor, the stables having only small slits like arrowloops for windows. Within, it smelled of sweat, festering wounds and other stale unpleasant odours. Panic rose in Peterson's breast. She did not like new situations. Especially situations in which she was about to feel the wrath of the army descending on her head. She was also fearful of deadly diseases like typhus or cholera, so she kept her distance from the apathetic men on the beds.

She waited in trepidation for several minutes, until finally a woman entered the room. Many of the regiment wives helped with the sick and wounded and Peterson assumed this person was one of those. She asked the woman if there was a Dr Barry there, or where he could be found. The woman said she knew of no Dr Barry, ' . . . but Assistant-Surgeon Lawson is in the next room.'

Peterson walked to the door of the room and looked in, to see a medical officer writing in a notebook. His head came up.

'What is it?' he asked. 'You're using my light. Come in, come in. Step aside from the doorway.'

Peterson entered the dim room and did a little nervous skip to the right.

'Sorry to be of a bother, sir, when you're so busy,' Peterson said, 'but I was — was sent to see if Dr Barry was anywhere to be found.'

'Here? I think not. Dr Barry has visited the

Crimea, but he is far too important to remain in this God-forsaken corner . . . ' The surgeon stared at Peterson keenly. 'Just what is it you want, soldier? Are you ill? You look somewhat shaken about. Have you a fever?'

'I — yes, sir. I think — I think I've got some sort of — pox.'

'Pox?' The surgeon stared at her. 'You mean a venereal disease? You have a discharge?'

'A — a what, sir?'

Lawson gave a sigh and put down his pen. 'Are you leaking fluids, man? Or do you have sores?'

'Oh,' said the dismayed Peterson, swallowing hard. 'Yes — leaking, sir. It burns a bit. I can't go to my regiment surgeon, sir, because I'm on special duties.'

'Well, I have no time to treat you myself. There's another surgeon due in — ah, here he is. Archie, this soldier has wandered in off the street. Perhaps you could deal with him? I believe he has a dose of gonorrhoea. You'll need to examine him further to find out. I haven't the time. I'm wanted at headquarters.'

A plump, elderly man with yellowy-white whiskers and red-veined nose and cheeks had entered the room. He glowered at Peterson.

'Gad! What have you been up to, you

naughty soldier? Didn't your mother tell you to stay away from painted harlots? As if the cholera and dysentery ain't enough. Two thousand deaths this month from diarrhoea and dysentery alone, and naughty cads like you have to go out and seek out something else to make you ill. It's not responsible behaviour.'

Peterson, who was frightened by the sound of the word the younger man had used for her complaint, asked. 'Am I going to die from it, sir?'

Lawson sighed and gathered his stuff together, putting it into a battered leather bag. 'Do we need to moralize, Archie? Just treat the man and get rid of him.'

Once Assistant-Surgeon Lawson had gone, the older man unpacked some instruments from the bag he too carried. There were a set of iron forceps, a formidable rusty saw, a long shiny spike with a hook at the end, and various other weapons of the surgeon's trade. They were tossed on to the table top, one after another. Peterson looked at these instruments of torture in horror and involuntarily her hand went to her genitals. A hammer went down on the wooden surface with a mighty thump. Then the clatter of a long curved knife not unlike those she had seen used in a butcher's shops.

'You — you're not going to cut me, are you, sir?'

'You're wasting my time, soldier,' said the old man, wearily. 'Now, describe the colour and smell of your discharge. Quickly now, I ain't got all day . . . '

Peterson did her best. The elderly surgeon's face remained sour throughout. When she was halfway through her faltering description he took out a pocket watch and stared at it for a full minute, his attention having wandered. Finally he interrupted her flow. It was the first time his voice sounded reasonable.

'I breed my own cultures, which I use in these cases.' He went to a shelf at the back and took down a large brown bottle full of vile-looking liquid. 'I've made an infusion of it.' When Peterson looked helplessly at him, he simplified it. 'A kind of tea. The symptoms should clear up in a week. If they don't, come back for some more. And soldier,' the old gentleman's voice became grave once more, 'stay away from those ladies of the night. I was young once too, y'know, but you've only got one hose. Y'don't want it to rot and drop off, do you? No. Well, then, mind my words.' He siphoned some of the potion off into a smaller bottle, corked it, and handed it to her. 'Two or three swallows of this every day before you eat, to give it a chance to reach your vital parts before food gets in its way. Take some now, before you go.'

He poured some out in a tin cup.

It tasted as terrible as it looked, Peterson asked the surgeon, 'Aren't you going to — to inspect me?'

A look of mild distaste crossed the medical man's face.

'You think I haven't seen enough in my time?' he told her. 'You told me what it looked like and how it smelled. I know what it is. Go away now and only come back if this lot doesn't clear itself. Any fresh condition will find me less than sympathetic. Go on, away with you.'

Peterson trudged back to the hovel. She had not been discovered and had not been dismissed from the army. Her secret was still safe. Yet now she had to face the lieutenant. She had disobeyed orders, or at least taken it on herself to jump ahead of them. Pirce-Smith was going to be furious with her. She had almost got them all killed. If only, she thought, the other half of the *peloton* had not escaped the Russians. It immediately appalled her that she could even think such a thing.

'Ah, Peterson,' said Pirce-Smith as she entered the hovel, her half-hopes dashed, 'I should like a word with you.' His face was indeed harbouring thunder clouds.

The others were all there, Gwilliams and Wynter included, so no one had lost his life. This was no time for heroics. She had to get out of this by devious methods, even if it meant she had to bend the truth. She did not believe she could face harsh punishment at the moment, ill as she was. However, Peterson found it difficult to lie. Her face always went red and her breath quickened. They did so now. Fortunately Pirce-Smith did not know of this quirk in her nature. He simply thought the reason for her flushed features was because she was being accused in front of the men.

'Sir — sir, my rifle just went off.'

'Went off? By accident?'

'Yes, sir. That is, I was all ready to fire and I — I had a sharp pain — in my belly. It made me squeeze the trigger too soon. I'm sorry, sir.'

Pirce-Smith's eyes narrowed. 'It was a damn good shot for an accident.'

'Well, sir, I was all lined up, ready — ready for your signal sir. Once I'd fired, well, they knew it was us there, didn't they? And everyone was firing then, so I kept on doing it. But the first one wasn't meant. I'm very sorry. I didn't mean to do it. It won't happen again.'

'I don't know quite what to do about this, Peterson,' said Pirce-Smith, frowning. 'I was all ready to haul you out, but you say it was an accident?'

'Yes.'

'I shall have to consider it. Just because it was an accident does not mean you were not negligent, Peterson. You may still have some punishment coming to you.'

'I realize that, sir.'

When Pirce-Smith had gone, Wynter swung his legs off his bed and snarled, 'Garn,' at Peterson.

'It was an horrible accident,' Peterson repeated, undaunted, 'like your birth.'

'You nearly got us all killed. You ought to have been flogged, like I was.'

Crossman intervened. 'You might still get your chance to die, Wynter. Did you not hear what the lieutenant was saying before Peterson came back? We're going to attack the Russians, in a few days' time. I haven't any doubt it will be the Redan again. If we walk away from that alive, we shall be very lucky.'

The colour drained from Wynter's face. 'He said he was only guessing.'

'You can feel it in the air, Wynter. Look at the face of any staff officer. Look how they're scurrying around the place like ants. Plans are afoot. General Simpson needs a victory. He needs the war to end here. The lieutenant doesn't know any more than we do, but he can see the hive is buzzing, ready to swarm. There's going to be a big battle.' Crossman paused, then continued in a quieter voice. 'In June the French failed to take the Malakoff and we failed to take the Redan. It follows that we have to assault them again and prove our worth. This time we cannot afford to fail. They will throw men at those fortifications until they fall. Those men will include you and I, Wynter. And Peterson. And any other soldier who can walk or crawl. Yorwarth may be the lucky one.'

Wynter stared at him for a minute, then lay on his cot and turned his face to the wall.

'Peterson,' Crossman said, 'did you visit the surgeon?'

'He gave me this.' She showed him her medicine.

'Good. Was it Dr Barry?'

'No. I asked for him, but he's some grand surgeon, that just travels around the army. There was a young surgeon, who was in a hurry, and then an old one. It was the old one who gave me this. He grumbled at me for going with whores. Said I was to stay away from them.'

Crossman joked, 'And so you should. But

— did he not . . . ?'

'No. He said he'd seen enough of it in his time and made me tell him what it was like.'

'Then your secret is still safe?'

'If I want it to be. I'm not sure I do now. But, sergeant, I'm worried about my prize money. They might take it away from me, if they know I'm a woman. I'm tired and sick though. I just want to go home now. I've done my duty as a soldier. If I tell them, will I lose my money?'

Crossman shrugged. 'It's a consideration. Lord knows they'll snatch at any excuse not to pay money out. But then again, I meant what I said before. We might not survive the coming battle. Any of us. Then what use will the money be to you?'

'I don't think I'm well enough to go into a battle. I'm not a coward, sergeant, but I'm sick and very tired.' There were tears in her eyes. Peterson had been through some terrible ordeals recently, not the least of which was her abduction and rape by the Cossacks. She looked frail and weak.

'I'll have a word with the lieutenant,' said Crossman. 'No one could call you a coward, Peterson. And what if they did? You are a woman who has done more than any other female I know. I have nothing but admiration for you. I'll do what I can.'

'Thank you.'

In the event, Lieutenant Pirce-Smith also thought it politic to bend the truth, when reporting to Colonel Hawke. He told the colonel that the supply train had been larger and better guarded than they had expected, but they had attacked it anyway, killing several cavalry and disrupting the supply wagons. He put forward the impression that the intention throughout was to attack the Russians, no matter that they outnumbered his force twenty-to-one. One of his men had fired too soon, but no harm had come of it.

'They'll think twice about using that route again, sir. We gave 'em a thrashing they won't forget in a hurry. It showed them how vulnerable they are up in the hills.'

Hawke nodded in approval. 'But you say one of our men let go a little too early?'

'Peterson, sir. But she hit her target, and her shot was as good as my signal for starting the whole show. I have of course reprimanded her for her eagerness, but I think I shall leave it at that.'

'Quite so. We have always admired Peterson's skill with the rifle-musket. God, I wish I had it. You can hear some of the quail laughing when I pick up a sporting gun.'

'I'm sure that's not the case, sir,' replied the lieutenant, diplomatically.

'And I can assure you, it is,' confirmed the colonel. 'Hares have been known to stop and cock a snoot after my bullet has whizzed by their ear. Well, that's all. You've heard about the coming attack?'

'Yes, sir — one of my fellow officers . . . '

'Quite. Well, there won't be any time to get another fox hunt in before we go into battle, so I suggest the men go back to their regiment, to prepare for the assault. My guess is this will be the final thrust. If we don't overrun 'em this time, we'll never do it.'

Pirce-Smith chanced a remark that a few months ago he would not have believed could have come from his lips.

'Sir,' he said, tentatively, 'do you not think the men deserve a rest? They've been hard at it for months now.'

Hawke's face was impassive. 'This is war, lieutenant. They must do their duty by their regiments. Men have been hard at it in the trenches too.' His voice grew softer. 'I appreciate your loyalty to your men, Pirce-Smith. It's a new feeling, isn't it? When the unit shrinks to around six or seven men, you know and are intimate with them, even though they are common soldiers. Out on a fox hunt you share your bread with them. You hear their stories and when your guard drops, as it must when you find yourself in dire circumstances every so often, they hear yours. The world is changing. Wellington called them scum, but you and I know they are men like us. Good men, and true. Perhaps not so refined, but then good breeding is not of much use out there in the hills, is it? The damn Cossacks pick their noses, eat with their fingers and fart in company, yet they're some of the best fighters in the business.' He paused for a moment, before adding, 'Yorwarth's dead, eh? That strong handsome Australian boy? Killed by bees. It strikes me as wicked, to go like that. Quite unfair. The Lord not only moves in mysterious ways, He smites His people in ironic ways too. Well, you'd better go and tell them to pack and make ready. They won't like it. Nor would I.'

'And the camel, sir? What about your zumbooruck?'

'Ah, that? It was an affectionate dream, lieutenant. But dreams must be put aside when the real fighting arrives.'

Pirce-Smith did as he was told. He returned to the hovel and spoke to the men, telling them they must return to their regiment. Gwilliams was to report to Hawke who would find use for his gentler talents, such as hair-cutting and bone-setting. Yusuf Ali was to return to the Bashi-Bazouks, those Turkish irregulars who could match the

Cossacks for wild horsemanship.

A group of them went out, to say goodbye to Betsy and Stik. The episode with the dromedary had been one of the more colourful experiences of their war. Crossman went to see Jane at her place. She was with Lavinia Durham. The pair of them looked grave as he approached. They too knew a battle was imminent. Lavinia was a warrior queen when it came to battles, often being among the first to reach a viewing point, but the last attempted assault on the Redan had cooled her ardour for that particular goal somewhat. To see men slaughtered like cattle was a sobering thing, even for an iron lady such as she.

'Alex,' said Lavinia. 'How nice to see you.' She pecked him on the cheek. 'I shall leave you two to talk.'

Lavinia left the room and went into the recesses of the house.

'Jane,' said Crossman, 'we are being sent back to our regiment.'

A look of pain crossed her face. 'You will be in the coming battle?'

'I fear so. I won't pretend I'm looking forward to it this time. I'm convinced it will be an attack on the Redan — there's no other real objective — and I saw what happened last time. Then I was standing on a safe hill

428

alongside Major Lovelace, with a spyglass to my eye. This time, I shall be in the thick of it.'

'And will your Major Lovelace be in the battle too?' she asked bitterly, knowing the answer.

'I doubt it. He is too valuable for the army to risk in such ventures.'

She stepped forward and gripped his sleeves with both hands.

'And you are too valuable to me! Priceless. Worth a thousand Major Lovelaces. I shall use all my influence to get you out of this battle, Alex. I shall.' Her eyes welled with tears. 'I do not want you dead. To die uselessly like that, as cannon fodder. It doesn't make sense. I can't bear it.'

'I wish you wouldn't, Jane. I implore you not to. I would not be able to live with myself afterwards, now would I? A woman pleads with the authorities to have them put one soldier aside, when there are thousands of others who have to fight? It won't wash, Jane. Generals will fall in that battle, let alone privates. I can promise you no heroics. I shall not join the Forlorn Hope. I shall do my duty, but I shall not put myself in the way of cannon or musket ball without good reason. I too am weary of this war. This will be the last battle, I'm convinced of it. Next week the war will be won or lost. There will be rejoicing in one camp or the other.'

'You promise to keep yourself safe?' she said, fiercely.

'I will do my duty, as I am able.'

'Oh, that? Duty. You just come back to me, you hear, Alexander Kirk, or Jack Crossman, whatever your name is. I cannot travel out here for the rest of my life, putting flowers on the grave of my beloved.'

'Your beloved?' His pulse quickened. He took her in his arms and was kissing her when Lavinia entered the room again in a flurry of silks and satins, only to wheel round and exit again as swiftly as she had come in. 'If for nothing else, I shall return for one of those,' he said.

She continued to clasp him until Lavinia coughed loudly from the other side of the doorway.

'You can come in, dear,' said Jane. 'We are not making love.'

'As to that,' said Lavinia, entering again, 'I am not convinced in the least. Here, I have some wine and some cakes. Let us enjoy ourselves for the next hour. I've sent for Mr Jarrard, too. I know he would wish to join us.'

'A last supper?' joked Crossman.

'That is not humorous, Alex,' said Lavinia. 'Look at how downcast you have made dear Jane by that remark.'

Jarrard duly arrived. 'Hey, Jack? The common soldier, off to war again, eh? I don't envy you. What's this, the last supper?'

The two women gave him looks that would have killed a camel at twenty yards.

'And how is Monique?' asked Crossman.

'As lovely as ever,' came the reply. 'I'm convinced I've found my soulmate, Jack. And she thinks me wonderful, which is, of course, a necessary thing in these relationships, don't you agree?'

Crossman smiled. 'I do indeed.'

The four friends continued to chat, until Lavinia's husband Bertie arrived home to find his wife hobnobbing with a mere private. Bertie however knew of Crossman's aristocratic connections and seemed oblivious of the fact that it was quite improper of him as a captain to share a bottle of wine with a private. In fact the amiable Bertie was soon exploring the possibility of visiting Crossman's father's estates in the shooting season.

' . . . once we all return home, of course.'

'Bertie, you can't invite yourself to Alexander's family home.'

'Can't I?' said Durham, looking round with a smile on his pleasant handsome features, his white teeth gleaming. He had broad shoulders, narrow hips, and looked magnificent in a uniform. His brain might not be all that his wife wished it to be, but many men would have died for his image. 'Why not?'

'Because it's — it's rude and unmannered of you.'

'D'you think it's rude?' he asked Crossman.

The common soldier shook his head. 'A gentleman must find his shooting where he can. There's not a lot of it about. Too many cliques, if you ask me. I'll have a word with my older brother, James. My father and I are not exactly on speaking terms at the moment.'

'No?' queried the captain. 'Why's that then?'

'Bertie,' cried Lavinia, 'that is also rude.'

Crossman was not concerned about the invasion of his privacy. 'My father does not enjoy having a common soldier for a son.'

'Ah.' Bertie Durham stared at Crossman's brick-red uniform as if noticing it for the first time. 'Can understand that. Wouldn't really like a son of mine amongst the ranks. Not now I've got out of 'em myself. But,' he added generously, 'I shouldn't stop speaking to him, if circumstances forced the issue. A father should speak to his son. A son should honour his father. Those have always been my sentiments. I expect you have yours, but they're mine.'

432

Lavinia Durham placed an ivory hand on her husband's sleeve to indicate that she approved of this little speech.

A long vacuum followed, which was finally broken by Rupert Jarrard. He said, 'I had occasion to shoot my own father once, when he failed to greet me at the breakfast table.'

They all stared at him, shocked and appalled by what went on in ex-colonies, now that they were governed by the sons of immigrants.

Jarrard grinned. 'Not really, but I felt the silence had gone on too long and I couldn't think of anything interesting by way of conversation.' He suddenly turned accusatory. 'Say! You believed me, too — didn't you? You actually believed I could shoot my own pa over a trivial matter like that. We're not that wild over there, you know.'

'Of course we didn't, Rupert,' said Crossman. 'You just caught us unawares.'

Jarrard was not mollified. He excused himself to the ladies and then went outside to smoke a cigar. Crossman joined him a few minutes later, with chibouque in hand. Together they puffed away. Once they were mellow with tobacco, Jarrard said, 'I hear it's going to be a rough one, this coming battle — rougher than usual.'

'So I'm told.'

Jarrard stuck out a hand. 'Good luck, old fellah.'

'Thank you, Rupert.'

'And if you don't come back, you can be sure I'll write a long and interesting obituary on the life and times of Fancy Jack Crossman. I'll have half America mourning your passing.'

'That's very kind.'

'Think nothing of it.'

★   ★   ★

A Russian man-of-war roared into a great pillar of flame, thus lighting up the small hours of the night. It had been hit by French guns and continued to burn beautifully as troops gathered in the early dawn to march down to the trenches. One soldier near Crossman likened it to the candle of God, saying it was a good omen for the coming battle.

Crossman thought the man an optimistic fool.

'Your objective,' said the captain who addressed Crossman's company, 'is the salient angle of the Redan.'

Crossman stared across the divide, unable to see the fortification which the officer was indicating, but able to picture it in his mind.

It was a very narrow objective — perhaps too narrow — and he knew this might indeed add to the difficulty of taking it. The Russians would have a happy time of it, firing their canister and grapeshot down such a lean avenue. Men would go down like ripe wheat under a shotgun blast. He heard a lieutenant mutter ominously, 'This looks like another eighteenth of June.'

It was the Light Division, of which Crossman's 88th Connaught Rangers were a part, who were to lead the assault on the Redan. To those veterans who had been in the Crimea since the first landing — perhaps a tenth of the whole division — it seemed a cruel choice. They had been bled of their seasoned troops by dint of defending the batteries and guarding the approaches to the Redan, for many a long weary day. For the most part, those men around Crossman, gathering in the 4th parallel on the morning of 8th September 1855, were mere boys. They were as green as the grass on the uplands and in their inexperience they felt they had to show nothing but bravado concerning the coming battle, whereas it was the veterans who quaked. They knew, from the numbers around them, that they were going in with a fraction of the force the French were using against the Malakoff. They knew that the slaughter of the last assault in June was going to be duplicated on this day. It seemed to them, and they could not understand the mindset of their commander-in-chief, that they were merely going to repeat the earlier mistake which had led to the carnage of their regiments.

'If we could go in with full regiments,' said one veteran, 'instead of these driblets that are left, we might stand a chance.'

A freshly arrived soldier answered cheerily, 'If ifs and ands were pots and pans, there'd be no need for tinkers.'

Crossman knew that this boy would most likely be a casualty before the evening came and this thought grieved him almost more than the death of Yorwarth. It grieved him because it could be prevented. Why had they chosen the Light Division to go in first? The division was worn out and weary from sickness, lack of sleep, culled numbers and sheer hard war-work. The Light Division should have been in reserve, not at the forefront of the battle. It was their right as battered troops from the last *identical* assault, to go to reserve. Yet here they were, ready to swarm out over that killing ground, to attempt in like fashion what had already failed.

Even now, while still in the trenches, one or

two were wounded, coming under fire from the Redan. The British batteries had been pounding the Redan, hour after hour, for several days now. A constant roar filled the air around the trenches, with the Russians replying in kind. An artillery man had told Crossman the previous evening that he believed over 100,000 shells and round shot had been sent winging towards the enemy.

'If each missile hit just one man,' the corporal had said, 'there would be no one left over there when the attack came.'

But of course it was not like that. In fact Crossman knew from experience that when the infantry attack came it would seem as if Russian numbers had hardly been affected. What happened to all that iron was beyond him, for it was enough to make a small mountain when gathered together. The French had recently begun firing their cannon in unison: up to 250 guns opening up at one instant. The reports were that this rain of heavy metal was creating havoc amongst the Russians. According to observers the enemy were suffering terrible losses. Yet Crossman would wager when it came to sending in the infantry there would be an army to meet them.

In the period before noon the Light and 2nd Divisions were given their tasks. There was to be a covering party of 200, a ladder party of 350, a storming party of 1,000, and 1,500 supporting troops. Crossman was in the supporting party. During the morning, fellow soldiers who knew him gave him nods, for though he had been an infantry sergeant, he had never been one of those who treated privates badly. He heard the name 'Fancy Jack' whispered a few times, usually from veterans to newly arrived troops, and they looked his way with wide eyes.

The wind was blowing straight from the north, raising the dust and driving into the faces of the 88th as they moved from one parallel to the next. The Russian guns fired grapeshot at the trenches, which zinged and whined from stone and metal, sometimes clattering amongst the hurrying soldiers. It fell not as the gentle rain from heaven, but came as hard hot iron from hell. They had a wicked time of it, moving along the shallow saps, some of them casualties before the charge had even begun.

At one point in their travels forward to the Quarries, they came upon a limping bewildered civilian, who was knocked roughly aside by a colour-sergeant. What this lame fool was doing out there on the battlefield was a matter for conjecture, for he simply allowed himself to be buffeted and pushed out of the way without a murmur. When Crossman looked back, astonished by the civilian's presence, he saw the man sitting on the ground with his trouser leg rolled up, inspecting his knee.

At noon the guns suddenly grew quieter and the high note of a French bugle replaced their thunder. At that moment Zouaves sprang out of the French trenches like a swarm of cats and began running towards the Malakoff. The French sappers took with them a secret weapon: a movable bridge, which they used to span the ditch in front of the Malakoff. Over this bridge they went in great numbers: far more than were being used by the British to attack the Redan. It seemed that despite the preliminary barrages over the last few days the Russians were not expecting an attack at such a time in the day. Attacks normally took place just after dawn, to get the most light out of the day, rather than at noon. The French soldiers were in the Malakoff before its commander knew what was happening.

A few moments later the French tricolour was hoisted above the ramparts. From that point on, hard fighting took place, as the Russians sought to drive the French back from whence they had come. An enemy Forlorn Hope was thrown at General

Pélissier's brave men, but was repulsed by the French soldiers who poured across the divide between their trenches and the Malakoff. Before long, French artillery was in place and pounding the Russian attackers with great thumps.

The raising of the tricolour found the British troops still waiting on their banquette, ready and eager to go, but unable to move without a signal from their commander. Crossman's heart was in his throat. Perhaps it would be all right? The French seemed to have taken the Malakoff with ease. Perhaps the fight had gone out of the enemy and this would be a victory for the British too. These were his hopes, as he waited impatiently for the call to charge. He had forgotten the fact that the British troops were so few in number, compared with the French, and that they had a more difficult fortification to scale.

Suddenly Crossman heard the call, 'Forward men! Come on! Come on!' Only some of the men moved at first, confused a little by the ragged response of their officers. There was no concerted attack, more a motley rush by the youngsters, and a more measured unhurried walk by the veterans. Crossman saw one or two old hands pause to light their pipes, leaning on their muskets as they did so. Only then they continued with narrowed eyes towards the Redan, puffing away on harsh tobacco.

When Crossman left the banquette and walked through the smoke of war towards the salient, he was cold and dead inside. He felt neither fear nor exultation. There were black blizzards of grapeshot sweeping towards him in hot waves. As they passed over and around him, leaving him unscathed, he saw others fall. Some were hit by a single piece and went down whole. Others were struck by a tight swarm, their bodies torn to shreds. A soldier to the left of him had his head taken off by a tight cloud of canister. His skull simply exploded into thousands of fragments. The corpse took another step forward, then fell sideways amongst the other dead and wounded. Crossman stepped around it, as if in some evil dream. A young ensign took a round shot in the stomach and was propelled, bent double, back a hundred yards, to land in a crumpled heap of flesh in the trench from which he had sprung just a few moments earlier.

The pungent smell of gunpowder bit into Crossman's nostrils, informing him that he was still alive. He found that hard to believe, watching men go down like skittles in an alley, some with musket balls, some with the cascading showers of exploded shell, some with canister and grape. How could the soldiers survive such squalls of metal, which swept across the battlefield, taking men's legs from under them, tearing off their arms, thwacking into chests protected by only a thin layer of cloth? Yet survive he did and with him several others. How strange it was to look around through the yellow gloom of gun-smoke, in the deafening thunder of rifle and gun, to see the ground littered with friends and strangers, yet still be standing.

He saw Wynter go past him, walking the other way, carrying an officer on his wiry shoulders. Wynter did not see him. Wynter's eyes were staring a thousand yards in front of him. The officer was still alive, though one of his legs was missing, the stump bleeding profusely down Wynter's back.

Crossman looked ahead again, saw the 88th rallying at the base of the salient, where the abattis had been shattered by allied guns. Looking up he could see the walls, bristling with muskets, some pointing down at him. Grey figures were up there, hordes of them, firing muskets, throwing down rocks. Cross-man raised his rifle and fired. The enemy were also falling like lone birds from the ramparts of the Russian defences above him. They came down as broken pigeons, their coats fluttering, their arms loose. Some screamed on the descent. Others were silent. They fell into the ditch below, in amongst the bodies of the redcoats, to be pierced by the bayonets of dead or wounded men whose weapons were jammed upright. It was a pit of spikes in there, a wild animal trap spearing careless men.

As the ladders went up, and Crossman began to climb, he told himself, *I must not fall*. Yet he did fall, when a rock struck his shoulder and dislodged him. He plummeted into that mass of bodies and spikes. His landing was soft and he fell between the bayonets. Still feeling numb inside, he automatically crawled out of the corpses, got to his feet, and started to climb the ladder again. It was pushed sideways from the wall at the top with a forked pole. This time the ladder fell on top of him and crushed his left hand. He sat up and held it out in front of him. It was floppy and useless below the elbow. There was a pain now, but it was distant, almost as if it belonged to someone a long way away. Reaching inside his coat he took out his private weapon, his revolver, and seeing a Russian leaning over the ramparts above, shot him dead.

Another ladder went up and he shinned up it quickly, hooking his good arm in the rungs. Men were ahead of him, others came after.

He found himself at the top and like his comrades who had gone before, jumped in amongst the Russians. He fired once, twice, a third time, into the mass of bodies, hearing only a single groan from a man whose nose was almost touching his, as the fellow's hands flew to the wound in his stomach. In the mass of heaving bodies, a burly Russian soldier, weaponless it seemed, grasped him by the shoulders and heaved him backwards.

Crossman slid headfirst down the ladder he had climbed, knocking men off on his way. His foot caught in the rungs halfway down and he dangled there. He started to haul himself up when a bullet pierced a hole through his cheek, tearing his lip on its way out of his open mouth. His leg suddenly gave way and he slid the rest of the journey to the bottom of the ladder, where a soldier stood yelling at him to, 'Get out of the way! You are blocking our climb!' Then the ladder was pushed off again, stranding those who had made it on to the ramparts, and crashed down upon the man who had been berating him, but this time missing Crossman.

Crossman blew a bloodspit-bubble and groggily got to his feet.

'Come on! Come on!' shouted a fresh-faced lieutenant, having reached Crossman's shoulder in another wave of attackers. The young man had his cap on the point of his sword, holding it high to encourage his company. Most of the soldiers in this company were mere boys, barely trained, and they faltered and fell back on being blasted from above by massed musket fire. The lieutenant cried to them, to remember their duty, and know who they were, but his words were cut short when a ball struck him in the temple and he dropped where he stood. His company scattered, looking for cover that was not there, using the bodies of their fallen comrades to attempt to block that withering fire from the sky.

Crossman had the horrible feeling that the day was already lost. He knew that they were charging the enemy with raw recruits, some of them barely able to use their rifles. He suspected there would be no Union flag flying from the Redan, as there was a tricolour on the Malakoff. Yet feverish hope still burned within him.

He picked up the lieutenant's sword and waved it in the air.

'Come on, men!' he cried, hoarsely. 'We can still take it!'

He turned to look at the salient, to see that only three of the original six or so ladders were still in place. There should have been twenty or more. Several of the ladders had been left behind in the trenches, an oversight for which someone would pay later. Others had been abandoned halfway somewhere along that deadly 250 yards to the Russian defences.

'Up, up!' he shrieked. 'Out of your holes, rabbits.'

A few dribs and drabs of the frightened young men darted forward from shell holes, but when several of these fell under the savage onslaught of musketry from above, the others stayed where they were, hunched down behind any sort of barrier they could find. They seemed paralysed by the noise and carnage around them. There was no fire in them, as there had been in those at the Alma and Inkerman. In his heart he could not blame them. Wicked iron was everywhere: a dust-storm of death. Looking around him, Crossman could see no senior officers. They seemed to have all gone down in the first wave. Near to him was the headless body of a major. Further over, in a tangled mass of dead men, the corpse of a colonel.

Crossman gave up on the young soldiers and limped over to where a Royal Engineer was trying to construct a ramp over the ditch. He stood by him, assisting him, waving encouragingly at those who dared to come to cross the ditch. His mouth kept filling with blood which he regularly spat out. The crushed hand was giving him great pain. But his head was clear for the first time during the battle. He felt as if he were there, really there, and not in some yellow-hazed dream. Yet it was as if the place on which he was standing was gradually sinking down into hell. The devil and his demons were dragging them into a morass of blood and fire.

Then he saw something which made him smile. Away on the right flank, a young officer, not much more than a boy, was coolly lighting a cigar. The youth was leading by example. Once his cigar was lit, the young officer urged his men on, pointing to the parapet, telling them it was but a step, no further. A great rock from above thumped into the mire at Crossman's feet, upending him with the force of the impact on the ground. When he regained his feet, another officer began prodding him towards the ladder. The sword was gone, so was his revolver. Still he did as he was expected to do, and began to climb again, hooking his left arm through the rungs, and using his good hand to heave himself aloft. The officer remained below, yelling, 'I want soldiers in formation and under obedience!'

For the second time Crossman actually stood on the ramparts of the Redan. But the whole works was jammed with men, mostly Russians. The enemy were heaving, surging forward in great numbers from the open rear of the fortification. A captain was trying to rally the British, to force back the oncoming mass. There were too many. There were far too many. They squeezed the British soldiers up against the stonework. A sergeant was crying, 'Where is that damned ammunition? We are out of it here! We have none to return fire!' Hand grenades flew through the air. A moan of defeat went through the British soldiery and some turned and jumped, down into the ditch below. Those lucky enough to land softly struggled out and ran. Others fell on broken ladders or bayonets, and suffered for it. Crossman was knocked over in the retreat and fell the whole way, to knock his head on the ground below. He lost consciousness.

When he came to, the battle was in its last throes. A bayonet pinned his left side to the ground. He tried to pull the blade out but had to give up, being too weak from loss of blood. Around him was a slumped mass of wounded or dead soldiers. Grapeshot still swept in swathes across the area from the Redan to the trenches. Retreating men were spinning over like hares caught by shotgun fire. It was ignominy. Crossman knew the day was lost and he groaned in sorrow, seeking refuge in unconsciousness again.

* * *

Some time later, during the dark hours, the bayonet was removed from his side. He felt himself lifted up and carried. He remained in a state of stupor, until the point where there was a grating, snarling pain that ripped through his body. It was too much to bear and he screamed with the horror of it. The pain stopped but he still lashed out at his attacker. A rag doused in chloroform was quickly placed over his nose and he swooned yet again. This time when he woke he had a raging headache. Too weak to move even a limb, he simply lay there, waiting for death to envelope him. At that moment he was careless of life: it mattered very little to him whether he stayed in this world, or let go and entered the next.

He continued in this state for several days, neither fully alive, yet not quite dead. A young man fed him with soup from time to time, forcing it between his lips with a wooden spoon. He drank it down in a desultory fashion, only vaguely aware that the person feeding him was speaking a foreign language. As he grew stronger and his mind began to clear, he realized he was answering. The language was French. Somehow he had ended up in the French camp. They had found him, with one of their parties out looking for wounded, and had taken him back to their own lines.

A period of high fever and anxiety followed. A bout of pneumonia almost carried him off. But he was well cared for and fought his way back, the will to live growing stronger in him every day. Once he poked his tongue through the hole in his cheek. For this he was chastised by a visiting surgeon, who spoke to him sternly. He promised the man that he would not do it again, yet like a child he did at the first opportunity. It held an irresistible fascination for him, that hole in his cheek.

'Am I to live?' he asked the young boy, who was not much more than fifteen years of age. 'Will I heal?'

'The surgeon says so.'

He was a round-faced youth with large muddy-brown eyes. A shock of dark hair sprouted from his head. His French dialect told Crossman he was from the south, probably Marseilles. He was eager to please and was forever hovering around Crossman's bed.

'What are my injuries?'

'You have a flesh wound in the side. Your cheek was shot through, but that is healing well. And of course, there is the arm, but there is no gangrene. You should be grateful for that. I'm the one who cauterized it,' said the boy, proudly. 'My name is Pierre. I am to be a surgeon when I go home.'

'My ankle hurts,' said Crossman, aware that he sounded ungrateful for the attention he had received.

The boy lifted the blanket at the bottom and looked, saying, 'It is no longer swollen, sir. It was quite bad, a blue colour, but the swelling has gone down now.'

Alarm suddenly shivered through Crossman as the full implication of the boy's previous speech entered his reasoning.

'What's the matter with my arm?'

Pity showed in the boy's eyes and Crossman lifted his right arm up to stare at it.

'The other one,' said Pierre.

He raised the left. It ended in a stump about halfway between the elbow and where the hand should be. He could not believe it. Using his right hand he wafted the air around the end of the stump, for he could *feel* his left hand. It was there, aching where it had been crushed. Yet, it was not there to view. A lump entered his throat as the realization flooded his brain. His hand had been amputated, up

451

beyond the wrist. He was crippled.

'Oh my God,' he murmured, appalled. 'Oh my dear God.'

'I'm sorry,' said Pierre, looking unhappy. 'You can do many things still.'

'Can I, by Jesus?' snapped Crossman, suddenly in a great fury. 'Who gave you permission to cut off my hand? Where the hell is the surgeon? Bring me the bastard who did this . . . ' He tried to raise himself from the straw pillow, but flopped back down again. Now he started sobbing, the shock rippling through him. 'Chloroform. I should have known. I should have stayed awake. Where have they put my hand, boy?' He started to look around him, seeking his severed appendage.

Pierre hurried away. Crossman looked around him, looking for sympathy, but the beds all down the long hut were full of men far worse off than he. There were those without legs, those without any arms whatsoever. Some had festering wounds of the trunk, the head, the arms, the legs. Others had bandages around their eyes and were temporarily or permanently blind. By the time Pierre returned with a surgeon, he was in remorse for his harsh words, although still feeling very sorry for himself at that moment. A talk with the doctor restored his dignity. By the time the surgeon left him, Crossman was bitter but accepting of his condition.

'I could be dead, I suppose,' he said to himself, strangely enough in French, presumably because that was all he had heard for some time now, 'but at least I am alive.'

'That's what I've been telling you,' cried Pierre. 'At least you are alive! Others have not been so lucky. And the Russians have gone, sir. The battles are over. There are no grey uniforms in the streets of Sebastopol.'

He cried, 'Sebastopol is empty?'

'There are some people there, but no soldiers.'

Another man then came to see him. A corporal clerk by his fussy looks and his quill and paper. He brought with him a stool on which he sat by Crossman's bed.

'Now that you are awake, Englishman,' said the newcomer, 'I must take your name and your regiment, so that we can report who you are to your people.'

'Serg — Private Jack Crossman, 88th Foot,' he said to the Frenchman. 'But I should like to get word to a Major Lovelace, of the Rifle Brigade.'

'Ah, yes — but you speak very good French? Have you a relative maybe, living in our country?'

'No — I was taught it at school.'

The corporal looked sceptical, knowing that a private in the British army was likely to be a peasant without access to a good education. He said nothing on the matter, however, but took down the meagre details. After asking a few more questions he left Crossman in the care of Pierre, who also had others to attend to in the hut. For the next few hours Crossman indulged in some deep thinking, trying to see beyond the sorrow of his lost hand, to a point beyond, where practical matters took precedence over feelings.

Crossman did not know why he asked to see Lovelace and not Pirce-Smith or even Jane. He wanted a person he knew reasonably well, yet not someone close enough to make for an emotional meeting. There was a need for a rational impartial discussion, without any melodrama. Not that Jane would have had hysterics — she was not the kind of female to indulge in such carnivals — but her eyes would show her feelings. Crossman needed someone who was cold and indifferent to suffering. That was Lovelace. Whether a major might feel it was beneath him to attend a private soldier's sick bed was another matter. Crossman thought he might come, though, considering their history. But who could tell, with field officers?

Lovelace duly arrived, six hours later.

'Hello, old chap, been in the wars?' he said, jovially.

Crossman gave the major a fierce look, but Lovelace was not to be stared down.

'So, I understand the injuries are pretty minor, except for the hand of course.'

'If you consider a hole in the cheek, a dislocated ankle and a bayonet which barely missed my kidneys minor, yes — I fare pretty well,' replied Crossman with a touch of frost. 'In fact I don't know why I'm not up and dancing a quadrille.'

'There's no need to be sarcastic, Private Crossman,' said Lovelace, 'I have come to your bedside as ordered.'

'I didn't order it, sir. I requested it.'

'Just so. Let me see the arm, old chap.' Crossman held up his stump, still covered in a bloody bandage. 'Ah, that dressing needs changing.' Lovelace took off his coat and rolled up his sleeves. 'I'm pretty good at these things. Boy?' he yelled in French. 'Another dressing here. Some clean water in a bowl and a sponge if you please.'

Pierre gave him a look that would have withered an oak, but he fetched the items. Lovelace then proceeded to change Crossman's dressing, swabbing down the stump, drying it, putting on some balm that Pierre had brought along with the water. When he had finished, the major put on his coat again, nodding at the limb. 'No gangrene. Excellent. They are good surgeons here, are they not? The French have always been skilful at this sort of thing. They have had to be I suppose, considering the drubbings we've given them in the past.'

'I — thank you for that, sir — but — I asked you here for a specific purpose. I must know. Have I been made sergeant again? For my part in the battle?'

Lovelace's facial muscles stiffened. He looked grim.

'I am afraid the answer to that must be *no*.'

Crossman, who had half-raised himself from his bed, fell back with a hollow groan.

Lovelace's face now broke into a smile.

'You've been made lieutenant instead.'

A hot wave of disbelief swamped over Crossman.

'Lieutenant?'

'Not even an ensign,' cried Lovelace, gleefully. 'You skipped over that one like a roe deer. The queen has been dishing out ensigns like confetti, but yours has been upped one. It was mostly Colonel Hawke's doing. He was prepared to fight for it like a tiger. Not that there was much opposition, for there are certain parties who have been aware of your wartime activities. Men of power who are behind our clandestine operations. They see how necessary such things are in modern warfare.'

'But the battle? Did someone see how well I fought?'

Lovelace shrugged. 'Perhaps, but you have received no mention for it, though all the reports are not yet in. Wait a bit, are you the soldier who assisted an engineer in constructing a makeshift bridge?'

'I didn't so much assist him, as give him my encouragement.'

'Then you have a witness! He said there was an 88th soldier, a sergeant without his stripes. There. A witness. He also saw you climb one of the ladders and throw yourself like a wildcat into the fray, even though you were unarmed at the time and sorely wounded.'

'And what of the others? I saw Wynter carrying a man.'

'He saved his company's captain and has been made sergeant for it, plus a big medal coming his way.'

Crossman ground his teeth. 'Wynter? A sergeant? What is the army coming to? It took me years to get that rank. Yet here he is, stripes on his arm, and still a whiner in his early twenties! Where is the justice?'

Lovelace was not sympathetic. 'Things happen in war that do not happen in peacetime. In the normal course of things, Wynter would have been discharged a private at age sixty. But you know, he has turned into the most strict disciplinarian. He is very keen that his men should be smartly dressed and the best at drill in the regiment. A tyrant for correctness, so I'm told. They are the worst, I understand, the reformed rebels. They turn into these satraps whom the troops both hate and admire.'

'I cannot believe it.'

'True, I'm afraid. And Peterson is gone, on a ship bound for England. You know she searched the battlefield for your body? Yusuf Ali and Gwilliams too. They scoured the land for your remains. Yet here you are, safe and well — an officer and a gentleman to boot. You have a servant now, of course. His name is Gwilliams. He was glad for the job. I've sent him to find Pirce-Smith, who will be directed to join us here.'

'I am hardly well, sir.'

'Call me Nathan.'

Crossman was puzzled. 'Call you what, sir?'

'By my Christian name, Nathan — we are brother officers now. Of course, in the line of duty, you will address me properly, but we are two friends here, one at the bedside of the other.'

'Nathan Lovelace? It sounds strange. I never knew you had a first name. It never occurred to me.'

He gave Crossman an amused smile.

'Too cold and hard, am I, to have been christened? I have three, actually. Charles Nathaniel Edward — but I prefer to be called Nathan by my acquaintances and friends.' He paused, then said, 'Now listen to me, and I will not take no for an answer. You will remember Lieutenant Dalton-James, the predecessor of Pirce-Smith? Yes, of course you do. You may also recall he was killed in civilian clothes? He rushed into the battle at Inkerman in his shooting jacket, boots and trousers. I still have his uniform. His note — one of those notes we all leave for our friends and relations should we fall — stated that I should find a good home for it. Well I have. He would be pleased if I passed it on to you. It is a particularly splendid uniform, for he was quite well-heeled, was our old lieutenant. You are about the same size. I'm almost sure it will fit perfectly. We can get one of the French *cantinières* to alter it if not. There is a sword and all that goes with it. What do you say?'

Crossman was close to tears. 'I have to be

honest and say that the lieutenant did not like me a great deal.'

'Oh, as to that, he admired you enormously, but it would not have done for him to say so. No — you are correct, he did not *like* you, but it is not his wife I'm asking you to accept, but his uniform. He knows, wherever he is now, that you will do it proud, I am certain.'

Crossman tried to wipe away the wetness from his cheeks, but unfortunately attempted it with his missing hand.

'Damn thing,' he said, crossly, to hide his emotion, 'I keep forgetting it isn't there.'

'Curious, ain't it? I'm told one has a ghost limb after the real one has been removed. But I've never seen anyone try to use it before now. I am truly sorry about the hand. But there are plenty of men with a limb missing who've gone far in the military. Look at old Raglan. He made marshal. And there was Nelson. A man for the ladies as well as a fighter. You'll soon find ways of getting around the handicap — oh, sorry, didn't mean that. I meant of course that you'll get used to the fact that it's missing.

'Now, there's one other thing before I leave you to your rest and to wallow in your promotion. Your Miss Mulinder. She has been going frantic. When I told her I believed

I had found you, she asked to come with me, but I said no. I was not sure whether you wished to see her.'

'Yes I do, but not yet.' Crossman struggled up and with Lovelace's help put a pillow between his back and the wall. 'I would like to be able to meet her in the new uniform. I know that sounds rather crass, but I have something special to ask her — something I am at last *able* to ask her. Could you stall her for a day or so? Until then? Say I am really bad-tempered at the moment and do not wish to see anyone at all. No, no, that wouldn't keep her away. Simply say I do not want visitors until I am on my feet, but don't tell her where I am, then she can't come looking for me. Does she know of my promotion?'

'No — I thought you would like to be the one to tell her.'

'Please keep it a secret for a while.'

The major nodded, then continued with, 'You've got a few medals coming too, by the way. Apart from one or two of ours, the French want to give you one — they seem to hand them out to all those wounded British soldiers they've found and subsequently nurtured, as if they've taken them for their own. And the Turks have given you a very impressive lump of metal — a huge heavy shiny thing of fake gold — quite garish and vulgar-looking if you ask me. I'm glad I didn't get one.'

'What is it for?'

'I understand it is for fighting alongside them — well, for fighting alongside *one* of them, namely Yusuf Ali. You'll probably topple over with the weight of the thing.' He hesitated before adding, 'Here's an idea. You could pin it to your left sleeve, to sort of restore your balance.'

'Your jokes, Nathan, are in appalling bad taste.'

'I know,' grinned the major, 'but I enjoy the telling.'

Crossman now wanted to know of the outcome of the war.

'Ah, as to that, I suppose you know Sebastopol was deserted by the Russian army. They built a bridge of boats over the harbour to the north side, as we suspected they were doing, and marched away without a by your leave. We tried to destroy it of course, but failed.' He grinned. 'We should have had your *peloton* do it, then the job would have been done well.'

'You know I never approved of that — letting them leave saved lives.'

'You would have done it, if ordered to do so, and you know it. That sack of morals you carry with you will help to hinder your progress in the army if you're not careful. Anyway, that is by the by. The Russians blew up their magazines and some of the forts before they left, as well as other buildings. I was one of the first to enter. Many of those left behind were in a terrible state, but they are being cared for. How strange it was to stand on the Redan amongst the ghosts.' He paused once more, for reflection, before continuing. 'I am not one of those who remains gloomy about the failure to take the Redan. It was but one event in a long war. There are two aspects to the battle. One is that we drew Russians away from the Malakoff, thus assisting the French in their successful endeavours. The other is that though we did not take the works, we showed our teeth, and the result was that they ran with their tails between their legs. It was a victory to be sure. Had they retreated after the Battle of Inkerman, we should have called it a resounding one. Because of this last hiccough, many have the blue devils. I say that is wrong. I say it was a great victory, overall, and never mind that such a few could not work a miracle on the last day. The sad thing is we didn't manage to blow up their pontoon bridge, as I planned. They got away scot free.'

'I know you particularly wanted that bridge destroyed.'

Lovelace shrugged. 'One can't have all that one wants. So, what about these medals? Do you want a formal presentation, on parade and all that, or shall I dump them on your bed tonight? You can have them either way. We're pretty much a law unto ourselves at the moment, Colonel Hawke and I.'

'Bring them to me, if you please, Nathan. No parades.'

'Very well. By the way, do you know who has also been highly decorated? Do you remember that little Russian girl, Dasha Aleksandrovna, at the Battle of the Alma? You will recall that she sold her possessions to buy a horse and cart, so that she could help the Russian wounded on the field. The Czar has given her a gold cross and a pension. Well deserved, I think. Eleven years of age and doing all that! If I had a daughter . . . '

While Lovelace was still in conversation with Crossman, Lieutenant Pirce-Smith arrived. Crossman watched him approach the bed, wondering how his promotion would affect the other man. Would he be galled that a private had been raised to his own level, just like that? But Crossman had no need to worry. Pirce-Smith seemed very pleased for him. He had brought Crossman

Dalton-James's sword, which he unsheathed and lay across the bed to be admired by his former sergeant.

'Give me your hand, sir,' said the lieutenant, solemnly, 'for we are now brothers of the blade.'

'I like the sound of that,' replied Crossman, reaching out with his right hand to shake that of Pirce-Smith. ' 'Brothers of the blade.' It has a nice ring. I shall wear the sword proudly and use it wisely.'

10

The American and the Anglo-Scot were in an orchard which was used by patients of the French hospital. He had contradictory feelings about the way he looked now, in his new finery, the uniform of the dead Dalton-James. On the one hand he felt quite grand, and on the other, a hypocrite. He had never expected to become a commissioned officer and had spent a great deal of his time despising them for popinjays and peacocks. Now he was one and he secretly rather liked it. In the way that Wynter had had a reversal of opinion on sergeants, he had done the same with officers. They had both been elevated to those positions which they had previously held in contempt. It was really rather bad of them now to parade themselves with the same aplomb as someone in carnival dress looking for compliments.

Crossman was staring at a newspaper article which Rupert Jarrard had passed to him as he sat convalescing in the late summer sun.

'I am listed among the dead,' said Crossman in dismay, 'and on top of that, they've spelt my name wrongly.'

'I thought it would please you,' Jarrard said, smugly, puffing on a cigar. 'A British paper of course. We wouldn't make that kind of mistake in New York.'

'Oh, no, of course you wouldn't. We all know how superior the Americans are, in all things.' Crossman put the paper down on his knees. 'Well, Rupert, it took you a time to come and see me.'

'Oh, hey!' cried the correspondent, 'Lovelace only just saw fit to inform me. I thought you were dead too. I even said a little prayer. As soon as I heard you were in here, I came running.'

'It was my fault, actually. I asked Lovelace to keep it a secret. I didn't want a horde of females descending on me, fussing over me. It is bad enough with that youth, Pierre. He will not let me do a thing for myself, and he should, for I shall forget how to lift a cup if I'm fussed over like this much longer.' Crossman's stump was strapped against his side, to prevent him from knocking it and opening the wound. He felt awkward, not really knowing what to do with the thing. It seemed to take over his whole attention. He must have been looking at it, for Jarrard said, 'Is it still raw?'

'Oh, this?' he replied, pretending to notice

it for the first time. 'Not really. Well, yes, it's as sore as hell, if you wish to know. I have to rub some more cream on it soon. The French surgeons did a marvellous job though. I am convinced the saws they use are superior to those employed by the British surgeons. Smaller teeth, I think, and sharper.'

'Did they keep your hand for you?'

'No, it was tossed on a pile of limbs in a waste bin. I suppose I could have sorted through them, later, but by that time they'd gone green.'

'There's no need for sarcasm. I know several fellahs who've been lopped like you and some of them went to great lengths to retrieve their lost branches. One of them put his leg in a glass case and gave it to his old university to put on display. Another had his buried in the grave he himself would occupy once the curtain came down. A third . . . '

'Please, Rupert . . . '

'No, no, this is the best — the third suggested his amputated hand be used in a parody of Shakespeare's *Merchant of Venice*, as the pound of flesh required by Shylock. Curiously, you see, a hand with a bit of wrist *does* weigh just about a pound.'

'How very interesting,' remarked Crossman, dryly. 'Now, if you'll excuse me, I must write to my mother to tell her I am not dead, but famously alive.'

'Hey, I only just got here!'

'Oh, all right. Did you remember to bring my chibouque? I'm feeling bereft without it. Ah, yes, you did,' he said, as Jarrard took the pipe from the bag he was carrying. 'And do you know if anyone found my Tranter after the battle? My revolver?'

'You think it would be handed over?' snorted the American.

'No, I suppose not.'

Crossman took some tobacco out of his right pocket, held the chibouque by the bowl with his knees, and proceeded to stuff it with tobacco. It was awkwardly done, but Jarrard did not move to help him. He knew his friend would have to begin to learn such tricks in order to survive. But, as he had said, he had known many amputees and they functioned as well as men with their full complement of limbs after a while. A match came out then and was eventually struck and the pipe lit. It was all rather laborious, but Crossman glowed with a sense of achievement when it was done.

'I knew a one-handed man who could load and fire a weapon quicker than he had done with both mitts,' confided Jarrard. 'He told me he had been all fingers and thumbs before he had been pollarded.'

'That sounds like a story, but thank you for it, Rupert. Ah, that's better. Nothing like tobacco to mellow a man's spirit. God knew what he was doing, giving us these golden leaves to sooth our troubled souls. Well, today I go to see Jane. Wish me luck, won't you? I intend asking for her for her — That is, I intend to marry her, if she'll have me.'

'Why won't she? A handsome fellah like you. Straight as a pole, still got your own hair, and dashing to boot. A uniform like that makes 'em go all wobbly at the knees. By God, sir, you look the bee's knees in that lootenant's uniform. I try to shine, with my sharp suits and all, but when you've got those golden spiders on your shoulders, a man can't compete.'

'You really think she will have me?' asked Crossman, anxiously.

'You know darned well she will.'

There fell between them one of those golden silences that drop naturally between two men who are comfortable in one another's company. They puffed away, staring at the leaves being lifted by the breezes. It was a charming day, not warm enough to sit without a coat, but certainly not chilly. Birds darted about in the bushes and trees. Small mammals scurried from here to there. Bees were murmuring and butterflies fluttering.

Wild flowers and herbs gave forth their fragrance. A poet like Tennyson would have gone into one of his reveries and come out of it with a masterpiece of euphonic verse.

'What will you do now, Rupert?' said Crossman, once the fuel in his pipe bowl had burned to ashes. He tapped it out on his chair leg. 'Now that the war is over?'

'Find another war, I guess. There's always something going on somewhere in the globe.'

'You don't think you might end up back home in America? I hear there are rumblings between the industrialized north and the agricultural south.'

Jarrard tossed away his cigar butt and shook his head.

'Americans will never fight each other. Hell, when we gave you fellahs a drubbing it was much like a civil war, many of us fighting our own relations. We'll go to war to keep our independence, but I can't see us killing our own brothers and cousins in our own streets.'

'When you put it like that, perhaps not. Well, I hope we cross each other's paths again, Rupert. I shall miss your company.'

'And I yours, old friend. Hell, Jack, you'll be in the thick of another fight soon, and I'll be there to write it all down for posterity.'

Crossman laughed. 'Or for the next day, at least.'

'Yeah, the fickle readership of newspapers.'

★ ★ ★

Later that same day, a clean-shaven Cross-man was riding a borrowed horse into Kadikoi. He dismounted and tethered the nag to a rail, before walking off towards Mrs Durham's place. On his way he saw a group of about two dozen 88th rangers marching towards him. A sergeant was keeping them in step with gruff timing and reminders that they were in the British army, and not a bunch of Hottentots from the middle of the continent of Darkest Africa. As Crossman passed them, the sergeant ordered a salute, which was carried out remarkably smartly for men who were obviously fatigued with working in Balaclava Harbour. Then suddenly the sergeant halted the men, as he and the officer recognized one another.

'Sergeant Harry Wynter, as I live and breathe,' said Lieutenant Jack Crossman. 'What a coincidence.'

Wynter looked about him as if tricked or thwarted by the Fates. 'You?' he said. 'I mean, it's you, sir. I thought you was still a private, damn it. I was goin' to come looking for you, once my duties allowed, to order you about a bit, just for fun, like. But I missed my chance, I see. You're an lieutenant. I hadn't heard. That's rich. That's very rich.'

'Richer than you think. This is Dalton-James's uniform.'

Wynter laughed out loud.

Crossman nodded towards the waiting soldiers. 'So, you've reached the dizzy heights of sergeant.'

Wynter nodded. 'I never realized what a job it was, to knock such turnip heads into shape. This lot?' he gave a snort of contempt. 'They don't know nothin'. Wet behind the ears, they are. You try to make decent soldiers of 'em and they resist. BAKER!' he yelled, loud and sharply enough to split a melon into two halves, 'DON'T LET ME CATCH YOU MOVIN' WHEN I AN'T PUT YOU AT EASE.'

'Yes, I see what you mean, Sergeant Wynter. That one twitched without warning, didn't he? Well,' Crossman stuck out his hand, 'I wish you all the best of luck, Wynter. I hear you did a courageous thing, saving the life of an officer.'

Wynter shook the proffered hand.

'I'd do the same for you, if you was to lose . . . ' Wynter stared at the loose end of the left sleeve of Crossman's coat and

473

suddenly became embarrassed. 'Thing is, sir,' his voice grew noticeably quieter, 'I did it without much thought, if you know what I mean. The officer had his limb shot away and the Ruskies moved in to stick him with their bayonets. I rushed up without thinkin', stuck a couple of them instead. Then I hoisted up the captain and carried him off. Yes, I threw meself into the teeth of the gale, but once out I was golden, see. I could carry this officer off the field and not have to fight in the rest of the battle. All the others I left behind, they went down. One or two got back, like you, with bits missing. I got a bash on the head and bled a good bit, but that was all.'

'You don't have to feel guilty, Wynter. You fought for me many times. Once, I believe, you saved my life.'

'When you was in Sebastopol,' said Wynter, his face brightening again. 'Yep, that were it. We had a time, didn't we, sir? We had a war all right. Now Peterson's gone home and there's no one else left. Now I have to bawl and shout at turnip heads all day long. It's not the same.'

'Good luck, Wynter.'

'And to you, sir.' Remarkably there were tears in Wynter's eyes. The reason was apparent on Wynter's breath.

'Have you been drinking, sergeant? You

seem a little emotional.'

'Oh, just a tipple,' replied Wynter, smirking. 'Just a little warmer after our work unloading the ships. You know how it is. Goodbye, sir.'

With that the new sergeant marched smartly back to his men and asked them in a voice that would have silenced Jove what the blamed hell they were looking at and to keep their eyes to the front or he would have them plucked out and thrown to the crows for horses' doovers. Crossman watched them march out of sight, wondering about the vagaries of war.

The door to the dwelling was thrown open before he even had time to knock. Obviously Jane had been watching from the window. She threw her arms around his neck and kissed him several times. Except that it was not Jane. It was Lavinia Durham and Crossman drew back in alarm, hoping no one had seen this unwanted display of affection.

'Lavinia, please! My new uniform!'

'We are so happy that you are safe,' she cried. 'Jane, Jane, here is Alex, that is to say, Jack. He is come home to us.'

Jane came up, almost shyly, behind her friend.

'So I see. Do stop fondling him like a spaniel, Lavinia, and let him come in. He looks a little bothered by your fuss. Hello, Jack.'

He stepped inside and removed his cap. 'Jack is it? I seemed to have scored a success at last.'

'I have taken to heart that you wish to be known by your army name. From now on, you will be Jack Crossman. I have taken the liberty of writing to your brother and parents to tell them just that. Alexander Kirk has been consigned to the attic, perhaps to be brought down and the dust blown off him at a later date. Jack Crossman is now a lieutenant, nominally of the 88th Foot, but actually on secret government business.' Her eyes were sparkling until she looked down and saw his empty sleeve, then they faded. 'Oh, Jack. Your hand. Does it hurt very much?'

He joked, 'I don't know, for wherever it is, any pain it feels never actually reaches me.'

Lavinia stared open-mouthed before saying, 'How will you manage without it? You'll need a good woman to look after you. I have to look after Bertie, so that only leaves Jane, doesn't it?'

'Lavinia, you have lost all decorum,' said Jane. 'Leave Jack alone. Come over here and sit down, lieutenant. Let us look at you. Doesn't he look fine, Lavinia?'

The other lady remarked, 'He must have been melted down and poured into that uniform. I wonder you can even bend, Jack, without the sound of ripping cloth?'

'Dalton-James was slightly smaller than I am.'

Captain Durham then walked into the room. Crossman stood up, his cap under his arm left arm, and gave the captain a slight bow. 'Your servant, Durham.'

'Good Lord!' cried Durham, moving forward with hand outstretched. 'You're here at last. The ladies have been going frantic for the past two hours. I'm so glad — they've been driving me mad. Anyone would have thought General Simpson was expected. Congratulations, old chap. Lieutenant, eh?' Durham nodded approvingly as Crossman shook his hand. 'More in keeping with your station, I have to say. A baronet's son? I should think so.' His voice dropped to a whisper. 'Are we still on for that shooting week, old chap? Looking forward to it enormously, you know.'

'Bertie!' snapped Lavinia.

'Yes, of course,' said Crossman, smiling. 'I'll speak to my father as soon as I get home. I'm on a ship leaving in two days. The *Waylander*. A small tub I understand, but I'm happy with anything.'

'Gad, but you look fit enough now. We was worried about you, weren't we, Lavinia? First reports said you was dead and Jane went into transports of grief. Buckets of tears. Couldn't stand it. Had to get out of the house. But then Lovelace came and told us you was alive, though a bit knocked about. The smiles came back and the house was sunny again. And here you are, looking as sharp and lean as a gypsy's lurcher on a frosty morning. I say, who's your tailor?'

'Borrowed uniform, I'm afraid, but I see by the label it was made by Joseph Rosenberg, of Savile Row.'

'Rosenberg, eh? I'll pay him a visit myself, when I get back. Nice and tight around the buttocks, ain't it? Old Cardigan's cherry-bums don't stretch that smooth.'

'Bertie, you are going beyond the bounds,' scolded Lavinia. 'There are ladies present. Now, *Jack*, you would like some refreshment I am sure. It is not quite ready, so perhaps you would wish to take Jane for a short walk, before we all sit down to eat? I'm sure you have lots to talk about,' she added, archly. 'Bertie, would you ask one of the servants to fetch the white wine? It's down in the harbour,' she explained to Crossman. 'We tie the bottle necks to a length of cord and keep them submerged under the water. The Black

Sea is quite cold you know? It's the currents, I'm told. It keeps the wine at a very nice temperature. Bertie's idea, of course. I never would have thought of it. He's so clever at things like that.'

'I've just met a drunken sergeant on the road — I hope he didn't discover your cache.'

Her face darkened. 'I hope so too, for his sake.'

Durham went off. Crossman was glad to take Jane out of the dwelling, even though the air was damp outside. It seemed that it might rain very shortly, but he had to ask her the question. Once he had her to himself, he did just that, coming out with it almost brusquely. The fact was, it had been waiting in there for such a long time, it seemed to bolt from his mouth like a frightened rabbit. Jane studied him with a frank expression, before replying.

'I'm sorry, Jack.' She looked down, obviously distressed. 'You — you don't know, you see.'

Her refusal shocked him to the core. He was so sure she loved him he had taken it for granted that the answer would be an unequivocal yes. Suddenly what had merely been a damp day was cold and bleak. He noticed the dark clouds scudding over a grey sky above. This was terrible! He fought against uttering a stiff 'By your leave!' and striding away, to nurse his shame and misery at being turned down.

'What don't I know?' he asked, eventually.

'I was engaged, you see.'

'Yes, to the oaf who jilted you.'

'But what you didn't understand — what I did not, nor could not tell you, was that — that . . . ' She fell silent, looking away to the black hills in the north.

'Ah!' He understood her at last. 'I see.'

'I'm spoiled goods, Jack.'

'You are not *goods*, Jane — you are a woman. A very beautiful one at that. I see no evidence of spoiling. I see a person with great spirit, with impeccable honesty, with a nature which outshines that of any other person, man or woman, I have ever met. If it is only an error of judgement that stops you from saying yes to my offer, then I have nothing to worry about. All you have done is rightly to trust a man who had given his word to you, to keep that word. The blame and the shame is his, not yours. I myself am not without stains on my character. Lavinia must have spoken to you?'

'It is different for a woman. It matters more.'

'Whether you think it does, or whether you think it doesn't, I am not influenced by this revelation. I don't give a fig for it. Will you marry me, Jane?'

She looked up, smiling now. 'Oh, I knew you would be like this — you are everything I want from a man, my honourable Fancy Jack. Yes, I will marry you. Nothing would make me happier.'

He took her in his arms, his good hand flat on her back, his shortened arm around her slim waist. They kissed, as if for the first time.

'This man,' he said, as they walked back to the house, 'I must know his name now.'

'Do you have to?'

'Yes.'

She told him.

He nodded, grimly. 'Don't worry, I won't go calling him out. I regard him as the poorest of losers, you see. He has made the gravest error of his life and will spend the rest of his days regretting it. He will stand on hilltops, staring off in the direction of Derby, biting his lip and cursing himself for a fool. No, no, I'm not saying this for your amusement, Jane. I mean it. He sounds like one of those men who want everything, and end up being frustrated and miserable because no man can have it all. You will sparkle and his soul will grow as cold and brittle as burnt coke. He will shrivel within. When you meet, *if* you ever meet, on social occasions, he will be so snarled up inside with his envy of me and his stupidity on letting you slip away, he will die inside.'

'Oh, Jack, how horrible.'

'He deserves no less. I shall look him straight in the eye and my stare will say, 'She is *my* wife, not yours, and you will never again know fulfilment.'' Crossman did not say out loud, 'May God damn him and rot his soul,' but the silent words were tagged on naturally to the end of his little speech.

Lavinia was waiting at the door for them. She knew what had passed between them from their looks. There were shades of envy in her, but she wafted them away with a determination to be glad for her ex-lover and her best friend. After all, she had chosen them for each other, and her plans had been carried out perfectly. She had her handsome, loving Bertie and now Jane was to have her Jack. They would make the perfect foursome, now that Jack was an officer. Of course, it did mean that Jack had to like Bertie, but though her husband was no genius thinker, he was very likeable. Jack could have no objection to him as a friend, for there was nothing about the captain quartermaster to dislike. He was bland, but not always boring, and he was a good sportsman and card player. That's what other men liked about him and there was no reason why Jack should feel differently.

'Luncheon is served,' she said, taking Jane's hand and whispering loudly into her friend's ear. 'How happy I am for you.'

★   ★   ★

Crossman had just said goodbye to his Bashi-Bazouk comrade, the Turk Yusuf Ali. They parted knowing they were the richer for ever meeting at all. They vowed eternal friendship for one another, as men do after a harrowing campaign. It is genuine, for there is nothing like war to weld men together, even previously bitter enemies. When the allied armies had first got together, he had seen senior French and British officers hug each other with tears in their eyes, as if finding lost brothers: old men who had been deadly foes in the Peninsula campaigns. He and Yusuf Ali were now closer than brothers. There was also that eastern code which bound one man to another, which the west to its detriment did not own. Crossman would do anything on earth for Yusuf Ali. But Yusuf Ali would have gone into hell for Crossman.

'I tell you they make you an officer,' said Ali, proudly, 'my wife says you are now her favourite son.'

Crossman was appalled. 'But what about

her — her other sons?'

'Bah,' Ali spat on the ground, 'they are ungrateful wretches. None of them have made themselves into officer like you.' He stroked Crossman's epaulettes as he spoke. 'They are lazy pigs with no ambition. Still,' he shrugged, 'the oldest is but sixteen. There is time. And he is not *my* son, of course, but the son of my wife's first husband, who died in the spice market in Constantinople, when he argue with a man who cheat him out of two grammes of saffron . . . ' The story went on for quite a while and involved several of Ali's wife's first husband's cousins and uncles, who sought revenge, and eventually found it. Finally, Crossman got away.

Crossman headed towards Balaclava Harbour, where he was to embark for England. Someone with a dog at his heels came up behind him and grabbed him roughly by the sleeve to whirl him round. The man who was accosting him was Captain Sterling Campbell, who now stared him up and down, taking in the lieutenant's uniform with a triumphant sneer on his countenance.

'Still up to your old tricks, I see!'

Crossman looked the man coldly in the eyes. He spoke with iron in his tone.

'Take your filthy hand off my uniform.'

Shock registered in Campbell's eyes. He

saw something in Crossman's expression that brought his racing brain up short. He let his hand drop, limply to his side. Crossman turned on his heel and walked on, leaving the captain staring after him.

★   ★   ★

Jack was with his brother James, striding over the heather-covered hills on part of the family estates. The air was clear. They had shotguns under their arms, but even when a stag broke cover they did not raise the hunting weapons. They were too engrossed in each other and in the scene around them. Every country on earth has its beauty, but there is nothing quite like the Scottish hills and uplands for its grandeur. On a good day the scent of the ground cover is invigorating, and the sight of the strong crooked shape of a rogue Scots pine fills a man with pride in his country.

'So, the old man has turned senile?' said Jack. 'And you must now manage the estates?'

He had met his father for the first time since seeing him in the Crimea just that morning. The baronet, Major Kirk, had been pottering amongst the vegetables of the house garden, with one of the stable grooms louring in the background. This groom was the same menacing dark-browed man that had quietly threatened to 'tak a pattle' to Jack when he and his father had almost come to blows in the yard on the day Jack left home. The man was very protective towards his father.

Jack had been warned by his mother of his father's present frail condition. The elderly baronet had lost all his original fire and spleen, however, and had smiled feebly at Jack.

'Hello, young man. Who are you?'

'I am your son, come home from the war.'

'Oh, are you? Here, look at these winter cabbage — aren't they splendid?'

Jack told his father — the father who until now would have spurned vegetables to hunt anything that had fur or feathers on its back — that he thought the cabbages quite magnificent.

'Who did you say you were?' the old man had asked, after another ten minutes. 'You remind me of someone. Oh, you seem to be without your left hand. Was it a hunting accident? I'm very fond of hunting, you know, but I should like to keep both my hands.'

The groom had remained within earshot and Jack, feeling uncomfortable under his gaze, left his father to his garden.

This meeting had upset Jack a great deal, naturally. He had despised his father as only a bastard son can. But now there was nothing left to hate and his former feelings turned on him. He had put his good arm around the old man's shoulders and given him a hug: a gesture that would have been impossible for both of them, before now. He hugged him as he would hug any simple, bent old man who needed assurance. Then he had gone in to see his stepmother and sought the comfort that only a mother can give.

James said yes, it was a shame, for the old man had even given up painting.

'He was a good artist, Jack.'

'I know, I saw some of his works, out in the Crimea. I wondered at the time how something so beautiful could come from such a man as he — a man whose soul to me was as black as pitch.'

'Ah, well,' replied James, generously, 'I had a different relationship with him, so I saw him differently.

'Did it make any difference to your feelings for me? Once you knew I was only your half-brother?'

'I do not agree with your use of the word *only*. A half-brother is a brother none the less. We were raised together from the cradle. Should I love you only half as much as I would a full brother? What rubbish you think about, Jack — I will have to get used to that name, I suppose, but it is still awkward on my tongue. You are my younger brother and childhood companion. I could not love you more if you were two brothers in one. Our mother — the only mother you have ever known — does not differentiate between us. We are her beloved sons. It is a shame about the rift between you and Father, but that is nothing to do with me. He was not a perfect man, of course — very flawed in his way — and I was always somewhat afraid of him — but there it is, now he is not much more sensible than one of those cabbages he raves about.'

'What is to be done with him?'

'Oh, Mother and I will see he is cared for here. Caleb McNiece, the groom, has said he wishes to see to his every need. You know he and Caleb were always tight together, both of them sporting men. Between you and me Caleb is rather tired of combing and brushing horses. He will live in the house and be at Father's beck and call.'

Jack said, 'Yes, I remember Father being the only one who could ever understand fully what Caleb was saying, with his broad highland accent. What is a pattle by the way?'

'It's a sickle. You and I should never have gone to Harrow, Jack. We should have received our education here.'

'What, gathering noils from the hedges?' But then he added, 'I feel as if Caleb McNiece has taken a pattle to me in any event.' He held up his shortened left arm. 'I have been cut about a bit, James, and I'm not feeling whole. You know Jane Mulinder has said she will have me, but I must gather my confidence again before going down to Derby to do the deed. You will be my best man, will you not?'

'I should be honoured and delighted, but you know, Jack, you have already asked me and I have gladly accepted.'

'I am getting almost as bad as father. War has shredded my brain, as well as my body. Have no concern. I shall remember henceforth.'

His brother James, shorter than Jack, but built in the stocky mould of their father, stopped and placed a fond hand on Jack's shoulder. There was to be a moment of genuine closeness between them, standing as they were on that heather-covered hillside above their childhood home. Both had dreamed of this time, when they were in the mud and mire of the Crimea, wondering if they would ever see each other again. Yet, here they were, together in the clear air of the land of their birth.

'My dear brother, home safe. It *is* good to

see you. Have I thanked you for the Russian sword? Of course, I must have done. It shall be placed above the inglenook fire in the drawing room, a position of honour. I pity the man you took it from, for I hear you have become a ferocious warrior. I find it hard to believe my gentle younger brother being such, but must accept what I hear from men who have no reason to tell other than the truth.'

A half-white hare ran a curving path from the patch of foliage at their feet to a safer haven amongst some grey stones, not because of the brothers, but because it had sighted an eagle.

'It is probably true, but not something I'm greatly proud of, James. I would rather you thought me the world's best engineer.'

'We must all follow our destinies, Alex — sorry, Jack. Yours is to be a soldier. It's an honourable profession. There are great engineers who would exchange places with you in a moment. The world is entrusted to men like you.'

'Not to me, James. To politicians. The army is the instrument.' Jack paused and thought about it for a minute, before going further. 'I suppose the only honourable soldier is a reluctant one.'

'Nonsense. Soldiers defend the country

from its enemies. There is great honour in that.'

'No, the *army* defends the country. The soldiers that make it up are there to kill other soldiers, soldiers in a different uniform.'

'But what choice do younger brothers have?'

'I could be a priest.'

'A most unlikely thing. I simply cannot see you in some seedy parish intoning litanies and liturgies. It won't do, Jack.'

'It might have made me a better man.'

James shook his head in disagreement. 'I think you're in a very sombre frame of mind, Jack, but I can see I shall be unable to change your mood. Perhaps it's the loss of the hand, or the end of a war, but something has brought you to this maudlin state. I refuse to believe that my brother, my *dear* brother, would do anything that was not honourable. There it is. The end of the argument. You may go out and be a highwayman now, I shall believe none of the sheriff's men when they call. Let us go home. The light fails.'

That evening the whole family sat down to dinner for the first time in many years. Their mother's face was shining with pleasure. Her sons had come home from the war: albeit not unscathed, but they were alive. Both had acquitted themselves with honour. Jack read in her eyes that inwardly she was tinged with sadness over the plight of her husband. Jack could not really see why she felt any melancholy concerning his father, who seemed now a much pleasanter man than he had ever been when his mind had been complete. He had gone from being an outright despot to being a rather mild-tempered spaniel. However, their mother obviously missed some part of the original tyrant, for Jack caught her looking quite low sometimes.

'How lovely it is, that we are all together,' she said, brightly. 'Isn't it quite wonderful, my dear?'

'Eh?' said the baronet. 'All together, is it?'

He smiled because his wife was smiling.

Caleb McNiece stood as stiff as a poker behind his master's chair, ready to do him any service. The servant was a dark brooding presence in the room which Jack tried to ignore, though it was difficult. The man breathed menace from his glowering face. Just before dinner there had been a confrontation between James and the groom.

McNiece had been helping the old man navigate the passageways to the dining room and came across James instructing one of the farm managers concerning the estate. McNiece had interrupted rudely with the comment, 'The laird's no dead yet. Ye should tak yer orders frae him, Hamish Calloway.'

James had reacted immediately. 'Keep a civil tongue in your head, McNiece, or you'll be sent on your way with a week's wages. Make no mistake about it, I'm the laird now. My father is not of sound mind, as well you know, and do not have any doubts that I shall dismiss you instantly if you are so foolish as to question my authority again.'

Jack had been standing nearby, and he added, 'McNiece, we are of one opinion in the family — my brother, my mother and me. We appreciate your long-standing loyalty to our father, but you will keep your place. Our father is mentally frail and we shall cope with that in our own way. You may have had power here while your laird was of full mind, but those days are gone.'

Neither Jack nor James could forget the thrashings administered by McNiece, under instruction from their father, when they were boys. Being a bully the groom had appeared to enjoy the exercise and it was a wonder that the brothers even consented to keep him in employment. The man had to be made to realize how precarious was his position now that James had power of attorney over their father.

Caleb McNiece's spiteful eyes had gone

from one brother to the other and his face seemed to sharpen in its aspect. The manager, Hamish Calloway, had said nothing, but he had clearly been put out by McNiece's hostility towards his employers. Finally McNiece had muttered something about 'ungrateful whelps' and then had continued assist the old man, who was fussing with the door handle to the dining room, turning it the wrong way and whimpering about the fact that the door would not open for him.

'We'll let that go,' James had said to the whole company, 'but do not think, McNiece, because my father was able to order me to do as he wished that I am soft with everyone in this life, or by God you will fly through the air so fast you will land beyond the border, believe me.'

This time the stable groom had taken note and wisely kept his own counsel, and had reached over and turned the doorknob, then ushered the baronet inside the dining room.

During dinner the amiable baronet kept up a stream of mindless chatter, but his voice was now so soft it did not intrude upon the general convivial atmosphere. Jack was able to tell his mother about his time in the Crimea, leaving out the really gory episodes. James now knew that his brother had saved his life on at least one occasion and since he had been ill at the time, he wanted to know the details. Jack of course played such events down, being even more modest with his own family than he was with strangers. He did however tell James about Campbell and described the man's face when Jack had snarled at him.

''Take your dirty hand off my uniform!' You actually said that to Captain Sterling Campbell, Jack? I can't believe it, though I know it must be true. Surely he wanted to run you through?'

'He was greatly provoked, it was true. I could see his hand was itching to unsheath his blade, brother, but he was so unsure of himself after seeing the fury in my eyes he hesitated too long — and then the moment was gone, his rage no longer sufficient to fuel any rash action.'

'I think this is all very childish,' said their mother, rebukingly. 'All this talk of insults and duels. We mothers have never understood why our sons have the souls of warriors. Why indeed did you need to be soldiers in the first instance? For my part, I wish you had both stayed at home. One moment playing with wooden horses, the next off to war. 'Arms I sing, and the man.' I should have removed that dreadful Virgil from our bookshelves and perhaps the pair of you would not have been so influenced by it.'

They both laughed at their mother, startling their father for a moment.

'Is it all right?' asked the old man nervously, turning round to face Caleb McNiece. 'Why are they making so much noise?'

'Dinnae fash yersel' laird, it's no-but brattle.'

The major then turned back to the table and spoke to Jack.

'You sir, can you pass the salt?' he asked, and when Jack reached for it, added, 'and the pepper pot too?'

When Jack became confused, trying to pick up both condiments with one hand and failing, the old man cackled in delight.

Jack smiled at what was obviously a joke. 'You've still a wicked streak in you, Father,' he said, 'and I'm inclined to admire you for it now.'

'Did I ever tell you the story,' said his father, 'of the time when the Duchess of Tyrol besieged Castle Hochosterwitz? It was in the fourteenth century, and those in the castle were close to starving . . . '

That evening there was a heavy snowfall. The baronet wandered out in the middle of the night, getting himself lost in the hills. They found him quickly enough by following his tracks. He had taken a sporting gun and was stalking deer by their spoor when they discovered him. Caleb McNiece carried the old man home on his shoulders, a full three miles, without complaint.

* * *

A week later Jack was down in Derbyshire. Gwilliams had now joined him after spending some time in London. Jane's father, Mr Mulinder, had asked to see Jack in the drawing room and greeted him sternly when he entered, throwing a brief glance at the missing hand. Jack was in uniform and he knew he looked impressive. He shook Mr Mulinder's hand and asked him how he did. Jane's father said he was doing rather well, thank you kindly, and what was all this about a wedding?

'I wish to marry Jane, sir, with your kind permission.'

'And how d'ye plan to keep her?' asked Mr Mulinder, one eye half-closed. 'Not on a lieutenant's pay, surely?'

Jane entered the room at that point.

'Oh, don't be so stuffy, Father, of course not. You know I have my own money, quite sufficient to keep two husbands, let alone one.' Then seeing Jack's face, added, 'Not that they would need keeping.'

'And who are these two husbands?' asked Mr Mulinder, getting muddled. 'And why d'ye need two?'

'They are Alexander Kirk and Jack Crossman,' replied his daughter, without hesitation. 'Both fine men, from good families, and they both admire your daughter immensely.'

Mr Mulinder grunted, realizing he was, as usual, having his pomposity pricked by his daughter.

'That's another thing. What's all this Jack Crossman business? Rather confusing if you ask me. What's wrong with your old name?'

'Nothing, sir, nothing at all, but I happened to join the army under an assumed name for reasons I would rather not go into, they being deeply personal. Having done so, it would be confusing for the army if I were to change it back again — they're not very bright, the army, and they become confused easily. It is better I remain Jack Crossman for the duration of my army career. I have even trained my own family into this usage and I feel that if my brother and mother are prepared to go along with my foibles, then surely acquaintances, friends and distant relations should do likewise.'

Jack had not meant this to sound so aggressive but he had become a little weary of being attacked for his use of an assumed name. Why he chose to live under such he saw as his business. However, he felt he might have gone too far with Jane's father, who stood there with a frown on his forehead while studying the toecaps of his shoes. But when Mr Mulinder looked up, he merely enquired mildly, 'And what does your father think?'

'Unfortunately, sir, my father is not of this world . . . ' Mulinder looked dreadfully shocked and darted an accusing glance at his daughter, but Jack realizing that the older man had mistaken his meaning, added quickly, 'That is to say, his mind is now so feeble he does not know where he is, who he is, or who we are.'

Mr Mulinder's expression cleared a little. 'Oh, I say, that is unfortunate. It does happen, I know — my own mother, your dear grandmother, Jane — but that is neither here nor there. So, Major Kirk has passed beyond the understanding of men. Do give your mother — I take it she is still *compos mentis*? Yes, yes, of course she is, why should she not be — just because your father . . . Well, do give her our sympathy. We feel for her situation gravely. Now Jane, what is it you were doing in your room? I heard the most frightful noise as I passed an hour ago.'

Mr Mulinder's mind, though not in any way feeble, did tend to dart like a silver fish between various rocks of enquiry.

'I was culling my collection of shoes, Father,' replied Jane with an amused look. 'Now I know the method of your delaying tactics, Father, and poor Jack is standing there in great anxiety awaiting your answer to his question as to whether you wish to burden him with me. Put him out of his agony, Father.'

'Wasn't there another chap here just a short while ago with the same request?'

Jane blushed with embarrassment. 'That was over a year ago, Father, and you know he cried off.'

The old man's head jerked back. 'Did he now? That's scandalous. I ought to do something about that, oughtn't I?'

'No, you oughtn't. We are far better off without him. You will please give us your blessing.'

'Oh, as to that — well then, there it is, congratulations my boy and you have my best wishes. Where will you live? Not here, I hope. I mean, I love my daughter, but I think young people should live on their own.'

'I quite agree, sir. I — I have been left a small house in Paris.' Jack did not add that it was an inheritance from an ex-lover, though

Jane was quite aware of the circumstances. 'We shall go there, initially, if Jane agrees. Then it will be off to wherever the army sends us. There has been talk of India.'

'India? Hmm. Lots of money to be made in India. Not so much trade these days, but revenues . . . '

The small round man then went to a decorated cigar box which he informed Jack had come from a place called Sarawak, where the local tribesmen collected each other's heads. 'They don't grow tobacco there of course — they just make the boxes.' He handed Jack a cigar and lit them both from a taper. They puffed away together for a few minutes, but Mr Mulinder was a business-man by choice and a landowner by inheritance, and having exhausted all his conversation about land use, he found that Jack knew very little about commerce. In order to escape the long silences that ensued between them he suggested Jack take Jane for a walk around the garden. Jack did so with great relief, much to Jane's chagrin.

'There's snow on the ground,' she said laughingly, tripping through the Italian Garden wrapped in warm clothes. 'We can't see a thing. This is complete madness, Jack.'

'I had to get away, Jane. I know nothing about commerce.'

'Oh, look, there's Mrs Robin.'

Jack stared at the bird on a snowy twig. 'Mr Robin, actually — you see it's breast is very red. Hers would be more of a light orange colour.'

'You know so much about nature, do you, Mr Naturalist? Let me take you round our extensive gardens, hidden deep under the winter snow. This is the Dovecote Lawn — you see how green it is below that mantle of white? — and there is the Citrus House and the Vinery, and over there the Southern Summerhouse — and, oh look, the Little Brothy with the Thunderbox Room next to it . . .'

'Ladies, especially the brides of commissioned officers, do not speak of thunderboxes, Jane. You will shock the commanding officer's wife.'

'Here is Hera's Garden.'

'Hera is here's garden?'

'No, silly . . .'

At that moment a figure familiar to both of them came striding down the West Path wearing a greatcoat, brown boots and army officer's cap. It was Major Lovelace. Jack was not as shocked as he should have been having had a premonition of this visit. He saluted out of courtesy, then shook the hand of the Rifle Brigade major, who had once been an artillery officer, but was now a spy and saboteur of no mean experience.

'Your servant, ma'am,' said Lovelace to Jane, saluting her in a rather less formal way than the army required. 'I hope I find you well.'

'Not only well, major, but blissfully happy.' She clutched and then hugged the arm of her beloved as if the major were about to try to take him away from her. 'You're not going to spoil our wedding plans, are you?'

'Good Lord, no. I was in the district and thought I'd call by to tell your bridegroom that he is to go to India.'

'India?' cried Jack, immediately excited by the prospect. 'When?'

'Oh, when you are ready to go,' said Lovelace, 'within reason of course.'

'And what will he do there?' asked Jane, not averse to going to India herself as the wife of a lieutenant. 'Is his regiment going?'

'Oh, who knows what his regiment is doing? That is not our concern. Jack is beyond regiments now. He is one of my little band. We go to the East India Company's army to further ourselves in the murky world of information-gathering. Colonel Hawke feels there would be mutual benefit from you attaching yourself to a chap called Hodson . . . '

'Of Hodson's Horse?' said Jack, now fired

by the idea that he might meet such men as John Nicholson and Neville Chamberlain, the men who had conquered the Punjab and scouted Kashmir and Afghanistan.

'The very man. He's not much liked, but that's neither here nor there. He could teach you much, and possibly learn a little himself. The North-West Frontier is the place to be at the moment. It might be that, as an infantry officer, you may prefer to attach yourself officially to a regiment of foot. Coke's Rifles, perhaps?'

'I would prefer Lumsden's Corp of Guides, and the infantry be damned — excuse me, Jane.'

'Well, that will depend on what Hawke arranges for you.' Lovelace took out a pocket watch and studied it. 'Now, I am due in London. I am going by train and strange to be said these steam machines have timetables which they keep to the minute. You will excuse me?'

Jane said, astonished, 'You are not staying for some warm refreshment, major?'

'No, do forgive my poor manners, I cannot.'

'But you will be coming to our wedding?'

Lovelace smiled. 'That I shall endeavour to work into my schedule.'

'We shall be pleased to see you there,' she said.

Later that night, while Gwilliams assisted him in undressing, Jack said, 'We might be going to India.'

'Well, there's a territory I ain't laid eyes on yet. You got any books on the place?'

'I'll find you one tomorrow.'

It struck Jack, at that moment, that Gwilliams might turn out to be another Caleb McNiece, standing by his chair when his mind had flown.

Lying in bed, once the candle had been snuffed, Jack considered where his life was going. He was to be married, that was certain, but what about this career he seemed to have found by default? Spy and saboteur? The job entailed destroying things, rather than creating them. All his young life he had admired inventors and engineers — men like Brunel — who raised things up — glorious things like iron bridges, great ships, steam trains. Yet now here he was consolidating a career in bringing such things down, blowing them up, smashing them to pieces. How contrary. Yet the subcontinent of India! Now that was a land to get the pulses racing and the brain in a fever of excitement. Heat and dust. Exotic cultures by the score. New peoples, new landscapes, new ideas and new revelations.

Could he turn down such an opportunity? Never in a million years.

We do hope that you have enjoyed reading this large print book.

Did you know that all of our titles are available for purchase?

We publish a wide range of high quality large print books including:
Romances, Mysteries, Classics
General Fiction
Non Fiction and Westerns

Special interest titles available in large print are:
The Little Oxford Dictionary
Music Book
Song Book
Hymn Book
Service Book

Also available from us courtesy of Oxford University Press:
Young Readers' Dictionary
(large print edition)
Young Readers' Thesaurus
(large print edition)

For further information or a free brochure, please contact us at:
Ulverscroft Large Print Books Ltd.,
The Green, Bradgate Road, Anstey,
Leicester, LE7 7FU, England.
Tel: (00 44) 0116 236 4325
Fax: (00 44) 0116 234 0205

Other titles published by
The House of Ulverscroft:

THE WINTER SOLDIERS

Garry Douglas Kilworth

After the battle of Inkerman on 5 November 1854 the British Army faces a terrible winter. Provisions and clothing for the troops are hopelessly inadequate. In this grim season Sergeant 'Fancy Jack' Crossman and his troop are billeted at Kadikoi village near Balaclava harbour - their official instructions to blow up the magazine in the Russian Star Fort. But it transpires this is not to be Crossman's main mission. His true, and infinitely more complex and dangerous task is to spy on a British general suspected of corruption, and to bring about his downfall . . .

LOOSE CANNON

June Drummond

A peace accord is due to be signed in Jerusalem in two weeks' time, but it is threatened when a Boeing airliner, leased by charity organization Dove International, catches fire and crashes in the Mediterranean, killing one hundred and fifty-five people. Political and commercial powers, fearing that charges of sabotage will enable extremists to wreck the frail truce, frustrate investigations and blame the crash on pilot or mechanical failure. It is left to individuals - the pilot's brother and ex-girlfriend, a forensic psychiatrist, a Roman policeman, an FBI investigator and a Mossad agent - to challenge authority and track down the criminals endangering world peace.

THE HORSE WITH MY NAME

Colin Bateman

Ex-journalist Dan Starkey is stuck in a grimy Belfast bedsit. His life is a disaster, and his only solace is the pub round the corner. He needs to get out more (particularly since the sessions at Relate with his wife Patricia have been cancelled and she's hooked up with new man Clive). He really, really needs something to get his teeth into. Fellow ex-journalist Mark Corkery provides that something. Corkery, whose secret persona is The Horse Whisperer, an internet horse-racing gossip, wants him to investigate Geordie McClean, the man behind Irish American Racing. Simple enough, surely? But Trouble is Dan's middle name – and trouble is what he finds.

THE GENERAL'S ENVOY

Anthony Conway

Seconded to China by a vengeful Indian Army high command, Captain John Caspasian finds Shanghai a cesspit of despair and corruption. He is glad to escape on a solo mission to contact a general whom the British see as a bulwark against the revolutionary leader Chiang Kai-shek. Once he has left the International Settlement for a gunboat on the Yangtze, though, Caspasian smells danger. The supposedly friendly General Mok turns out to be a bloodthirsty sadist. And Caspasian has made two implacable enemies. One is a Chinese criminal. The other is a former British officer . . .

DEADLINE

Vernon Coleman

After losing his job on a national newspaper, Mark Watson is approached by a former colleague whose wife has been mysteriously kidnapped. Despite his total lack of experience, Watson finds himself offering to help locate the missing woman, and before he knows it he has embarked on a new career - that of a private investigator. Soon, he finds himself in a terrifying race against the deadline date which would mean certain death for his friend's wife.

THE BLUE EDGE OF MIDNIGHT

Jonathon King

Max Freeman's old life as a cop ended the night he killed a twelve-year-old child in self-defence in a Philadelphia shootout. Now he lives alone on the edge of the Florida Everglades, where the demons eat away at his conscience. But when he finds the corpse of a child beside an ancient river, Freeman is thrust into the search for a serial killer. Distrusted as an outsider by the longtime residents of the Glades and considered a suspect by the police, Freeman walks a tightrope of suspicion. Then another child goes missing and the ex-cop knows that he must hunt down the murderer himself . . .